THE ROMANCES OF GEORGE SAND

ANNA FAKTOROVICH

ANAPHORA LITERARY PRESS

TUCSON, ARIZONA

ANAPHORA LITERARY PRESS
5755 E. River Rd., #2201
Tucson, AZ 85750
http://anaphoraliterary.com

Book design by Anna Faktorovich, Ph.D.

Cover Images: "Honorable Mrs. Seymour Bathurst," by Sir Thomas Lawrence, 1828.
"George Sand," anonymous portrait.
"George Sand," by Auguste Charpentier, 1838.
"George Sand," signature, 1873.

Published in 2014 by Anaphora Literary Press

The Romances of George Sand
Anna Faktorovich—1st edition.

Paperback ISBN-13: 978-1-937536-68-8
ISBN-10: 1-937536-68-8
Hardback ISBN-13: 978-1-937536-69-5
ISBN-10: 1937536696
EBook: ISBN-10: 193753670X
ISBN-13: 978-1-937536-70-1

Library of Congress Control Number: 2014908816

THE ROMANCES OF GEORGE SAND

ANNA FAKTOROVICH

CONTENTS

beggars attempting to seize her money. —Marie Dorval and George Sand begin their sixteen-year love affair after George sends an admiring letter about her performance in *Antony*. —Sand ends her affair with Jules after catching him with a washerwoman.

Alfred de Musset has a tragic affair with a consumptive lady, who is in love with another man. —Alfred and George meet, and strike up a literary friendship. —Prosper Merimee attempts to seal the deal with George, but fails to rise to the occasion. —Alexander Dumas spreads rumors about the encounter. —Gustave Planche, George's one-time lover, defends her honor, so Dumas invites him to a duel. —George and Musset begin a love affair. —Planche explains he's not Sand's lover, so Dumas calls off the duel. —Sand and Musset's affair intensifies. —Planche challenges Cap de Feuillide to a duel upon reading his negative review of Sand, and the two fight, without hitting each other. —Musset is threatened by Planche's rivalry, so he writes a satirical poem about the failed duel. —Musset and George go to Venice together. —Musset begins womanizing with society and lowly women across the islands.

Both Musset and George get sick with typhoid fever, and George recovers early on, while Musset becomes violent and delirious. —George brings in Dr. Pagello to help him. —Pagello and George begin an affair once Musset begins recovering. —Musset starts to suspect something and nearly kills both of them with a knife, and threatens a duel. —Musset continues raging until George confesses that she is having an affair, so Musset offers to leave Venice and the two lovers alone. —George and Pagello have an adventurous romance in Venice. —The Canut labor uprising calls George back to Paris. —Musset and George keep getting back together and then breaking up. —George ends her relationship with Pagello, who returns to his medical practice in Venice. —Upon returning to Nohant, George demands that the woman hired to care for her daughter, but who was actually beating her and having an affair with George's husband, be fired, and this leads to a break with Casimir that forces George to prepare to file for divorce. —Musset challenges George's prior lover, Planche, to a duel because he joked about his being cuckolded in Venice. —George and Musset keep bouncing between love and hate, until they finally brake up after a string of violent and mad incidents.

George begins her legal studies under her tutor and lover, Michel de Bourges. —George begins legal negotiations for a separation or divorce from her husband. —George helps Bourges compose a radical manifesto against corruption and for the rights of labor that puts Bourges in prison for contempt during the Mammoth Canut trial. —George writes a rebellion novel and an insult against the King, which lead to her being blacklisted, and put under police surveillance. —George and Casimir go through an extremely long divorce trial that is published in its entirety and outs a few of George's extramarital affairs. —George's son, Maurice, befriends Prince Antoine, and is nearly killed in a new republican assassination plot. —The affair between George and Bourges ends.

She has a brief affair with an acting friend of Marie Dorval, Bocage. —George's mother dies after over a decade of the two barely speaking. —George has an affair with Felicien Mallefille, a younger play writer and her children's tutor. —When George begins a new affair with Frederic Chopin, Mallefille nearly kills both of them. —George withdraws from politics and spends a decade taking care of Chopin's consumption. —George writes a satirical novel, *Lucrezia* about her affair with Chopin, and after understanding the allusion Chopin ends their affair.

George's daughter, Solange marries a sculpture, Clesinger, who was after her money, so the two divorce tragically after a few years. —Chopin dies in London, without reconciling with George. —George's half-brother, Hyppolite, dies from alcoholism. —George founds a string of radical presses, newspapers and reviews, as part of her duties as the unofficial Minister of Propaganda in the period around the 1848 Revolutions. —Marie dies after learning about the ending of her acting career, and several personal tragic events, confessing her love for George on her deathbed. —George begins a string of light love affairs across the last decades of her life with young residential artist lovers: Victor Borie, Hermann Muller-Strubing, Alexandre Manceau, and Marchal le Gigantesque. —George meets twice with Napoleon III after his coup d'état to arrange for the liberty of her republican friends. —George dies on her bed in Nohant, uttering to the illustrious gathered friends, "Love live greenery."

Introduction

This book is a work of fiction, and not a biography, but it is based on a close study of Aurore Dupin's or George Sand's autobiography, and a biography of Sand's life. As the only major female novelist in the French Romantic Movement, George Sand had an extremely painful experience as she attempted to find love, but discovered that for a woman to survive heartbreak, she has to continuously end painful affairs, and venture into new stormy romances. Despite numerous near-death experiences, George continued struggling both in political and in personal battles. She wrote in her autobiography, "I believe, that one must love with one's being, or live in complete chastity no matter what the consequences. This will not impress men at all, I am well aware, but women, who have at their disposal a sense of shame and propriety, can accept this doctrine, no matter what their station in life, when they feel they are worthy of complying with it" (Sand 1012). As a child, Sand wanted to become a nun, and soon after her marriage she regretted not joining the Sisterhood so much that she spent some time at the convent when she first started having marital problems. Of course, it was too late for her to take back her marriage and her son Maurice was already learning to walk. So, Sand flew to other men, who were also cold in the end, and this flight in an attempt to find affection ended in nympholepsy, or the yearning for the unattainable ideal that she was writing about in her novels (Sand, "Critical Introduction"). Her addiction to love and search for affection earlier in life cost her millions of francs in charitable and "friendly" donations, an unparalleled work ethic to fund these, and her health as she ignored it. She was surrounded by a gang of manipulating charity seekers that fed on her desire to finally find a positive romantic relationship to bleed her of funds. Her downfall started when she married an abusive husband, Casimir, at seventeen, and had to fight for a decade through a romantic rebellion in relationships with other hurtful men, before finally gaining a divorce and regaining control over her Nohant estate with the help of a notorious and revolutionary lawyer. To prove that Casimir was only contesting the divorce because of George's money, Michel de Bourges brought up a letter where Casimir confessed, "I am going to Paris; I will not stay with you, because I do not wish to inconvenience you any more than I wish to be further inconvenienced by you" (Sand 1070). Sand detested writing romance novels across this turbulent period, when romance seemed to be as dead as her marriage, but was forced into the genre by a lack of other routes for professional advancement for a woman. One of the more frank accounts of an intimate encounter with Sand is one where Sand tells Prosper Merimee in response to his advances, "Very well, I am disposed. Let it be as you wish, since it gives you such pleasure. But for my part I must tell you that I am sure it will give me none whatsoever" (Cate 244). After saying this, Sand allowed Merimee to accompany to her apartment, undressed with the help of her maid, out of her boy's costume, and non-ceremoniously got into bed, and was so still and irresponsive that Merimee failed to rise to the occasion. There are very few other accounts with this level of detail of Sand's romantic misadventures, but I believe that the majority had a similar tone, even if Sand didn't say the same lines aloud. Her lesbian love affair with Marie Dorval, the actress she befriend when they were both at the peak of their fame, was perhaps the most satisfying among her sexual adventures, but it was tragic because both women were also married and involved with other men across their sixteen-year "friendship."

This novel is of interest to modern women who are fighting similar pressures between work, marriage, children, lovers, and their own needs and desires. It is a novel full of revolutions both political and personal, as well as back-stabbing social intrigue, social climbing, military defeats, and a string of outrageous romances, which while they all turned out badly, clearly offered some extraordinarily varied pleasures that kept Sand hooked on love until her final years. This is an anti-romance, which does not end when George finds her "true love," but continues from one great love to another, and lets love be what it is in reality, an emotion that does not know fidelity. Hopefully, it will speak to readers who have not found their rollercoaster love stories in traditional romance novels. With the current divorce rates, the asexuality movement, and the devastating state of modern dating and relationships, there must be readers out there who also see the world from this inverse perspective, where the traditionally glorified self-less love for others kills a spirited female soul, while a selfish love for the self can expand an individual and the world around her.

Works Cited

Cate, Curtis. *George Sand: A Biography.* New York: Avon, 1975.

Sand, George. *Story of My Life: The Autobiography of George Sand.* Thelma Jurgrau, Ed. Albany: State University of New York Press, 1991.

Chapter 1

The Revolution and the Social Contract

Marie-Aurore Dupin de Francueil was sitting in her boudoir, reading over the last lines of Jean-Jacques Rousseau's *La Nouvelle Heloise*, "Blind as we are, we each waste an existence in the pursuit of different chimeras, and refuse to see, that, of all the illusions of humanity, those of the just man alone lead to happiness." Her eyes were wet, and her face convulsing. She looked up at the mirror and saw that her soft, white round shoulders were trembling. A couple of tears had fallen onto her purple dress, outlined with finely embroidered lace, and she now wiped them away. Half of her hair were up in a high bun, and the rest were curled and running down her back. Her lips were painted a bright red, and her cheeks were running a pink blush that her maid had put on minutes earlier. The maid ran back into the room now and seeing the havoc the tears had caused, she wiped the tears away, and put on fresh makeup, until only the red veins in Aurore's eyes and the puffiness around them gave away the emotional distress the lady was in.

Aurore inhaled to gain courage, fighting against her corset, when her childhood friend, Mme. d'Esparbes de Lussan, rushed into the room on her fine heels, throwing her hands up with exasperation. D'Esparbes' back had been deformed by a fall from a pony she suffered years earlier, and her cross-eyes had difficulty focusing on Aurore's face.

"My darling Aurore," d'Esparbes gasped, "they are waiting for you! He's in such a mood, he looks like he might jump up and run off at any minute."

Aurore hopped up, checking her attire one more time in the mirror. "Yes, I'm sorry. I wanted to review the book before going down, and I just lost control of myself." The maid made a few adjustments to the back of

the dress, as Aurore walked out of the boudoir, and hurried down the spi-
ral central staircase to the back door. A servant opened the door for her,
and she was hit with the heavy smell of the surrounding roses, the rays
of the afternoon sun, and the sound of birds chirping on the branches
of ancient trees surrounding the garden. A small party was sitting at
a delicately laid out table in the center of this finely cut and arranged
courtly garden. Aurore's husband, M. de Francueil, was on one side of
the table, beaming at Aurore as she approached, while the other side of
the table was occupied by an awkward, scowling, short man in a worn out
traveling outfit, whom Aurore immediately recognized as Jean-Jacques
Rousseau.

It was 1776, and Jean-Jacques had been in withdrawal from society for the previous two years, as his political writings had led him to
view the world and the monarchy in a progressively darker light, until he could barely chat with an aristocrat without expressing his bitter
criticism. His writings were later to inspire the French Revolution, but
in the final years of his life, he attempted to shield his work from censorship by closing himself off from external influences. M. de Francueil had
roped Jean-Jacques into a visit by expressing a similar radical sentiment
because he wanted to impress his young wife, who was impervious to
nearly everything aside from her books. The two had been friends for two
decades, but Rousseau withdrew from Francueil, as from everybody else.
At the same time, Aurore had a few close friends, but she preferred reading in the library to most social interactions. Aurore was the illegitimate
daughter of Maurice de Saxe, a famous military hero, who was the de-
scendant of August II the Strong, King of Poland, so her family had the
best connections to the aristocracy of France, but she was not as well received in society as her relations due to her illegitimacy, an uncomfortable
detail that made her prone to withdrawing from society. Knowing how
much Aurore had adored Rousseau's work, M. de Francueil approached
bringing Rousseau over for a visit as he would have approached a diplo-
matic negotiation. But, it had taken Aurore hours to get ready and come
down, and meanwhile M. de Francueil was driving Rousseau to distraction by chatting about agriculture, current fashion, and a string of other
topics to which Rousseau only replied by throwing more of his dinner
to the doves that were jumping after it in a pack. Rousseau had tolerated
these subjects when he wanted to be polite in society, but now he had lost
all taste for them.

Aurore gently sat down at the table, shyly glancing over at Rousseau's aggressive movements and furrowed brow.

"...So, you think we should all grow our own garden on a little farm?"
M. de Francueil was finishing a thought.

"Yes, it's much better for people to reconnect with nature, to live on the land."

"Are you really gardening then? I mean you have an estate, surely you have men helping you?"

"Of course, but I don't see a point in working my peasants until exhaustion just so I can buy a better cane, or a better horse."

"They sign a contract with their lord, to obey and serve him. There is nothing sinful about holding them to their agreement."

"Why did you ask me to come here?!" Rousseau stood up, throwing an armful of crumbs to the birds. "You just like the rest of them. You think I haven't heard your replies dozens of times before, you wanted to lay on a bit more on me, so that what? Who put you up to this?"

"No one. I have been trying to understand your side of the debate. I'm sorry if I have offended you."

Aurore blushed scarlet, and opened her mouth, thinking of stepping in and defending Rousseau's position, but Jean-Jacques looked over at her with scorn, and she remained silent, casting her eyes down at the tablecloth. Rousseau nodded and walked away from the table, and around the Chateauroux, towards the place where a servant was already holding the reins of his aging, brown horse. Aurore was stunned by this sudden exit, and was devastated that she had not been able to express her deep admiration for Rousseau's political and literary genius. But, all Rousseau saw was a short and plump little aristocratic socialite, who was two hours late for dinner, and apparently not gracious enough to even look directly at her distinguished guest.

These events untraveled a couple months after Aurore's wedding to Dupin, and in a few months her only child, George Sand's father, Maurice Dupin, was born, and nine after this M. Francueil died in 1786, leaving a ruined estate to his wife and young son. Aurore had a basic education, and it was enough for her to be able to manage her accounts and to recover from this loss. Aurore and Maurice might have eventually regained their fine family's former glory if the French Revolution did not derail them, shifting the course of their lives into a radical new direction.

In the years before the Revolution, Aurore acquired and moved into the apartment in Paris that Sand later inherited on Rue du Roi-de-Sicile, which was decorated with Chinese rugs, gilded fireplaces, and pastel-blue damask furnishings, and overlooked a luxurious garden. Maurice had several qualified tutors up till that point, and despite her financial distress, Aurore felt that it was essential to hire the best available tutor in Paris for him, and the man for the job was Abbe Francois Deschartres, who was teaching at the College du Cardinal Lemoine and studying medicine under M. Desault, at the time, but eventually became a permanent tutor in residence on the Dupin estate after the Revolution.

Between 1786 and 1793, France went through a period of drastic changes from feudalism to capitalism, from prosperity to poverty, and from monarchy to a temporary republic. The trouble started with an element that seemed inessential at the time to the rich, but was devastating to the poor, and pushed them towards desperate actions. Grain was getting more expensive, and like the Potato Famine in the next century, when grain and bread became barely accessible to the poor, their stomachs reported a major problem in the social order. The feudal system in France had passed its peak centuries earlier, but while there was now a way to make a living from capitalist wages, and one could start a business to work one's way up into the bourgeoisie class, most peasants, and they were the overwhelming majority in France, preferred to live on their ancestral land, under the same feudal families as for the prior millennium. But, history aligned not only high grain prices, but also a rise in dues and rents for the peasants, and a reduction in wages for the city laborers in 1788, and the strain broke the workers' backs. While France had a strict policy against sedition in the press up to that point, the monarchy made the mistake of loosening censorship just at that crucial moment, and July saw an explosion in radical, revolutionary newspapers and pamphlets. Aurore joined the ecstasy of this outcry by writing some lampoons on Marie-Antoinette herself, which George Sand burned when she was twenty and hoping to live a dignified high-society life. A year into this outpouring of hatred towards the spending-crazed monarchy, in June of 1789, Louis XVI decided to seal a gaping wound by pouring liquor on it, and attempted a *coup d'etat* to dismiss the Estates General, and to reclaim power over the French nation. The attempt failed and in the following month a mob, among whom few could sign their own name, stormed the Bastille, and, with the help of the force of freeing the political prisoners held there, demanded that the king recognize that he did not have a "divine" right to rule granted to him by God, but rather that he only had the power that the people allowed him. This was an idea that spread in pamphlets since the American Revolution years earlier, in works of theorists like Thomas Paine, but it came in simpler phrases and slogans down to this mob that was fighting with an animal hunger for bread and wages, rather than with memorized quotations in mind. Weeks later, the new national Assembly abolished feudalism, loosening a burden of paying fees despite near-starvation conditions on the peasants. After the Revolution, land was redistributed from aristocratic and church hands to the peasants, but it would take years for the country to recover from the devastation that the violence and fires of the revolution brought.

The peak of Revolutionary violence occurred years later. The hottest riots occurred after the Louis XVI attempted to flee Paris for Germany in June of 1791, only to be returned with dishonor, and to be overthrown a year later in August of 1792. The overthrow signaled the end of the monarchy, and the new power held by the proletariat, so riots intensified. Among these rioters was Jean-Paul Marat, who fought alongside a murderous gang in the September Massacres of 1792, who took out thousands of prisoners in the Parisian goals, and then was elected for this loyalty to the National Convention that same year, only to be murdered in his bath by a monarchist sympathizer, Charlotte Corday, and to become one of the more famous martyrs of the French Revolution. When the September Massacres had ended, on September 21, universal male suffrage was proclaimed, slavery was abolished, divorce was legalized. The rebels were hungry for blood, and the military began to war with most of their European neighbors, while also fighting a civil war at home with the Vendee and Chouans rebels, of the latter around two hundred thousand were executed. Aurore was right to have remained in Paris when the Revolution started because there were only three thousand executions in the city, while nationally several hundred thousand people were executed, a million "suspects" were imprisoned, and a hundred-fifty thousand were forced to emigrate. Two of those executed were the deposed king Louis XVI, and his successor, who attempted renaming himself as "Philip Equality," and voted for the execution of his predecessor, in an attempt to save himself. Aurore had observed these events, reading about them in the revolutionary press, and seeing them in the streets of Paris.

Putting business ahead of personal safety, early in 1793, Aurore bought the Nohant estate that remained in the family for the following three generations. It was a place in central France, near the childhood home that was lost after the death of her husband. But, before she could move to this new domicile, her Parisian apartment was raided as part of the revolutionary Terror on November 26, 1793, and she was arrested for hiding her wealth in the walls of the apartment. Aurore was jailed in an English convent on Rue des Fosses-Saint-Victor, while Maurice and Deschartres remained in the apartment on Rue de Roi. A couple of days passed between the initial arrest and a more thorough search of the apartment and in that time Deschartres and Maurice were able to destroy documents that proved that Aurore had made a loan to aid the escape of the later King of France, Charles X, because she was a cousin of Louis XVI, or a near-relation of the Bourbon dynasty. If these papers were found, Aurore would have been immediately executed. Instead, Aurore spent a month at the convent before the apartment was closely searched for nine hours, and because nothing besides the initially discovered hidden wealth was found, Aurore was released from the convent prison on

August 22, 1794, having been imprisoned for nine months. On August 22, Aurore was released without any money and in convent rags, but instead of finding a carriage to take her, she walked, for the first time in her life, all the way to Passy, on the other side of the city, to see Maurice and to give him the good news. After regrouping, Aurore, Maurice and Deschartres moved into their new chateau at Nohant. But, this detention left a scar on all three of them because Aurore prided herself with being a radical, and a supporter of revolutionary change, but suddenly they had a sense that regardless of their beliefs, they would always be titled and members of the aristocracy in the eyes of the peasants and the proletariat.

Chapter 2

Conscription Service and the Fight for Legitimacy

It was a warm and clear night in September of 1795, and a new riot had broken out in Paris. The administration was by now attempting to crush these uprisings, as the Terror had served its purpose, and there was a need for peace at home, while France began aggressive campaigns abroad. A group of unemployed and barely employed hooligans had picked up bricks and other projectiles and were throwing them at a public building, which had just been restored after earlier vandalisms. A few of the rougher men in this gang had already broken some noses of those shopkeepers, and employees at the building who dared to intervene, and there was a threat of deadly violence. The rioters suddenly heard the trot of a few horses approaching. They stopped, with stones-in-hand and looked in the direction of the noise. In moments, a short Corsican general, with long, straight black hair, a sharply cut nose, and a blue uniform with gilded buttons trotted towards the front of the crowd on his horse. He was followed by a few other soldiers, all heavily armed.

"Disperse immediately!" Napoleon Buonaparte commanded, for it was indeed the man who would name himself Emperor of France within the coming decade, but who at this moment was only a minor general, attending to his nightly duties in Paris. "You are causing an unsanctioned disruption, and if you do not cease your harassments, we will be forced to make a suitable response."

"Disperse yourself," shouted a drunkard, nearly falling over to the stones of the street, as he made an attempt to be heard.

"You've been warned," Napoleon proclaimed. "Fire the grapeshot."

The men behind him wheeled out a carronade with grapeshot ammunition that had been tied to one of their horses, and began aligning it with the center of the crowd. Seeing that the small troop was about to carry out the threat, most of the gang dispersed, running in all directions away from the center of the attack, screaming and screeching, as they stumbled over each other to get away. A couple of drunks, including the one that made the response, had more difficulty escaping than the majority, and they were still crawling or stumbling away when the grapeshot was fired. The drunkard got a flash-wound on his shoulder, and there were a few other scrapes, but all of the rebels managed to leave the scene on-foot, rather than in a box. In minutes, the street was empty of all onlookers and rioters, and Napoleon and his men were left alone to survey the result of their efforts.

The success was complete and was achieved with a single shot of grapeshot, without any loss of life. Napoleon reported to his superior officers later that night, and they congratulated him warmly on his bravery and decisive action. The Terror had hardly subsided, so fighting back against an angry mob would have required more than the usual bit of bravery, as they were likely to be armed and could've turned their weapons on the troops, as the government was new and some of the rebels did not supports its actions. An easy victory allowed the military to encourage other military men to also show bravery when responding to unrest in the city. The achievement was significant enough for Bonaparte, who took out the Italian "u" from his name, to be promoted to Commander of the Interior, and given command of the campaign in Northern Italy.

This acclaim attracted the attention of the women who circulated with the top military circles. Napoleon had been engaged to Desiree Clary, who he met in 1794, when she had made an appeal on her brother's behalf to the War Ministry, where Napoleon's brother, Joseph, worked at the time, who was about to be executed during the Terror because his father had applied to become a noble before the Revolution, to rise above his bourgeoisie mercantile roots. Desiree and Napoleon had a year-long courtship, when the riot incident suddenly catapulted Napoleon's reputation.

Paul Francois Jean Nicolas, the vicomte de Barras, at that time the executive leader of the Directory had given a dinner at his luxurious Parisian residence. Napoleon found himself in a circle of gossiping ladies at the dinner table, and the woman who made the strongest impression on him was the one dressed in the finest fashionable dress for the period, who was sitting next to Barras because she was his mistress. This lady was none other than Rose, or as Napoleon preferred to call her, Josephine de Beauharnais, whose first husband was executed during the Terror, an event that did not stop her from going to bed with his executioners.

While she endured love affairs with revolutionaries, Josephine held a suppressed hatred for those who wronged her family, which she hid below her smile, her rose garden, and her flirtatious coquetry. Josephine flirted furiously with Napoleon, and he fell for this attention because he had never been courted by a strong, ambitious woman like Josephine before. The two began an affair, and within a year Napoleon was so smitten that he proposed marriage, and they were married civilly before an officer of the court in Paris, on March 6, 1796. Only two days after the wedding, Napoleon left for the Italian campaign. Barras was furious about this wedding, and this anger was partially why Napoleon was particularly attracted to Josephine, as he did not want to be exiled to Italy, while the revolutionary government's bureaucrats maneuvered in Paris for top leadership positions. Winning over Barras' mistress was a symbolic victory for Napoleon while he could not reject the Command of the Italian troops without going out of favor with the Directory government. But, this rebellious action made Napoleon into an aggrieved enemy in Barras' eyes and he decided that he wanted to keep Napoleon abroad as long as possible. The affair also isolated Napoleon from his own family, who were outraged by Josephine being six years older than Napoleon, her prior two children, and her superior attitude.

The Italian campaign involved strenuous travel, as Napoleon had to cross the Saint-Bernard on a mule to gain a position, and it was successful enough for Napoleon to have continued in honorable service in the following years. The distance from Paris plunged Napoleon back into obscurity. Napoleon hated being out of the spotlight, the harsh conditions involved in living in distant encampments, the diseases and malnutrition among the troops, the long marches, and the constant threat of death on the field. What was he fighting for? He gained some distinction for suppressing a riot, but as time passed, and promotions passed him by, he began to believe that the only way to gain real power was to seize it by force by helping an uprising, instead of blindly obeying his superiors' orders. History was teaching him this lesson, as he saw that incompetent men with little experience had gained the top positions in the military and in the government that were out of reach to him despite his aristocratic birth, and loyalty. Napoleon might have continued contemplating greatness without seizing power, if it hadn't been for a tragic personal development.

Within months of Napoleon's departure, Josephine went to a social gathering for the troops, where she was introduced to a Hussar officer, nine-years her junior, Hippolyte Charles. The two began a love affair, visited Napoleon together in Milan later that same year, and stayed together for the following two years. In 1798, Napoleon was told repeatedly by his counselors about the affair, and these reports were so infuriating that he drew up the divorce papers. Napoleon's letters regarding the affair were seized by the British and published in the radical press in London and Paris, a publication that mortified him, and made him hungry for a bitter revenge. Upon reading Napoleon's letter regarding the affair in a Parisian paper one morning, Josephine stopped her affair with Hippolyte, and put her seductive powers towards seducing Napoleon into staying married. These news drove Napoleon to distraction, as he wanted to be in Paris, keeping a watchful eye on his wife, instead of in Egypt on end-less campaigns. He started an affair with the wife of one of his officers to regain some manly pretentions, but while it won him some supporters among the Casanovas among his troops, it did not sooth his internal agi-tation and building hatred towards humanity in general, which he saw as conspiring against him in war and in love.

Finally, flabbergasted by years of strenuous campaigns and news that France might be invaded on its home soil, Napoleon deserted his troops in Egypt and returned to Paris in August of 1799. While the circum-stances were hazy, the Directory, and more specifically his old enemy, Barras, accused him of desertion, but stopped short of executing him. The threat of potential death after all those years of dedicated military service brought Napoleon to the edge of desperation and to a stone-cold hatred of the Directory regime. He took some time to recuperate from all those years of harsh living conditions, and by the end of October he was alert and eager to find a way to turn his years of military experience into a conquest on his home soil. It was on November 2, 1799, when he sud-denly jumped into center-stage, taking charge of leading a *coup d'etat* that managed to overthrow the Directory, and founded the Consulate regime, of which Napoleon Bonaparte gained unchallengeable power. The years that followed were among the most aggressive in France's military his-tory, and they moved political debates in the country from radical social-ism to totalitarian compliance, a shift that once again made an enormous redirection in the story of the Dupin family.

Five years after Aurore's imprisonment and a year before Napoleon's *coup d'etat*, in September of 1798, Maurice, who was twenty by that time, enlisted in the French Army. He was called into service by the universal military conscription that had been in-place since 1793, as the French army ballooned into a force of a million men and continued its war with Europe and for colonial dominance. Maurice attempted to work his way up the ranks honorably, without asking or paying for favors, which meant that he spent five years at the rank of lieutenant, while most men with his aristocratic title surpassed him years earlier. Maurice had a good deal in common with the young Napoleon, but his passion was for drama and for love, while Napoleon thirsted for conquest and power. Maurice was also miserable traveling between encampments, and only found relief in his occasional trips to Paris and to Nohant to rest and recuperate.

In 1800, a couple of years into his stint as a lieutenant, while Napoleon's family began gaining royal titles across Europe, Maurice was in Milan during the Italian campaign. During a break in the fighting, Maurice wandered through the cobblestone streets of Milan, looking at the beauty of that ancient city. He was not looking at anything in particular when he noticed a delicate woman, who stood out sharply amidst a crowd of Italians. She was bargaining loudly in a heavy French accent with a shopkeeper about the price of a skirt. Her dress was outrageous, and yet tasteful, as it mixed colors and materials that hardly matched, and yet created a strong positive impression. Maurice came closer and as she was turning to go, with the acquired skirt in-hand, Sophie-Victoire Antoinette Delaborde met eyes with his, and the two shared a moment of tense embarrassment.

"Well Monsieur, how can I help you?" Sophie blurted out after a moment of silence.

"I was just admiring your taste in skirts. I was thinking of buying something for my mother, while I'm in Milan."

"You've asked the right person, as it so happens I own a hat-shop, so I should be able to be of help."

Sophie introduced herself and pointed out the benefits of different outfits that the merchant was selling, and after Maurice chose a piece, she bargained on his behalf with the merchant until the price was to her satisfaction.

Noticing a bit of sweat on Sophie's forehead, Maurice exclaimed, "I've exhausted you, please let me take you to dinner at a nice restaurant, so I can repay you for your kind assistance."

Sophie blushed, and nodded in agreement.

Maurice took Sophie to the finest restaurant in Milan, and the two chatted at-length about their past, as both were homesick for France. At first Sophie attempted to hold back the details about her past, but then they started talking about the Terror, and it turned out that Sophie was imprisoned at the English convent at the same time as Aurore, and this detail raised the flood-gate that was holding her back from being entirely truthful with the handsome stranger she met only hours earlier. Sophie became orphaned as a young child, and married at seventeen to find some protection, but this marriage was disrupted by her imprisonment during the Terror only three years later. Sophie had a child from her first marriage, and had given birth to a second child out-of-wedlock a year before meeting Maurice. This child, Caroline, was now waiting for her in a dim apartment and Sophie was distraught from the lack of certainty about how she would care for this new babe, as she was now twenty-seven, and while she had found an elderly gentlemen that was kind enough to bring her with him to Milan, he did not appear to be willing to commit to marrying her, or to taking permanent care of her family. Sophie glossed over the details a bit, but she revealed enough for Maurice to have entirely comprehended her delicate situation. He was touched by this story, and offered to pay for her hotel stay in La Chatre, inviting her to visit him in his home region of Berry, where the Nohant estate was. Maurice was not outraged or surprised by Sophie's story, as he also strayed by fathering an illegitimate son with a peasant on the Nohant estate, Hippolyte, who was being raised at Nohant, under a vague cover-up. Hippolyte was named after Empress Josephine's young Hussar lover, Hippolyte Charles. Sophie agreed and the two started an affair that lasted casually for three years before it experienced a major development.

The couple met infrequently over these three years due to Maurice's duties, their separate domiciles, and other obstacles between them. They had been practicing *coitus interruptus* during intercourse to avoid insemination, but shortly after the start of the year 1804, it became clear that Sophie was with child. Maurice was twenty-six and Sophie was thirty, and since there were now three illegitimate children between them, and they both wanted to stay together indefinitely, they decided that a marriage between them would simplify life for the forthcoming child, and would make both of them happy. A religious marriage was out of the question, and even a civil marriage was difficult to arrange because the father needed a promissory signature from a parent before he could marry, and Maurice had already had the debate with Aurore regarding the youthful affair that resulted in Hippolyte, and at that time she outright forbade him from marrying the illiterate peasant girl that carried the child. Maurice knew that asking would result in a retaliatory action in addition to a rejection, so he forged his mother's signature to pull off a civil marriage ceremony.

A few months later, with Sophie in an advanced stage of the pregnancy, the couple was joined civilly. Sophie wore a thin and airy, dimity dress, which was a bit uncharacteristic for her eccentric taste, but which brought a glow to Maurice's eyes, as he put a thin gold band on her finger, and they exchanged vows.

Maurice was lucky enough to have some months he could spend in Paris after the wedding, and the couple engaged in a bohemian reverie, as they settled into living on 15 Rue Meslay in Paris. On July 5th of 1804, the family was listening to Maurice playing his Cremona violin, while Caroline, Sophie and six other guests were dancing the quadrilles, performing the square shaped formation maneuvers with *L'etes* and accidents. Quadrilles only became widely popular among the poorer population a decade later, while at this point it was a very push social activity, only practiced among the aristocracy, and Maurice had brought in a dancing instructor to demonstrate this intricate dance. Still smiling widely, and a bit out of breath, Sophie separated herself from the dancers, nodding while lifting the sides of her "pretty pink dress." The dance resumed, though the perfect symmetry was interrupted, while Sophie quietly made her way into her bedroom down the hall. When Maurice finished playing a piece and was about to start a new variation, Sophie's sister, Lucie, also extricated herself from the arrangement and upon entering the bedroom screamed loud enough for all to hear over the violin, "Maurice, you have a daughter!"

Maurice rushed into the room and found Sophie on the bed, trying to push all of her pink skirt up high enough to avoid the blood and placenta that were on the sheets around a baby girl. Lucie had rushed into the bathroom and brought out a wet towel that she used to wipe the baby, giving Sophie another towel to adjust herself. The birth took less than an hour, and for half of that time Sophie was still dancing the quadrilles. The baby was clearly anxious to get out of the dark womb and to study the spectacle she was only hearing when locked in. A maid came in and straightened up the room, while the party dispersed in the living room, giving the family time to make arrangements. The guests whispered and laughed with delight as they exited the apartment into the summer night.

"Let's call her Aurore," Maurice pronounced after everything was arranged, and Aurore was sleeping majestically in the center of the refreshed bed.

"After your mother?" Sophie asked.

"It will help us convince her to approve of the marriage. We have to try our best to appease her."

The process of sealing the marriage and Aurore's legitimacy proved to be a difficult one, but both of the parents knew, looking down at Aurore that there was something unusual about the child, and that she was destined for greatness despite her sex.

Chapter 3

Escorting the Emperor

There were many parallels between the lives of the Napoleon's family and the path of the Dupin family. The matriarch of the Dupin clan, Aurore, had funded the king's escape attempt during the Terror, and this was only one intrigue that happened to come out into the open because of the extensive search of Aurore's Parisian apartment. There were many other ties between Dupin aristocratic roots and the new regime that Napoleon was building by focusing on strengthening his family's ties with the aristocracy of Europe. Maurice was unusual in his minor role in the Empire. One Dupin family relation was Marquis de Caulaincourt, who began his military career at fifteen, before the Terror, and served as the master of horses to the Emperor from 1812. Then there was General Harville, who began as a Divisional General in the Revolution and in the Napoleonic Wars, and later had a similar post to Caulaincourt's, or Master of Horse, but to Empress Josephine.

Maurice's nephew, Rene, served as the chamberlain to Prince Louis, Napoleon's brother, who served as the King of Holland between 1806 and 1810. Rene's wife served as the lady's companion to Prince Louis' wife, the Princess. One of their relations that were of particular historical significance was M. de Segur, who had assisted in the American War of Independence, then wrote comedies for the Russian Empress Catherine II, then retired during the French Revolution, only to be brought back into politics as an elected member of the senate by Napoleon in 1801. Comte M. de Segur later became the master dignitary of the Empire and grand master of ceremonies, which offered a handsome salary of a hundred thousand francs, and forty thousand on top of this for serving as the councilor of state. If Maurice had played his cards correctly, he could have become obscenely wealthy and successful through an introduction by any one of these great relations. Instead, he chose to work his way up as if he was one of those bourgeoisie that were attempting to enter the new careers open to "talent" that Napoleon had put in place to appear to democratize his inner circle, meanwhile working to surround himself with the top aristocrats to give his regime legitimacy.

The stress of having fathered a child and married without his mother's consent, on top of continuing his habitation in the barracks among lower-class soldiers finally exhausted Maurice's constitution in 1804, and he fell deadly ill with scarlet fever. As Maurice was tossing and turning on his floor mat, he received a letter from Octave de Segur's mother. Octave was a close relation of Comte M. de Segur, and Octave worked in the Comte's office years earlier, before serving as the sub-prefect at Soissons. Maurice had frequently spoken with Octave at dinners, fetes, and other gatherings organized by Comte M. de Segur. On their last meeting, Octave confessed that his lover was unfaithful to him, and that when he attempted to berate her for her actions, she had told him that she could no longer see him, if he was going to be flying into rages. Maurice attempted to ease Octave's mind by saying that he was better off without her, but Octave was hardly hearing him, and then suddenly left in the middle of Maurice's remarks. Maurice had called on his apartment several times, asked the servants about him, wrote to all of his relations, and otherwise searched for Octave over the following two years, but no clues about his whereabouts surfaced. Maurice's eyes swelled with tears now, as he read the letter from Octave's mother that informed him that Octave was found dead in a river in Milan. The circumstances of the death clearly pointed to a suicide, and the fever made Maurice so delusional that he imagined that this outcome was entirely his fault, and that had he told Octave just the right words, he could have pointed him on a path that would have led to happiness instead of this disastrous end.

In a couple of weeks the fever cleared, and Maurice felt a sudden burst of productive energy, as he felt as if life was flying by him, and that if he failed to make a play to get ahead at that moment, he might end up as a body fished out of a Milan river himself. So, he took a long bath, received the best grooming services, bought a new wig and outfit, and thus dressed and arranged in the best finery his mother's allowance could afford, he made his way to meet with Emperor Napoleon on November 20 of 1804. The title just used was the other chief motivator for Maurice's desire to present himself, as Napoleon had just named himself Emperor days earlier, and while this move upset the higher sentiments of his mother and other radicals, if Maurice was to continue to serve in the army, he felt that now was the best time for ambition.

Maurice took a carriage to the Tuileries imperial palace. He entered through the central doorway and was greeted by an army of servants and military men. He was escorted through the southern gallery, which was decorated in the Neoclassical style by Fontaine, and furnished in gilded chairs, tables and chandeliers, into the Napoleon's study, an enormous room. Emperor Napoleon was sitting at the table, and was signing a stack of letters and decrees on the table in front of him. Maurice was struck by the site of a jeweled cabinet at Napoleon's side, and the gilt-bronze ornaments that decorated the edge of the table.

Emperor Napoleon looked up as Maurice stopped and bowed a few steps from the table.

"Your Imperial Majesty, it is an honor to meet you. Thank you for agreeing to see me," Maurice proclaimed, saluting in the military style, and standing at attention.

"At your ease," Napoleon replied. "Comte M. de Segur has highly recommended you. So, let's get to the point, what is this all about?"

"Comte M. de Segur was too kind, thank you. I requested this meeting because I have served in the army for around five years and I still hold the rank of lieutenant, and I have been hoping to be promoted to the title of captain, if it pleases you?"

"I'm afraid that it does not please me."

"I'm sorry, is there something wrong with the request? Should I present it in writing?"

"No, We will not need the request in writing."

"It's just that I have recently married, and my wife has given birth to a daughter, and as my family's needs are growing, a promotion would help me to keep my affairs in order."

"While that is clearly the case, all promotions have been postponed for a year, as I adjust the government to my new needs as Emperor."

"Of course, Your Majesty. I'm sorry that I was so forward."

"By all means, I asked you to be direct."

Maurice bowed, as the Emperor nodded, dismissing him. Maurice exited backwards, bowing a few more times. As Maurice was turning around in the hallway he met with Comte M. de Segur who was on his way into the Emperor's study. The two gave each other a small bow of the head.

"How did it go?" Comte de Segur inquired.

"Not well. Did you know that the Emperor is delaying all promotions for a year?"

"Ah, I suspected, but it has not yet been formally announced. I will be sure to send a note to you when this limit is lifted. Be well, I'm sure it won't be long until your services are recognized."

They bowed to each other again, and Maurice continued towards the exit, while Comte de Segur stepped into the study.

"Ah, Segur come here, there's much to discuss. What a good chap that cousin of yours, Maurice, is. Too bad about the delay with his promotion, he looks like he needs it."

"Yes Your Majesty, but he'll manage." Comte de Segur bowed and approached close enough to see the papers the Emperor was working on.

"I have completed the composition of the Civil Code. You will review it before it goes to the delegates?"

"Yes, of course, Your Majesty."

"Women are going to once again have the legal rights of minors. Divorce laws from the revolutionary period will be repealed. These are all points we discussed before, in reply to the requests that have come in regarding unruliness among the women, Josephine being only a sharp example of the havoc out there. If somebody doesn't brittle them, they'll ruin the whole country with their disobedience."

"Yes, Your Majesty, I agree it's best to regain control over the situation."

Napoleon handed the Comte a stack of letters, "These should go out to a number of architects, painters, and musicians I'd like to commission to serve at the palace. This place needs a northern wing, to connect the Tuileries to the Louvre, and I described some of the other projects I would like to focus on to the artists. I'll need your help supervising some of this work."

"I would be delighted to help, Your Majesty."

"And then there is the other matter… Do you recall the Dagger Conspiracy from that evening at the opera house in 1800, right after the *coup d'etat*? And the royalist infernal machine plot from December of that same year?"

"Of course, Your Majesty, I believe you called me into the senate a few months after the second plot to assist you with preventing similar disasters."

"And you have done a great job protecting my interests, simply superb… But, of course, you are aware that the royalists have become active again in the plot earlier this year by the Duke of Enghien, you helped with his recapture and execution. So, do you think it worked, has my recent adoption of the title Emperor of France meant that there is no point of continued assassinations because the crown would pass down to my sons, instead of to the Bourbons, if they succeed in assassinating me?"

"There hasn't been a new assassination plot in recent months, Your Majesty, so I believe that our plot did work, as planned."

"We must have a coronation by the Pope, or they can raise questions of legitimacy of the title."

"Pope Pius VII has replied that he will only anoint you as Emperor if you and Empress Josephine have a religious marriage, before God, as he does not recognize the civil ceremony under which you were wed."

Napoleon furrowed his brows and supported his chin with his hand, looking momentarily at the distant corner of the room.

"That would affirm the marriage, and would detract the one stipulation that currently exists that can annul the marriage."

"Your Majesty, do you want to annul the marriage?"

"No, of course not. We discussed the point already. There's no point of dwelling on it, if the Pope requires a religious marriage, regardless of how I feel about Catholicism, religion, or about marriage, it is a necessary step to guarantee that my sons will inherit my title, and that the assassination attempts will become mute-strategies. If I have to marry for the sake of the safety of my family and the Empire, I guess We must take the plunge once more."

"Cardinal Fesch has volunteered to run the ceremony, Your Majesty, is this agreeable?"

"Yes, he will do. And once all this is settled, then we can look around to figure out who has been loyal and who is in league with the royalists. I know that your family has been an enormous help, but with so many aristocrats keen on stabbing me in the back, even somebody as loyal as Maurice can be a threat if I let him come to close without some retrospection."

"Yes, I would advise Your Majesty to be cautious with all appointments until Your Majesty has the reins fully in-hand."

The Emperor nodded and dismissed the good Comte, who exited gracefully, carrying the letters and the Code that he was asked to process. The Emperor returned to the pile of letters before him, becoming engrossed in their content before the Comte fully left the study.

***

A year after this meeting, Maurice found himself in the ranks of the Hussars in the middle of a brutal Moravian winter. Camping in the thin tents at night, with only goulash, and basic army provisions to keep warm, Maurice, in his thin navy-blue uniform, could barely feel his fingers as he grabbed onto his Charleville .69-caliber musket, which at five-feet was Maurice's height when stretched upwards. He also had a substantial sword dangling at his side, and, between the two of these, travel by means other than horseback, even between the tent and the horse was a strenuous exercise. The troops had been marching and fighting across Europe since a few days after Maurice's meeting with Napoleon, and it was now December 2nd, twelve months since Maurice last saw a warm Parisian bed. The size of the army astounded Maurice, as he felt lost and insignificant in a sea of two-hundred thousand soldiers. The fighting had escalated in the months leading up to December, as Napoleon was attempting to make a dent in the struggle before the middle of the winter. France lost at sea, but gained thousands of Prussian prisoners on land. The previous month had engaged Maurice's creativity more than the previous year, as he assisted Napoleon in a covert maneuver that was aimed to persuade the Russo-Austrian army that the French troops were weakened and that they were preparing for surrender. Maurice accompanied the Emperor on his meeting with the Russian Emperor's aide, Count Dolgorouki on November 28th. Napoleon was hiding the truth strength of his forces, and baiting the Russian Czar to attack first, and Maurice anticipated that an attack could come at any hour.

It was 7am on December 2nd, and between the heavy clouds and the slow-rising sun, there was barely enough light for Maurice to see outlines of the terrain. Maurice barely slept that night as he felt and believed that the battle would start that morning, a premonition that was aided by the fact that Napoleon had asked to be awakened at 5am, and was already holding council with his top commanders. Maurice studied the peak of Santon Hill and the village clusters spread across his field of vision. Both armies formed straight lines along the low-lying parts between the surrounding hills. Most of the French army was now up, and were busy with breakfast, and before long the commanders emerged from Napoleon's tent and spread out for a round of inspections.

At exactly 8am, Maurice heard the first round of cannon file from the direction of the village of Telnitz, and within moments the French army was on their feet, in formation and executing a carefully planned strategy. The columns performed a complex maneuver, and Maurice joined in, taking his assigned place among the Hussars. The fighting continued steadily until 4pm, when France became the clear winner in the conflict, and the Russo-Austrian army surrendered and signed a truce two days later, having suffered the loss of 27,000 soldiers, while the French lost 9,000. The battlefield was covered in bodies, and while fewer Frenchmen lost their lives, Maurice was shaken by the violence of this clash, and retreated to his tent, away from the stench of the bodies, as soon as the surrender was called out. After recuperating for a few moments in his tent, Maurice realized that Napoleon would look for him as he tallied the dead, and made plans for the coming days, so he overcame his momentary weakness and approached the war-tent.

The commanders were once again in a meeting, and when a few of them exited to smoke cigars, several shook Maurice's hand, congratulating him on his bravery, as he fought in decisive positions that saw the heaviest losses, and held his ground, striking down dozens of enemy troops with his musket, firing up to five volleys a minute, and striking soldiers that were over a hundred yards away. Maurice had learned to shoot from hunting on his home estates since he was a child with his father, then with Deschartres, and later on his own or with hunting parties. He also received fencing and military training from professional tutors, who had served in the royal army before conscribing, this being one of the reasons he was willing to conscript, as his military skills were superior and he managed to hold his own on the battlefield across his many years of service.

Maurice accompanied Napoleon to the political negotiations that followed this victory, and on December 20th, he was called in by the Emperor.

Maurice had some trouble cleaning the blood and mud off his official uniform, which he had to wear on the negotiation visits he made with Napoleon in the previous weeks, but enough of it came out for Maurice to count himself as modestly presentable.

Maurice bowed as he entered the Emperor's tent. The Emperor was having dinner with his top advisors, and invited him to dine with them, pointing to a seat near enough to him for the two to be able to talk.

Maurice sat down and they indulged in an unusually fine dinner for a gathering in the field of battle. The table included lobster thermidor, chicken marengo and napoleons pastries. Maurice forgot about the battle, and nearly forgot that he was dining with Napoleon himself, as he did his best to mind his manners while he ate morsels of these delicatessens, after a year of only eating canned food. When Maurice had finished his second napoleon, the Emperor caught his eye and announced loudly enough for the entire gathering to hear.

"Maurice Dupin, your conduct during this campaign has been out-standing, as all gathered here can attest. You have dedicated many years to the honorable service of the Empire, and I would be doing a disservice to the military profession if I failed to immediately promote you to a rank you so rightly deserve. So, you are hereby granted the rank of captain of the 1st Hussars."

Maurice stood up, and gave the Emperor a low courtly bow, beaming with excitement, and thinking about his wife and daughters, and how they would react to his military victory, and to this new title.

As if reading Maurice's mind, Napoleon added, "I know that you have a family waiting for you at home. I have felt home-sick myself when I was away from my family years ago. It is hard on a marriage, when a husband is away for too long, and I can't be selfish with your time. You have duties in France, and you must attend to them, so you are hereby granted the right to return to France, and to serve us from there."

Maurice bowed again, "Thank you Your Majesty. It is an honor to have served you on this glorious campaign, but you see through me, I miss my wife and child, and I thank you for your kind words, and for this leave, which I accept with wholehearted gratitude."

"We will want you back with Us Maurice, there is too much of Europe left to conquer, but the fighting will still be here when you return."

With the Emperor's permission, Maurice returned to Paris and received some much-needed rest from the battlefield. By the time he returned, his baby girl, Aurore, was already walking steadily around the apartment. Maurice spent a couple of months in Paris with Aurore, Sophie and Caroline, before returning to the battlefield, which once again became critically hot, despite Maurice's assumption that the fighting would fade out after some of their enormous victories. Napoleon's success in military stratagem was unprecedented, so most of the French troops were in awe of the grandeur and enormity of the continued victories, and in 1806 it seemed to them that Napoleon could expand his reach across the entire globe.

Maurice didn't have too many other meetings with the Emperor, so that when he had a brief encounter with Napoleon on October 2nd of 1806, he recorded the event in a detailed letter to Sophie, writing that he spent three days making thirty-six leagues on horseback, escorting the Emperor to Wurzburg. At one point, Maurice took a position at the side of the Emperor's carriage. When the Emperor looked out, he recognized Maurice, and since their eyes met, he asked him, "What's the status of the regiment?" The Emperor was curious if the regiment was keeping to formation, and if they were tired after a three-day march, but the rocky dirt road was moving the carriage around, as if it was in a storm at sea, and the other members of the guard around the carriage were stomping out-of-rhythm, so that the overall noise was deafening. By watching the Emperor's mouth and guessing what he must have wanted to know Maurice surmised the question, and shouted back a basic status report on the organization of the troop, and their fitness.

"Did you say they the back of the line is falling behind?"

"Yes, Sire."

"Why don't you go and encourage them to pull up?"

Maurice listened closely, but he could not distinguish what the Emperor said, so he decided to repeat, "Yes, Sire."

The Emperor stared back at Maurice, waiting for him to go check on the back of the line, but Maurice sheepishly stared back at the Emperor, hoping he would repeat the message if it was important enough, or if the Emperor needed an answer.

The Emperor smiled after a stretched silence. Maurice kept looking over at Napoleon hoping for a clue to the message, but the Emperor decided that the troops must not have fallen far enough behind if Maurice didn't guess what he was asking, and reclined in the carriage, while Maurice remained high in the saddle, his mind racing over what command or question the Emperor could've made.

That night he wrote to Sophie, "I guess I must have committed some gross stupidity. If he sees fit to retire me for idiocy or deafness, I would easily be consoled by returning to you!"

It was around this time that Aurore was mishandled by a drunk servant, who dropped her onto a red marble fireplace, injuring Aurore's head. The servant was dismissed. In parallel in time and traumatically for some of the parties involved, Napoleon's first child was born that December, named Charles Leon, to his mistress Eleonore Denuelle de la Plaigne, who had been accompanying the troops during the military engagements. The latter event of the two was more significant for the Empire, as Napoleon was surprised to discover that he wasn't sterile and that Josephine was the cause of his prior childlessness. This turned his mind back to divorce, and he spent the following years plotting the best way to divorce from Josephine.

Maurice's next chance to distinguish himself came on February 25th of 1807. The Russians were once again fooled by the French army's inactivity into thinking that it was the ideal time to charge, and began closing in on the town of Braunsburg in Prussia near the Baltic Sea. Observing the approach, General Dupont, with Maurice's help, repelled the advancing Russian division back over the Passarge River, captured ten thousand soldiers and their cannon in the process. Shortly after these events, on April 4th, Maurice was granted the title of squadron chief, and this distinction attracted the attention of general Joachim Murat, who took him on as his aide-de-camp. Murat was Napoleon's brother-in-law via a marriage to Napoleon's sister, Caroline Bonaparte, and served as the Grand Duke of Berg during this period. The latter offer distressed Maurice as he weighed how much time he would have to spend away from his family and the enormous expense of the required uniform, gallant horses and various other luxuries that were required at court to work in Murat's service, against the small benefits in glory and fame that came with the title. Maurice could not afford a fraction of these fineries on his military salary, so he wrote to his mother, and left the decision up to her judgment. Since becoming an aide-de-camp to Murat was closer to the outcome she had hoped for Maurice's military career than the years he previously spent in the trenches, she decided that it was a worthy maneuver and sponsored the cost of the venture.

After spending the bulk of 1807 with Murat, Maurice returned home to his family for the winter between 1807 and 1808. This was a period when Maurice's young daughter, Aurore, became aware of herself, as her memories of her childhood begin at this point in her life, when her father gained a position of prominence and she began to be treated as an aristocratic heir, even though they still lived in the small Parisian apartment that Aurore's grandmother had owned since before the Terror. Of all things that Aurore could have chosen as a first memory, she focused on the repeated candlelight dinners she had with her family, eating sugar milk soaked vermicelli. The next flash that Aurore later recalled with warmth was the time she spent reading and writing in those early days, when these tasks were new and amazing to the developing child.

Perhaps, it is possible to point out the writer in a group of kids by studying who begins reading first, who keeps reading until stopped, and who begins writing and making up stories before they develop an interest in most of the other things that enthrall all the other kids. Out of a thousand children, only one might push aside the puzzles, blocks, jump rope, and all the other toys and entertainments, and instead just sit down in the quietest and darkest corner of the room and stare at a book until the letters turn into words, and words into stories, and the stories suddenly open a fantastic dimension that was just the simple "now" of mundane reality moments earlier. Sophie gave Aurore a few brief reading lessons, pointing out the letters, explaining how they sound separately and when they form words, nearly exhausting her own limited linguistic knowledge, as Sophie never had a formal education. Aurore also started to understand the learning process, when her cousin Clotilde taught her how to recite her prayers and La Fontaine's fables. When Aurore started to glaze over after hours of recitation, Clotilde would jump up, pulling

Aurore up with her and they would dance around in a circle, singing:

> We'll no more to the woods,
> The laurels are cut down.

One of the reasons Aurore had to escape into the written word was because her home life was one that demanded escape. Aurore had the same nature as her father and grandmother, but she had spent most of her first four years in the sole company of her mother, and a few other poorly educated girls from the middle and lower classes, who could help her take the first steps into learning, but who eventually abandoned Aurore to these ventures, withdrawing from this strange child that lived in her unseen fantasies. Aurore made some attempts to mimic Clotilde and Caroline's giddiness and boisterousness, running around and trying to play, but these bursts of energy maddened her mother to distraction. Sophie would be cooking or doing housework when Aurore would run through the kitchen, dancing around the table or the stove. Sophie would try to continue with her work, but Aurore was not a child that one could block out like a cat or a parrot, or like so many other children that feebly cry or whine or tap gently around. When Aurore ran, she kept running, and developed enough muscles early on to make a ruckus as she galloped around the room. This must be another trait that talented children have that others lack, a limitless need to be noticed, watched, admired, and appreciated. Other children might be satisfied when they are told that they are pretty good at something, but a few kids out of many are never satisfied even when they are told that they are great at something. They must be at the front of the theater, or on the cover of a best-selling novel, or at the head of a procession. It might seem that most kids want to be good at something, but there is almost a defect in a few kids that sets the bar of recognition that they expect to receive above what the vast majority ever contemplates. Sophie belonged to this vast majority, which when they notice a member of this small group with unbridled ambition, are filled with a deep-seated hatred without a clear sense that they are feeling, which typically results in waves of hostility pouring over those who have this bug of ambition from the ocean of "happy" and self-satisfied "common" people circling around them. Sophie would imprison Aurore between four chairs, putting an unlit foot warmer in the middle of them, where she would sit Aurore, preventing her from venturing out. A common child might have started screaming and crying, begging to be let out of this prison. In contrast, Aurore was a child that had a unique focus, or the ability to be hyper-attentive to details even when she was locked in a dungeon, or in this case between four dull chairs. To Sophie the scene must have looked very strange. After being locked in the prison, Aurore would glaze over, staring into empty space, silently. But, inside of Aurore's mind, she was developing the information she was getting from the books she was reading and from the world around her into her first novels. A shadow running over a chair suddenly turned into a prince, or a princess, a fairy, or an evil witch, and these characters would interact, some times in the same ways as in the stories she read earlier that day, and sometimes in ways that were not in those stories, mixing and mingling in ways that Aurore wanted them to play and fight. Then, when Sophie would let her out, Aurore would run up to Clotilde, insisting that she should play a general or a commander, an Amazonian princess, or a noble king, and they would wage battles that echoed what Aurore had just dreamed up, and echoed the stories her father had related from his actual battlefield experiences.

Once, Maurice walked into the kitchen in the middle of one of these scenes. Aurore was stabbing Clotilde with an imaginary sword, represented by a spoon, and Clotilde fell backwards as if wounded and threw a pillow aside, bending her leg in half, and thrashing the pillow around, as if half of her leg had been cut off by Aurore's mighty blade. Tears came up in Maurice's eyes as he watched the scene, and he rushed out of the kitchen and into the bedroom, and locked himself in to recover. Aurore didn't notice the tears, but she was left with a sense that her little play made a powerful impression, and this small burst of power inspired Aurore with the notion that make-believe could affect people in reality, and that her fantasies could spill into the world, making real changes in it. Aurore could not dream of becoming a General, or leading men in battle, but she suddenly felt that her lifelong battle would be fought with fiction.

Chapter 4

The Spanish Excursion

Maurice was sent on a new campaign in February of 1808, and arrived in Barcelona, Spain on February 27th, just as Napoleon issued orders to commanders to pretend as if they were still fighting on Spain's side in the Peninsular War, while they actually turned around and attempted to capture key Spanish cities with the few thousand French soldiers that were in the area, as if to help Spain win the War. Within two days of Maurice's arrival, the maneuver was executed and France had captured Barcelona. The maneuver was a variation on the Trojan Horse, as Maurice was in a column of what looked like wounded soldiers, who attacked as soon as they were past the city's gates, without meeting much resistance as the commanders in the city were hostile towards the Spanish government. There was hardly an injury to show for this relatively silent battle.

Maurice spent a few days seeing the sights in Barcelona, pretending to be inspecting the fortress at Montjuic for structural faults, and the Santa Maria del Pi gothic church for possible religious adversaries to the French invasion, while really studying the architecture of the arches, the vaulted ceilings, and the enormous ancient stones. Maurice walked across Barcelona on-foot to see these sites, disguising himself in local garbs, and stayed in a little inn overlooking Santa Maria and the ocean. He always took advantage of sight-seeing while on campaigns to break the monotony of tent-living, marching and fighting. After a few days without any major rebellions against the French take-over, Maurice was ordered to head for Madrid, and made the long journey to the center of the country on horseback, arriving in Madrid on March 18, and writing a letter to Sophie immediately upon putting his luggage down in a tent, as there were no convenient ways to send out a note along the journey. Murat was preparing for the siege of Madrid over the next few days, but Maurice had a few moments to write about his progress.

At almost the same time as when Maurice sat down to write a note home, Sophie and Aurore felt closer to him than in all the prior months. Sophie, Aurore and their old man servant M. Pierret dressed in their finest formal clothing and took a carriage ride to the Madeleine, where they had to stop because a large crowd was blocking further approach. They left the carriage and made the rest of the trip on foot, with M. Pierret walking in front to clear a path to the front of the crowd. They were suddenly at the front, near a neatly lined-up formation of soldiers. The Emperor was striding on his grand white horse along the line, inspecting each of the soldiers, captains and commanders for any flaws in their uniforms, gait, or other problems in his army. The Emperor was coming closer, so M. Pierret lifted Aurore up over the crowd and placed her on his soldiers. She gasped in surprise, and then froze in amazement, studying all the details of the scene. The soldiers in front of them all wore tall red and black shakos on their heads that blocked the details from most in the crowd. She was mesmerized by the variations in uniform colors, the sparkling bayonets, the hanging swords, and the fanciful formation. Then, her eyes followed the line of sight of most of the commanders that were not staring straight ahead, and she saw Emperor Napoleon coming towards the spot where she sat. Aurore was surprised by this sight. She had been told that they were joining the spectacle because the Emperor was there, and the grandeur of this announcement made him seem like a supernatural being that would glow with a halo of light and majesty. The reality of the man struck Aurore as a contradiction with the fairytale. Napoleon was a short, balding, bluish-gray, oily, plump, in a knee-length black frock coat that was preventing his embroidered coat, cuffs, lapels and gold buttons from being displayed in their full magnificence, and the cahouk hat he held in his hands spoiled his posture, as he had slumped over it.

The Emperor's eyes were coldly calculating the arrangement of the troops, and he was thinking about the hot sun and about how pointless the review of the troops was after his commanders already ran minor inspections that morning, and about the fact that he had to find a way to divorce Josephine despite unsurmountable odds, and about the fact that the crowd around the troops was noisy and disrespectful to their Emperor. Suddenly, he saw a child sitting on the shoulders of a servant directly behind the back line's shakos, and their eyes met for a long moment. Napoleon thought that the child looked familiar, and thought for a moment about his own illegitimate child, Count Charles Leon, who was almost a year and a half now, but who Napoleon hardly ever saw, and who was destined to live a long life in obscurity, while Napoleon's legitimate heirs lived in the light of international politics.

Aurore saw the cold glance and felt a chill, but studying the stare further she realized that he wasn't really looking at her, or even at the troops, but at political or personal reflections that were far away from that particular moment in time. Aurore suddenly felt sympathy with this great man, who appeared to be troubled by an unseen burden, and she looked closer at his dress and appearance, trying to figure out what he was thinking about.

The Emperor's eye moved away from Aurore's, back down to the line of soldiers, as he once again returned to processing the flaws in uniform arrangements, and the other items that he was looking for during the inspection.

"He looked at you. It will bring you good luck!" Sophie cried, startling Aurore out of her reflections. She looked down at Sophie and smiled, but looked puzzled, as she was trying to figure out how that cold and tired man's glance could be a sign of good fortune.

Days later, on around March 25th, they received a letter from Maurice, who reported that after a successful attack, the French gained control of Madrid on March 23rd, and that at that point he received grand accommodations in the center of the city, because of his status as Murat's aide-de-camp. While Murat, now the French Marshal in command of Madrid, was traveling with the troops, he had to make-due with shabby living arrangements for his assistants, but in Madrid, the aristocracy made an entire palace available for him and his staff, and Maurice suddenly felt the advantages of seeking higher appointments. Maurice described his enormous room, the palace, Madrid, Murat's populated staff and servants, and all this made Sophie jump in her thoughts between ecstasy, envy, and suspicion. Sophie last saw Maurice in Paris six months earlier, when they had a few intimate months, while Maurice was stationed in the city for the winter. They had known that Sophie was pregnant when Maurice left at the end of the winter, and now knowing that she would give birth in a matter of months, Maurice seemed intent on staying indefinitely amidst all that luxury in Madrid, leaving his growing family to make-due without him. Sophie imagined the courtesans and loose ladies of the court swooning over her young and upcoming military officer, and she could imagine him finding a permanent mistress and staying in the front with her for years, without returning home, and perhaps without sending funds home for her and the kids to live on. She was bored with their small apartment, and tired of performing household chores, and her thoughts kept churning and growing darker, until she saw no other way to be rid of them but to travel to Madrid and to have her child in the luxury of a palace, and not in a damp Parisian apartment without her husband.

In April, Sophie, Aurore, a twelve-year old groom, Mackenzie, and the wife of an army supplier, Joan Dieulafoy, set out in a travel carriage from Maris to Madrid. The trip was inexpensive because the supplier's wife was traveling on business to assist her husband with sending supplies to the front, and had rented the carriage for this purpose. A wife of one of Murat's other staff members had put Aurore in touch with Joan and recommended that they should make the trip together, to assure safety in numbers, as the trip into a warzone was a hazardous one for any single woman. In the first couple of days of the trip they traveled uneventfully through France, then after they crossed the border into Spain everything went smoothly too. The group ate grilled, peppered and melted fat covered pigeons at many of the inns along the way, a delicacy that Spain was known for. Then, a couple of days along the journey into the heart of Spain, the scene outside the carriage mutated, and suddenly all the horrors of war were just outside the carriage's windows.

The dirt road took the group through a string of hilly-mountains that were covered with a dense forest. We saw a couple of palm trees out of the windows, and there was a heavy fog in the air from the evaporating heat, which was more intense than earlier in the day despite the approaching sunset. As they were making their way around one of the taller hills, they saw smoke coming over it. When they were on the other side, they could see the scorched grass, and the cindered huts at the outskirts of the village. The coachman started pulling on the reins to stop the horses.

"No, we can't stop here," Sophie yelled to the coachman, looking out of the window.

"There are no other villages on our way for many more miles, and it's getting dark. We don't want to be caught on these roads at night. It's not safe," the driver replied over his shoulder.

"How is it safe for us to stay here? Why, these people were ramshackle by the French army just earlier today? Wouldn't they be a bit mad with the French?"

"Honey," Mme. Joan Dieulafoy commented, bending her eyebrows in disbelief, "you are heading into the line of fighting. Everybody in Spain is pretty mad with the French by now. Why would it be any different in the next village?"

"So, we might be murdered in our sleep for being French?"

"Perhaps. But, it's more likely that the villagers will leave us alone to avoid having the French troops return to burn down what's left of the village."

This eased Sophie's mind well enough, and Aurore tried to accept this reasoning too, seeing that they were already deep in the middle of Spain, and she doubted her request to return to Paris would be seriously considered. She was too young to have stayed in Paris with Caroline, and she had no means of returning to Paris on her own now.

The carriage stopped in front of an old inn, which was only spared because most of it was built out of stone, but because the staple and the side additions were wooden only the central stone room remained, while the rest had burned down. Aurore wondered what the point was of staying in this foul-smelling place, when they could just sleep on the ground or in the carriage with a much more satisfying result. A small part of the front door was still smoking, as the fire that touched it was only recently put out with a bucket of water. The mistress of the inn saw them approaching and shook her head from the doorway.

"We have no hay—"

"No hay?" the driver asked.

"For your horses? It burned down. It was in the barn."

"I'll take them down to the posture instead, it's all right. We are more concerned about a place to sleep for ourselves. I mean, mostly the ladies here, me and the Mack here will manage."

"We've got a bench and a table. You fellows want to pay to sleep on them?"

"It looks like yours are the only accommodations around."

The innkeeper chortled, shook her head, but nodded in agreement.

"What do you have in the way of dinner?" Sophie asked, feeling a bit better about speaking up after that exchange.

"Raw onions, that's about it."

"Why not cooked?" Sophie looked around for the stove. The wooden components of the stove in the neighboring room had burned down, and it didn't look like they could be resurrected. Suggesting a cook-out outside would have been in poor taste, as starting a forest fire on top of the destruction brought on by the French troops would've been seen as a deliberate attack by the villagers. "All right, I understand, raw onions it is. Thank you," she finally shrieked, sitting down at the edge of the bench.

The innkeeper brought out a few peeled raw onions, which she picked out of the backyard garden that survived the attack. Looking out at the vegetation, Aurore became suspicious that there were potatoes and other vegetables growing there, but that the innkeeper only gave them onions out of spite; she didn't comment on this to the gathered party, as their eyes watered-up from chewing this bitter vegetable.

Aurore slept on the table with her mother. Joan did her best to sleep on her back on the bench, while the driver and Mack slept on the floor. Joan, Aurore and Sophie used the three cushions from the carriage as pillows, and while none of them slept well, they did drift off for a couple of hours, and managed to spend the night in a relatively safe haven.

The following couple of weeks were equally naturalistic, as the group progressively found themselves in more and more miserable accommodations, until they reached Burgos.

***

Before Maurice arrived in Madrid, on March 19, the Mutiny of Aranjuez, in the town of the same name in Spain led to the overthrow of the pro-French King Charles IV, and his replacement with his son, Ferdinand VII. After a reign that only lasted a few days, Napoleon insisted on having both the father and the newly crowned son meet him in Bayonne, France, feigning a desire to reconcile them. Before his departure from the Royal Palace of Madrid, Ferdinand VII had a premonition of what was to transpire, and he looked around the French commanders that were invading the Palace, as he was being forced out of it. He had been given a crazed horse by one of his hussars, who was a daredevil and enjoyed riding wild beasts, and he knew that the horse in the hands of any less skilled rider would cause serious injury. He decided to offer a number of different items to Murat to tempt him with the appearance of bribing him, and to slip this terrible horse into the deal.

"I hope you will find the accommodations for your staff at the Palace to your liking," Ferdinand VII was telling Murat that evening.

"Yes, I have had wonderful compliments about just about everything at the Palace. Thank you for your hospitality."

"Since I'll be away temporarily, you are welcome to use anything that you might find useful, the clothing makers, the jewelry, the dresses, the stables with the horses in them. There is one fine new steed, Leopardo, which we recently acquired that should be to your liking, very strong, great breeding."

Murat had dealt with foreign dignitaries on invaded soil long enough that he knew exactly what "strong" meant in reference to an offered horse, and he was more likely to have put his head into a hot stove than accept such a present from a soon to be deposed monarch. Ferdinand also made the mistake of putting too much stresses on the horses in his excitement to convince Murat to take advantage of them, and this was the final red flag that led Murat to a full-stop on the idea. But, he could not refuse anything at that moment as Napoleon relied on him to be as gentle as possible and to avoid all suspicion, thus leading Ferdinand into some sense of false security, so that he would agree to meet with Napoleon on the French soil, instead of remaining where he had military and political clout. Murat decided on a course of action after a momentary consideration.

"My stables are full at the moment, and I couldn't possibly accept any more horses, but my aide-de-camp here," he pointed to Maurice, "will take good care of your steed while you are away. He is a trained hussar, and he will appreciate the fine breeding of your horses."

Maurice nodded and bowed. Ferdinand studied Maurice, and decided that one French military man was as bad as another. "Yes, wonderful. I hope you will form a great bond with Leopardo, and that he will serve you well."

Maurice bowed again, "Thank you, Your Majesty. I will take care of Leopardo as if he was my own son."

With this and a few other maneuvers, Ferdinand and Charles IV obliged Napoleon's request and found themselves on enemy soil, surrounded by the French troops, without a Spanish army behind them. Under these hostile circumstances, Napoleon convinced them to surrender their Spanish crown to him, and passed it over to his brother, Joseph Bonaparte. To avoid a civil war, Joseph and Napoleon insisted that all remaining Spanish royal family members immediately leave Spain. This pronouncement reached the Royal Palace of Madrid on May 2nd. There were two chief royal family members left in the Palace, Infante Francisco de Paula and the daughter of Charles IV, the Infanta, Queen of Etruria, or three if one counted the Infanta's eight-year old daughter. Murat announced the news to them in their waiting room, with Maurice attending at his heels once again, in his duties as aide-de-camp.

"We must leave the Palace? Permanently?" Francisco murmured.

"The council approved the request for your departure. They have received a letter from your father, who has requested that you join him in France."

Francisco was only fourteen, and while the Infanta was twenty-seven and a mother, she had lived a sheltered life, and both had not been away from the Palace for an extended period of time previously. Now they realized that all of their elders were already abroad, and that any resistance could be met with violence. Francisco was turning the options in his head, hoping to think of some strategy that would delay or turn the events, but failing at this he felt his eyes swell up with oncoming tears. The Queen of Etruria was significantly calmer because she was not contemplating an escape, merely going along with the flow of the historical events.

"And you must leave today, there cannot be any hesitation. This is all for your own safety."

"What about our belongings? Can we bring all of our servants? Are there any enough carriages for all of them?" Francisco was working through the items that he knew his father would have asked about had he been there.

"No, there is no time for all of that. There can be unrest if you delay even by a day. You must leave immediately."

Francisco and the Infanta stood up, as they heard a pinch of anger in Murat's rising voice. They made a small bow and began approaching the door. The Infanta's daughter was waiting for her mother in a gilded chair in the hallway, and the Infanta now waved for her to follow her. They were about to leave the only home they knew, without checking their rooms even to grab a small trinket to remind them of their youth. All of them were also leaving their nurses and tutors, who had stayed on with them, and there was a risk that they would not be gently handled, but rather treated as spies or enemy hostages, after the last of the royal family deserted the Palace. As they came out of the Palace, Francisco saw a crowd of his countrymen gathered around and his frailty turned into weakness and a few tears burst out of his eyes. Those at the front of the crowd could clearly see the tears, and the fact that the royalty were leaving in a rush, without any of their royal retainers, attired in their daily clothing, instead of the finery they were used to seeing them in at public gatherings. The crowd was made up of a few councilmen and other politicians who had attempted to fight the removal politically, but failed, as well as by some of the poorer rowdy element of the city that was enraged by these actions. The crowd was standing in the palace grounds, despite a battalion of grenadiers of the Imperial Guard and artillery detachments that were approaching the Palace to oversee the departure. The moment the crowd noticed Francisco's tears, and the other details about the departure, they sprang into action. They hurled stones and sticks at the Guard that had closed in, and one of the men had come armed, and he fired a shot, hitting one of the Guard on the leg, which caused the guardsman to fall to the ground.

"Attack, fire!" screamed Murat, infuriated at such an outrageous attack carried out right in front of him, and by a such poorly organized common troop of rebels. Receiving this direct command, the Guard and the artillery, which rushed to the scene, assumed full battle formations and fired at the rebellious crowd. A few in the crowd continued throwing projectiles, a couple fired weapons, while some of the weaker members ran away from the fighting. The Infante, Infanta and her daughter made it into a carriage safely, where they remained while the fighting continued on the Palace grounds. Many of the rebels fell dead, but a couple of the French troops were also seriously injured. A few of the rebels that managed to run away, and spread the word about the violent suppression and about Infante's planned exit from Madrid. They were met with violent emotion by the city dwellers, which up until that point were indifferent about the country that ran their city. Several small gangs of rebels began guerrilla warfare against the French troops, damaging horses, supply lines, and finding some weapons with which they managed to spill some more French blood.

Murat was still agitated over the long battles and marches that came before he occupied Madrid, and the idea that on the eve when he was finally taking charge of the Royal Palace, about to become the ruler of the city, and perhaps later of all of Spain, he was facing such an annoying insurrection, infuriated him and he overreacted with Napoleonic zeal. Afraid that a few rebels might seize the Palace by sheer luck or trickery, he called the entire French army in the region, the majority of which was encamped around Madrid, rather than in the city center, into the city. He imposed martial law, and ordered all inhabitants that wanted to have their lives spared to stay indoors. Then, the French troops combed the city and took out all of the rebels that remained in the streets, counting as rebellious anybody that spoke, sang, or moved in even a slightly threatening fashion. By the evening of May 2nd, hundreds of rebels were dead, the Peninsular War for Spanish independence had started, and the last of the remaining Spanish royals were being galloped to France.

It was on the evening of May 2nd, when Aurore and Sophie met the Infanta and her daughter in Burgos, as both were staying in the best inn in that small city, with two of them heading from Paris to Madrid, and the other two from Madrid to Paris, and both by the shortest possible route. The Infante had gone to his room, without eating, while the Infanta and her daughter came down to the dining hall for supper. It was a small dining area, so Sophie and Aurore occupied one table, while the Infanta with her child occupied the only other available table. They were all served grilled pigeons, with bread and wine.

The driver slowly approached Sophie and whispered who was dining at the table next to them. Aurore's eyes widened as she realized that she was sitting next to a real Spanish princess. She stole a few glances in their direction, and once again her sense of what somebody royal was supposed to look like was shocked by the simple, overgrown white dresses that both of these young women were wearing, the mud on their skirts, and the speed with which they were eating the small wings and breasts of the pigeons, as if they hadn't eaten anything else that day (and indeed they hadn't). Aurore tried not to stare too closely to avoid making the Infanta feel uncomfortable, and looked away entirely after she once caught the Infanta's eye and saw the tint of hatred in her stare, as the Infanta observed the French fashion and heard the French royal accent, which were both offensive to her sentiment at this particular moment in her life. Of course, Aurore had not heard anything about the insurrection, or about the maneuvers that Napoleon was playing with Spanish royalty, so the moment stayed with her as a scene from a fairytale in an otherwise mostly unpleasant journey into the war-torn Spain.

Before evening on the following day, Aurore and Sophie arrived in their carriage at the Palace. The driver and the supplier's wife were aghast at the spectacular domicile their traveling companions were about to enter, and Joan was suddenly extremely polite, in contrast with her usual rough manners. Aurore and Sophie were greeted by a troop of servants at the entrance, and their belongings flew up the stairs to their rooms and were arranged in their closets before the pair got out of their carriage. Aurore took in every detail of the Palace's architecture, the luxurious furniture, the Spanish garb of the servants, the fancy military uniforms of the French Guard, and all the other tiny details, like the Chinese carpets, and the paintings of the Spanish royalty that made up the most luxurious residence in Spain, which was now going to be her home.

The fourth-floor apartment that Aurore was assigned previously belonged to the Infanta and her daughter. The view from the tall windows with gilded cornices was spectacular, as a good portion of Madrid was visible over the flat terrain. The walls were hung with a crimson silk damask, The Spanish royalty were fond of domestic animals, so the Palace was full of unusual well-bred beasts, including cats, dogs, and hamsters. Aurore was most impressed by a large rabbit, with snowy white long hair, which belonged to the Infanta, and was already residing in her new apartment, so she adopted it as her own.

On the following morning, Aurore was anxious to become involved in the life of the Palace. She had played with Murat's children in Paris, and she was curious to learn what the residents of the Palace did for work and play. When she told her mother about her intention of going down to Murat's study while he was engaging in politics, Sophie suggested a military uniform that would disguise Aurore's sex. Since George Sand is perhaps most stereotypically known for wearing men's clothing, the detail that she began this practice as a political maneuver to enter Murat's inner circle when she was four adds a unique twist to the standard interpretation. Wearing men's clothing was never a fashion statement meant to stress something abnormal about her unfemininity, but simply to join ranks with the sex that held more political power in her time than her own. Decades later when she wrote her autobiography, Aurore remembered every detail of this uniform, from the gold-buttoned cassimere dolman, to the black-fur trimmed pelisse, to the purplish cassimere trousers, and the still more masculine Moroccan leather boots with golden spurs, and a saber in her braided silk belt. The tailor and the hairdresser worked on making Aurore look like a little boy, and the job worked so well that Murat assumed that she was Maurice's son, and introduced her as his aide-de-camp, allowing her to oversee public meetings with dignitaries, the council, and various other military and government affairs from which all other women in the household were barred. This was an early lesson for Aurore in the fact that it was not her intellect, manners or actions that might derail her ambitions, but simply her gender, and that this barrier could be erased simply by putting on a man's mask.

Aurore spent a bit over a month in the idyllic lifestyle of a young aide-de-camp to a general before a sudden string of tragic events brought this grand appointment to a bad end.

Murat was not cautious enough in his choices for manservants, and he had left a good majority of the old servants that worked for the Spanish royalty. Some of them received regular communications from the decrowned kings and princes, or had friends and relatives who lost their lives in the insurrection on May 2nd. Within a month of this insurrection, Murat started to suspect, with good reason, that he was being poisoned. His intestines were inflamed, and he was suffering from violent pains. Murat believed that it was arsenic poisoning, and since Napoleon showed similar symptoms and has been believed to have died from long-term arsenic poisoning, it is most probable that Murat was being poisoned. What saved Murat were his keen observation, and the fact that he identified the possible cause of his problems. One night, upon waking up and pulling an armful of hair from his scalp and feeling a stabbing pain in his gut, he screamed, "Murder!"

Maurice was in the room adjoining Murat's and he grabbed a saber and ran into Murat's room to assist him, expecting to find an assassination attempt. Observing that Murat was alone in the room, he stopped, studying the distant corners for an enemy who might be getting away.

"There's nobody here," Murat gasped. "I've been poisoned!"

"Poisoned? By whom? When?"

"It must be in the food. Those Spanish dogs want us all dead and gone!"

"Are you sure—"

"Yes, look," Murat showed the hair he had just pulled out just by brushing his hand through them. "All the signs are there."

"Should I call a physician?"

"What do they know!? A bunch of fools. No, just fire them all. I don't want any Spaniards working at the Palace."

"Yes, of course Sire. I will dismiss them first-thing in the morning."

"Good."

Maurice sat down in the chair across from Murat's bed, and remained there all night. Murat was tossing in pain, and did not sleep, but he did not scream again, refusing to let anybody who might be responsible hear that he was suffering at their hand.

That morning Maurice carried out Murat's order by firing all of Murat's cooks and Spanish domestics. Within a few weeks, Murat's symptoms cleared, and he was strong enough to ride on horseback, a part of his usual morning exercise routine.

While Maurice obeyed Murat's order, he did not believe that there might be actual poisoners living so close to them in the Palace. When it came time to find a doctor for his newborns birth, he brought in a Spanish surgeon on June 30th. The baby in Sophie's womb had too many obstacles stocked against it, as Sophie had traveled for a month in the last months of the pregnancy, and the pressure of the sitting position and the rocking of the carriage could have crushed the baby's eyes, but sitting is hardly life-threatening for a baby in the womb. The surgeon invited Maurice to leave, and gave Sophie alcohol, saying that it was for the pain. The labor lasted many hours until the baby finally emerged, and when it did the surgeon pressed his fingers into the infant's eyes and said, "This one won't see the sun of Spain." When the baby was put into Sophie's hands, its pupils were pale from crystalline, as the baby boy was born blind.

"It's him! He pressed his fingers into his eyes! He blinded my baby!" Sophie shouted, as she cried and screamed, throwing her fists in the surgeon's direction, hoping to smite him for his horrid deed. Maurice grabbed her hands and held them down.

"Shh. Calm down darling. It wasn't the surgeon."

"But, you weren't here. He said, 'This one won't see the sun of Spain.' Have him executed! He deserves to die for what he did!"

"No, you don't know what you are saying. It's the alcohol. Just calm down. He might still be able to see?"

"You don't believe me!? How can you? Look at him standing there! Look at how he's looking at my baby! It's your son! Don't you care about your son?!"

Maurice kept trying to calm her down, but she became delirious, for which the surgeon prescribed a stronger sedative, which eventually forced Sophie into a deep sleep, and when she awoke the surgeon was no longer in the Palace.

Two weeks later, on July 13th, as soon as she was strong enough to travel, Sophie left the Palace with Aurore, and headed back for Paris. Maurice came with them because he did not think that Sophie was strong enough to make the trip alone, and the fighting was so hot across Spain that sending Aurore and Sophie alone without a convoy would have been extremely reckless.

They made their first stop at Burgos without incident, but as they were departing to continue on their journey, Maurice received news that the Spanish troops were forming ahead of them with the intention of blocking France's supply routes and the main central road between Paris and Madrid. Maurice was called on to assist with the coming battle. He told Sophie and Aurore to attempt crossing out of the danger area before the battle started. They took a carriage and made it through several tall hills until they could see the slowly moving flanks of the two armies. Aurore looked out of the window at the green countryside and at the two armies, and for some time they were moving slowly but surely, and it looked like they might make it across the path around the armies before the fighting started, but then they heard the first cannon fire. The carriage was just far enough away to have been out of the direct line of the fighting, so they froze at this high vantage point, to avoid becoming a threatening moving target.

The battle was a blur of fireworks, blazes of fire and voluminous noise for Aurore because she was preoccupied with the intensifying itching and feverishness she was feeling. In the month the family spent living in the Palace, they were all infected with the scabies. Since scabies are passed by skin-to-skin contact and take around a month before symptoms of itching manifest, it was likely to have been one of the exiting Spanish servants, most likely the one poisoning Murat, who also handled the Dupins and spread the infection to them. Aurore manifested symptoms first, so it must have been one of the servants that helped to tailor her new manly outfit that passed the disease.

Maurice was not yet symptomatic. He joined the commanders at a meeting regarding battle strategy before the fighting broke out. The events of July 14th would later be called the Battle of Medina de Rioseco. The Spanish troops had been fighting in small scattered battles between the insurrection in Madrid upon the exit of the Infante and this new incident. The commanders discussed the poor positioning of the Army of Galicia, and decided to exploit the ridge between the armies to split the Spanish in two and then crush them amidst the chaos. The strategy worked, and the bulk of the Spanish militia ran away from the scene of the battle, after losing many of their men, and this defeat was a major blow to the Spanish fight for independence from France. After the meeting in the tent, the captains and generals went into the field, and Maurice was among those who immediately noticed specific weaknesses in the Spanish line and exploited them with precision. His military stratagem must have made a significant difference because after he left the fight, the Spanish won many of the battles that followed, outsmarting the French and recapturing control of many of the key Spanish cities. Maurice was particularly vigilant in this fight because he knew that his wife and children were parked on a neighboring hill and that a loss or any retreat before the Spanish could mean his family's capture and possible execution.

The sight of the battle made Aurore hungry, as she wanted to be alert to see the details, so she asked for a snack and Sophie gave her an apple from her travel bag, which kept Aurore alert despite her fever. The sun was setting and there was a red glow in the sky, which made the scene look like a symbolic painting, with the sub-tropical greenery hiding the soldiers on the sides of a hilly terrain, while the swords and muskets of others were sparkling red as they reflected the rays of the sun. Aurore finished eating the apple and threw it out of the window. Just as the apple fell, the last shots sounded. The positioning of the army had changed radically in minutes, and Aurore could see some of the Spanish militia was still trying to run away through distant hills, and a few were nearing a river they intended to cross. A messenger approached their driver and gave an order that Aurore didn't make out, and their carriage started moving again. In a couple minutes, they were downhill, near the ridge, where the center of the battle had been. A new messenger approached and this time addressed Sophie, leaning into the window.

"Madame, would you be so kind as to let us use your carriage? We have several wounded men here and they won't make it if they don't have a place to recline."

"Of course, Sire. Please. We would be honored to be of help."

"Thank you, Madame." He made a small bow and briskly turned to bring in the wounded.

Sophie, with her new born baby in her arms, and Aurore behind her made it gently out of the carriage. Their driver took down their luggage and put them at the side of the road next to them.

The soldier was back in moments with a couple of infantrymen, who were carrying six wounded on stretchers. The sun had just gone down, and little could be distinguished aside from the grunting, and muffled screams of the wounded as they were carried up into the carriage, and Aurore noticed some sparkling gold buttons that suggested that those wounded were of the upper echelons of the military, and there was a moment when Aurore wondered if it might be her father, but she dropped this idea recalling that he had been in many battles before and was unlikely to have fallen in the one battle where his family was with him. They waited at the side of the road as their old carriage departed speedily, and then watched a few other carriages pass them until a farm wagon stopped for them. The driver was informed that they had their carriage requisitioned, and was asked to take them in, along with the army baggage and lightly wounded soldiers that he was already carrying. Because it was a wagon for key baggage and equipment, they could not leave the area, and they spent the night attempting to sleep in a sitting position, parked in a central place in the battlefield. A few of the soldiers next to them were bleeding from their battle wounds, their stomachs growling, and their feet aching with sores. Because Aurore was feverish she drifted into sleep, despite all these horrors that might have kept any healthy child awake for months.

Aurore woke up when a couple of soldiers sitting near her stood up and left the wagon. Sophie wasn't sleeping, as she was kept awake with holding the baby and checking on Sophie across the night. In the first moments upon opening her eyes, Aurore felt relieved from seeing the bright rays of the rising sun, but then she could smell the thick aroma of blood that was coming from the wounded in their wagon and from the field outside. She looked out and saw an enormous battlefield covered with thousands of bodies of Spanish and French soldiers. This was the first time Aurore was near somebody who had died, and it was a lesson that would have been overwhelming for most young ladies. Aurore did not faint, or swoon, instead looking at the details, the way the blood was crusted over the soldiers' uniforms, the fact that there had been little effort made to burry these bodies despite hours having passed since the battle, the fact that nobody seemed to be inspecting these bodies to check who was wounded and who was dead, and the strange absence of muskets and swords from among the wounded all registered and was analyzed in Aurore's mind. She didn't ask Sophie or the soldiers in the wagon about these things because she was aware of the dress she was wearing, and it felt indelicate for a girl to ask about death, instead of trembling from its sight.

The soldiers in the wagon all filed out, and as a few began returning, Sophie took Aurore aside and led her behind a somewhat isolated bush, suggesting that she do her business there, and awkwardly enough, with dead bodies only feet away, Aurore managed to obey nature's call.

When everybody was back in the wagon, and some of the baggage that was needed for the army that would stay behind to clear the battle-field was taken down, the wagon continued down the road that led to-wards Paris. A couple of minutes later, they heard something crunch under the wheels of the wagon, and in moments they all connected the sound with the sound of large bones breaking, and they all couldn't help but look through the open back of the wagon at the body of a dead sol-dier that the wagon had just rolled over. The body had a few markings on it, and it looked like their wagon was not the first go tread on it, but nobody was around attempting to move it out of the way, as the wagon continued its steady movement down the path.

The sun started to make its way towards the zenith, and the putrid wagon started to steam up from the heavy breathing of the two dozen people that were crammed into it. Aurore was already sweating from her fever, and how she could feel that her dress was drenched in her sweat. Her threat became so parched that it felt as if saliva had stopped generat-ing, as all water had left her body. The soldiers were also licking their lips and looking around the wagon, searching for supplies.

"Do we have any water on us?" one of the soldiers finally asked.

The driver heard him from the front of the wagon, "No. We had to leave most of our supplies with the main troops."

"What are we going to do for water then?"

"I guess we gotta stop and try to think of something."

The wagon stopped. They attempted stopping a few of the wagons and carriages that were following the same road after them, but they ei-ther did not have any water and food, or they did not want to share what they had.

"There, look, there is a ditch, does that look like water?" one of the soldiers exclaimed.

The group moved in the direction he was pointing to and looked into the ditch. The water was reddish-green, and there were sections of clot-ted blood at the bottom among the mud.

"We can't drink that. We'd all die if we tried," the driver observed, turning back to the wagon.

They all climbed back into the wagon, and a few soldiers were finally hungry and thirsty enough to show the supplies they did have. Green lemons, raw onions and sunflower seeds were thrown into a community pot, and passed out as rations. Aurore's thirst was hardly quenched with these, but there was enough water in these groceries for the group to survive until that evening. For dinner the group gathered around a fire at a French encampment and managed to get water from a mess pot of soup, which, Aurore learned after enjoying it, was made with candle ends. That night they slept in a tent with eight people sleeping side-by-side in a cramped space, but the air had cleared somewhat as they were further away from the field of battle, and the wounded soldiers had time to clean their wounds before going to sleep.

Most of the troops that were at first traveling with them stayed behind in cities, villages and troop gathering points along the way, so as the family continued down their path, they left the war behind, and there was suddenly enough space in the local inns for them to stay indoors. At this point Maurice joined them, as his military duties fell away with the decrease of accompanying soldiers. In the first inn they stayed in, the family indulged in large cups of tea with cheese and sweet pastries. Immediately after dinner, Sophie applied pallets of ground up mix of yellow crystal sulfur, butter and sugar to Aurore's dry skin to kill the scabies, a regiment that the family endured over the following two months before they finally exterminated the last of these intruders.

The next morning, over tea and a light breakfast, Sophie made a suggestion.

"Why don't we return by sea to Bordeaux, instead of following the same road we took to Madrid?"

Sophie was severally affected by being so close to a violent battle, and she understood better than Aurore that they ran a great risk by the proximity to the fighting. Sophie was also emotionally overwhelmed by the scenes of the dead and wounded that were all around them in the first days of the trip, and she had never lived in the unbearable accommodations that came with living with the troops. She had worked for years in the hat shop, and had married Maurice to rise above her unfortunate background and into society, where she would have fine clothing and a delicate place to live, and suddenly she found herself in the Royal Palace in Madrid, only to be plunged down into the lowest possible living quarters within days after giving birth to a blinded baby. Even if the smell of blood had cleared, Sophie was suffocating and felt a desperate need for a change of scenery, as if a new setting outside the carriage's windows would shift the turn her mind was taking as well. Maurice was also exhausted from worrying about his family during the battle, and then looking for them for a day before he caught up with them in the chaos of the aftermath of the battle. So, he agreed to Sophie's proposal, and the family directed the carriage driver towards the sea.

The carriage stopped at a small port, and they boarded a small boat, pulling their carriage aboard. The weight of the carriage and the passengers shifted the ship dangerously from side to side, but the captain reassured them that they were safe. The first hours of the trip were calming, as the boat rolled gently, and the family looked out at the beautiful coast-line of Spain, and then the first curves of the French soil. The water was green with seaweed. The coastline was covered by a dense forest, and tall thick grass. A few boats were tied to small harbors near mansions, cas-tles and towns along the coast. Aurore was standing at the stern, when she was suddenly thrown backwards by a strong wave. She recovered and moved to the center of the boat, taking some cover. The rocking of the boat intensified in the choppy sea as they sailed along the coast of Gascogne through the Bay of Biscay, where Alexander Dumas' fictional hero, d'Artagnan, was born. Aurore saw a tall, gray reef ahead of them, as the ship was attempting to navigate into the mouth of the Gironde, and a moment later the front of the boat hit the reef, and they all heard some of the wood crunch from the impact. The captain maneuvered the ship masterfully away from the reef, and continued to progress further towards the docks, but water started entering the hold, and it was clear that the ship was gradually sinking. The family watched in horror as the ship barely managed to make it to the dock. Aurore skipped to the front of the ship, and jumped onto the dock ahead of the rest of the family, as Maurice helped Sophie and the baby out. Meanwhile, the captain had just enough time to pull the carriage up onto the dock, with the help of some ropes, horses and many helpful deckhands, before the ship sunk further so that the entire deck was under water. The captain busied himself with saving the ship from drowning in the dock, as the Dupins got back into their saved carriage and continued the trip to Paris. Across this incident, Aurore was composed, and even amused by this sudden excitement, in place of the mundane rocking of the boat before the turn of events. It was during this trip to Spain that Aurore's constitution began to solidify. Her family life, and her politically charged environment were the initial ingredients that separated her from other young girls, but this trip into a warzone, the service she did as a mini aide-de-camp, and the adventurous militant journey back to France created precedents of toughness that Aurore lived up to across her later travels and adventures.

On the same day when the Dupins barely escaped drowning, August 1st, Murat was named the King of Naples and Sicily, and if Sophie had not gone to join Maurice in Madrid, he would have suddenly acquired a very different title, becoming a chief advisor to a King. But, this alterna-tive was not to be, and Maurice only found out about this development in September after he was back in Nohant, and this news must have weighed heavily on him, as he regretted leaving his post at just the moment when his military career could have bloomed into a triumph. It is likely that he was pining over this loss during the events that unraveled next.

Chapter 5

The Fateful Leopardo

On August 30th, after a month and a half on the road, the Dupins arrived in Berry. The village of Berry was spread out and Aurore studied the huts along the road. She watched the peasants ploughing the fields, and from the conversation between her parents realized that they were entering a region where her family owned the bulk of the land. She would benefit from the work those peasants were doing, and she might even one day be responsible over them, as her grandmother was at that time. Amidst this reverie, Aurore saw for the first time a grand mansion enter her line of vision. It immediately appealed to her as an idyllic setting even in comparison with the Royal Palace. The Palace was positioned in the middle of a busy Madrid street, and only had a few trees around it, while Nohant was surrounded by a forest, fields, flowers, and various structures and houses that were all a part of this grand estate. The carriage drove past a beige-bricked barn, a village church, a small cemetery, and then down a path along a delicately trimmed garden at the back of the main house, and to the circular courtyard. The carriage stopped and a few servants approached, helped them out of the carriage, took their luggage, and otherwise made them feel comfortable. As they started walking towards the mansion, a sixty-years old lady in a fine gown appeared in the entrance and made a few steps towards them. It was Marie-Aurore, as she must be called from this point forward, to distinguish her from Aurore, who at five-foot was still taller than Aurore, and made a powerful impression of feminine strength on the child. Marie-Aurore was meeting her grandchildren for the first time and she embraced Aurore, who twitched at this contact, bursting with an urge to tell her grandmother about the scabies, but too embarrassed to open her mouth. Marie-Aurore then pointed to a young man, dressed in a fine cashmere outfit, who was standing in the living room, studying the new arrivals.

"This is Hippolyte," and then pointing to Aurore, "and this is Aurore. Now you will have somebody your own age in the household."

Hippolyte went up to Aurore and they kissed each other. From that moment, the two formed an automatic bond, without knowing that they were siblings.

"Come with me, I want to show you something," Hippolyte said right away, dragging Aurore by the arm. He led her to the backyard, where he began aggressively piling sand into a number of buckets.

"Are you going to help?" he asked Aurore, staring up at her, as if to measure her daring.

Aurore couldn't help but crouch down next to him fighting against her dress, and helping him collect the sand. Then they ran to the well and pulled up a bucket of water. Hippolyte pulled out a metal tray and proceeded to mixing water and sand in a new bucket and shaping them into ovals, which he placed on the tray. Aurore helped him, following his movements, as she did her best to learn the technique. When the tray was full, Hippolyte ran into the house with it, and to Aurore's surprise put it in the oven, taking out the loaves of bread that were cooking there.

"Shhh!" he hushed Aurore, who was about to protest.

They sat down at a table in the kitchen and waited for a few minutes. Then one of the cooks entered the kitchen, and Hippolyte closed his mouth to avoid having her hear his suppressed giggle. The cook opened the stove, hoping to take out the bread, and threw her hands up.

"Hippolyte!" she exclaimed in frustration. "Are you making dung pies again!? You naughty boy!"

Hippolyte jumped up and pulled Aurore out of the kitchen and up to his room on the second floor of the mansion. The two formed a fast-friendship, as Aurore kept up with him as he ran, and was eager to engage in his rough-play. The friendship was rocky despite Aurore's attempts to appease Hippolyte's whims, as Hippolyte enjoyed bringing misery to everybody around him. He would bury the dolls, which she imported from the Spanish court, in the backyard, marking the graves with crosses, but failing to wrap them up to avoid spoiling the fine material of the dolls' dresses. At other times, Hippolyte would challenge her into eating raw lemons whole with seeds, or would dare her to eat unripe strawberries they would pick from the backyard garden. Because the peasant children were unwilling to engage Aurore in play, Hippolyte was the only game around, so Aurore had to be extremely flexible with him, and could not risk losing him as a friend. As was mentioned earlier, Aurore had an urge to please and to be perceived in a positive light by everybody. She wanted Hippolyte, the older boy, to admire her courage, and she was willing to go beyond her own moral limits, or tolerance for emotional and physical pain to meet with his approval. This relation, along with most of the other people that were around Aurore in her youth, hurt her self-esteem, pride, and her ability to trust and love people, as she began to associate love with misery.

That evening, after Hippolyte left to work on something on his own in his room, Marie-Aurore introduced Aurore to Deschartres as the chief doctor at Nohant. Deschartres was wearing yellow gaiters, knee breeches, white stockings, bellows cap, and a brown coat. After inspecting her skin, Deschartres confirmed that she had scabies, and administered a curative regiment, which he also recommended to other members of the family that were starting to show similar symptoms.

A week passed when the family began settling into the routine at Nohant. They breakfasted and dined together, went on group walks around the enormous garden, played cards and dominoes together, and otherwise entertained themselves. Aurore's fever subsided soon after arriving at Nohant, and she began exploring the barn, the church, and the various nooks and corners of the estate. While Aurore recovered her strength, the other members of the party that had traveled to Spain were progressively becoming more dejected. Sophie and Maurice did not share the details of what was troubling them with Aurore, but Deschartres had discovered that the baby's blindness was a sign of a serious illness, and he could not find a cure before the baby grew colder and colder, and on September 8th died in its sleep. When the death was discovered, the baby was immediately buried in the family cemetery. Sophie made an attempt to be strong, and to carry on with life at Nohant, but she was constantly destructed by the haunting image of the Spanish surgeon's fingers on the baby's eyes, and she was being driven mad by the guilt of going to Spain at such an advanced stage in her pregnancy, and then letting a hostile doctor injure her baby. The fact that Maurice mistook her certainty about the homicide for a light insanity also caused a greater strain on her self-composure. She had nightmares, and thought she saw the ghost of a baby in a white robe that was covered in blood on the first night, and as she was preparing for bed on the following night, Sophie turned to Maurice and was forced exclaim:

"Maurice, we forgot to wash the baby, and it's wearing that old rag, we should've prepared it better, it is going to meet God, and how can it go dressed like it is, like some poor urchin?!"

Maurice looked up at Sophie with fright, "No, we can't disturb the grave!"

"Please darling, I can't go to sleep. It's haunting him. I keep seeing its little face!"

Sophie looked so distressed that Maurice wondered what she might request next if he allowed her agitation to continue. Opening the grave and following her request seemed like the quickest way to bring a resolution and some peace to their minds.

Maurice grabbed a shovel right then, in the middle of the night, and dug up a grave, but because it was dark he dug up the wrong grave, which turned out to belong to a peasant that was buried a couple of weeks earlier. The sight and smell of the peasant upset Maurice, but he composed himself as much as he could and dug up the neighboring grave, taking out the baby and brining him to his mother. They washed and dressed him, perfuming the decomposing body, before once again burying it, but this time in the garden under a tall pear tree.

In the week after the re-burial, Maurice attempted to return to normalcy, by attending to the daily business at Nohant, but as he was looking over the accounts, or reading a military history, his mind returned to the horrors of the preceding weeks. He had seen death at dozens of battlefields, assisted in political intrigues that led to executions and violent suppressions of revolt, all this after spending his early years constantly worried that the Revolution might send both him and his mother to the guillotine, but he suddenly thought back to Murat's claims of poisoning, and started to wonder if there might be some truth in Sophie's claims about the surgeon. What if there was a complex plot involved in all this, one that took Maurice out of the Palace right before Murat was named king? Could anything be accidental when it involved the change of dynasties? Had he been a victim of royal manipulations? Was his family still in danger, even after he had left the court behind? Should he go back and attempt to claim a title next to Murat? Why did he agree to dig the baby up? The image of the still corpse distressed him amidst all these other worries, and brought on the darkest imaginings and the darkest conclusions about humanity.

On Friday, September 17th, Maurice finally could not be alone with his thoughts any more. He needed a distraction to take his mind off all these reflections. He went to the stables and found the old horse he rode as a child, but then he noticed Leopardo, and recalling that he was given that horse by a man who was the King of Spain at the time, he could not help but want to ride it. Leopardo had been dragged along at the back of the carriage that Aurore and Sophie took to return to France for over a month, and between feeding him and otherwise caring for this vigorous horse, it seemed to be an error to keep from riding him now that it had been imported. With the help of a stable hand, Maurice inspected Leopardo and found him to be in excellent health. He gently mounted him and the first few steps did not betray anything unusual, so Maurice took Leopardo onto the main road, and slowly began the trip to the neighboring town of La Chatre, accompanied by his manservant, Weber. Maurice was received in the biggest house in La Chatre, which belong to a family that was composed on an aristocratic wife, and a wealthy merchant husband, who were delighted to have such a noble distinguished captain in their abode, and entertained him with fine piano playing and melodic singing, dancing of the quadrilles, a bit of gambling at cards, and a good deal of fine wine across this long evening. It was the middle of the night, and it was raining profusely by the time Maurice and Weber emerged out of that fine house. The rain agitated Maurice, as he did not bring a coat and was chilled by the downpour. Because he was intoxicated, the solution that came to his mind was racing to beat the rain. He jumped onto Leopardo's back and hit the spurs with all his might. Weber did his best to keep up, and had to work his own horse to its limit to stay ten paces behind Maurice, as Leopardo began to gallop at a speed that for him was equivalent to a light jog. This wild run might have only lasted a minute before they were at the edge of La Chatre, a hundred paces past a little wooden bridge, when the road, surrounded by dense poplar trees, took a sharp turn, and as Leopardo was landing from a tall jump he hit a pile of stones and garbage that some careless peasant left there the day before. Leopardo was too strong to fall, but the stones frightened him and he reared instinctively to a near vertical position, which threw Maurice ten paces backwards, so that Weber's horse nearly hit him as he fell. Weber managed to maneuver his horse out of the way and jumped down to help his master.

"Come to me Weber, I'm dead," Maurice whispered, as he lay, trembling, on his torn neck. Weber was startled and as he was trying to think of some way to help his master, Maurice's body grew still, and he was dead.

Weber ran to a neighboring inn, and brought the owner and his servants out, and had them carry Maurice's body into the inn. Weber still had hope and galloped to get Deschartres, but as the innkeeper put the lifeless body onto a bed, he knew that there was no hope.

While Deschartres was mounting a horse, Marie-Aurore was being told about the incident by Weber. She was wearing her slippers, sitting up in her bed. She stood up slowly and walked to the front door. She saw Deschartres speeding away towards La Chatre. She considered getting a carriage, or a horse, but she was suddenly overcome with a sense of finality. Weber left no hope for a recovery, as a broken neck and a lifeless body could only mean that her only son was dead. She felt tears bubbling up in her eyes, so she waved the servants off, telling them to go back in, and she slowly began walking as-she-was, in her slippers, down the muddy road towards the small dot that was Deschartres, as he advanced. It was the second time she took a long walk, after the trip she took across Paris when she was let out of prison. Her thin gown was immediately soaked through by the rain. The mud was sticking to the edge of the gown, making it heavier. The silk on the slippers was sagging and wet. But, she did not notice any of these details, as her memory rushed backwards to the walk she took during the Revolution, to all the effort she made to rescue enough resources to provide for Maurice's education and career, and across the lifetime she dedicated to Maurice's ambitions. What was her life now adding up to, when the child in whom she had put all the dreams she could never realize for herself was gone? She recalled her meeting with Rousseau, all those things she did not tell him, and she thought about the long silences she had with her son over the past weeks during dinner, and she realized that her life was full of silences, and that there wouldn't even be a goodbye between Maurice and her, even a simple short communication where she might summarize all the things that were left unsaid. She kept walking steadily for a long time, and finally arrived at the little inn. She stood over her son's body, and studied its features, observing the similarities with her own, without considering what she might say on such an occasion, as words were failing her again. The innkeeper had been struck by Marie-Aurore's appearance as she entered, but he did not dare to interrupt her until she glanced up and met his gaze, after a few minutes of silence. Then, he brought out a change of clothing, new shoes, and several towels, and the servants took Marie-Aurore into one of the rooms and helped to pat her dry and change her to keep her from catching a cold. She was as if paralyzed during all this, and merely allowed herself to be led, clothed, and then lifted up into a carriage, and carted back to Nohant.

Later that night, Deschartres, Hippolyte and a few of the servants thought that they saw Maurice's ghost floating around in his distinguished uniform, and Deschartres shot it to make sure it wasn't somebody playing a practical joke on the grieving family. After hearing about the death of her husband, Sophie developed a migraine that kept her in bed for at least a day out of the week across the following twenty-years of her life. On the day after the burial, Marie-Aurore was lying in bed. Aurore entered and greeted her.

Marie-Aurore said gently, "Maurice darling, stand up straight, and go see to your lessons."

Aurore was about to correct her, but then thought that she was simply drifting off to sleep and had made a simple slip. Aurore stood up straighter, and left the room. But, over the following weeks, Marie-Aurore made a few similar slips, and it became clear that her mind was refusing to accept the death of her son, and that she wanted to see his image and his potential in the one legitimate child that he fathered.

Chapter 6

Imperial Divorce and the Fatal War with Russia

Aurore spent the years after her father's death at Nohant, and they were full of emotional rollercoasters between the family members, as historical events swept French history to some of its most dramatic moments. Aurore was starting to form the features that later attracted some of the best-known men in Europe, gypsy-like dark hair and eyes, very light skin, a strong nose, a small chin, and all in what would eventually become a short and thin four feet, ten inches frame.

As was mentioned earlier, Sophie hated Aurore. How can a mother hate a child? Sophie hated the fact that Aurore was accepted and legitimized by Marie-Aurore, while she was ostracized as a peasant that got ahead by marrying up. After teaching Aurore how to read, Sophie abandoned her education, and was bitter to see tutors teaching her things that she would never be able to learn or understand, even if she married the Emperor. Hamlet's mother betrayed her husband, and in real biographies, there are as many parents that hate their children, as those that love them. Not all animals have an instinctual attachment to their young, with some abandoning them at birth, others eating their weaker spawn, and only a few staying in family units or tribes permanently. Sophie was broken by a string of enormous hardships, from imprisonment, to illegitimate birth, to years of living in sin with Maurice before he finally agreed to marry her only to legitimize Aurore. When Sophie expressed "herself," she was naturally violent, both emotionally and physically, and focused her rage on Aurore. Sophie would scold Aurore for being too respectful, hit her as part of a penance, smack her hard enough to leave a mark, or would push her with all her strength into a bed or an armchair.

All the while, Sophie was flirting with Deschartres, and once he fell in love with her, she mocked his affection, which enraged his sentiments and created a cold war between them. When they played cards at night with Marie-Aurore, Sophie would cheat by hiding cards up her sleeve, put good cards at the bottom of the deck and drew them when she shuffled, and sneaked a peak at her opponents cards while pretending to be going to get a bit more tea. She was usually very good at these tricks, as she had gambled a bit when times got hard with her hat shop, but because they were not playing for money, she occasionally got sloppy and betrayed the trick she was playing. Once Deschartres noticed that she was taking a card out of her sleeve.

He threw his cards onto the table, jumped up and said, "You just took that card out of your sleeve! You are cheating!"

"I most certainly am not!" Sophie protested, blinking innocently.

"Somebody should throw the cards in her face!"

"If *somebody* did throw the cards in our dear daughter's face, I would be sure to give that somebody a *big* slap!" Marie-Aurore interjected. She recovered most of her mental faculties from the emotional breakdown, which resulted from the stress of her son's death, a couple of weeks after the event, but she was still strained and tense, and this hypertension eventually turned into the stroke that led to her final decline.

Sophie couldn't help but break out in a laugh upon hearing that noble woman say something as outrageous as that she would actually slap somebody with her own hand. The absurdity also struck Deschartres, and he made a suppressed chortle, sitting back down at the card table.

It was during this period, in 1809, when Sand began intensive studies in French writing, grammar and the classics. She read the fairytales of Charles Perrault, including the original 1697 edition of *Histoires ou contes du temps passé* (*The Mother Goose Tales*), which contained the story of *Le Petit Poucet* (*Little Poucet*), where a boy defeats an ogre. Another favorite of Aurore's from this period was Madame d'Aulnoy's *Belle-Belle ou le Chevalier Fortune* (*Beautiful-Beautiful or Chevalier Fortune*), which related the story of an emperor that demanded a soldier to serve in an army from every family, but one old man had no sons, so his three daughters attempted to volunteer, the one that managed to go dressed as a man, and then because she made a mistake she revealed her true gender to the king, who ended up marrying her. This fairytale was especially significant for Aurore, as she had already started cross-dressing at Murat's court, and was encouraged to continue by reading this fairytale.

Aurore already spent most of her time in Nohant's grand library, which contained an enormous collection of classical and modern literature, which was enlarged by Marie-Aurore on top of the judicial library that the previous noble owner left behind. Marie-Aurore encouraged her spend even more time among books because the noise of Aurore's playing with Hippolyte and the children of the staff distressed Marie-Aurore as much as it annoyed Sophie. Marie-Aurore was undergoing a hypochondriac phase, when she was worried that a cold wind might turn into a deadly plague. Marie-Aurore was even more distressed about the poor manners her granddaughter was picking up from her middle class mother. She instructed Aurore to talk quietly without using Berrichon, to stand erect, to curtsy visitors, and to speak with her in the third person. Aurore attempted to take this advice, but curtsying and forced politeness went against her nature. Instead of seeing sense in these refined mannerisms, Aurore saw a woman who was gradually becoming paralyzed by a total lack of physical activity and boisterousness across her life. Doctors were not prescribing exercise in that era, but Aurore felt an urge to run out of her grandma's stuffy room and to run and play with abandon to avoid a similar fate of gradual immobilization instinctively.

One day, a gray and white donkey from the barn, which was used for gardening and by children for transportation over muddy roads, casually entered the main house. It walked with determination and conviction, as if it was the narrator of Apuleius' *The Golden Ass*, inwardly a wise writer, and only outwardly a stubborn ass. Aurore saw it enter the kitchen, and along with Hyppolite Chatiron followed it as it made it through the house, sniffing every closet and doorway for food. It didn't manage to find any food in the kitchen because the cook shooed it away, though the children stopped her from escorting the donkey out of the house. The kids could see that the donkey had made the wrong turn, towards the grandmother's quarters, but it was too late to stop it without bringing more attention to the incident. So, the donkey continued rummaging through all of the rooms and finally stumbled into Marie-Aurore's. Seeing a smelly donkey in her neatly arranged room, Marie-Aurore rang the bell, a signal of extreme alarm, to which the chamberlain, Mlle. Julie, ran up from her room down the hall, tripping over the donkey as she ran in.

"Dear girl," Marie-Aurore told Aurore, who she noticed in the doorway, as the chamberlain fell, "you are too big for such foolery. Why didn't you have somebody escort the donkey out?!"

"I'm sorry dear grandmother. I was just curious to see what it would do."

"It's an ass, so it does what all asses do! Now go and play somewhere quietly, while the chamberlain leads the donkey to greener pastures."

***

While Aurore was entertaining herself with asses, Napoleon was busy with much more stubborn asses in his court. The two stories are also linked by Frederic Chopin, and to explain the connection we have to move back in time momentarily to 1799, when Marie Countess Walewska of Poland was tutored by Frederic Chopin's father, Nicholas Chopin, in French (he was a Frenchman who migrated to Poland) for six years until her marriage in 1805 to a man four times older than her, count Walewski. The marriage was rushed and she gave birth to a son around six months after the wedding, which cast some suspicion on Nicholas Chopin for potential paternity. A year after the Countess' marriage, in 1806, Nicholas Chopin married a poor relation of an aristocratic family that he started working for after leaving Countess Marie, and fathered Frederic Chopin as part of this union shortly thereafter, in 1810. As will be seen later in this story, Frederic Chopin was to play a major part in Aurore Dupin's life, so it seems the noble families of Europe had more intersections among them than horses bred in the same barn. But, to return to Napoleon, during the Prussian war, the Russo-Austrian Army encouraged Marie Countess Walewska to have an affair with Napoleon in order to encourage Napoleon to grand Poland independence from Russia. After some hesitation, Marie obliged this request and in August of 1809, she became pregnant with Napoleon's second illegitimate child, Alexandre Joseph.

The two had been having an affair for a couple of years. Then in August of 1809, Napoleon invited Marie to join him to Vienna during the late stages of the Prussian war. Napoleon conquered Vienna in July of 1809, after a period when it was out of his control, Napoleon having previously occupied Vienna in 1805, but then having given it to the dominated Italians for their supervision. Napoleon paid for Marie to stay in a mansion near his Schonbrunn Palace. He paid an enormous sum for her residence in luxury from this point in Vienna to her later divorce from Count Walewski in 1812. The news that Marie was pregnant affected Napoleon more than the news about his first illegitimate child. Unlike Eleonore Denuelle, who mothered Napoleon's first illegitimate son, Count Leon, while her husband was in prison for fraud, and from whom she gained a divorce at around the time of the birth of the son, Marie's marriage to Count Walewski would take many more years to break, and Napoleon was starting to see a pattern where the women he was involved with engaging in extramarital affairs on an equal footing with him, and mothering children that legally belonged to their husbands, and not to him. Thus, Napoleon decided that he had to resolve the problem of parental illegitimacy by divorcing his wife, and forming a union with any other aristocratic child-bearing woman in Europe. Aside from his parental concerns, the union with Marie was also expensive for Napoleon financially and politically, as she did not enter the relationship for love, and could have rebelled by disclosing the affair to the public, or with another move that could have tarnished Napoleon's reputation. The last component that sealed Napoleon's determination to win a divorce was a new assassination attempt in Vienna in October, while he was negotiating the Treaty of Schonbrunn, which meant that he could not merely call himself Emperor, but he actually had to produce legitimate heirs who would receive the crown if an assassination attempt succeeded.

Three months after learning about Marie's pregnancy, on November 22nd, Napoleon locked himself away in his study with the 1st Duc de Cadore, Jean-Baptiste de Nompere de Champagny, who retired during the French Revolution like many other top politicians in Napoleon's ranks, and was brought back in by Napoleon with the lure of great titles and honors. Champagny had just negotiated the Peace of Vienna, and he assumed that Napoleon wanted to discuss this matter further, but Napoleon had a very different subject on his mind.

"My dear Champagny, there is a matter of great importance that you must try to assist me with."

"Yes Your Majesty, how can I be of assistance?"

"It is a delicate matter, and I count on your discretion."

"As always, Your Majesty."

"The assassination attempt last month has been troubling me more than prior attempts. It seems that somebody makes an attempt at least once every year, but when it happens during treaty negotiations, it hints at weakness and can be disastrous for our interests."

"Yes, Your Majesty. I agree that something should be done."

"Well, what I think must be done is that I must gain a divorce from Josephine as soon as legally possible."

"A divorce," Champagny's eyebrows rose momentarily, "yes, Your Majesty."

"Only a full civil and religious break will allow me to remarry, and to father legitimate heirs that would make the assassination attempts ineffective for contesting monarchs."

Napoleon was being poisoned with arsenic across most of the years he spent as Emperor, so he was immune to this and most other poisoned through their over-use. He was also a brilliant general and escaped assassination attempts like pesky mosquitos. Among other measures, he wore a newly improved protective vast at all times, which blocked at least one of the assassins' bullets. But, he could not have been the great general that he was, if he did not think twenty moves ahead, and if he did not consider that a simple marital annulment could prevent further assassinations more readily than numerous military stratagems.

"So, take down the following dictation…"

Champagny found some official paper, and took out the ink pen, and sat down in a chair opposite Napoleon, preparing to record the message.

"November, 1809: Dear Czar Alexander: I am delighted that the naval war with Britain is going in your favor, and I was confident of this outcome since your initial engagement. Please do not hesitate to inform me if I can be of any assistance as the fighting progresses. I am confident that the Franco-Russian alliance will lead us to joint dominance across Europe. I write on this occasion to express my great admiration for your younger sister, the grand-duchess, Anna Pavlovna. I have acquired a print of her image by George Dawe, and it left a wonderfully warm impression on me. The warmth I feel towards your sister prompts me to inquire if you might be inclined to give me her hand in marriage. I am planning to file for divorce from Josephine, which should be finalized shortly, and I wanted to send this letter of inquiry first to gage your ideas and feelings on the matter. Sincerely yours, Napoleon."

Champagny finished the transcription and looked up. The Emperor imprinted the letter with an official seal, and signed it.

"Let's see what he'll say, and once we have an alternative marriage plan, we can proceed with ending the current engagement."

On the morning of November 30th, Napoleon received a letter back from Alexander:

November 27, 1809

My Dear Emperor Napoleon:

I was honored to receive your proposal for Anna Pavlovna's hand in marriage. However, I cannot grant my permission for this union because I do not believe Anna is mature enough yet to wed, as she is only fourteen, and is engaged in her education. She has not yet considered any marital proposals, and I'm afraid her mother, the Empress, would not consent for her to begin courtships before her find has fully matured. I am very sorry to bring you this news, and it would have been a delight to me to have you for a brother-in-law. The naval battles are steadily progressing in our favor, and I will write separately at a later date with a full report on those matters.

With admiration,

Alexander

Napoleon was distressed by this news, as it also meant that Russia was not as strong of an ally as he had previously imagined. He had Cham-

pagny transcribe a better asking for the land of archduchess Marie Louise, and from that point forward the alliance between Russia and France
was irrevocably injured. That evening Napoleon informed Josephine at
dinner that he was seeking a separation, at which she has a nervous fit
and fainted. Napoleon lifted her in his arms and carried her back to her
chamber, where she recovered with the help of her ladies in waiting. Two
weeks later, on December 15th, the dissolution of the civil marriage was
announced. The dissolution was adopted by the Senate on the 16th, and on
January 14th, the Tribunal took the final step of annulling the marriage
between Napoleon and Josephine, due to Josephine being sterile, and thus
the marriage not being fully consummated. The string of divorces that
surrounded Napoleon's personal history were political and legal precedents that were indirectly used by Aurore Dupin's lawyer later during her
own divorce proceedings. Napoleon oversaw the creation of strict anti-
divorce laws that took decades after his reign to repeal, but he assisted
with the divorces of his mistresses and himself gained a divorce, which
meant that an aristocrat like Aurore could also claim that she was different from commoners seeking divorce because she had political or societal
needs for this tactical move. But, we are getting ahead of the story.

***

Both Aurore and the Emperor were battling for their survival by
1810. Aurore was assigned a supervisor by Sophie, who was in-tune with
Sophie's temperament. With Sophie's blessing, Rose beat Aurore regularly for four years between 1810 and 1814, when Aurore was finally too old
to allow herself to be beaten by a servant. In those same years, Aurore
continued to be harassed by Hippolyte's steady progression into madness,
and his insistence on taking Aurore there with him. Hippolyte started
drinking as a child, though Aurore interpreted his early revelry as a wild
imagination similar to her own. When he was drunk, he would pretend to
be sacrificing pigs to the Gods, or pretended to be Calchas, a high-priest,
or Ajax, the warrior who committed suicide because he came in second.
While Aurore also loved to make-believe, Hippolyte would actually burn
pigs, stump plants, and otherwise would explode his psychotic hilarity on
all objects and people that were nearby. And on top of dealing with Sophie, Marie-Aurore, Hippolyte and Rose, Aurore was also given a rustic
playmate that was mad enough to claw, fist, scratch, and hit with hands
and feet the granddaughter of the mistress of the great house, Ursule,
Mlle. Julie's daughter. Most of these relationships had some kisses, and
some good times that made up for the prolonged nightmarish tortures
that Aurore endured on a regular basis, which kept her from isolating

herself completely from these negative people.

Over these four formative years, Aurore advanced in her studies by learning Latin and Greek, in addition to French. She closely studied the Bible, and was given drawing lessons by Mlle. Valery Greuze, the daughter of Jean-Baptiste Greuze, the famous painter, who died in 1805, having been honored by the Academy, but criticized by Rousseau for painting aristocratic subjects to gain notice. Mlle. Greuze gained some repute in her own right with the publication of comedie-vaudeville, *Greuze, ou l'accorde de village* (*Greuze, or grant village*) in 1813, around the time when she was tutoring Aurore. Needless to say that between Descecretes and Mlle. Greuze, Aurore was taught by some of the best tutors in France at a level that her father was trained before starting his military career, as opposed to the basic reading and writing needed for prayers and obedience that the vast majority of women in France were allowed. Aurore even studied chemistry, medicine and poison brewing, and various other complex subjects with Descecretes, who discussed the subjects that he was practicing as the estate doctor, manager and mayor of Nohant. Aurore's one weakness was the study of agriculture and business economics, as she was repelled by the idea of estate management, as a practical task that did not catch her creative interest. Aurore preferred teaching to management, as she started teaching a peasant, two-years her junior, Liset, spelling, reading, geography and history, when he accompanied her on her outings.

Amidst these intense studies, Aurore gradually began developing her first complex narrative, which remained in her imagination, without being put to paper. She continued gradually developing this story for over five years, from twelve through around the time of her marriage. Perhaps because of studying Greek and Roman mythology with Descecretes, or as a result of Hyppolite's passion for the subject, this story was an invented pagan religion, centered on the fictitious god, Corambe. Corambe was exiled from heaven to live on earth because he had too much pity and love for humans. The idea of meeting Corambe in the woods and gardens around Nohant thrilled Aurore, so she created an alter to Corambe on a rocky grotto under three joined maple trees, placing wreaths of flowers, seashells, and a number of other decorative objects to honor her god. She gave Corambe offerings of goldfinch, redbreast, and beetle. Aurore reclined in that grotto for hours, day-dreaming what Corambe would say if he was there. Today she would be said to have had an imaginary friend, but over the prior centuries creative children who later became novelists always had to invent characters in their imaginations or daydreams, before they could write their first fictional story on paper. Repeatedly imagine Corambe and considering the possible variations of what he might do or say in different environments and situations is a step Aurore had to take to learn the process of crafting a fictional story. What is fiction after all? Fiction writers invent lies out of their imaginations, and turn blank pages into a Bible, a novel, or a play. If somebody fails to conjure an "imaginary" character, friend or foe, as a child, one does not have the ability to instinctually lie on cue. Aurore's alter was discovered by Liset, and she buried all signs of it shortly after erecting it, but the story of Corambe kept running through her mind, and she had no intention of expelling it.

***

In 1812, the Napoleonic Wars took a turn towards catastrophe. Napoleon's re-marriage might have prevented a successful assassination, but the break with Czar Alexander cost Napoleon the Wars, and eventually his life. Just as Napoleon started in politics out of vengeance over a disappointing love affair, his fortune in politics turned because of the two affairs that were previously described. The first of these was the affair he had with the Polish Countess, Marie Walewska, who, as you might recall, agreed to have an affair with Napoleon in exchange for him supporting Poland in its fight for independence from Russia. Anyone that looks on nineteenth century or current maps of Europe and Asia might easily surmise that Russia, even without its republics, stretches from Europe to China and all the way up to the Pole, and down to near the tropics. Both Napoleon and Hitler made the same mistakes. First, they attempted to play the same manipulations and false treaty games on Russia, as they did on the rest of Europe; a flaw because the Russians succeeded at that very game, taking over an enormous part of the map, and continued to play those games across the last three centuries, losing some countries, while gaining others. Czar Alexander and Stalin assumed that Napoleon and Hitler were lying, and they were simultaneously lying, and thinking of ways to double-cross the other side before they agreed to peace treaties with the enemy. The second mistake both of these great generals made is marching towards Moscow in the summer, or only three months or so before the onset of the extremely brutal Russian winter. France and Germany must be in approximately the same climate, and they both must not have counted on the fact that a Russian ruler sacrifices all of his peasant troops to save the capital, and that this makes the march towards the Moscow or Saint Petersburg, a long one that cannot be completed before the first snow falls. If they had started their progress towards Moscow in March, they might have fought through the long ranks before the following winter. Napoleon must have been in love to have decided to side with Poland against Russia, without any direct provocation from the Czar other than the fact that the Czar was trading with United Kingdom. The second affair that was bringing about an irrational response in Napoleon was the fact that Alexander I refused his marriage proposal for his sister, Anna.

But to explain how Napoleon was feeling as things declined, we have to first look in on an elderly, aristocratic woman, M. de Lafayette, who was reading Voltaire's *Candide*, reclining on her bed, in a light, black dressing gown, when her bedroom's door flew open. She covered her breast with her book, as a six-foot tall hooligan, with mud all over his bearded face, clotted hair, and old, torn army uniform, turned the knob aggressively, and ran into the room like a madman, rushing directly at her and grabbing her, lifting her halfway off her bed, and shaking her in his arms convulsively. M. de Lafayette gave a few shrieks of horror and then caught the man's light blue eyes, while they were jumping with nervous intensity, she clearly recognized the hue of the iris. It was her son, Louis, who had left to fight in the Napoleonic Wars six years earlier, when he was only sixteen. He grew half a foot in the interim and the long absence and rough army living conditions made him unrecognizable even to his own mother.

"I thought you were dead! Oh, darling boy! My Louis!" M. de Lafayette exclaimed with joy.

"Yes, maman, it's me. I was finally granted leave! It's finally over!"

He broke down into tears, and held her tightly enough that she thought he would strangle her.

Louis was similarly distracted upon his return as Maurice, and he met a near-identical death, though he was not given a horse by a foreign king. He too rode his horse recklessly, in a semi-suicidal manic state, smashing into a wagon shaft and dying upon impact.

The news reached Napoleon, and Aurore reported in her autobiography his exact "brusque" words upon hearing the news of Louis' demise, "The mothers claim I get all their children killed in the war. Yet here is one whose death I am not responsible for, as was the case with Monsieur Dupin. If someone is killed on a wicked horse, is it still my fault?" Aurore thought that Napoleon was "reflecting on his destiny" when he said these lines, but that she could not understand why he felt the need to stress that mothers hated him. It is likely that Aurore over-thought the statement. Dozens of men and women made direct attempts to assassinate Napoleon in the approximately fifteen years that he was in power, working to maintain totalitarian control domestically, while also fighting for dominance across most of Europe. Tens of thousands of soldiers died in a few single battles of the Napoleonic Wars. So, Napoleon was hated by mothers in a very direct and standard way, as in some of them attempted to assassinate him for leading their sons into slaughter. It is more likely that Aurore was trying to fool the censors into a radical statement about her own hatred for Napoleon by subversively disguising it in uncertainty.

The same events must have looked very different from Napoleon's perspective. His mind was warped from the arsenic, the constant stress of wearing the vast daily, juggling the conflicting interests of multiple manipulative social climbing female partners, and the constant travel to war camps all over Europe, all created a warped reality that Napoleon couldn't escape. Since the moment he succeeded in a *coup d'etat* in 1799, he could not retrace his steps, as moving backwards or stepping down from power would have cost him his life. Attempting to surrender his position would have been seen as weakness, and loosening his grip on power and declaring a republic would have given the assassins and less violent backstabbers a chance to get rid of him and seize power. His situation was similar to a middle school English teacher who starts to sense that the students are about to throw their books at her; she can expel some, suspend others, yell at yet others, but she cannot suddenly become lenient, allowing some of the students to throw paper planes, as leniency is likely to cause an immediate uprising. The early military victories that Napoleon did have heightened his sense of infallibility, when they were frequently the result of kings, like the Spanish Infante, simply leaving their kingdoms behind and surrendering power to avoid the threat of death. Julius Caeser, Attila the Hun, Alexander the Great, and Napoleon are among a handful of leaders that attempted to take over the world, and the attempt always leads to eventual failure, but figuring out why they keep trying is like trying to figure out why kings or presidents attempt to seize leadership power to begin with, it's just something a certain type of men can't help doing. Napoleon must have reflected at the end of his life about all this, and he clearly came to the conclusion that if given the choice he would repeat the same maneuvers every time.

Napoleon began the Moscow campaign in 1812, and he was defeated by a coalition of European powers, having lost an army of half a million men, which would have included Maurice if he hadn't died riding Leopardo because Murat died on May 19th of 1815 after a period of imprisonment from a death by a firing squad, and his aide-de-camp would have certainly been included in the list of men that had to be executed alongside with him. After Moscow, Napoleon lost Germany and France in the following couple of years, until he was deposed at the end of 1814 and sent to the small island of Elba in Italy. As mentioned a bit earlier, Napoleon did do the same thing all over again, returning to France in 1815, and attempting to do what a middle school teacher should never do, or being liberal towards those one used to discipline. After the infamous "Hundred Days" of trying to offer the people of France liberty, he once again lost a battle at Waterloo, and was sent to spend the rest of his days in a mansion on the idyllic volcanic island of Saint Helena, a territory of the United Kingdom, in the South Atlantic Ocean. While Napoleon rested, France lost all of the territories they had gained since 1792, the Bourbon dynasty regained the throne, in the person of Louis XVIII.

France was in ruins, and Aurore's life took a tragic turn as if in reflection to the country's fate, but really due to her grandmother's sensibilities and emotional response to this devastating loss. Aurore was in Paris before the invasion of Paris by the Cossacks, when on January 13th a cannon ball broke through the floor of their apartment, and Sophie and Aurore retreated to Nohant. Back in 1810, Aurora had seen the hung cadavers of robbers in the Forest of Orleans on her trip towards Paris, a part of the harsh repressions Napoleon was instituting to bring the country into compliance. Now, on her way back to Nohant, Aurora saw long lines of starving soldiers, even hungrier and thinner than how she remembered them from her Spanish campaign. Marie-Aurore sacrificed her storage boxes and wine cellar and fed as many of these soldiers as she could because the sight of them reminded her of Maurice, and this memory made financial concerns inconsequential. As part of these charitable efforts, Marie-Aurore played host to General Colbert and General Subervie, as well as their aides-de-camp and staff for a couple of months before the order to disband came in.

It was after the generals and the soldiers had gone and Nohant returned to its natural rural appearance, when Marie-Aurore had a disagreement with Aurore over some minor misbehavior, but instead of telling her to go study in her room, Marie-Aurore told her, "Aurore, if you keep on behaving like you've been behaving, I'm going to send you back to your mother!"

Sophie had returned to Paris a month earlier. Sophie and Marie-Aurore had never gotten along, as Marie-Aurore was forced into accepting the marriage between Sophie and Maurice after-the-fact, and she hired a legal representative in an attempt to annul the marriage. This attempt failed, and when she learned that Maurice was returning from the Spanish campaign, she invited him to stay at Nohant, agreeing to accompany his new family as well. She resigned herself to the fact that the couple was married and that a divorce would have been near-impossible if the marriage could not be annulled, and the two had already had a child. She did not resign herself to having a common, uneducated shopkeeper for a daughter-in-law, and she offered her money to move to Paris, away from Nohant after Maurice's death, leaving Aurore with her at Nohant because she reminded her of Maurice, and because she was the only legitimate heir to the estate.

"That's exactly what I want. I just want to be in Paris with maman!"

"Ah, so after all I've done for you, that's all you want?! Go to your room then, and I'll think of what we should do."

Aurore went to her room, and she was surprised to find that her grandmother did not call on her again, and did not ask her to dine together with her over the next few days. Finally, one morning, her grandmother called her into her room and said, "Aurore, you've made your wishes clear, and from where I'm looking there is only one way I can help you child, and that's to send you to the English Convent that helped me get my bearing when I was young and lost, and it will help you to grow up and become the polite, mannered young lady that your position and title demand you to be."

Aurore tried to object, "But, why can't I stay with my mother?"

"You are too old to stay with your mother. What you need now is a proper education."

Aurore tried to think of a way to get out of the matter, but then she considered the adventure of it all, and realizing that her grandmother's word was surely binding, she resigned herself to going along with the matter, and departed for Paris without any further fuss.

Chapter 7

The English Augustines Convent

There was a period of civil freedom for women in France between the Revolution and the Napoleonic Code, which was reversed at that point and women remained as minors across Aurore's lifetime. Because marriages granted all of the power to the men, and did not allow women to gain a divorce, many women escaped to the convents, and joined the nunnery to avoid being forced into marriage by their families or by their impoverished circumstances. Even if a wife was battered, or if her husband abandoned her, she could not legally leave a marital contract. There was also only one place where women could obtain an education outside the home, and that was in convents and religious institutions.

Marie-Aurore had followed these legal developments in the radical press, while Aurore played, read and dreamed.

She had proposed that Aurore marry Maurice's nephew Rene's son, Septime, who lived in a townhouse in Paris on Rue de Gramont in 1812. As was mentioned earlier, Rene served as the chamberlain to Prince Louis, including the period when he served as the King of Holland until 1810. Thus, Rene and his son were among the best aristocratic connections the Dupin family had, and a marriage between Septime and Aurore would have satisfied Marie-Aurore's noble ambitions for her. The proposal came in when Aurore was only eight, and at a time when Aurore was in her first years at Nohant, a couple of years after her father's death, when Sophie was in a vicious battle with Maurice's side of the family over her allowance and Aurore's fate. Aurore was hearing regular complaints and insults addressed at her mother at family dinners and dances, and she recalled that Rene was among the chief gossipers, so she was repelled by the idea of joining his family. Between this early proposed marriage and 1817, when at thirteen Aurore entered the convent, she had not shown any interest in marriage, or young men. Marie-Aurore had to conclude that the girl was either too young for marriage, or did not yet have the mind frame necessary to marry for convenience and social progression. Marie-Aurore thought that seeing the only other alternative she had, the convent, would bring Aurore to her senses, and that she would begin seriously considering marriage. To Marie-Aurore's surprise she had read that the English Convent where she was imprisoned during the Terror had become the most popular convent for the aristocracy, including the Mortemars and Montmorencys, to send their heiresses, perhaps because distinguished women like Marie-Aurore were confined there just a couple of decades earlier, and there was a renewed revolutionary spirit in 1817, which made the aristocracy want to blend in with the liberal spirit of the times, and yet to be somewhere exclusive where they would not have too many people from the other classes to mingle with.

Aurore was taken by carriage to Paris. She was watching the scenery change outside, and was curious to see a side of Paris she hadn't frequented before. The carriage stopped on the cobblestone pavement of Rue des Boulangers next to a short black fence. Looking out of the carriage's window, Aurore saw the Baroque façade that was made up of a wall of dark grayish-green stones, seeded with tall black iron-sealed rounded windows. A few of the windows were not sealed shut with iron, but still had their casements hung with thick canvas screens that prevented all visibility of Paris from inside the convent. The walls were designed in an unusual pattern, as there were indentations and protruding geometric shapes scattered along the wall, and in one portion three windows formed a misshapen rectangle that stood out from the main wall, as if somebody began by building a balcony and then built a few floors with sealed windows under the top balcony. Aurore could see four floors looking up, and a rounded, multi-sided tower with three extra floors to it, all under a dome. A few scattered trees lined the road. The wall stretched as if continuously, and was longer than the walls of the Royal Palace in Madrid. But, unlike the gilded white of the Palace's walls, these walls looked like they hadn't been washed on the outside for two hundred years, a timeline Aurore estimated based on the gothic architectural style of the structure.

The driver brought down Aurore's luggage, and helped her out of the carriage. Meanwhile, an elderly man in a loose suite and brimmed hat identified him as the porter came out of a small single door with shaded windows and took Aurore's bags, waving her to come inside after him. Aurore looked back at the dusty carriage and the driver and then followed.

They went through a narrower corridor, past a room that was cluttered with packages, then a couple of rooms meant for lodging visitors, and a large grilled parlor that smelled like spicy chicken. This corridor also connected to a room used by nuns and visitors, a room for private lessons, and the largest room where resident students went to meet with visiting relatives. The last and largest room had its door open, so Aurore looked in and saw a salon decorated in a gilded and elegant Parisian style that reminded her of their family's Paris apartment; this was the room that Mother Superior used to receive members of society that were considering bringing their daughters to study at the convent, or donating to the establishment. Finally, they reached the courtyard gray-stone door armed with grating, and stepped back out into the sunlight to the screeching noise of the heavy echoing door. The porter's small wooden lodge was near this door, and Aurore could see most of his small room and essential possessions through its windows. On the other side of the porter's lodge was a little house that was rented by boarders and private matrons, the latter of which Aurore would later become. Aurore's attention was arrested by a complex set of gardens that made up the majority of the center of the interior double courtyard. The gardens were thickly planted with chestnut trees, golden grapes and melons, vegetables, and flowers. Amidst the gardens, there was a fenced in poultry yard with a chicken coop, a well, a laundry room, the refectory used for communal meals, and a chapter house used for religious meetings. The students were housed in the main square building that surrounded the courtyard, on the other side of the structure from the porter's house. The lower class was housed in a top-floor room directly under the attic roof with thirty beds in a single small room with a pealing ceiling and yellow wallpaper. The nuns that had duties cleaning that room enjoyed beating the students more than mopping the place up, so the place was entirely abandoned to mice and spiders, along with thick layers of dust, and the soot from the smoking stove. Aside from the hard and bare bed-like items reserved for sleeping, there were a few decomposing benches and stools that could be used for reading and eating, when the room was not extremely hot or freezing cold, and sitting was a viable option. The kitchen, cellar, and a maze of galleries, storage rooms, linen closets, musical practice rooms were on the first and second floors under the lower class's room.

The other three sides of the quadrangular cloister, lined with barred arched windows were used on the lower floor by the members of the upper class and the nuns. The nuns' work rooms were on the mezzanine level above them.

The porter took Aurore to Mother Superior's office. At that time, Madame Canning held the position, and she was an enormous sixty-year old woman, who began dictating the rules at the convent as soon as Aurore took a wooden chair in front of her, and the porter left the office, closing the door, and leaving a purple serve uniform on the chair next to Aurore's.

"You must wear the uniform at all times. You will have to pull your hair down over your temples; it's indecent how you have it pulled up now." Madame Canning was speaking in English, so Aurore had difficulty grasping the few words she had learned in English from Deschartres over the years.

"Yes, Mother Superior," Aurore managed to mumble with a thick accent.

"You are allowed to leave the convent twice a month, but you can only sleep outside the convent's walls once a year."

"Yes, Mother Superior."

Marie-Aurore only visited twice in the two and a half years Aurore spent at the convent, and while her Parisian cousins wanted to take her out with them, she insisted that if she was forbidden from seeing her mother, she would not see them either. The lack of visibility of the outside world made Aurore a bit claustrophobic for a few momentary instances, but most of the time she used the cloister to go inwards and to develop her mind, as the distractions of the outside world were barred from entry. Her reverie had three main stages during her stay at the convent, at first she escaped into boisterous play and fantastic escapism, then she was possessed by an extreme piety, and finally she became calmly observant, as she was seriously considering becoming a nun.

The first year that Aurore spent in the lower class during her rebellious phase was especially full of abuses by nuns like Miss D., who would make the girls kiss the ground, pushing their aristocratic faces into the dust, and then make them wear their nightcap to class.

Aurore attempted to bond with the other students, but this effort cost her too much heartache, so that she only had one close female friend later in life, Mme. Marie Dorval. Aurore sympathized the most with a girl nicknamed Boy, Mary Gillibrand, who was eleven when they met, but already tall, awkward and violent, with a deep voice, that left Aurore puzzled if indeed Mary might by a male in a girl's disguise. Boy called Aurore "Dawn of Bread," a play on the meaning of her name, as *aurore* means "dawn" and Dupin sounds like "*du pain*," or "of bread." Boy would hit Aurore on the shoulder, and the two would run around together. Boy belonged to a third of the class that was called "devils," whose favorite pastime was wandering into restricted hallways in search for "the prisoner," who their imaginations suspected was still hidden away somewhere in the convent, and in need of a rescue.

A typical day at the convent for Aurore in the lower class began at 6am, when the girls were awoken by their regular "servant," Marie-Joseph. Then they dressed by candlelight, broke the ice in the wintertime to wash, and had mass praying on their knees. The kneeling would aggravate the rough, narrow shoes, and blood would seep through them, past the swelling. At seven, they had tea with bread, and then go together to the classroom, where finally there would be a bit of fire in the stove. Aurore was wick with colds and pains in her limbs across her stay, and for fifteen years afterwards.

Aurore was relieved from this nightmare when Mother Superior discovered satirical letters she was sending to her grandmother, and she was transferred into the upper class, which had better living arrangements, as that room had some open windows, a stove that didn't smoke, and was supervised by a nun called the Countess, who was well-born and much more gentle and agreeable than Miss D.

The atmosphere in the upper class was positive enough for Aurore to have had the energy to write the first novel she put on paper. This was an asexual novel about Fitz Gerald who meets a heroine during prayers, but instead of following conventions and falling in love they do not and instead become "ardently pious," and joyously became a nun and a priest. After this attempt, Aurore also tried a pastoral, but both were "lifeless," and she returned in her imagination to her epic of Corambe, abandoning serious novel writing for many years. The conventional love plot is a difficult one for most female writers because it does not comply with instinctual or logical ways in which women perceive love or fall in love. For the man, it might be logical that simply looking at a woman's eyes or figure awakens attraction and love, which only needs a few syllables of expression before it blooms into a relationship worthy of a marriage. Eventually, Aurore was able to write about love, but most of her stories avoid the simple romantic plotline. Jane Austen wrote about relationships by focusing on the youth and development of a female character, and then the long period of getting to know a male character before the female character realizes that she might be feeling some love for him. And there have been few female writers that have been able to step away from the male-dominated love plot, and into their feminine ideal love plot, instead most simply learn the movements of the male-authored plot and mimic it for the sake of experience and convention. Aurore recalled this early failure at the novel in her autobiography because it was a problem that haunted her literary career, and led her to step away from regular novel writing once she regained control of her estate and fortune because she followed the conventional plot under the duress of financial responsibilities, rather than out of a conviction in the reality of this conventional romance structure.

In 1819, when she was fifteen, her situation improved still further, as she was given a private cell, which while it put her back into the attic, and had a low sloping ceiling, also had a window that allowed her to feed the sparrows. She also suddenly had a dresser, a wicker chair, a threadbare rug, and even a Louis XV harp, which she could practice on in her spare time, without any interruptions.

It was during her stay in this private room that Aurore developed an extremist religious piety. Aurore gives an exact day and time for this moment as August 4th, 1819 at 4pm, in her autobiography, while the rest of her convent stay lacks concrete dates. At this time she picked up *The Lives of the Saints* in the chapel and began reading about Saint Simeon Stylites. At first Aurore laughed at the poorly constructed story that was out-of-place in Christian mythology, but then she found it to be strangely poetic, and read the other stories in the book. Aurore's imagination was engulfed and she snuck back into the chapel that night to pray for the first time in her life with real devotion, and belief in God, as if she was transferring her passion for Corambe into this newly discovered divinity. In the days that followed, Aurore read the Bible, psalms, and other religious texts more closely until she started perceiving sins in the simplest actions, and started to feel an overwhelming guilt. The majority of the billions of people living on earth have experienced what Aurore experienced in those weeks she spent in ecstatic religious faith, only most of them manage to keep this faith across their lives. People are told that while most imagined fiction is pure lies, fantasies about religious figures are real. In other words, there is really an elderly man watching our every move, who knows if we are good or evil, and will send us to hell if we are the latter or if we fail to believe in the correct religion. Aurore was affected by this story because she was placed in a convent where she was only taught about religious rules, and finding a well-written mythological book about the saints brought her out of the mundane repetitions of catechisms and daily prayers and into the more complex elements of the Christian mythology. Being in a place where all of the adults insist that the old man that sends people to hell is real warps a child's imagination and perception of reality. We learn about what is real from touching and sensing it, but also from books and from oral reports from others. When the "wise" men or women in a community insist that God exists, the children must accept this belief, or risk burning in hell or being ostracized by the community. However, there was a boundary along this path for Aurore, and it was her prior secular reading, which exposed her to science and mythology, and which meant that there were always doubts and questions that awakened Aurore from slipping into blind faith. Thus, when Aurore encountered a confessor who told her that she was too apologetic in her confession without a due cause, and that she should instead be joyous and helpful to others, Aurore snapped out of the spell religion had temporarily held her in. But, it took a few other traumatic events for Aurore to regain some of her earlier atheism.

By August 15th, Aurore had stopped eating and drinking. Then, on that day she encountered Sister Helene, who was only eighteen, a lay sister, with pale consumptive-like skin, but white teeth, and a robust frame. Realizing that Aurore was going through a pious streak, Helene faked extreme consumptive illness when Aurore was passing by her, sitting in place on a staircase and staring out, slouched over, as if dying. Without explaining much of what exactly was ailing her, Helene guilted Aurore into doing all of her chores for her, so that Aurore spent a full day washing and waxing floors, dusting, polishing the nuns' stalls, and making all the beds in the two dormitories. Just as Aurore was finishing the last of the beds in the upper class dormitory, Helene walked in to check on her and realized that she was not folding the sheets according to Mother Superior's orders, so she told her that she would take over and redid the sheets. The next day, Helene had a new plot for taking advantage of Aurore, as she asked her to tutor her in French, a task that would have been expensive had she hired a tutor. Aurore joined Helene in her stall, and fought through the odor that Helene's lack of cleanliness had left there, and Helene's persistent yawns and unbearable boredom with learning. By the end of two hours of tutoring, Helene had realized that she had no business attempting to learn French, when she barely knew any English. Meanwhile, Aurore was suddenly inspired with the idea that to avoid marriage, but without committing to becoming a nun, she could work as a servant in a convent like Helene, an idea that she continued to have in the back of her mind in the following years. Aurore never figured out what Helene was playing at, but the fact that Helene did not ask her again to help with cleaning or tutoring left a sense of inadequacy in Aurore. She felt that she had failed Helene and while she fantasized about being a servant, this experience taught her that it was likely she would fail at servitude if she made the attempt.

For a period after this incident, Aurore attempted the other alternative available at the convent, by joining the Sisters, who welcomed her participation as if she was a new Sister in training. The life of the nuns at the convent consisted of having tea in the workroom, alter adornments arrangement, chorus practice, and jasmine and rose flower gardening. Aurore might have become accustomed to this gentle and peaceful routine if it wasn't for the sudden death of Mother Alippe of endemic pulmonary catarrh, a disease that also nearly killed Mother Superior and some of the other nuns. This death was so gruesome and sudden that Aurore began to suspect that living permanently at the convent would be dangerous for her health, as she understood a good deal about medicine from Deschartres' lessons. Aurore attended the burial with all its ceremonies: chants, service and the planting of pansies on the tomb. Just as they were singing Ava Maria with bowed heads, they all looked up at the sound of a horrific shriek from Elisa, who fell to the ground in convulsions due in part to the infection and mental distress she caught from sleeping next to Mother Alippe's stall as she went through the death agonies the night before. Aurore saw the ghost of Mother Alippe in a white robe that night, and after this she was plunged into a depression, so that she couldn't pray, had severe stomach cramps, and felt a resurgence of her doubts about her faith. She kept recalling the line, "Many are called, but few are chosen." Prayers once again started to feel formulaic and lacking in mysticism. Her confessor once again pulled her further away from her reverie, and helped her to focus on her present reality, as opposed to on an unseen spirituality. While Aurore now had strong doubts about becoming a nun, she spent the following six months in tranquility, assisting the nuns in their daily tasks without any overly emotional ecstasy or despondency.

During this period of peaceful coexistence at the convent, Aurore reverted to the one activity that she felt instinctually drawn to since she first learned to read. Aurore was bored by the monotony of two years of convent life, even if she did not admit this weakness to herself, and she felt that the tensions and violence at the convent were the result of a shared ennui that was misdirected into hostility. When she thought about the type of entertainment that might be allowed at the convent, she decided that comedy skits would be the most amusing activity that would pass the convent's censorship regulations. Aurore made herself the producer, acting director, casting director, costume and set designer, writer and central actor in each of her plays. She thought back to plays she read, and wrote skits based on what she could recall from them. After the first few shabby experiments, Aurore learned the skills involved in play organization, and began displaying the shows not only to students in her classroom, but also to the nuns. At this point, aristocratic relatives began donating costumes, screens for the wings, and other props that improved the appearance of the shows. The clothing was so fancy that the nuns even allowed cross-dressing, as for example once Aurore dressed up in a Louis XIII costume. Male costumes and other unique sets required Aurore to put her sewing, embroidery and other household skills to work, which she thankfully acquired during her eclectic early education. The stage sets were less elaborate than the costumes, as they had to rely on stools and tables, that were given symbolic meanings with the color that covered them, or green for grass, and gray for stone. Before long, the lower class and Mother Superior were coming to the performances. Aurore suddenly had to develop four-hour full-length plays, and while perhaps any other child would have fumbled at this enormous pressure, Aurore ravished it, and succeeded at running every element of this extremely complex set of productions.

The biggest show Aurore organized was an imitation of Jean-Baptiste Poquelin's, better known as Moliere, French play that was first-performed in 1673, *The Imaginary Invalid*. Aurore remembered the name of this play in particular because it was Moliere's last and most masterly play, and because she had been shocked to learn that he died during its fourth performance. The plot of the play on which Aurore did a variation was that a hypochondriac, Argan, is constantly calling in his physician, Mr. Purgon (who was played by Aurore herself), to check on his health, and decides to marry his daughter, Angelique, to a man that plans on becoming a doctor, Thomas Diafoirus, but Angelique is already in love with Cleante, so Argan threatens to change the will taking Angelique out of it if she fails to marry a doctor. Argan homes to have a live-in permanent doctor if Angelique consents to marrying a doctor. A string of comedic incidents and disagreements follow until at the end Argan consents to his daughter marrying for love as long as Cleante agrees to becoming a doctor, at which he is told that he could just as well become a doctor himself. This idea excited Argan, but he dies shortly thereafter. Aurore managed to take out the love plot and the medical details to make the play more appropriate for the convent's audience. The plot that Aurore devised was that instead of a daughter, Argan had a son, who he insisted had to become a physician, or risk losing his inheritance, and the comedy was primarily the conflict between the artistic ambitions of the son, and the coy remarks of the physician, which were in conflict with Argan's wishes. Because all of her actors were new to the craft, she allowed them to improvise lines instead of memorizing a script. Only one heiress in the audience recognized the play because she saw it at a Parisian theater.

"Don't tell anybody it's Moliere, or they'll close the theater," she whispered to Aurore during the reception after the show.

Shortly before the end of Aurore's stay at the convent, France underwent a new wave of liberalism under the Restoration leadership of Duke Elie Decazes, who served under Napoleon, then became a royalist and served as the Minister of Police and then as the Prime Minister, the latter through 1820. Decazes' leadership came to a sad end when he was accused of assisting the revolution in Spain, and the forthcoming assassination of the Duke of Berry. Aside from those achievements, Decazes loosened censorship and also allowed for mutual schools that broke up the Catholic dominance among French primary schools. The creation of these new schools was not entirely peaceful, as some students rebelled and insisted on the change before the government agreed to its necessity.

"Can't we have our little revolution? Can't we have our own little notice in the newspapers?!" Aurore cried out once in class, raising the rebel, in the midst of their laughter at one of her jokes, when the Countess was momentarily outside of the classroom.

Suddenly, the Countess came back, "What's all this noise?" she asked looking at Aurore, who was towering above the class, on top of her chair. "And get off that chair!"

"Let us raise!" Aurore shouted, raising her fist up into the air.

All the girls stood up immediately, crossed their arms in a threatening fashion, and made mean, angry faces, pretending as if they are about to begin a real rebellion.

In that age of revolutions, the Countess assumed that if the students are looking and talking like they are about to start a revolt, then clearly they were about to start one, so she ran out and hid in her room on the other side of the convent. What started as a joke, suddenly threw Aurora into an actual rebellious ecstasy, a feeling she had been suppressing in the prior months, as she worked to piously assist the nuns. The other students were far more crazed than she was due to the enormous suppression of emotions and words that girls at the time endured daily. Aurore at least expressed her frustration with her plays, and in her reading and writing, but most of the other students had no similar outlets for aggressive emotions and thoughts. A couple of them grabbed torches and candles out of the Countess' desk and threw them at walls and windows. One of the girls even grabbed a footstool and smashed it into the floor.

"Revolt!" Aurore screamed, jumping around and also throwing some candles around.

"Revolt! Revolt!" the other girls echoed.

A full hour passed of this mad running around and screaming before Mother Superior and her full staff of the elder nuns arrived.

"Now girls, you clean this mess up this instant," Mother Superior said, with her hands on her hips.

The girls were suddenly embarrassed by their childish behavior, and Sand blushed red at the thought that her gardening co-workers were all looking at her as if she was an infanta terrible, too spoiled to obey rules of basic human decency. So, she nodded obediently, and the girls cleaned up the signs of their shanty rebellion in an hour until it was just a distant, silly outburst.

It was shortly after this uprising among the girls that Duke de Berry was stabbed to death by Louis Pierre Louvel, a bonapartist, as he was in the entrance, leaving the old Opera house, which was rebuilt at a safer isolated location because of this incident. The fact that the rebels succeeded in such a public assassination allowed Louis XVIII to reverse some of the liberal education, censorship and other types of policies that had just been turned by Decazes' administration. The incident occurred on February 14, the American Valentine's Day, which was celebrated as a day to express love since before the nineteenth century, so the killers must have seen irony in killing Berry after a performance of a love-themed opera on the day meant for the expression of love. The assassination perhaps had to do with the fact that Berry resigned during the Hundred Days period, a loss that partially precipitated Napoleon's final loss. In addition, Berry had just married into the royal family, and his son was a likely contender for the crown, in direct opposition with the bonapartist cause he swore to fight for with Napoleon. Aurore read about these events in the papers in the months that followed this event, and it affected her with a strong sympathy with Louvel's bonapartist radicalism. In general, Aurore had gotten a taste for rebellion and insurrection, regardless of the party responsible for the intended overthrow, a preference that she kept until sometime after the 1848 Revolutions, when she changed her mind about the effectiveness in the long-term or for people of violent overthrows.

Meanwhile, a week after Berry's assassination, Marie-Aurore came to visit Aurore to check on the impact the assassination was having on the convent. Marie-Aurore was distressed by the news of the assassination because she had known Duke de Berry across the decades she lived in Berry, and she knew that the bonapartists might have just as easily misinterpreted one of her family members of switching sides too frequently in accordance with changing political climates. To her surprise,

Marie-Aurore was told by Mother Superior that Aurore was seriously considering becoming a nun. This idea terrified Marie-Aurore more so than Berry's assassination, so that she exclaimed the moment she heard this tragic news.

"I'm taking her with me. She is educated enough, and I intend for her to marry. If in three years she's still not married, then it would be prudent to review this option."

Mother Superior nodded, brought in Aurore, and related to her this news. Later that day, Aurore was in a carriage headed for their Parisian apartment with her grandmother.

Chapter 8

Independence and Confinement

Some girls must anticipate marriage as a fairytale conclusion to their childhood, and the beginning of their life as a wife and as a mother. They must develop a flutter in their stomachs, and a yearning for love and companionship. They must anticipate that they will be adored, loved, admired, esteemed, and worshipped by a man who will provide for them, and will be exactly what they need. Aurore did not see any evidence in her life that this was what a marriage would bring with it. Her father had died on a mad horse after surviving a decade in the army, moments after she was recognized as a legitimate heir by the Dupins. Her mother was malicious and abusive, and Aurore only understood later in life just how manipulative and cold-hearted she was. Her grandmother had actually sent her to the convent where she was imprisoned during the Terror, and while Aurore tried to explain this action as a positive, resilience-building gesture, it was clearly not the actions of a warm and caring matriarch. And she had taken Aurore out of the convent just as it was finally becoming Aurore's home, and as she indeed became the resilient and hard-skinned woman that a convent can mold when its fire hits a suitable metal. Aurore also knew that her grandmother's husband died young like her father, and that this meant that Marie-Aurore had to fight through a Revolution and the decades of hardship that came after it on her own. The women in her family were single mothers, who were used to managing estates and shops because the men they married failed them or died too soon. Marrying somebody from the middle class brought about a social war between Marie-Aurore and Sophie. But, marrying up could mean marrying a much older men, or somebody that was intellectually repelling to Aurore. Each of these memories and scenarios entered into Aurore's imagination as she contemplated that she was taken out of the convent with the sole purpose of marrying in the near-future. Her marriage could be immediately arranged, and she might not have a chance to express all these objections and preferences. She might be dressed in a wedding gown one morning and be at a church for the wedding that afternoon, without a chance to get to know the character or temperament of her new husband. The second she married she was agreeing to remain a legal minor across her entire life, until the death of her husband. Aurore had just found a passion for the theater, for writing, for theological study, and this new master over her might forbid her from pursuing all of these interests. Will he allow her to even go to the theater or the opera? Will she be locked away in a bedroom, and would not be allowed friends, or tutors? There was no romance in these horrific options, only the dread of equally miserable alternatives. Aurore attempted to find a solution, but she was too young to calculate the course that would have led her to a positive marital life, so she allowed her relatives to propose suitors.

A number of suitors were immediately presented to Aurore upon her entrance into Parisian society. Aurore had spent the majority of her life in Paris, but she was suddenly welcomed into the upper echelons of Parisian society, as Marie-Aurore made a final effort to find the husband that she felt was suitable for the Dupin family name. Marie-Aurore approached these negotiations as a military campaign equal to helping her son become aide-de-camp to Murat. She brought in the military leaders who worked around Murat in Madrid to help her with this new central venture in the life of her aristocratic family.

The first relation that came to mind was Marquis de Caulaincourt, known to the family as Armand, and to those in his district as the Duke of Vicenza. He had served as the Master of Horse to the Emperor after successfully negotiating with the Russians in 1807, a period when he and Maurice maintained both military and familial communications. Because he had already established positive relations with Czar Alexander I, he was the representative charged with negotiating the peace treaty after Napoleon's defeat, which allowed Napoleon to be taken to the island of Elba. He was Napoleon's minister of foreign affairs during his Hundred Days return, and despite this, he was not executed during the Second White Terror that followed the second defeat because Czar Alexander personally interfered on his behalf. Armand spent the last decade of his life in retirement, writing a memoire of his time with Napoleon, while also enjoying some quiet time with his extended family. The Duke of Vicenza happened to be residing in Paris in the period when Aurore was coming into society, and Marie-Aurore inquired with him regarding possible suitors for Aurore. Armand's oldest son, M. Louis de Caulaincourt, was twenty-two at this time, and had begun a career as a cavalry officer. He later served as a senator under Napoleon III, but at this time he was merely a somewhat awkward, but handsome military man, with dark curly hair and sideburns.

To romanticize the meeting, Armand and Marie-Aurore plotted to have the two cross paths in a setting that might be pleasant for both of them. Aurore had recalled that Duke de Berry was assassinated only months earlier at the opera house, and she had an irresistible urge to see the opera that he saw before his untimely death, which was still playing, *La Cenerentola, ossia La bonta in trionfo* (*Cinderella, or Goodness Triumphant*) by Gioachino Antonio Rossini, who was enormously popular in Paris at the time, and later spent his last decades in Paris on an enormous pension from King George IV. *Cinderella* was a modernized variation on the traditional fairytale, with a wicked stepfather, Don Magnifico, and the Prince's tutor instead of a Fairy Godmother. It was a materialistic get-rick through social climbing plotline, as Cinderella is identified by a bracelet and reaches a happy ending by marrying the Prince. The old Theatre National de la rue de la Loi was closed a couple of months later because it was deemed to be unsafe by the King, and this was one of the last times it was crowded with thousands of theatergoers. Since Aurore was eager to see *Cinderella*, Armand and Marie-Aurore invited Louis to attend the performance as well, and both sat in the same front box of the opera.

A tailor had designed a fashionable high-waisted, cropped, short-sleeved chemise dress and a Spencer jacket. The light material of the dress made the outline of Aurore's developing breasts visible, which made her feel awkward and uncomfortable, as she imagined what Mother Superior would have said if she had seen her in that dress. At the same time, Marie-Aurore was shocked by the tailor's suggestions, as the last time she had researched fashion to make an impression on Parisian society was when the corset was still in style, and she had been teaching Aurore those outmoded tastes before this tailor explained the radical developments in fashion that took place between the French Revolution and 1820. Aurore liked some of these changes, as she could suddenly breathe in her dress, but she wished she could go further, back to the comfortable aide-de-camp outfit she wore in Murat's court. She did not express this sentiment, and focused on becoming more comfortable in this rather revealing dress.

It was hardly the first time Aurore had gone to the old opera house, and she had frequented most of the other cultural establishments in Paris as a child, but she suddenly saw it in a new light. The light, showing dresses were almost in contrast with the gold mirrors, and busts of Roman emperors along the walls of the gallery. The heavy jewels of the chandeliers contrasted with the simpler pearls and elegant jewelry the ladies were wearing. There was also a freshness to the air, as perfumes had lighter, flowery scents. Guests gradually filed into the main hall's tall doorways, and took their seats, assisted by gallant valets, in long jackets. The seats in Aurore's box were made out of an enormous piece of marble that was outlined with fine gold leaves, and covered on top of the pillows with thick, dark-red cashmere. The wall behind them was also covered in the same color of cashmere, and was also decorated with a few paintings by French masters. A long table at the front of the box was covered with candles that set a relaxing and romantic mood for the occasion. Aurore and Louis curtsied to each other as Marie-Aurore and Armand took the side seats out of the four, and left Louis and Aurore to sit next to each other in the center.

"I hear you recently resided at the Augustine Convent, our cousin Jane told me she asked you to attend some gatherings in Paris with her, but you could not leave your studies?"

"Yes, I couldn't go with them, though I would have liked to have gone to the opera more."

"You like the opera?"

"Yes, I helped to organize some plays at the convent."

"I think I heard about those, they were a bit of a talk-of-the-town. You must be very proud of your achievement."

Aurore blushed, "I guess. I mostly did it for fun. There's so little to do at a convent. I think we'll do some plays at Nohant later this Spring, if I can find enough volunteers."

"I would be delighted to join you. I did a bit of amateur theater years earlier."

Aurore's imagination flew away from her as she saw a way for her to continue running a theater even outside of the convent, a notion she had not previously seriously considered. "Yes, that would indeed be delightful."

The main lights were dimmed and *Cinderella* began. Louis snuck a few quick glances at Aurore's defined chest, as her breasts heaved with the trepidations of Cinderella's voice. Aurore was trained in operetta singing by Marie-Aurore, and she was imagining singing the part of Cinderella. She studied and performed the part on her home piano in the following weeks, and she was now so engulfed in studying the singer's performance that she did not notice Louis's glances, and if she had she would have thought there was a stain on her dress.

"Au revoir," Aurore said to Louis as they were leaving the box.

"Au revoir," Louis replied, curtseying.

Marie-Aurore and Armand exchanged quizzical glances, and both seemed puzzled about if their plot had succeeded or failed. When Louis told Armand that Aurore had invited him to perform in a play she was putting on at Nohant, the plotters decided that it was best to wait and see. Meanwhile, since no immediate plans for a meeting were arranged, Marie-Aurore pursued several other fitting alternatives. On the following occasions Marie-Aurore simply proposed suitors as such, without setting up a meeting, and these Aurore flatly refused until Marie-Aurore had gone through all eligible bachelors related to General Harville, M. de Segur and all of her other aristocratic friends and connections. Aurore called one too old, another too rich, and yet another too stupid, after brief introductions at masquerade balls, dances, dinners and various other social gatherings through which Aurore and her grandmother ploughed through with amazing speed. Before the season was over, Aurore's old abusive governess, Rose, had married in a small civil ceremony in Paris and went to live with her new husband in La Chatre, but Aurore was further away from finding a husband than she had been when she was eight. After one particularly biting rejection when Aurore laughed and shook her head openly upon seeing an elderly, wrinkled postal worker that had thrown his hat into the mix enter a dining room, Marie-Aurore gave up and proposed that Aurore take at least six months off from searching for a suitable mate, and the two returned to Nohant for a rest.

Marie-Aurore had suffered a stroke which was gradually limiting her ability to perform simple tasks, and her withdrawal into her room, and her abandonment of household and estate business meant that the servants and staff of Nohant started to see Aurore as the new young manager of the estate, even if she was more interested in the arts than in keeping the estate books. While at Paris, Marie-Aurore had kept to a strict schedule, waking up early, and going to several meetings daily with Aurore, but when she said that she was now giving Aurore a respite for half-a-year, she knew that she was permanently resigning the responsibility of marrying Aurore off before her decline incapacitated her. Marie-Aurore was starting to go deaf, and had difficulty making it through more than an hour of her regular salons. She decided that if she had managed Nohant without a husband with Deschartres' help, so could Aurore when the time came. Thus, suddenly, there were no restrictions on Aurore's time, and she could sleep in, run around, or do just about anything she imagined, as long as she could not be heard doing it by Marie-Aurore from her bedroom. Of all things she could have done with her free time, she chose her studies, and made a strict schedule so that she spent an hour each day on history, sketching, music, Enlgish and Italian.

When Aurore sent note that she was preparing a play for her grandmother's upcoming birthday, Louis came for a visit as-promised, along with Mme. De Pontcarre and her classically beautiful daughter, Pauline.

Aurore once again took on the main male part, as she was accustomed to cross-dressing at the theater because it elicited laughter, and subconsciously she did not want to wear a revealing dress because she now clearly distinguished Louis studying her breasts over dinner before they began their first rehearsal. She did not want to be distracted from her work as the theater director by worrying about Louis's sexual or marital motives. Seeing the cold manner with which Aurore treated Louis, who clearly expressed a growing passion for the girl, and on top of this seeing Aurore in a man's costume made Marie-Aurore realize that there was something queer about Aurore, and that even if the handsomest and richest man in France fell on Aurore's head and begged her to marry him, she would flee the scene, and would flatly refuse this threatening entreaty. Louis made a few attempts to engage Aurore in conversation, and constantly ended up in technical debates about the arts, instead of on personal matters. He also attempted to be alone with Aurore to find a moment to express his feelings, but Aurore would suddenly sprint forward in a run during a walk through the garden, and dodged all of his attempts at a romantic *tete-a-tete*. Finally, after the play was over and Pauline and her mother departed for Paris, he felt awkward about staying, and so he too departed, and while the two exchanged a few letters after this point, Louis did not propose marriage directly because he knew he would have been rejected.

A more lasting relationship was about to come into Aurore's life, one that took her over rough terrains, and always put her in good spirits, the one that involved none-other than Colette, her thin, ugly, untamed and awkward horse. Hippolyte had joined the army and was now at twenty, a hussar sergeant. Hippolyte casually invited Aurore to come riding with him one morning, and was shocked to hear that Aurore had never been on a horse. So, Hippolyte took her out to the barn, where he mounted General Pepe, the grandson of the terrible Leopardo that their father died on. As part of his military service, Hippolyte was teaching new cadets at the Ecole d'Instruction des Troupes a cheval, or School for the Education of Troops on Horseback in Saumur, France at the intersection of the Loire and Thouet rivers, which was housed in a large u-shaped building, and the surrounding spacious fields.

"Are you sure it's safe? Don't you want to explain how it all works first?" Aurore inquired.

"I pretend to be Deschartres when I teach in Saumur, I don't want to bore you as well with my attempts at serious lecturing."

"But, I've never been on a horse before. I'm sure there are rules I have to know."

"From teaching a lot of recruits, I've figured out that most of them forget my theories on horse-riding as soon as I utter them. Do you really want to know how to put in a horseshoe?"

"No, I'm just a bit nervous."

"Just remember this, in horse riding two things can happen, either you are going to fall, or you are not going to fall. Since it will be your first time, you will definitely fall, so we'll go to a nice grassy spot and will take it slow, so that when you fall it won't be too bad."

This didn't reassure Aurore, but she decided that getting on a horse for a few moments to gauge its reaction wouldn't be too bad. She led the horse by the reins until they reached a flat, grassy field behind the main house. Colette was at this time only four, had never been mounted, and served Aurore for the next fourteen years until 1834, when Aurore's fast life demanded speedier horses and carriages, and Colette was honorably retired. Hippolyte helped Aurore up into the saddle, explaining how she could get on herself in the future, and said that she should avoid riding side-saddle if she wanted to go faster than a trot, an advice that Aurore readily accepted. Aurore prepared to take a couple of cautious steps, but Hippolyte whipped Colette and she took off at a gallop, bucking over branches and rocks, as one might see at a rodeo, and occasionally kicking in the air, as if attempting to throw Aurore off.

"Just don't fall off! Grab the mane if you have to, just hold on!" Hippolyte yelled as Aurore came around a circle back past him.

Aurore was indeed holding on to the mane, the reins, and once Colette's ears, but still she almost left the seat at least six times. Yet, despite Hippolyte's and Colette's efforts, Aurore never fully left the seat, and managed to stay on Colette for an hour before she came to a stop and dismounted, having briskly learned all she would ever receive as part of her horsemanship instructions. A week later, she was safely jumping over ditches and hedges, climbing slopes, and even once crossed a deep river on horseback. The time she spent in the heat and icy cold of the convent strengthened her constitution and she readily jumped into this and other manly challenges. One incident almost put a permanent stop to her riding. She took General Pepe for a ride instead of Colette, and had a dangerous fall in the exact spot where her father was killed, but she only had a few bruises, so she managed to hide it from the household, and continued riding as gingerly as ever.

One of the reasons Aurore was tolerant of the bruises that came with extreme physical exercise is that she wanted to separate herself from her grandmother's immobility. Marie-Aurore gradually became confined to her bed, where she rested in her lace bonnets, wearing exotic perfumes and rings, indulging in her snuff-box, and sleeping sitting up. One night, as she was attempting to get out of bed, she was hit with apoplexy and was half-paralyzed, blinded and stuttering, so that Julie had to lift her off the floor. They sent for Dr. Decerfz, who bled her, and eventually she regained some of her faculty, but she was diminished and Aurore felt as if her soul had left her, as she lacked the spirited vitality of mind that she previously identified with Marie-Aurore. Several months later, Marie-Aurore experienced a temporary recovery, so that she was able to sit in an arm-chair in the garden, but a few months after that she relapsed into complete lethargy. This gradual decline left a scar on Aurore's sensitive nerves, so she started using Marie-Aurore's snuff-box to deal with the smell of Marie-Aurore's decaying body and mind. Aurore also took to drinking black coffee without sugar, and sipped on brandy to have the courage to stay up for most of the night with her grandmother without much sleep.

In a period when Marie-Aurore was clearly near-death, and yet had regained some of her mental faculties, so that she could communicate with those around her, Archbishop of Arles, or M. Leblanc de Beaulieu, the "bastard uncle" as Marie-Aurore called him, as he was the result of a publicized love affair between Marie-Aurore's husband, M. Francueil, and the famous Mme. Louise Florence D'Epinay, who also had an affair with Rousseau in 1756, even buying him a cottage, before the two became bitter enemies. Rousseau was introduced to D'Epinay by M. Francueil, who had been having an affair with D'Epinay since 1752, when she became pregnant with the "bastard uncle," who was then born in 1753. For the first forty years of his life, Leblanc lived in a small village, having taken the orders early in life, but only gaining the title Father Maugras in 1798. Thus, he never married and only rose above abject poverty when he turned thirty-nine. The Archbishop first became a bishop in 1799, a year after Maurice enlisted in the French army after the Terror. Leblanc had to endure exile in London in 1815 after Napoleon's overthrow. The Archbishop had just resigned his post as the Archbishop of Soisson, a year before this present moment, in 1820, which meant that he was facing a modest and obscure retirement, unless he reclaimed his inheritance. In 1821, the Archbishop was sixty-eight, while Marie Aurore was only five years older than him, having married a significantly older man with this enormous complication in his romantic past. The Archbishop was the cause of much friction in the marriage between Marie-Aurore and her husband, so he was put in a monastery as a child, and then for a while Marie-Aurore took care of him as her own child, before he started a career and left the family estate. He hadn't visited Marie-Aurore for at least two decades when he suddenly arrived to bring out a religious confession in Marie-Aurore before her forthcoming death. When he threatened that Aurore would go to hell if her grandmother did not confess, Marie-Aurore confessed that she has nothing to confess, and that she has lost faith in God since her son's death.

To this the Archbishop said, "That is meaningless."

On the next day, the Archbishop attempted to get a confession out of Aurore, and when she refused he set fire to her books, ripping a few of the other books to shreds. Amidst this wild and crazed destruction of extremely valuable hundreds of year old books, Deschartres rushed in and exclaimed that he had the power to stop him by the authority of being the Mayor of Nohant.

"I can bring charges against vandals, archbishops or not."

This cooled the Archbishop, and he left, but the fact that Marie-Aurore had gotten the last word ate away at him, and he dedicated the following decades to spreading false or exaggerated rumors about Aurore around Berry, and this came around to Aurore because the priests in that city became hostile towards her, demanding that she repent her sins, a move that furthered deepened Aurore's anti-organized-religion sentiment. While Marie-Aurore imagined that she had mothered the good Archbishop, in his memory she had sent him away, and had led to his loss of inheritance of the family estate, which he hoped to regain upon Marie-Aurore's death, but now realized was going to Aurore, a child of a mixed-class union, but still one more legitimate than his own origin. If he had succeeded in convincing the people of La Chatre that Aurore deserved to be disinherited, he would have eventually succeeded, but the rumors mostly fanned the flames of Aurore's literary fame, and eventually helped her to gain a divorce and full independence.

Meanwhile, by July 5th of 1821, Aurore felt like she was the mistress of Nohant, as everybody called her "Mademoiselle," and obeyed her wishes. She was now accompanied by a squire, Andre, a Berrichon, who carried a pistol for protection in his holster, and had a steady nature that was unique when compared with all the other people Aurore knew up until that point, who were always quick to yell, and panic. The pair usually traveled accompanied by two of their dogs, and if they spotted game, they proceeded to hunt after it with the dogs' help. They rode ten leagues together every morning, drinking goat milk at a farm mid-trip, before returning at noon. Their favorite farm to stop in belonged to a spinster called Clara, who besides the goats, also had chickens, a wheat field, an orchard and a vegetable and fruit garden. Clara was defamed in Berry and La Chatre as having had many affairs, and was suspected of being a witch, and Aurore's frequent visits to her farm and her defense of Clara's character in public won Aurore many enemies in her neighboring cities, as she was contradicting their statements, and collaborating by somebody shunned by the community. At one town dance, while engaged in a bourree, Aurore was almost stoned by the townspeople, but she was defended by her tutor and peasant male friends, who surrounded her to protect her from an attack. Meanwhile, aside from hunting and meeting interesting people in the area, Aurore used these outings to study nature, recording the details she was observing in the back of her mind for future literary use.

It was Aurore's habit at that time to read to Marie-Aurore in the evenings, and one evening she read Rousseau's *La Nouvelle Heloise,* and she was surprised to discover a tear in Marie-Aurore's left eye, as she was reading the last few lines. Aurore attributed it to the late hour, and excused herself, asking if Marie-Aurore was all right. After Aurore left the room, Marie-Aurore picked up the book again and recalled the connection between Rousseau and her husband via Mme. D'Epinay, and she re-read the lines, "Blind as we are, we each waste an existence in the pursuit of different chimeras, and refuse to see, that, of all the illusions of humanity, those of the just man alone lead to happiness." She had wasted her existence when she lost her son, and now her illegitimate son, an Archbishop, was haunting her for her failure to fully accept him when her pride was hurt by the affair. Who was the "just man" in her life's story? Clearly even men of God, like the Archbishop, were sinful and vain. It was too late to discover how she could become just, and it was too late to tell Aurore all the lessons she had learned from her own painful existence. She would try, she promised herself, to explain it all to that dear girl, who was spending all that time sitting with her and trying to make her last days bearable. Perhaps, of all the people Marie-Aurore knew the one that was innocent and just was this little girl, who was refusing to marry, but was reaching for artistic ambitions that Marie-Aurore might have unconsciously dreamed of, without ever having the courage to attempt them.

***

As Deschartres felt that Marie-Aurore was fading, and as he realized that Aurore was receptive to difficult study, and that she could be a useful assistant in his work, he took her on as an apprentice. From the earlier rudimentary lessons in science, he moved on to teaching her complex physics, anatomy, osteology and even surgery. Deschartres would have Aurore assist with the cutting off of arms, amputations of fingers, re-setting of wrists, and even the patching up of cracked skulls. It was during her surgical trips with Deschartres that Aurore met the heir of the noblest family in the Berry region, Claudius, who was handsome, intelligent, witty and was in medical school, preparing for a career in scientific research. Sadly, Claudius was consumptive, and died shortly after this period of this disease, a fact that later created sympathy in Aurore for consumptives, and explained her dedication to consumptive men like Chopin, even when they were severely ill, and being around them endangered her own health and the health of her family.

They formed a bond, when Deschartres assigned Claudius to tutor Aurore in physics. The three of them would study full skeletons together, and for a period during her grandmother's decline Aurore had a skeleton of a little girl in her dresser, which frequently startled her at night at first, but then helped her to get over her fear of death and of human body parts, as Deschartres thought it would. The maidservant did not discover the skeleton in the closet because Aurore's room was cluttered with a piano, a harp, a guitar, books of musical scores, and various other books and projects, so that the cleaning staff only swept up and straightened up the bed.

While Aurore barely got to know Louis, the time she spent working and studying with Claudius meant that she allowed herself to form a serious connection with him, which started to feel like love, even if it was only the love between friends.

Because Aurore started to trust and to feel comfortable around Claudius, one evening when they were dissecting a pig together in Claudius's office, Aurore said casually, "Isn't it a bleak world we live in?"

"How so? I don't see what you mean?"

"I mean when I was in Paris, in society, it was also so unnatural and forced, like everybody was playing a part."

"That's called manners, people act in public, that's the proper thing to do."

"It's appalling. I hope I'll never have to go back into Parisian society again. It was exhausting."

"But, how can you not? Don't you want to get married? Certainly, you'd have to look in Paris. Berry is so small, there are few people that might be…"

"I think I'd rather become a nun. I wanted to, but then grandma took me out. I think I'd be a lot happier now if I had just taken the veil."

"What! That's absurd! How can you take the veil?! It's not real. To marry God? That's not like marrying a real, warm human being!"

"What's so good about real human beings? It's so complicating, so painful. I don't think I can love another person, as much as I can love an abstract idea… It's easy to love an idea, it can't disappoint you."

"You are a truly philosophic soul, Aurore. You are right. You are always right. But, it's that kind of truth that kills!"

"Kills!? Claudius, what's the matter with you? You are overreacting.

Who cares if I become a nun? It would hardly kill anybody…"

Deschartres leaned in towards Aurore and whispered, "I think he might be confessing that he loves you."

Aurore looked back up at Claudius, who was staring at Deschartres and her in horror, as he overheard a bit of what Deschartres had whispered, and the fact that he had to explain the matter to Aurore was not a good sign.

"Claudius, I really don't think I'm ready for marriage. As you can see, I'm still considering becoming a nun. I'm not in the right state of mind to answer your affection. And maybe I could come up with a better answer if we weren't in the middle of dissecting this pig… maybe I'm just a bit too rational-minded at the moment, maybe after we put the pig away…"

Claudius turned a pale white and glared at Aurore in complete horror.

"How can you be so cruel Aurore! What if I die of grief?!" His face convulsed, but he didn't break out in tears. Because he anticipated that he might start crying, he ran out of the lab, and did not see Aurore much after this point. They exchanged some letters, but Claudius was never brave enough again to attempt asking Aurore directly for her hand in marriage. And Aurore was waiting for him to make a move, and assumed that he was merely overly dramatic, but unwilling to make a more focused effort in winning her love. That's how it worked in novels, after all, the girl always rejected the boy across the entire saga, until she finally agreed to the union at the very end. In reality, Aurore started to realize, if a man was making an effort to join with her, she had to accept immediately or he would permanently lose the courage to try again.

Aurore did not ponder long about this potential engagement because her mind was occupied with new challenges she was taking on. Deschartres started taking her quail hunting at dawn every morning, which involved rummaging through the thorny thicket, setting up the trammel net, lying in the dewy furrow, calling the quail, and then shooting around ten of them out of the pack. All then were eaten for lunch, primarily my Marie-Aurore, with Aurore and Deschartres taking one each. Aurore started wearing boy's clothing, including a smock, gaiters and a cap for these outings because her dresses would become see-through if she lay down on the wet grass in that material, and a thicker material made it difficult for her to ride Colette with impediment. An unpleated skirt that got caught in the reins or tangled her legs up could have caused a fatal accident on that lively beast. Riding and hunting in boys' clothing was starting to be in fashion among the aristocracy in the Berry region, as Aurore knew of Count V., whose daughter followed this style. In addition, Deschartres had diagnosed her with rheumatism, most likely caused by the cold, damp nights at the convent, and prescribed strenuous exercise and masculine attire. Once she started wearing trousers regularly, Deschartres' lessons intensified still more, as if he was suddenly mistaking Aurore for one of his collegian male students, or for Maurice.

Why is it easier for people to take seriously a person who is dressed simply, casually and without embellishment? If you have attempted teaching, tutoring or mentoring employees at work, you might have noticed that it is difficult to focus when you are talking with somebody in an extremely short skirt or baggy pants that are revealing boxers, not because one is attracted to the person one is speaking to, but because they are aware of this element and are calling attention to it, without focusing themselves on the lesson at hand. Aurore never considered herself a feminist, instead she thought that she had taken on the clothing, attitude and reasoning of a man, or had become a man when she made the choices that she did. She did not see this transformation as sex-related, but simply a performance that allowed her to stop being a minor, and to become the master of her estate. Wearing skirts involved performing vulnerability and inferiority, and cutting open a pig or calmly studying the bones of a skeleton were not activities that one could engage in while worrying about looking feminine, a gender that required the wearer to look distressed by the site of blood and bones.

One day, while on an exposition with Deschartres, Aurore was mesmerized by the sight of the river they were traveling along. She looked at the water, and let her mind escape from the moment into her reflections. She suddenly realized that the year at most she was given for respite from deciding the marriage question was almost up. She might be forced into a decision on the following day, or month. She wished she could push the decision back by a decade, to a time when she might be a skilled physician, in charge of an estate, or after she sang in an Opera, or wrote a play, or otherwise achieved something grand and significant. She recalled the last letter she received from Claudius, which included atheist, extremist statements, and implied that he was engaging in outrageous behavior in Paris. She did not plan on replying to that letter, despite knowing that Claudius was suffering from the advanced stages of consumption. Aurore was more concerned with her own ambitions that would be suppressed as soon as she married. Her husband might not let her ride Colette, and she might end up paralyzed and voiceless like Marie-Aurore. Suddenly, the water had a comforting feeling to it, and Aurore felt a dizziness seize her, and she desperately needed some rest, and the water felt like a bed she could fall into to find complete peace. Then, she became conscious that she wanted to end her life right at that moment, when she was happy riding through the woods with the beautiful river and the flowers along the bank. She did not want to see the life that would unravel ahead of her, the life she would have as a wife and mother, or the old age and eventual slow death that followed those functions. Her nature was in complete opposition to all of the things she was supposed to want, love or strive for. She could not go to medical school like Claudius, or become a professor or abbe like Deschartres. She had read all the classics, modern masterpieces, and devoured her lessons in various advanced subjects with distinction, and she would certainly be forbidden from running dissections or bleedings after she was married. If she jumped into the water and drowned now, her life, while difficult, would have been lived without her making a conscious compromise to settle for something she was not forced to accept. She was forced to go to a convent, forced to live at Nohant without her mother, but with the death of Marie-Aurore she would have to make a conscious decision to marry and to give up her ambitions despite the various ways she could have rebelled, like running away and becoming a cleaning woman, joining a convent as a nun, or some other outrageous option that would have let her remain independent. She had not found friends at Nohant, in her family, at the convent, or in Berry or La Chatre, and she expected that she would never find those that sympathized with her rebellious ideals, and that she would always be surrounded by poisoners, assassins, and manipulators, who would be keen to take her money and estate, and would not see beyond her sex to the creative genius that was trapped in her small, pale body.

All these thoughts rushed through Aurore's mind in moments, and as they were flooding her, she pulled the reins and suddenly Colette gave a start and jumped into the river. The ford was twenty feet deep, but Aurore was overcome with joy and laughter, as she felt the water splashing against her skin, and as she sank lower with Colette under her. After a moment of confusion, Colette realized they were in deep water, and began to swim towards the riverbank, despite her rider's apparent lack of interest in navigation. When Colette got to the bank, she could not scale it because it was too steep, but under Deschartres' prompting, Aurore grabbed a hanging branch, and pulled herself out. With Aurore's weight off her, Colette swam ahead past the ford and came out next to General Pepe, on the accessible part of the bank. Deschartres studied Aurore all over, checking for damages, and seeing that she was all right turned General Pepe around and got in the stirrup.

"Let's head back. We need to get you dried up, Mademoiselle."

"Yes, Deschartres, you are right."

Aurore got back on Colette, who gave a brief start at having Aurore back on top of her, but as they rode away from the spot of the incident Colette seemed to forget all about it, and continued at her regular steady pace.

"What happened back there?" Deschartres asked.

"Can I confide in you, as my doctor?"

"Yes, of course you can."

"Well, I pulled Colette into that river."

"Why did you do that?"

"I wanted to drown?"

"To drown? You mean you had a dizzy spell? They run in the family. Your father used to have them."

"He jumped in a river."

"No, but also had a few desperate moments."

"What was he sad about?"

"It's a miserable world. There is a lot to be sad about."

"But, didn't he have a lot going for him?"

"He did, and so do you."

"Like what?"

"Well you are young."

"Why is that a good thing?"

"It means you aren't old, you have your health…"

"What else?"

"You are wealthy. There are a lot of poor people out there, but they are too busy working to be jumping into rivers. You just need to find something to do, to keep busy and it will keep you from thinking about such things."

"Like what?"

"You have to decide what you are best at, and what you can do at an advantage."

"Like your teaching?"

"I have other ambitions. I actually just bought a piece of land near Nohant that I hope to develop into a profitable farm."

"Is that your ambition, do you want to be a great farmer?"

"I guess, we'll see. I have to become independent. I always planned on striking out on my own and having my own estate. Nobody wants to be working for somebody else all their life."

"Yes, that's exactly what I think too."

The two continued slowly on their ride, and Deschartres cleaned Aurore up before anybody in the household realized that she had taken a dive into a river. They didn't discuss the incident again, but somehow Aurore got a sense that Deschartres had the same dizzy spells that he thought were hereditary in her family, and when he looked at that river, he also had a compulsion to rest in it. The idea of suicide reappeared in Aurore's mind after that point, but she never made another definitive attempt.

***

One night, on December 22nd or 1821, Aurore was sitting in Marie-Aurore's room, chewing snuff, and sipping brandy. Marie-Aurore was asleep for most of that day, but suddenly she woke up. Marie-Aurore looked around the room. She was startled out of a dream about her husband's illegitimate son, the Archbishop. In 1786, when her husband, M. Francueil, died she was faced with the decision of what to do about his two illegitimate children from D'Epinay, who were both living in a village some distance away from her residence. At the moment, she was faced with an extremely difficult financial situation, as her husband had been liberal with offering money to D'Epinay and his other lovers, which meant that the estate was near bankruptcy when it passed into Marie-Aurore's hands. She made the decision to cut that family out of her accounts, and wrote a letter explaining her financial difficulty. This put enormous strain on Leblanc who had to get away from his usual drunkenness and reverie to provide for himself and his family. He only managed to recover in 1798, after over a decade of extreme poverty. While Marie-Aurore was not exactly comfortable for most of those years, during the Revolution and the Terror, she did not come to his aid even after she had moved into Nohant, and regained a share of her earlier wealth.

In her troubled mind, she suddenly recalled the smell of burning books from several days earlier, when the Archbishop attempted to "convert" her, and ended up starting a fire in her precious library. The past and the present got mixed up, and she momentarily imagined that it was 1786, and her husband had just died, and somehow Leblanc had entered the household and was setting fire to her house, hoping to burn it down with her in it. She opened the drawer at the top of the cabinet next to her bed, and took out a knife with a finely cut and decorated gold and mother-of-pearl encrusted handle. Marie-Aurore grabbed this knife, as if ready to defend herself if Leblanc broke into her room. She stared wildly at the knife for a moment, inspecting its sharp edge, but then she realized that there was somebody else in the room. She looked up and met eyes with Aurore, who was sitting in the recliner. For a moment she only saw Aurore's face in the dim candlelight and thought it must be Maurice, but then she saw Aurore's white dress and this brought her fully into the present. She looked back at the knife and realized that she must look awfully ridiculous grabbing a knife without any threat around, as she remembered that the Archbishop had left many days earlier. Then, she looked back at Aurore and thought about the decisions she would have to make after she took over the estate, and wondered if she too would have to disinherit some, and enrich others, and she realized that Aurore would have much more need to have a knife in her cabinet than she would in the few days she had left. Her throat was sore, and she didn't have the strength to speak, but she had the energy to stretch the knife out towards Aurore. Aurore hopped up from the recliner and approached her grandmother. She took the knife and studied the pearls. With the knife out of her hand, Marie-Aurore let her head drop back to her pillow, and she drifted back into sleep.

The noise of Aurore walking over to the bed was heard by Deschartres, who was in the next room to be available in case of an emergency, and he stormed into the bedroom. The noise of him walking in did not disturb Marie-Aurore in the slightest. Aurore showed Deschartres the knife she was just given, signaling that Marie-Aurore gave it to her. Deschartres studied the knife and realized that it was the knife that Marie-Aurore had hid in a wall during the Revolution because it was given to her by her husband shortly before his own death, and she saved it, while she left most of her jewelry in the open to be found, to keep the hounds away from the more incriminating papers that were hidden in that same apartment. Deschartres recalled how he started tutoring Maurice at a time before the Revolution, when he was contemplating either a career as a full-time lecturer and researcher at the College du Cardinal Lemoine, or an even more distinguished career in the sciences, hoping to publish grand books on the new discoveries he would make. The Revolution and the Terror had changed his plans entirely, and he had not considered leaving the Dupins in three decades, even after the death of his first pupil. He hadn't realized it until that moment, but he had fallen in love with Marie-Aurore during the Terror, and felt as if he was married to her since spending a year taking care of Maurice as if he was his own child during the year Marie-Aurore spent confined in the convent. He never married, and never achieved any of the plans he set in medical school, and how Marie-Aurore was dying, and it was too late to tell her how he felt. He would never have given up all his dreams and wishes unless he had been in love. This thought brought a tear to his eye. Looking up at Deschartres, and noticing the tear, Aurore suddenly realized that the knife had some greater symbolic, personal, or historic significance that she was not aware of. She considered that her grandmother might be telling her that she is in danger, and even if Marie-Aurore was delusional due to her illness, there was something awfully eerie about this gift, and something even more troubling about seeing Deschartres crying, so her eyes also teared-up, and in a few moments both Aurore and Deschartres were shedding tears in torrents, an act that was painful for both of them because it was so uncommon in their eyes.

Marie-Aurore slept without waking for the following two days until the night of December 24ᵗʰ. Aurore was drifting off in the recliner, when she heard a shuffling on the bed. She opened her eyes, and saw that Marie-Aurore had just woken up, and had moved up slightly against her pillow. Aurore approached and stood, touching the bed, right next to Marie-Aurore's face. Marie-Aurore had been recalling her life across that long slumber, and studying its details, trying to make sense of it. She looked at Aurore, and recalled that she had sent her to the convent where she spent the Terror, and she felt momentarily guilty for this action, but then she thought of the unique artist Aurore had become at the convent and under Deschartres' instruction, and she felt as if she was just and correct in the steps she took to raise Aurore up. She inhaled and decided that she had to tell Aurore this point to summarize all the things she felt and had failed to express. She coughed to clear her throat, and softly at first and a bit louder at the end she said, "You are losing your best friend."

Aurore nodded, but didn't reply, in case Marie-Aurore wanted to say something else. But, the effort exhausted her grandmother, and she fell back into sleep, and into her contemplations. She died in a coma when the day broke on December 25ᵗʰ, and their little church at Nohant played the Christmas bells. When Deschartres pronounced that Marie-Aurore was dead, Aurore was partially relieved that there wouldn't be the death agony that she had heard down the hall from her stall when Mother Alippe died at the convent. Nobody at the household cried upon hearing the news, as all had been prepared for this eventuality, and most had a private cry days earlier. Julie arranged a lace bonnet with ribbons on her head, put on her best rings, and positioned a large gold crucifix and a prayer book into her hands. While these arrangements were being made, Aurore went to her own room and read a bit from the Bible, and some prayers and psalms, as she considered what this death meant. The day went by slowly, and she had a long discussion with Deschartres about what they had to do next to manage Nohant, about the funeral, going through all the mundane and monumental tasks that were before them. When they looked at the clock it was 1am. Both of them knew that they could not go to sleep with Marie-Aurore's body down the hall.

"Let's go take a bit of a walk, my dear girl," Deschartres said, putting on a thick coat, as it was snowing outside.

Aurore followed him out, and they both fell a few times over the frosty ice that covered the snow. They walked through the back entrance to the little cemetery. The ground had been opened for the burial planned for the next day. Maurice's grave had been unearthed because it was directly next to the one planned for Marie-Aurore. And under Deschartres encouragement, the two of them got down to her father's grave, and kissed his skeleton.

"You never got to kiss him goodbye," Deschartres said to explain why this action was necessary. "But, don't speak about this to anyone."

The funeral on the next day was loud and harassing, as beggars nearly pushed the grieving party into the grave, trying to get alms, while whaling with exaggerated emotion. Aurore ran away from this throng as soon as the service was over and locked herself in her grandmother's room, lying down to smell the sheets where her grandmother was just resting, and burning incense, while resting in the recliner and listening to the sound of a lone cricket hiding somewhere in the room; this sound at first disturbing, suddenly lulled Aurore into sleep, and hours passed before she awoke, looked around the room, and had a cry, which relieved the agitation she had felt over the last few days. When she was done, she quietly left the room, and changed in her own room, creating a list of tasks she had procrastinated for days. Returning to a routine was a sure way for Aurore to move forward with new strength that was needed now more than in all other difficult parts of Aurore's life.

Chapter 9

Casimir Dudevant

A couple of days later, Aurore took a carriage over the crusted snow to Paris. She stayed the night in the Rue du Roi-de-Sicile apartment that her mother inhabited at the time. In the morning, cousin Rene de Villeneuve, Marquis de Caulaincourt and their wives joined Aurore and her mother for the reading of Marie-Aurore's will. The attorney proceeded directly into the reading, and Aurore learned that she would inherit the majority of the estate and that her noblest relative, Rene de Villeneuve was assigned to be her guardian. Aurore only saw him as a child, and did not know at the time the details of his royal duties, so she did not appreciate this assignment. Sophie objected that she was the legal guardian, as Aurore's mother, and while Marie-Aurore would have had the power to overturn this objection, the others present, including Rene did not have the courage to prevent a mother from living with her daughter, so the two were reunited, and began living at Marie-Aurore's Reue Neuve-des-Mathurins apartment. Caroline had gotten married shortly before this, so they were alone there with a single servant.

Sophie spent the majority of the following weeks studying Nohant's poorly managed accounts, which indicated that there wouldn't be as much coming in from the estate as Sophie had imagined. She brought the lawyer that read the will back in and had several consultations with him. The lawyer advised that the party who had managed the books while Marie-Aurora was ill over the last three years was Deschartres, so he was invited for a family meeting to "render an account of his administration." The same relatives present at the reading of the will returned, as well as a couple more lawyers, one that was representing Deschartres, and a second that was representing Rene. Sophie's lawyer explained that there were accounts of payments coming in for crops sold, but eighteen thousand francs of those payments were not turned over as part of the estate

by Deschartres. The old Abbe explained that he had bought a farm a couple of years earlier, while also paying a lease at Nohant, and that while he
expected to have become profitable in the first year, there were problems
with the land that he did not anticipate that caused him to lose money,
and that he had to pay for these losses out of his government pension,
and income from rents on an apartment he owned at Rue de la Harpe.
Thus, he had indeed taken out the money in question that belonged to
Nohant, but he thought of it as a loan due to his stressful circumstances.

"If you took out a loan you are supposed to pay it back," Sophie exclaimed.

"I have been trying to pay it back, but I just don't have the money to
do it at this time. I do hope I can sell the farm. I am trying to do everything I can to return that money."

"If you can't return it, I don't see how you can avoid debtor's prison."

Aurore looked at Deschartres and was frightened at how pale he became, remembering their talk by the river, she imagined that he would
commit suicide if his honor was degraded with a trip to debtor's prison.
She also thought about the debt she owed him for educating her for the
last decade at a level that matched a top-level college education.

"He already did pay me back. I'm sorry. I forgot, and I just remembered, it was a few months ago."

"Do you have receipts to prove this?" the lawyer asked.

"No, I didn't think to keep receipts."

"So, you received eighteen thousand francs. Where is the money?"
Sophie screamed in frustration.

"Apparently, I spent it, since I no longer have it."

"You have to show proof, you can't just say that he paid you!"

"No, as the sole beneficiary, Aurore does not have to prove how she
spent the money," the lawyer corrected her.

"She's lying! Pious prig! Philosophist! She's lying and stealing from
herself!"

"She certainly has the right and is only defrauding her dowry."

"I'm going to take both of you to court, and then we'll see if it's legal
to steal from yourself and your family!"

"Mam, you will be told the same thing there as I have been telling
you here. She has the right to have spent the money as she chose fit, even
if she simply never collected it from Dschartres," the lawyer intervened.

Sophie steamed and offered a few other brief objections, but finally
she agreed to a defeat and the debt was crossed off the ledger. All the
relatives left the room and Aurore was briefly left with Deschartres.

"I promise I'll pay you back. I'm so sorry for the trouble this is causing."

"I know you will Deschartres, I'm sorry for the way my mother has handled this matter, it's just awful."

"Thank you."

Deschartres departed, without finding much more to say.

In the hallway, Aurore came across M. de Villeneuve, who said, "Will you come for dinner tonight?"

Aurore was about to agree politely, when her mother, who had overhead interceded. "She most certainly will not."

M. de Villeneuve was shocked by this answer, as he couldn't imagine why Sophie would want to bar her daughter entrance from one of the most aristocratic and wealthy houses in Paris. But, studying Sophie's stern expression and posture he realized that she was holding a grudge against him for receiving Aurore's guardianship, and this seemed so petty to him that after making a brief goodbye, he left, and never interacted with Aurore during Sophie's lifetime.

After he had gone, Sophie immediately gave away Aurore's dog and dismissed the maid to show her displeasure. Aurore replied by attempting to become a nun, but her application was rejected because she was told there wasn't an available place for her. There were three years left before Aurore would reach absolute majority, and Sophie made all efforts to make such a term unendurable to force Aurore into marriage. One of the worst of these offenses was that she forbade Aurore from reading the complex philosophical material that she had become accustomed to studying. Sophie was also incredibly irritable and anxious, and was constantly worrying about the appearance of her clothing and hair, changing them many times daily, until it was an all-consuming obsession. In addition, Sophie believed that her indigestion meant that she was being poisoned. Since Aurore was the only party present that would stand to gain financial independence from her death, she suggested that Aurore was the responsible poisoner. The suggestion distressed Aurore, who started to feel like she was living with somebody who felt she was her mortal enemy. She couldn't imagine who could benefit from poisoning Sophie, but the fact that Sophie might take her to court for an attempt even if she wasn't capable of considering such an act made Aurore watchful and tense around Sophie, so the time they spent living together was one of the most stressful and painful times in Aurore's life.

Sophie frankly did not think that Aurore or anybody else was poisoning her. The accusation did what it was supposed to by making Aurore feel extremely uncomfortable, and helped to force Aurore into an early marriage.

Around four months after Marie-Aurore's death, Sophie decided that while she could push Aurore into wanting to marry, she did not have the resources to find a suitable husband that Aurore could accept. She started taking her to various functions with friends and relations. One time they were dining with their cousin, Gustave de Beaumont, who was twenty at the time, and would later go on to write a well-known book about reforms needed in the American prison system. For now, he was a carefree, young man, recently out of the university, who had many connections with the bourgeoisie of Paris. On this particular occasion, they were joined by Mme. Angele Roettiers du Plessis, the twenty-seven year old, thin and tall wife of James Roettiers, who was in his forties, balding, but had bright blue eyes, and was in charge of running the Manufacture des Gobelins, a tapestry factory, located at 42 Rue des Gobelins in Paris. The factory had recently been reopened as part of the Restoration, after having been closed since the French Revolution because it primarily catered to the tapestry needs of the aristocracy.

"The tapestry your artisans designed for me is simply divine. It is amazing that you could commission such an established artist. I was recently at the Louvre, and I was told that Battle of Zama tapestry that hangs in the main hall is the work of your predecessors at the factory, designed for Louis XIV," Gustave gushed with pride.

"I was lucky to win that post. It is a delight to work in such a historic place. The timing for the reopening couldn't have been better," James replied, showing pride in the work of his staff.

"Do they hand-paint the tapestries?" Aurore inquired, curious about the design process.

"Yes, it's very fine work. They use the tapestries as a canvas. Typically it takes a few layers of faint before the color is solid enough. But, you have to be careful with the details, so it looks realistic."

"Do you think I could get a little piece of the tapestry and paint that you use to try it at home?"

"No, you certainly can't take advantage of Monsieur Roettiers' kindness to take all his tapestry. And how would you paint it in our apartment?! You'd get paint all over the floor!" Sophie objected, outraged at the suggestion.

"No, it wouldn't be any trouble. The raw-materials are very inexpensive. If it was a small piece, you could use newspapers over a table without too much of a mess."

"No, no, we couldn't impose on you," Sophie insisted.

"But, I insist, I'd really like to help a young person to explore her interests."

"There are things this young mademoiselle needs more than painting tapestries…"

"Really, what do you need, it would be my pleasure to help."

"Well, it so happens that Aurore is in need of a husband."

"Mother!" Aurore exclaimed, horrified.

"Now, now, it's ok to ask for tapestry, but you are shy about your marital needs."

"We happen to know many eligible bachelors, we'd be happy to introduce you to some of them. We have five daughters of our own, and a few bachelors have already asked to come and visit us in the coming months."

"Aurore, why don't you go with Monsieur Roettiers? It can be good for you." Then, Sophie addressed James, "I've simply given up. I can't find anybody that she'd even consider."

"What do you think Aurore, do you want to come with us. We have an estate in the country, not too far from Paris. You would be welcome to stay as long as you like."

"It can be a nice little week to look around and maybe try something a bit different."

Aurore was puzzled by this proposal, as Sophie previously prevented her from having cousin Rene for a guardian, and now she was shipping her off to some strangers country house that they had just met. But, she had learned that when her mother gets an idea she never yielded, so to spare herself the embarrassment of begging not to go somewhere she would then be forced to go, Aurore accepted the proposal, and the next morning she was picked up by the Routtiers and they set of for their country house.

✳✳✳

Chateau de Brie was only a short drive out of Paris. It stood at the top of a hill, overlooking a few village houses below it. To enter the main grounds, a porter had to open the main black, decorated, 8-feet tall iron gates. The road took the group past a row of tall oak trees to the main entrance. The castle was made up of three towers. There were also a barn, a church, and a couple of other buildings on the property. It all reminded Aurore of Nohant, but instead of a flat roof, this structure had the appearance of an ancient castle of yore, and some of the large stones that the walls were made from could indeed be placed back to 1215, when the castle was initially constructed. Most of the rooms were in the square structure that was in the middle of the three towers because that was where the main chimney was, which heated all of the apartments. The servants lived in the cottages that surrounded the chateau. James Routtiers was a relative of Casimir Louis-Victurnien Rochechouart Mortemart, a Prince and Baron, who stayed in politics and the military across the Napoleonic Wars and the Restoration, only retiring after the 1848 Revolution. James was thus a member of the aristocracy, but he supported his enormous estate by working in manufacturing management, as farming, while still profitable, was not as respected as aristocratic tapestry making.

James Roettiers' five daughters included the eleven-years old Alice Felicia, the eight-years old Henrietta Emma, the six-years old Alexandrine Charlotte, the five-years old Cecile Victurnienne, and the two-years old Marie. All five of them dressed in trousers, imitation-military jackets with silver buttons, and played aggressive outdoor games and rode horses and ponies. Only Alice was near Aurore in age, so instead of encouraging them to be more mature, Aurore recalled her own youth before the convent and engaged with them in their games. She only had Hyppolite and domestic and field servants as playmates as a child, so she was eager to engage with these strong and ambitious young girls, with whom she identified more so than with all of her previous playmates.

Aurore woke up late, breakfasted in her room, read the classics from the castle's historical library, then met up with the girls and they took the horses out through the tall grass and into the virgin forest that was on the other side of their extensive vegetable garden. They strolled slowly, studying the archways of branches, wild flowers, and old trees that made for a romantic setting. They deliberately went in search of isolated pools, and glades, as if they were explorers in search for hidden gems in their terrain.

This existence was so relaxing that Aurore nearly forgot that she was left there on her own by her family with a set purpose in mind. While Aurore put these plots out of her head, James Roettiers vigilantly looked out for an appropriate match. Almost every evening, James brought a new suitor or two for dinner. Aurore usually did not associate the men dining with them as potential husbands as they were frequently older. One of these was a retired army offer, who she found out from Alice was the pensioned son of a peasant. Many of these suitors were rejected by James after seeing them interact with Aurore over dinner, and many more were considered over private conversations between Mme. and M. Roettiers, without ever being invited to dinner at all. Offers of marriage also came in via the mail, as Rene de Villeneuve, and Marquis de Caulaincourt, each had a dozen acquaintances and relations in mind that they thought would be an excellent match for Aurore. Marie-Aurore in part focused on Aurore's education because she knew that she might be used in a political marriage to unite their family closer to other aristocratic families of France, a position for which Aurore had to be mentally prepared. But, while Aurore had indeed developed a brilliant mind, this made it difficult for her to see her personal life as nothing more than a political play. In addition, when the Marquis or Rene offered her hand in marriage, they typically stressed her enormous dowry, so when these suitors managed to get past Mme. and M. Roettiers and were invited for dinner, they occasionally slipped into discussing Aurore's Nohant estate in a way that sounded as if they were considering a business acquisition, and this repelled Aurore from their advances.

There was one suitor that managed to slip into this mix by accident and caused a good deal of havoc in the Roettiers' plans. The youngest of the Roettiers sisters developed a fever, and Doctor Tessier was invited to take care of her. He brought his son, Prosper Tessier, a thirty-years old infantry lieutenant, with him and he dined with the family that night, after Doctor Tessier diagnosed the fever as part of a simple flue. Prosper was different from all the other aristocrats, bourgeoisie business owners, and young chevaliers that came to visit the Roettiers. He was charming and downright seductive.

Aurore walked into the dining room and immediately met his large, brown eyes, which radiated with joy, and vigor. He had thick black eyebrows, and thick, dark curly hair, and he was wearing a dandy, colorful outfit that could have been a played-down version of a court jester. When Aurore curtsied to the group, Prosper stood up, leaped towards her and gently kissed the top of her hand for several moments with his thick lips, looking up into her eyes, and battering his eyelashes. He then pulled out a chair for her, and bowed as she sat down in it.

They had quail for the main course, and Aurore couldn't help giggling at watching Prosper cut off extremely tiny pieces with his knife in order to appear and gentle as possible, as he was constantly trying to impress Aurore with each of his movements and mannerisms.

"We caught the quail ourselves," Aurore burst forth, as she couldn't help but dim Prosper's embarrassment in such aristocratic company by shifting the focus onto her.

"You go hunting," Prosper was both amazed and amused.

"Yes, me and the girls," Aurore pointed with her eyes to the Roettiers daughters sitting at the other end of the table.

"We are better at it than papa, he hates hunting," Alice commented, glancing at Roettiers to check that it was all right to make such an observation.

"It's true. When I was younger, I would roll around in the grass with the lads, but in the last decade I've become accustomed to my daughters taking over hunting duties. And they do a fine job of it."

"I thought the quail was especially good, I guess it tastes better when it's caught fresh."

"You should come quail hunting with us," Aurore said, blushing slightly from excitement.

"We can't possibly impose," Doctor Tessier said, embarrassed that his son was taking liberties.

"Yes, the girls would enjoy hearing about your sons army exploits. You simply must stay at least for a night. And I think it would be best if you stayed for a week, until Marie is better."

"There is nothing to worry about regarding Marie's health. She should recover shortly."

"Meanwhile, the girls might fall and scrape their knees tomorrow quail hunting, and there you go, we'll have need of you again. Trust me, you are doing us an honor and a great service by staying."

"Yes, of course, we will stay, if that's the case."

The family rose early on the next morning and Prosper and the girls ventured out on the hunt. Aurore rode ahead of the group, as she was the fastest rider. She dismounted by jumping off the horse before it came to a complete stop, and quickly tied the horse to a tree, taking out her quail hunting equipment. As she was finishing, Prosper and the girls caught up to her, and also tied their horses. Aurore must have hunted hundreds of times, so she knew just where to go, made perfect calls, spread the net expertly, and gave Prosper several tips that Deschartres had taught her on their expeditions. Prosper had gone on a couple of hunts before, but clearly was no match for Aurore's dexterity. Similarly to Louis at the opera some years earlier, Prosper's eyes were repeatedly drawn to Aurore's chest, but this time there was a much better reason for Prosper's distraction. Aurore was wearing a cotton shirt with her trousers, and while she was wearing a second shirt under it, the dew was so thick that both shirts were drenched in water, and Aurore's nipples were as visible as her nose. Her body was thin at the time, but her breasts had completed maturing. As she lay on the ground, she was comforted by them as if by cushions, so it wasn't until close to the end of the quail hunt that Aurore looked down to check what Prosper kept glancing over at. She had assumed that he was studying her posture, as she was working to explain the best shooting positions to him. Realizing what was making Prosper blush, Aurore became highly embarrassed and rushed over to her horse, grabbing a jacket to cover her chest. Her movement led the other girls towards the horses, so Aurore declared that the hunting trip was over, and got up on her horse. Prosper came up and also hopped onto his horse. Aurore rode ahead as usual, and her shirts were reasonably dry by the time she arrived back at the chateau.

As she was riding, she kept looking back at Prosper riding behind her, in contrast with her usual focus. While the incident was extremely embarrassing, she felt an uncharacteristic flush in her chest and cheeks.

And as she rode the horse, she suddenly felt the sensual touch of the mane and leathery skin, as she had never experienced them before. It was as if her sense of touch was fully awakened, and she rode faster to reach the maximum potential of this new feeling. She ran into the chateau and hid in her room before the other members of the party could catch up to her.

That evening she put on her best dress because she suddenly felt as if this was required and that she would be embarrassed to be seen in anything else. Dinner was awkward, as Prosper and Aurore kept exchanging glances, but both uncharacteristically said very little.

"Would you like to take a walk with me in the garden," Prosper asked as the dinner was ending.

"Yes," Aurore's throat was a bit sore as she spoke up, "yes, let's do that."

There was a beautiful red sunset over the hill. The couple strolled over the sandy walkways through the garden. They were walking through the flower section, and the smell of the multi-colored rose bushes, tulips, and gardenias put them in a sensuous mood. Prosper gently took Aurore by the hand and led her gently forward. They kept walking until they reached a distant part of the garden that could not be seen from the chateau. There was an elegant bench there, and Prosper helped Aurore take a seat, and then sat at the edge of the bench himself. They looked out at the sunset, which was now turning purple-yellow, as the sun was extinguishing at the horizon. It was a warm May evening, and there was only a very light breath. Aurore listened to the chirping of birds above them in the trees. Prosper took Aurore's hand into his. He held it there for a moment longer than casual friends would, and when Aurore did not remove it, he bent down and kissed it gently, but this time he parted his lips and they trembled and then moved up the hand. Aurore felt the tingling in her chest again, and this time there was a warm tingling on her skin between his lips and her chest, and her whole body started to feel flushed as he continued kissing her hand, then moving up to her arm. Aurore felt Prosper take her other arm and begin massaging its end, and she reciprocated by gently massaging his hand with hers. Prosper jumped up from the arm to her neck, and after a gentle peck, began to kiss her neck with moistened lips. Aurore was overwhelmed as if she was about to faint, as a weakness seized her body, together with an urge to kiss Prosper as well to return this sensuous pleasure. As if hearing her thoughts, Prosper bent closer and kissed Aurore's closed mouth. She involuntarily parted her lips, and Prosper slipped in his soft, moist tongue, which fluttered against her tongue like a hummingbird. This fluttering was waking up something in Aurore that might remain permanently dormant in women that enter marriages of convenience, but which creates an aching yearning for an ideal of sensual love in women like Aurore who have felt this seductive mating ritual. Most men fail to understand that the fluttering of a tongue, or a kiss on the neck takes women's whole bodies to the same place men reach in one point of theirs at the end of intercourse. Needless to say, Aurore was not thinking logically as she began to kiss Prosper on the mouth with full force, and as their hands began to travel over the other's back, shoulders, and arms. But, suddenly she felt his hand slip down to the bottom of her skirt, and that he was pulling her skirt upwards. At this moment, some women might surrender to the impulse in them to continue to be caressed, but Aurore could not indulge her desire because she had never reasoned through what engaging in sexual intercourse before marriage would do to her reputation or her chances of finding a good husband, or even of becoming a nun. She suddenly recalled her "bastard uncle" and thought about the women she had met who had illegitimate children, and despite the fact that Prosper's lips were still fluttering around her mouth and neck, Aurore was suddenly stiffer and colder than she had been once when she took a bath in the convent's ice-cold water.

Aurore stopped caressing Prosper and became limp. Prosper immediately noticed the complete change about Aurore and lowered her skirt, taking his hands and lips away.

"What's the matter?"

"What's the matter with you?! What are you doing?"

"I'm just... I thought that you were also doing... it with me?"

"Yes, but no. I mean, what are we doing? What's your intention here?"

"It's just to do what we began doing..."

"No, I'm interested in that."

"I mean, I would like for you to become my mistress. You could stay in my apartment in Paris. You wouldn't have to keep living with the Roettiers."

"I want to live with them, what makes you think otherwise. And what do you mean, I should be your 'mistress.' What kind of a woman do you think I am?!"

"There's nothing wrong with being a mistress. We could keep it from other people. You could say you want to live in an apartment of your own in the city."

"No. I have obligations to other people, to my family, to all of workers at Nohant. I can't just run away with you. It's absurd."

"Absurd?! You are here with me, alone, and I don't think you've responded so far as if you think this has been absurd."

"Well now I think that it is absurd, and I don't have anything else to say about it."

Aurore stood up and started walking towards the chateau. Prosper followed a few steps behind her, finally catching up to avoid their separate returns from causing gossip at the castle. Prosper stayed for the next few days until the week that Roettiers had invited him and his father to stay ended. Aurore and Prosper did not speak at dinner, and neither of them volunteered to go on any joint outings. Aurore even rejected the idea of going quail hunting when the girls invited her to go with them one of those mornings. When the appointed day came, Prosper and the Doctor left. The departure had an odd effect on Aurore. While she was uncomfortable with having him at the table, and wished that he wasn't there to taunt her in the days between their *tete-a-tete* and his departure, after he left she felt a deep sadness, which kept her in her room for most of the following couple of days. She woke at twelve, and then would stay in her bed, looking up at the ceiling. She was imagining Corambe coming into her room to cheer her up and to offer his help in escaping the castle and flying off to Milan or Madrid. But, the reverie about Corambe would suddenly blend into a fantasy about Prosper, as she imagined going to live with him in Paris, and what it would be like to walk with him at night across the city, going to the theater and to the opera, and how happy she might be kissing him, and being with him in a blissful eternal honeymoon, as they would love each other without the stress of a wedding and marriage and without him becoming a master under law over her.

Aurore's unusual absence from the children's playtime and from a few family breakfasts and dinners became apparent to the Roettiers, so they divined a plot to pull her out of this reverie. They had an acquaintance with whom they had briefly discussed Aurore's hand in marriage, but who was not the best choice out of the bunch, so they had not brought him around to introduce him to Aurore.

"She will feel better if she feels wanted again. That Prosper he must have said or done something to her. She's been affected by something about their meetings."

"Yes, if we could set up a meeting between her and Casimir, they will cheer each other up."

The Roettiers knew that Francois Casimir Dudevant, who was twenty-seven at the time, made for amusing company at the card and wine tables, and that he could amuse the dead into waking. So, they wrote to him and explained the situation to him.

A couple of days later, the Roettiers invited Aurore to go to the theater and for ice cream with them to Paris. It was a short two-hour trip from Brie to Paris, and Aurore had wanted to see a new Parisian play, so she did not resist and got dressed gingerly. They departed early and

Aurore was so captivated by the Cirque performance that she forgot all about Corambe and Prosper.

It was June 5th, and Mme. and M. Pouttiers took her to the same place where she had first met them with her mother, Tortoni's, a fancy Parisian ice cream parlor. They were sitting at a table, eating large portions of colorful ice cream, when Mme. Pouttiers pointed and exclaimed: "Look, isn't that Casimir!"

"Yes, I believe it is!" M. Pouttiers also exclaimed, and waved for Casimir to approach them.

Aurore looked in the direction they had pointed to and saw a muscular, elegant, grinning young man in foppish attire, which was approaching them. Casimir Dudevant was born from an illegitimate union between the Scottish Baron Jean-Francois Dudevant and his Spanish housemaid mistress, Augustine Soule. Baron Dudevant had married into a wealthy family after this affair, but his marriage failed to produce any children, so Casimir had an inheritance to look forward to, or so he hoped.

"Ah, Casimir. We haven't seen you in some time. How is your father?"

"He is doing very well, he has retired somewhat in Gascony after the busy days he had as the Officer of the Legion of Honor under Napoleon."

"Please have a seat," M. Pouttiers asked Casimir.

Casimir bowed and sat down across from Aurore.

"And who is this lovely lady?"

"This is my daughter," Mme. Pouttiers replied with pride.

"I see," Casimir said, and then in a loud whisper he asked Mme. Pouttiers, "So, she is to be my wife? You did promise me the hand of your oldest daughter. We had discussed Alice, but this girl's age is clearly closer to my own. If she is the one intended for me, I full-heartily accept."

Angela suppressed a chuckle, and then broke out in a laugh. Aurore had heard this entire communication, as Casimir was deliberately speaking just loud enough for all at the table to hear him. Angela and James expected that Casimir would play some joke, as he usually did. But, this was just charming, as Casimir had interpreted the need to cheer up Aurore and give her courage as an invitation to make an all-out assault on her hand in marriage. Meanwhile, Aurore was stunned by this direct approach, while also doubting herself and wondering if Casimir was making fun of her. At the same time, she did not know enough about Casimir's background to have formed an opinion about him as a potential husband. The fact that the Pouttiers knew him well suggested that he was a good match, but then why was Angela laughing instead of allowing her to respond to the proposal. When James finally burst out in laughter as well, Aurore decided that it was all a bit of a joke either way and with a smile began to coyly chat with Casimir about his father, Napoleon and the ice cream.

Aurore and the Pouttiers departed back for the chateau after they finished the ice cream. Aurore was refreshed by this trip, and went quail hunting on the next day. She also returned to playing with girls, and otherwise reverted to her earlier routine.

A few days later, Casimir Dudevant suddenly appeared at the chateau, apparently without warning the Pouttiers, but they readily welcomed him to stay. When he saw that Aurore ran to play a game of tag with the young girls, he instinctively joined the group of playing children. He was over a foot taller than all of them, and his age made it difficult for him to blend in with the girls. But he had a round jovial face, and he made good natured fun of them as he pretended to fall and to have trouble catching them until he blended in with the group, and Aurore felt that it was natural to have him running around with them.

When they ran past Mme. and M. Pouttiers, Casimir would shout out, "What a good chap your daughter is!"

"And you son-in-law has been a good little boy," Aurore would retort, belittling Casimir in her turn, while also acknowledging their mock engagement. In the back of her mind, she knew that Casimir might have been serious, but she had decided not to worry about that possibility. The affair with Prosper was still fresh in her mind. She felt a need to be wanted and admired, and the attention that Casimir was giving her by bluntly and playfully proposing marriage was just the sort of flattery that was healing this open wound. The Pouttiers started calling Aurore and Casimir husband and wife, and the other members of the family joined in.

One evening, Aurore was last to leave the dinner table together with Father Stanislas, the priest responsible for the church at the chateau.

"I see you are calling Casimir your 'husband.' What do you mean by this?" Father Stanislas asked. This was the first time he heard the family using these names, and he was shocked that the girl who was there on a hunt for a husband had found one without him knowing about it.

"Oh, it's just good fun. There's nothing to it."

"Good, because you have to be realistic. His inheritance will be over sixty thousand francs in income, why would he want to have you for a wife?"

Father Stanislas had heard that there was a chance that Casimir would have a significant inheritance, but he also knew that he was illegitimate, while in contrast Aurore had already inherited her fortune and definitely had an income that at least matched Casimir's. He knew Casimir from his visits to the Pouttiers and he wanted to encourage Aurore to think more seriously about this potential marriage, as he knew that Casimir would not be joking about matrimony without having a firm intention of pursuing the union. If he played on Aurore's sense of inferiority, he expected that she would put a higher value on Casimir and that the two might seal a union.

This ploy worked, and Aurore went to bed that night weighing what a marriage with Casimir might be like. So, she was particularly saddened when Casimir left the next morning, having been advised by Father Stanislas that absence might make the heart grow fonder. And indeed it did, as Aurore missed Casimir while he was away.

Casimir returned on the following weekend.

He asked Aurore to take a walk in the garden with him immediately upon his arrival, and this request unnerved Aurore, as she expected a repetition of the scene that unraveled with Prosper. They walked over to the same distant bench, and Casimir also took her hand. His thin, light hair circled his round face, and he looked unusually serious as he looked up into Aurore's startled eyes.

"This is probably not the way I'm supposed to do this, but I need to know your feelings on this matter first before I approach your family. If you don't think that I'm repelling for some reason… Well, maybe you need some time to think about it… to consider your options… you can take as long as you need… and then when you reach a decision, you could let me know if you would like me to ask your mother…"

"Ask my mother for what?"

"For your hand in marriage."

"Why?"

"What do you mean, because I want to marry you."

"I mean," Aurore was search for the words that would describe her confusion, "why do you think we should marry?"

"I think we could be great friends. I think that friendship is more important in a marriage. I think it's wonderful that I wasn't immediately attracted by your beauty, but rather that we have developed a comradery."

While in most romance novels a line like this one would have cooled the heroine, it warmed Aurore up. Men might misunderstand the importance that a calm friendship plays on the woman's ability to love a man. It is extremely rare to find a male partner who is capable of speaking with an intelligent, strong-willed woman on equal terms, and placing their intellectual and emotional bond above her physical appearance, or their physical attraction to each other. When a single tryst between a man and a woman is involved, the physical attraction alone is enough for a woman to agree to it, if she is inclined to that sort of affairs. But, when a woman imagines being with a single man for the rest of her life, what stands out in her mind are all those breakfasts and dinners they will have together, and that if he cannot chat with her on friendly terms during those times, she will be living in continuous hell, constantly distressed about finding something to say, while saying nothing at all, because she knows that her thoughts and emotions are not respected or considered. What happens in the bedroom might take five minutes or all night, but those brief chats, or their absolute lack is what either brings a woman into desperation and misery, or rises her up into a sense that she has made the right decision in choosing her spouse, and that her marriage is a happy one.

"Yes, perhaps it is possible for us to get married. I don't know if your father, or my mother might have an objection, so if you think this is for the best, go ahead and ask them."

This was good enough for Casimir as well, and he proceeded to writing to his father, and to Aurore's mother, asking them for Aurore's hand in marriage. The Colonel arrived in military-style a day after receiving the letter, and taking Aurore by the arm and walking with her through the garden, discussing farming and estate management, he lightly switched to the topic of the marriage and expressed his complete satisfaction with Aurore, and his delight at the prospect of having her for his daughter. Aurore's mother arrived on the next day from Paris, and at first she was relieved to find that there was this great news, which she was afraid might never come. She immediately agreed to the match, and both parents left the chateau happy, deciding to allow Aurore and Casimir two more weeks to become fully acquainted. The pair took full advantage of this opportunity to talk about their past histories, their future hopes, as well as to ride and walk together, allowing their rhythms to become linked, and for them to become familiar with the other's tastes and preferences.

Sophie suddenly returned a day earlier than expected and immediately upon her arrival exclaimed in front of the entire household, "This marriage just can't happen! I was told in Paris he used to be a waiter!"

Casimir was standing in the spacious guest room and his mouth dropped open upon hearing this startling news that he had never imagined was possible before. Who could have said that he worked as a waiter?

"A waiter?" he finally managed to pronounce. "While it's a wonderful profession, I simply haven't had time to be a waiter…"

"A young man, who said that he was a good friend of yours, told me."

"Who?"

"I can't give his name. That would be inappropriate."

"I don't know about that, but I know that after leaving the military academy, I served as a second lieutenant, and I only recently finished a law degree in Paris. In the last few months after I completed the degree I lived with my father in the country. I simply never had the leisure time available to spend working at a café. Maybe you heard that I met Aurore at a café? It was really an ice cream shop, but I can see how the two are similar…"

"Hm…" Sophie was puzzled by this denial, as she had not expected the chance that the news might not be entirely truthful. Why would
somebody in high society outright lie to her about her future son-in-law?
"Well, I don't know what to say to that. I just don't want to see you Aurore being taken advantage of by being married to some adventurer."

"Mam!" M. Pouttiers interjected. "We have known Casimir for many
years, and he is certainly no adventurer!"

"Well perhaps somebody is soiling some pots on all ends…"

"Now you are just being outrageous!"

"Mother, please stop it!" Aurore was mortified.

"I see, now you are taking their side. Very well, maybe I'm just crazy."

"No, nobody is calling you crazy. It's just that it can't be true that
Casimir was a waiter. Haven't you heard about the Colonel? He served
under Napoleon? It makes no sense that his son would have to work as a
waiter!?" Aurore was eager to change her mother's mind and to stop her
from continuing that awful scene.

"I see. All right. I'm going to go back to Paris, and I will do some
research, and I'll come back when I have some proof."

Sophie stormed out, leaving Aurore in an awkward situation as she
attempted to mend the wound that Sophie left behind with her accusation.

Sophie returned from Paris much calmer, and took Aurore with her
to Paris, as if she had forgotten her when she last stormed out. She did
report that the earlier gossip about Casimir serving as a waiter appeared
to be unfounded. Aurore lived temporarily with Sophie and Hippolyte in
a newly rented small apartment on Rue St. Lazare. Hippolyte had completed a tour of duty, and did not renew military service because the hard
life of an officer without a war did not appeal to him. As they were settling into their life in Paris, Aurore having assumed that her mother's behavior outraged the Dudevants into no longer wanting the union, Mme.
Dudevant came for a visit, despite her weak physical state, and managed
to convince Sophie to agree to the marriage by treating her as if she was
a foreign dignitary, and not a hat-maker. However, the marriage was broken off once more and the terms were renegotiated all the way through
the autumn. The final agreement, reached under the dotal system, provided the Nohant estate as a dowry to Casimir, who in exchange offered
a marriage settlement of sixty thousand francs. Casimir had wanted to
sell Nohant and use the money from the sale to create more free capital,
but Aurore was too attached to this now ancestral home to consider this
proposal.

On the day of the marriage ceremony, Aurore was fitted into a
cropped wedding dress without a trail. Aurore had to once again wear a

corset with it because it had a very firm center. It also had some hoops in circles around the hips under the fanned out skirts. The color of the dress was a mix of light purple, covered all over with embroidered beige lace. The sleeves were composed of multiple layers of lace, and there was a long lace border around the shoulders, covering the low-cut neckline. She also wore a flower headdress, and a large pearl necklace and earrings. The outfit made her look more mature than her eighteen years, but she also felt awkward in it and her mother corrected her a couple of times not to slouch before she made it to the alter.

Casimir met them at a judge's office on the morning of September 17th, 1822 for a civil ceremony that was attended only by the couple, their parents, Hyppolite, the judge and the clerk. Then, the immediate family traveled on a couple of carriages to the Church of Saint Louis d'Antin. The church's exterior was made out of a purplish-beige stone that was similar in color to Aurore's wedding dress. A porter held the tall wooden door open for Aurore and the other members of the party as they scaled the six short steps and entered. Aurore looked on the walls that were hung with sixteenth century fine paintings of Jesus and Mary, performing various holy tasks, such as anointing and blessing people, below the half-circle painted glass windows that provided the main hall of the church with a dim but clear light. Casimir went inside to wait by the priest. The church was full with visitors that were sitting on velvet-cushioned chairs. These visitors sparkled with half of the aristocracy of France. Marquis de Caulaincourt, Rene, and Comte M. de Segur had invited the princes, counts, barons, and other notable officials, nobles, and socialites in France, and everybody who was invited was honored to come to the event of the season, with a few bring additional honorable guests. Thus, everybody short of the king and the queen were there, and Louis XVIII, King of France and of Navarre, noticed that his court was unusually empty that day, as he sat on his throne for his daily audience and was only attended by his minister, and a couple of devoted courtiers. The marital music started playing and Aurore moved down the wood-floored isle to the front of the church, which was decorated with a fresco over a bright-blue background. She tried to imagine that all of the guests were beautiful decorations to stay calm, and because they were as still as marble adorned with previous jewels, this was easy enough.

A few witnesses were standing behind Aurore on one side and Casimir on the other side of the aisle. The priest was standing on a step that led to the alter. He was dressed in white petticoats with long sleeves, and a red yoke with long ends over his neck. The priest was holding a finely designed bible in his hands. A twelve-year old boy dressed in a similarly designed outfit to the priest's was assisting the priest by holding a whisk with holy water. The priest asked Casimir and then Aurore if they would take each other in marriage, and both agreed. Then, the priest joined their hands, and then took a ring from Casimir's hand and placed it onto Aurore's finger. The couple knelt down, as a protracted piece of textile was extended that hid them from the congregation. The priest read several traditional prayers from the Bible, made the appropriate gestures with his finger, and when he closed the Bible and said, "Amen," the congregation followed and all also said, "Amen." The material hiding the couple was removed, and they stood up. Several of the dignitaries in the audience came up and congratulated Aurore, Casimir and their families on the union.

From this ceremony the couple was taken by carriage to the Pouttiers' chateau, as both felt most at home as a couple there. When the carriage arrived, Casimir helped Aurore down, and escorted her to the largest guestroom in the house, which was assigned to them for this monumental occasion. They were both hungry by the time they arrived from Paris, so they had a light snack of caviar on toast and tea in their room. By that point, Aurore was incredibly uncomfortable in her corset, and asked Casimir to help her out of the dress primarily to regain her ability to breathe. Once the corset was untied and removed along with the wedding dress, Aurore was left in her white cotton chemise with short sleeves, a low neckline, and a plain hem to her ankles.

A note is needed on this point about how men typically do not understand women's sexual needs. A bull or a cock approaches the mate and goes to town in the traditional fashion of the species, and most men attempt the same strategy. Casimir gave Aurore a single kiss on the mouth, undid her chemise, and then proceeded to get on top of her body under the sheets, beginning with somewhat slow penetration, and then moving up to his personal best speed and vigor and carrying on with this activity until he ejaculated. If this was a pornographic film, Aurore would have been sighing and moaning across this process, rolling her eyes, and finally squirming, as if in orgasm. But, this was a period long before pornography and film itself were created, so Aurore was not aware of these customs and responded to this procedure naturally by lying there and waiting for Casimir to finish. At first she was uncomfortable with the odd pressure, but when Casimir kept going, hardly looking down at her, Aurore relaxed and she could barely feel any pressure, or any other sensations down below. Because Casimir seemed to be fully engaged without any interaction from her, she shifted her eyes to the window and studied the leaves of the willow tree just outside. She almost started thinking about Corambe, but the current activity was so repelling that she did not want Corambe coming around to see it. She switched to thinking about how she would manage the Nohant estate in the upcoming year, as she was given the management responsibility, with a limit of spending no more than ten thousand francs annually. She imagined buying fancy dresses and jewels and then thought better and decided to re-decorate and update some of the rooms that had remain the same since the Terror. The thought of the Terror brought her back to the present moment. Thankfully, Casimir was reaching a climax, and before Aurore knew it, he ejaculated inside of her. The sensation of having somebody else's bodily fluids inside of her was grotesque, and she wished she could wipe them off, but there was no tissue of suitable size nearby.

This was where Aurore's logic had led her astray, while friendship was a wonderful foundation for a marriage, just because Casimir said he felt about her as a close friend, did not mean he would be considerate or friendly in bed, or that he would really think about her thoughts or feelings after the marriage. Aurore also did not count on the role that physical attraction might have played in their nightly intercourse, and now it seemed that their mutual coolness towards each other's bodies meant that Casimir could focus his energies on his climax ignoring the rest of Aurore's body, while Aurore was left with a wifely task she had to perform to beget children. But, while this activity was grotesque at times, and boring at others, Aurore was optimistic about its short duration, as Casimir never managed to carry on with it for over fifteen minutes. Thus, Aurore lied down and took a bit of a rest nightly for a month, while Casimir huffed and puffed, and otherwise became awfully excited, and then afterwards looked like he had run from Paris to Brie, falling back as if near-death onto the pillows. Within moments he was dead-asleep, snoring like a tea-kettle. Aurore would occasionally read during these times, as she couldn't sleep over the snoring. When she read romances in those hours, she couldn't help but laugh aloud at the happy endings, where the books ended with a marriage, and she wished there were a few more pages to describe what exactly was happy about those marriages, and if there was anything she could do to make her marriage any happier than it was.

They spent a month at the Pouttiers' as part of their honeymoon, and on October 15th, they left the Pouttiers' place for Nohant. Aurore was managing accounts, and to show his financial independence, Casimir bought her a new piano. Aurore immediately began rehearsing Ludwig van Beethoven's sonatas, focusing on the Moonlight Sonata, using a booklet of his notes that was recently imported from Germany and which contained his latest projects. She began to slowly hit the notes of the Moonlight composition. Her face became serious and a bit sad, as she measured the sounds rhythmically and gradually moved through the melody. The music would climb, but would always fall on a note, and then try to climb up again… There were many repetitions, and then improvisations that hypnotized the imagination. Aurore spent fifteen minutes playing it from start to end, and after a short pause she started playing it from the beginning because she was happier listening to that complex melody than in the best Italian operas she had heard in Paris. In the first couple of minutes of this second round she heard somebody sniff and shuffle on the sofa. She looked up, continuing playing the notes because she had now memorized that section. Her eyes met Casimir's. They were hysterically annoyed, and his eyebrows were crossed and contorted.

Why is he sitting there if he doesn't want to listen to the music? Aurore thought, puzzled.

"Do you want me to play something else?" Aurore asked aloud.

She was now nine minutes into the Sonata, the quick section and she had to look back on the notes to keep up with the flying and rushing music, which sounded like a summer hurricane, yellow and red leaves flying past, and then like a ballerina flying across the stage in an intricate dance. Aurore's fingers flew all over the keyboard, as she kept pace with her foot. Her fingers were just long enough to keep up with this tempo. She hit the keys with precision, without missing a single note. The purring and rolling notes in this latter half of the Sonata engaged all of her attention, as her fingers curled and flexed, and touching them was a sensuous experience, as intense as riding a horse or running through the woods. And just as Aurore ran her fingers across the length of most of the keyboard in one of the final movements, Casimir stood up and left the room.

The conversations she had with Casimir when they first met focused on his military career, on estate management, on the games they were playing, and on other light and serious matters that either amused them, or were necessary topics for discussion for them to become acquainted with each other. When Casimir walked out after frowning to her spectacular professional-grade performance of the most highly respected musical composition from the period, Aurore suddenly realized that there was something strange about her husband, aside from his bedroom manners. She started casually introducing popular and classical writers and their works into their dinner conversations, and found that Casimir could not discuss any of them because he was not familiar with any of the names. He seemed to have a vague idea about a narrow set of classical writers that were required for his legal studies, but aside from these Aurore suspected he had never read an entire book for enjoyment. It was difficult to imagine how a man with a colonel and a baron for a father, and who had an advanced legal degree could have missed some of the basic classics that Deschartres explained were the required texts for a basic classical education. This deficiency in Casimir proved to be a devastating problem in their marriage, as Aurore realized that Casimir was not the sort of friend she expected in an adult, as she anticipated he would treat her like Deschartres had, but instead Casimir treated her as if she was indeed a minor child, and he treated all friends as drinking and chatting companions, and not as people who might help him expand his mind or bounce his ideas on. At first Aurore let this vacancy pull her towards Casimir's attitudes, but eventually she could not let her mind air any longer and she had to rebel or she would have died of intellectual boredom.

One of the reasons Aurore initially gravitated towards Casimir's way of thinking was because she became pregnant soon after the wedding, and this process made her feel maternal, and awakened feelings in her even for Casimir, who she felt close to even when he was withdrawn and cold. Reading also did not seem practical with a baby coming, as she suddenly wanted to spend all of her time sewing, preparing the layette, whipstitching, needle working, and embroidering bonnets. For the last six months of the pregnancy, starting in the winter between 1822 and 1823, Aurora was in bed engaging in these activities, while Casimir went out to hunt. Domestic activities can be surprisingly calming and creative, when a woman allows herself to become engulfed in them. Stitching can turn into artful decoration with unique designs, and sewing can produce practical and fashionable clothing. Thus, as a multi-dimensional artist, Aurore became just as enthusiastic about needle work as about composing on the piano, as both created something unique, and Casimir seemed to appreciate the needle work a lot more than her attempts at improvisation on the piano.

Other matters that occupied Aurore at this time included the fact that Deschartres' lease was ending, and despite her requests for him to stay on permanently at Nohant, he was flatly refusing. In parallel, Hippolyte, now twenty-eight, married Mlle. Emilie de Villeneuve, who was thirty-seven with a house of her own, in Paris. She later inherited her family's estate near Nohant, but Hippolyte squandered it away with his gambling and wine drinking.

On June 24th, Deschartres' lease ended and he departed for Paris. Because the Dupins did not have another adequate doctor in the region, and Aurore did not trust that she could deliver the baby herself, Aurore and Casimir traveled to Paris with Deschartres to find a physician there that could assist them. They spent a couple of days with the Pouttiers, and then rented a furnished apartment on Rue Neuve-des-Mathurins at the Hotel de Florence, which was the home of the Emperor's former chef, Gallyot, and his wife, who served as Empress Josephine's chambermaid. One night Gallyot boasted to them as he was serving them roasted chicken that during his decade in the Emperor's service he slept the entire time in a chair fully dressed, ready to make that chicken dish whenever the emperor wanted it. Considering that Napoleon died of arsenic poisoning, it is very likely that the good Gallyot disliked sleeping in that sturdy chair. Aurore never connected the two, and in fact she never knew that arsenic was found in Napoleon's stomach, so she was comforted by eating Gallyot's cooking during the last stage of her pregnancy.

On June 30th, Aurore went into labor in the garden in a pavilion. The pains of her ribs being pushed aside and a massive infant moving through her body were stronger than any pains Aurore felt before, but they proceeded without any complications and Aurore gave birth shortly to a healthy baby boy, Maurice. She only slept for an hour after the birth before waking to adore the beautiful baby sleeping in a silky little outfit she made herself on the pillow next to her. After Aurore was watching the baby sleep for a bit, Deschartres came in and inspected Maurice, concluding after a close exam that he was in perfect health. The baby had fallen back to sleep at the end of the exam, and not wanting to wake him Deschartres let him sleep in his lap, as he glanced at this fine new baby and contemplated for some time. Deschartres recalled that he was not present at the birth of either the elder Maurice, because he joined the staff when Maurice was old enough to need a tutor, nor at Aurore's birth, as she was born in Paris before Marie-Aurore was notified of the marriage. This was the first baby in the Dupin family that Deschartres was seeing on the day he was delivered in his decades of service. He also reflected that working as a teacher had meant that he never got married himself, and that this baby was as close as he could come to a grandchild. He had to tell himself at that moment that he never wanted any children in order to avoid breaking down into sobs or to avoid allowing his deep-seated depression about how his life turned out to overwhelm him in front of Aurore. To do this, he physically pushed the baby away from himself and gave her to Aurore. He stood up and said: "It's time for me to live for myself."

Aurore contemplated this statement. It had a lot of philosophical weight, and she wanted to consider its possible implications before replying.

Meanwhile, the silence grew long, and Deschartres turned around and walked out of the room. Had he lived for himself when he decided to indulge in teaching and research, instead of settling down with a wife? What could he do now in his old age to "live for himself?" Aurore remained in bed for the next few hours, and was kept awake by these questions, and by a sudden silence where a philosopher's words hung moments and then hours earlier.

Chapter 10

Postpartum Depression

Two months after the birth of Maurice, Aurore was fully recovered, but amidst her pregnancy she had gone over by four thousand francs above her ten thousand francs limit on spending for that year. This became apparent they she added up the accounts in September. Casimir had suggested several of the luxury items that Aurore bought during her year in charge of accounts because he hoped that she would go over so that he would have a legitimate reason aside from his sex to seize control over the books. He was responsible for their extended stay in Paris, when they could have used the Pouttiers' doctor at their chateau at a minimum cost. Casimir lived a wild lifestyle before his marriage, indulging in women and alcohol. But, without an allowance from his side of the family, and the books in Aurore's hands, he hardly had enough resources to buy a single extra unaccounted for bottle of wine. So, he began screaming an intimidating Aurore, stressing that it was entirely the fault of her flighty female mind that was leading them into ruin. After several weeks when he kept screaming at her at almost every one of their meetings, berating and humiliating her, Aurore gave up control of the finances, and even surrendered the one thousand and five hundred francs allowance she was due under their marital contract. This surrender served as a precedent that lost Aurore control over their money for the following decade, and meant that she had to file for a divorce to gain any financial independence. Powerlessness did not suite Aurore and she slumped into a severe depression. Immediately upon taking control of the assets, Casimir ordered extensive renovations to Nohant, fixing everything from the straightness of the paths, to trimming trees, to firing old servants, and even killing Aurore's old dog, Phanor. Sophie had killed one of her prior dogs when they moved to Paris some years earlier, and the pattern that those closest to her kept killing animals that were equivalent to her best friends, especially amidst her isolation in Nohant, was devastating, and suggested that she lived among enemies. Aurore was thinking about Phanor when she burst into tears over her quail egg breakfast the morning after he was killed.

"What's the matter?"

"I miss Phanor," Aurore cried.

"Why didn't you say that you were this attached to him before he was shot?"

"I should've, I'm sorry."

"This just goes to show that despite the renovation, I think we both need a change of scenery, maybe if we were somewhere else?"

"But, our budget, we can't go to Paris now."

"Why don't we go stay with the Pouttiers for a bit?"

"Yes, I think that should help."

One evening, at the Pouttiers, Maurice was brought out to the dinner tables, and M. Pouttiers gave him a sip of wine. Maurice liked it, and took a full sip out of M. Pouttiers' glass. Seeing that the wine settled nicely, M. Pouttiers then gave Maurice a small piece of his chicken wing, which Maurice munched on with his newly developing teeth. Meanwhile, Aurore was running around the sand-covered terrace with the girls in the household. She was carrying a bucket of sand, which she was playfully threatening to spill on Alice, who was running away from her, when they came near the table where the adults were dining. Aurore spilled a few grains of sand into Casimir's coffee cup as she hopped past him.

"Stop this instant! You are acting alike a spoiled child!"

"It was an accident! How dare you speak to me that way?!"

"I said stop right now, or I'll… I'll slap you!"

"You wouldn't dare!"

Aurore shook her bucket over his cup, spilling a few new grains into it.

Casimir reacted immediately by slapping her with the full force of his open hand over the face. The slap resonated through Aurore's head and she felt rage burning where the slap had hit. She ran away from the terrace and his in her room. She had not been hit by anybody since she resided at the convent, around four years earlier. When she returned to Nohant, she was the mademoiselle in charge of the estate, and there were no adults, house servants, or tutors above her in these last years that could have dared to slap the mistress of the house. She could tolerate the awful nightly intercourse, the lack of control over her inheritance, and being treated as a minor, but she would not tolerate being assaulted, and especially when it was in front of the people that she considered being her second parents. Once again, despite popular perception to the otherwise, intelligent women cannot tolerate being hit or slapped, playfully or not in their relationships. Slapping can symbolize the powerlessness of the person being slapped, and a power play like this is likely to lock up any woman with ambition to gain power. Aurore had tolerated everything about her awful marriage with a cheerful optimism, but that single slap pushed her past suppressed discontent and into complete severance of her emotional attachment to Casimir, and when this happened she suddenly could not tolerate having him in her bed for even one more night. When Casimir attempted to fondle her that night, she insisted: "I am sharing your bed under duress!"

"Duress? How do you mean? You are my wife!"

"You are an abusive brute, and I want you to know it."

"All right, if that's what you want. I can stay in the other guest bedroom…"

"Yes, I think that would be best."

Casimir was tempted to argue and insist on having intercourse, but knowing that the Pouttiers were down the hall, he decided to withdraw.

***

Casimir was in a meeting with his public notary, Jean-Louis Lambert, in the office of his Parisian apartment. They were discussing laws related to the Nohant estate and its business dealings.

"So, you have a right to keep control over your finances, because Aurore is a legal minor, and cannot contest this matter in court," Jean-Louis was saying.

"Can I extricate an affirmation or an oath statement from her that she would not attempt to reclaim control over our finances in the future?"

"No, you cannot force her to do it. And there some circumstances under which she might be able to reclaim control over running the books. But those are very unusual. Your best option is to let things go on as they are, without causing any disruptions in your arrangements. You are currently in the best possible position."

"But, you will compose the ship's protest against the damages that were inquired in the incident we had when we shipped out crops to Spain last season?"

"Yes, as we agreed, I will complete that document before our next meeting, and after you review it, will submit it to the ship's captain."

"Very good."

"Now, if you excuse me, I have to get going, as there is an urgent appointment I have on the other side of Paris."

"Yes, of course, please don't let me keep you."

Lambert grabbed his jacket and tall hat and rushed out of the door, without looking back at Casimir, who made a few slow steps as if to follow him, but then strolled into the dining room.

Laure sitting at the dining table, sipping a cup of tea, and taking a bite out of a napoleon pastry. Casimir sat down at the table next to her, and took a bite of her napoleon, taking it with his hands.

"Oh! Casimir! What are you doing?! Look you got a bit of cake on your ruffles."

Laure brushed the crème off the silky ruffles.

Casimir bent towards her as she did it and kissed her on the mouth. She kissed him back and the two were suddenly wrapped up in each other, caressing all possible body parts, and kissing whatever bits of skin were accessible over their formal dress. They didn't make it out of the living room, and had a prolonged rump on the dining room table. For some reason, while he was usually premature with Aurore, Casimir lasted for an incredibly long time with Laure, and they were still in an awkward position with Laure sitting on the table when her husband, Jean-Louis, returned from his meeting, and after putting down his umbrella, began climbing the stairs to the second floor. Casimir immediately retreated, pulled his pants up, straightened his ruffles, patted down his hair, which was standing somewhat on-ends, and sat down in a velvet chair, taking a new pastry from the tray bit it, a bit more aggressively than the pastry deserved. In the same few moments, Laure pulled up her undergarments, straightened her dress, twisted and pinned back in her disheveled hair and sat back down in her chair, taking a sip of her cold tea, and a bite out of her dried napoleon. At this very instant, Jean-Louis entered the room.

"Casimir, what are you still doing here?!"

"I forgot to ask you if I should prepare something for the complaint you are making with the ship's captain."

"No, my good man, you don't need to worry about it. You gave me all the information I need to finish a detailed report."

"Ah, I feel embarrassed then, it's silly of me to be so airheaded. Well, see you next week," Casimir said, standing up and quickly moving out of the room, with a brief curtsey, and rushing down the stairs, nearly skipping a step.

Casimir was on one of his "business" trips to Paris, which he started taking nearly every other weekend. Aurore had become completely frigid and would not let him near her, so he began exploring all other possible options, and the wife of the notary he could say he was seeing on business was the most logical option he could conceive. She was surprisingly willing, warm, and receptive, and appeared to enjoy these encounters, in complete contrast with Aurore. Laure's enthusiasm also sparked Casimir's intimate impulses and he felt re-awakened and young again. He almost started to think about his break with Aurore as a blessing, as it had allowed him to find a new partner that was satisfying urges he was unaware of.

Chapter 11

A Change of Regimes and Aurelien de Seze

While Casimir was engaging in amorous encounters, Aurore gained a new interest in social gatherings and political events. Her interest in intrigue and political maneuvers was sparked at the funeral of Louis XVIII. The reign of Louis XVIII was one of relative stability, despite the backwards steps he took away from revolutionary policies that were enacted before he took the reins. Louis XVIII had one of the stormiest reigns in French history, as the two preceding monarchs, Louis XVI and Louis XVII, died during the French Revolution. Only after Napoleon was exiled to Elba in 1814 did Louis XVIII seize power, and he lost it again a year later during Napoleon's Hundred Days return. Marie-Aurore had supplied funds that assisted some members of the Bourbon dynasty in escaping out of France and into exile during the French Revolution, so her family enjoyed good favor across Louis XVIII's reign. The funds that Louis XVIII was offered or managed to take with him only afforded him a small two-bedroom apartment above a shop for the first couple years of his exile, but later he lived in the Jelgava Palace in Latvia, and leased the Gosfield Hall in England. By the time Louis XVIII returned to power in France, he was fifty-nine, and due to a near total lack of physical activity and a veracious appetite across his life, he couldn't walk. Thus, he could not lead the troops and failed to launch a response to stop from Napoleon's return for the Hundred Days. In the decade that followed Louis XVIII stayed out of politics, and allowed the council and assembly to rule in the new constitutional monarchy. He died of obesity and the gout after a very gradual decline.

When news of Louis XVIII's death reached the Dupin family, they were very interested to learn in what direction French politics would swing after this major event. Aurore was staying in Paris at the time, and when she received the news on September 16, 1824 of the King's death, she met with her neighbors and relatives for dinner to discuss the event. Aurore's aristocratic relations, Marquis de Caulaincourt, General Harville, Rene and his wife, and M. de Segur, all attended. The neighbors that joined them were the Richardot, and Malus families. None of them wanted to buy tickets for the funeral coming up on September 23rd, as this seemed to be awfully bourgeois, but they did want to see how many people would attend and the exterior appearance of the church, so they all decided to venture out to the Saint-Denis church on the appointed date. When they departed from Aurore's apartment at 7am, the party was sixteen in all, with most of them politically allied against the forthcoming regime of Charles X, and for the bonapartist or liberal opposition. They all dressed in black, but most of them wore a smile. Aurore's neighbor, Mme. Richardot, was the one that stepped forward to negotiate with the officials at the church regarding their entry, but the officials looked past her at the Marquis, the General and the prior Master of Horse, and the man at the front who recognized all three of them simply muttered, "If there aren't too many of you..." He really meant to say, "If there were any more of you, I'd think you are staging a coup d'etat.

"Oh, my dear man," Mme. Richardot fluttered, unaware of who most of Aurore's relations were, "there are only sixteen of us."

The officer did not chuckle or smile at this remark and merely curtseyed and let the party in, pointing them to the seats at the front of the church, reserved for dignitaries. This was the first full monarchical funeral procession that Aurore saw, and it was the last of its kind that was scene in France, as all later monarchs did not die in office. It is possible that the people abdicated the later monarchs prior to their deaths simply to avoid watching a similar funeral again. The first impression was mildly positive, as the church was luxuriously decorated with votive candles, embroidered hangings, a flaming cross, and a draperied basilica. But, the music could only be heard within a few feet of the piano, and the priest had a sore throat that made his shaky voice similarly inaudible. The ceremony lasted all day, from eight till four, as the princes, priests, the new King, and various other dukes and counts all made varied traditional bows, kneelings, and other movements and gestures, the meaning of which escaped all present. The repetition was broken when, as Louis XVIII was lowered into the open vault, the rope holding the casket broke, nearly crushing the pallbearers. This startled the entire audience out of their sleepy reverie, and forced some of the more excitable women to break out in violent sobs.

After the funeral, Aurore spent the winter alone with Maurice in

Paris, studying the *Essais* of Montaigne and Jean-Jacques Rousseau *Of the Social Contract*. This was the first time in Aurore's life when she was entirely in control of her daily activities, without a master or a mistress in the house to tell her when to eat breakfast, or what books to read. Those who go from living under the control of parents into living under the control of a husband or wife perhaps never realize how liberating and empowering living on one's own is. Aurore did not experience what Woolf was idealizing in *A Room of One's Own*, because she had Maurice with her, but she still suddenly felt a sense that she could seize her moments and could attempt ambitious projects that would have seemed forbidden under the protective gaze of her husband. Could she start or assist a revolution? If she lived alone, there was nobody next door who might criticize her for taking such a radical political action. Aurore spent the winter thinking about what the change of regimes meant for France and for her, personally. She began considering why she was not taking responsibility for the social ills around her, and why with all of her privileges, she had a right to abstain from direct political action, remaining merely a wife and mother, when there might be a new revolution around the corner, or a new reformist movement in need of recruits.

Aurore's reflections were interrupted when Casimir moved her and Maurice with him into a new apartment on Rue du Faubourg Saint-Honore, and preceded to opening a salon for friends, which was a guise for inviting his female companions over without facing objections.

These regular salons and once again living in the same space with Casimir brought back Aurore's ennui, and to resolve this psychological and spiritual crisis she went to see Abbe de Premord, who advised her to spend some time back at the English convent to regain her moral courage. The idea struck Aurore as a relief from her turmoil, so she asked for permission for the stay from Mother Superior, then Madame Eugenie, who welcomed Aurore, as she would have any society lady that wanted to visit the convent. The time she spent once again living with Casimir made her regret that she had not become a nun four years earlier, and the cloister seemed to be a more comfortable place to habituate, despite its lack of luxury, than the largest castle in France with a cruel and detached husband. Aurore spent some time in the convent's chapel, recalling her earlier religious ecstasy, without regaining those long-gone feelings. She also watched with cool detachment students in classrooms, and a performance on Mother Superior's birthday of a tearful morality play by Madame de Genlis, recalling how she founded these now regular events, but there were fewer students at the convent now because it lost its popularity as more bourgeoisie sent their children there, and the aristocrats reacted by withdrawing their daughters. Watching the children interact only reminded her that she was no longer a child, and made her yearn for Maurice, who, upon request, was allowed to join them. Aurore might have stayed on much longer, but Sister Helene, who had feigned illness years earlier to get Aurore to do her chores, now retaliated for her earlier failure by telling Aurore that Maurice's pink face and slight cough meant that he must be consumptive. Aurore took Maurice out of the convent within an hour of hearing this remark, and despite the physician finding Maurice to be in excellent health, Aurore could not bring herself to return to the convent.

Before returning to Nohant, Aurore visited Deschartres at his furnished apartment at Place Royale, the oldest square in the city of Paris, which was initially used by royalty, but then was rebuilt for nobles and the bourgeoisie. Deschartres mansion was later occupied and remodeled by Victor Hugo, between 1832 and 1848, a period when Aurore knew this great man and made several visits back into this abode. When Deschartres stayed there, its two floors were already made out of the fine, carved red oak, and chairs were covered in red velvet. The apartment did not reflect Deschartres' extremely troubled finances, as he explained to Aurore briefly that he lost money on his speculations in rape oil and colza, because he invested without supervising these enterprises. The chat leaned towards business, a topic Aurore disliked, and the apartment seemed to indicate that Deschartres was still ahead financially, so Aurore only asked a few questions and made some polite comments before excusing herself, and returning from Paris to Nohant.

It was soon spring in Nohant in the year 1825, and Aurore had not heard a word from Deschartres, in reply to her letters. Aurore wrote to a letter to Colonel Dudevant, who was staying in Paris at the time, and asked him to check on Deschartres' apartment. The Colonel obliged her, and to his surprise was told that Deschartres had died some weeks earlier, having lost his fortune before what looked like a suicide. Aurore received this news in a letter, while she was sitting at a little closet-desk in her room, which she no longer shared with Casimir. Reading the line, "Deschartres passed away..." gave Aurore a jolt, as this was extremely surprising. There were no apparent clues that he might have been ill when she last saw him. When she read that "suicide" was suspected, she trembled and felt her eyes watering. She recalled the day she had jumped into the river, and the talk she had with Deschartres on the way back to Nohant.

Deschartres was not surprised by her confession that she was suicidal, and instead shared a few thoughts that Aurore just now fully recalled, "On the day when I was called in to examine your father's body at the inn, I nearly blew my brains out when I got back to Nohant. Before I checked his pulse, I was horrified that he might still be faintly alive and that he might suffer agony before he died, and I felt a bit of relief when I discovered that his spirit had already fled. So, just know that if you find me deadly injured beyond all hope of recovery, I hope you will help me to end my life. I think you'd find a bit of opium in my medicine cabinet, and around double the regular dosage should do it. I'd do it myself without telling anybody, if I could reach the cabinet."

If no illness incapacitated Deschartres, was complete ruin enough for him to have sought such a solution. She wished she had a chance to inspect the body for clues as to the cause of this sudden end. Learning about Deschartres' suicide had an enormous impact on Aurore's decisions from that point forward. She came to suspect that complete independence could lead a person to not have anybody to live for, and while her artistic nature might have demanded that she obtain a room of her own to work in, she continued to cohabitate with others, in part for protection against what she perceived to be as a deadly loneliness. In addition, Deschartres and Casimir's investment failures kept her from engaging in investing herself, or in other forms of business outside of agriculture. On a personal level, it took Aurore a long time to recover from the loss of her tutor, and she actively sought intelligent men out as companions across her life because she was missing the gap Deschartres suddenly left.

Aurore's depression was intensified when Hippolyte moved to Nohant with his wife and daughter, Leontine. Hippolyte had just concluded squandering away his own fortune, and after moving to Nohant he continued drinking and womanizing as usual. Aurore suddenly realized that what was previously harmless fun was now a clear case of alcoholism that was turning Hippolyte into an unfeeling, brutalizing, and fully absent-minded egotist. The couple was so troubled that they even left Leontine with Aurore, while they left for a couple of seasons to stay in Paris, in a period when their finances temporarily rebounded.

All of these traumatic events made Aurore want to escape, and when Casimir suggested them taking a trip to Cauterets, Aurore hardly realized that she would be going there with her husband, only focusing on the idea that she would be going somewhere else. Aurore had passed by the Cauterets before on her childhood trip to Spain, as they were on the border between the two countries, towards the center between the two borders with the Tyrrhenian Sea and Atlantic Ocean, or the Bay of Biscay. On the last trip through the region they had gone around the Cauterets because they were difficult to scale, but this time they gradually directed their carriage up the mountains until they were in the valley of the Gave de Cauterets, among snowy mountains. The town of Cauterets was known for its high-end spa establishment. While Aurore was taking part in the regular rituals of the place, like drinking mineral water, taking showerbaths, and being mummy wrapped in a sedan chair, she met an aristocratic young lady who had ties in the town and could explain some of the stranger activities, Zoe Leroy. The two went with the men on hunts and hikes up the mountains. Then Zoe insisted that Aurore accompany her to her country house, in the nearby town of La Brede. On the trip there, they went through the countryside and saw shepherds tending to their sheep, goats, cows, and calves, and Aurore started a fantastic story in her mind about what it would be like if she came to live with these calm and caring people, instead of continuing to live in her tumultuous family. The fantasy overwhelmed Aurore with its realistic intensity, as she studied the details of how these shepherds lived and worked. Aurore managed to eat dinner without breaking down with the Leroy family. Zoe introduced her to her friend, Aurelien de Seze, who was five years older than Aurore, and had just become the Deputy Prosecutor General. After dinner, Aurelien offered to show her a covered terrace that looked out on a great view of the mountains at the back of the house. Aurore agreed and soon they were sitting on a couch on the terrace.

Aurore asked him about what he did, and when he told her about his distinguished legal career, at which he was excelling in his young age, she was overcome with a feeling on inadequacy, and the fact that she was no longer a girl, and that she was now a woman whose sole achievement was motherhood. She expected that she would be able to sit in the carriage next to Casimir without really noticing his presence, but he was glum across the trip, and even as he laughed with the friends that accompanied them, she sensed his anger and resentment, and this cold treatment was just now piling up and severally affecting Aurore's emotional state. Tears came up in Aurore's eyes, and then a torrent was pouring out. Aurelien nudged her head gently towards his shoulder, and Aurore felt some relief from feeling his strong, but soft shoulder under her cheek. Her tears were falling on his jacket, but Aurelien showed no signs of hesitation, and instead he gently took her in his arms and kissed her.

Did I tell him I have a husband? Aurore wondered a moment after letting herself become lost in a sensuous kiss. Then she heard the terrace's door opening.

Casimir walked into the terrace in the middle of this long kiss. There could be no confusion that the kiss was mutual.

"Sir! What are you doing kissing my wife?!"

Aurelien pulled his lips away, pulled his hands away from Aurore, and jumped up.

"I'm sorry. I don't know what came over me. It's inexcusable."

"It certainly is. So, please be so good as to leave me alone with my wife, as we clearly have some things to discuss!"

"Yes, of course, again, I'm very sorry…"

Aurelien left the terrace, curtseying to Aurore as he went.

Aurore was speechless. She did not understand how Casimir had a right to stop her from kissing other men, when she had heard from her housekeeping staff and from the neighbors that Casimir was having a few simultaneous affairs. She also glimpsed him kissing one of these women after a salon at their house several months ago, so there was no doubt about the truth in the rumors. She also had not had intercourse with her husband for a very long time, and she considered the intimate part of her marriage over, so it was unclear how he had a right to dictate her intimate affairs.

"Aurore, how can you be so indelicate!"

"Casimir, it was a bit of an accident. I'm not even sure how it happened."

"Well, I need you to promise me that you will never see him again."

Aurore felt outraged, angry, but even more so she felt powerless, and that one of the only people that had cared for her, and was kind and gentle was being torn away, just as she was bonding with him, and just as she started to feel a bit of happiness. Aurore felt as if she was about to faint, so she sank down to her knees on the floor of the terrace, and broke out into the sobs that she had momentarily suppressed during the kiss. Her legs were as if paralyzed, and she remained on the floor for some time, crying, with Casimir looking down at her with contempt. She eventually stopped crying and stood up, her feet still shaky. Aurore never answered the question, but Casimir took the sobbing and kneeling to mean that she repented and was agreeing to his demand. They went back to their hotel rooms, and carried on with their planned schedule for the next day.

In the morning, Casimir went out mountain goat hunting, while Aurore stayed at the hotel, as if to continue with the massages and soaks. She had received a secret letter from Aurelien on the previous evening, which invited her to meet him at the café near the hotel. She threw on her best dress, and ran down to the café.

Casimir entering when he did was no accident. Casimir knew that Aurore had discovered his affairs, and his lawyer informed him that multiple affairs and other indiscretions could strengthen Aurore's case for a divorce, if they had also stopped all intimate relations. Casimir hoped that if he could catch Aurore in an indiscrete situation this would be proof that she was unfaithful, and would stop her from filing an infidelity complaint against him. He explained it to Zoe in other terms, hinting that Aurore was loose already and that they had a somewhat open marriage, and Zoe had taken these hints and in her turn encouraged Aurelien to make the first move. Zoe told him in advance of the dinner that she knew a man who might be eager for intimacy with a beautiful woman and who would also attend, so Casimir followed them to the country house, and with Zoe's help was watching at the door of the terrace until the exact moment Aurelien kissed Aurore. Casimir assumed that since Aurore did not show any signs of wanting intercourse with him, she was generally asexual and might even resist the kiss, but that he would see Aurelien kissing her, even if she did not respond by kissing him back. But, the suspicion that Casimir was partially responsible for this incident, and the bitter anger at him for being pompous enough to insist that she never see Aurelien again, suddenly boiled out of furious rage and into an intense physical attraction. Aurore was once again the little girl sitting on a bench with a boy who was making her feel a tingling yearning all over her body, only this time both of them were adults. She found herself in the café, looking at Aurelien and seeing a handsome judicial official, who was a much better match for her intellect and social status than Casimir could ever become. And as they chatted about the fog that morning that covered the mountains, and the unique flavor of the coffee in that region, Aurelien gently began massaging Aurore's hand, which she had delicately placed on the table between them, and Aurore was once again swept up in fantasies of romance.

They wrote love letters to each other in the following months, as Aurelien returned to his job, and Aurore returned to Nohant. Casimir discovered one of these letters and confronted Aurore about it.

"What does this mean, didn't you agree not to see Aurelien again?"

"No, I did not. You didn't wait for my answer."

"So, you want to continue writing to him, despite my objections?"

"Yes, I heard about your affairs, how can you have a right to tell me who I can't write to?"

Casimir was struck by this. In part, he wanted to insist that he was the master of the house, and that she was forbidden from actually indulging in an affair. But, at the same time, the revolutionary spirit had swept him up into a liberal frame of mind, and he reconsidered. If Aurore had an affair, and was aware of his affairs, and they managed to keep their marriage, and to keep their finances intact, this seemed to be a logical solution to all of their problems.

"If you feel that you have to keep exchanging letters with him… and even if you two want to meet alone together, I will consent to it, if that's what you want?"

"Yes, I want both of us to stay out of each other's personal lives, and to live together as business partners. You proposed to live as friends, well at least let's not leave as enemies."

"If that's what you think is best, I agree. Let's try it."

Casimir put the letter that he had intercepted back into the postman's hand himself, and pretended as if this turn of events was exactly what he initially wanted. Meanwhile, he began frequenting the Nohant library, and attempted reading up on some of the classics Aurore had mentioned over the years. He suddenly felt that there was a chance his marriage would slip away. He knew that a single slap in Aurore's face had permanently ended their sexual relations, and he knew that if he attempted to force her into refraining from corresponding with Aurelien, it would have the same impact as a slap. While Aurore's guilt over having had what looked like an affair would have worked in Casimir's favor, having Aurore actually engage in an extramarital affair could have caused a deeper rapture in their marriage than what was already between them. The only solution Casimir could imagine was developing in the one area that Aurelien was clearly his better, in the mind. But, Casimir did not have the patience or the discipline for consistent reading, and after turning a few pages, and pretending to read a few times as Aurore walked by, he gave up and reverted to his old habits.

A few months later, the couple's financial situation changed when Colonel Dudevant died in his estate in Guillery from an attack of the goat of the stomach. Casimir and Aurore traveled to Guillery to comfort Mme. Dudevant during this time. But, this experience hardly brought the marital couple together, as they witnessed a Mme. Dudevant, who despite being deathly ill and frail herself, was doing everything in her power not to let any of Colonel Dudevant's inheritance end up with an illegitimate son, even if she did not have any children of her own.

Because Casimir did not receive an inheritance from his father that he promised when he married Aurore, they were forced to spend the years between the summer of 1826 and 1831 in permanent residence in Nohant, with only very brief departures, as they did not have the means to travel or to rent additional apartments that might have let them live separate lives.

Being in tight proximity of each other, while they were both engaging in extramarital affairs, and were hardly speaking for half a decade created a violently strained atmosphere. Hyppolite and Casimir would spend the entire evening and night drinking, until they could not utter more than a phrase across the following day, left vomit on the floor, and laughed obnoxiously as they should obscenities and vulgarities through the night. Hyppolite was the more unstable of the two, as he would begin shouting with rage at a servant for putting his bottle in the wrong closet one moment, and then would suddenly break down and start crying while chatting with Aurore about the best color for a baby's shoes or blanket. While at first Aurore even joined them in their first few drinks, she soon learned that she could not stomach even a few minutes of their destructive conversations, and the moment Hyppolite and Casimir took out their bottles of wine, Aurore retreated into her room and began reading or writing because she knew that she could not get sleep until both of them passed out or managed to find a bed to sleep in. Both Hyppolite and Casimir made the decision to permanently escape from the stress of ambitions and responsibilities in the bottle. When they drank, they felt truly free from all the negative burdens, such as social, political or economic problems, as well as marital and emotional complications. In addition, both felt frustrated with the vacancy of their intellects, or with their inadequate capacity for concentrated perception. They had been bred around people who were becoming colonels, barons, business owners, or great authors, but they did not have the desire or the ability to rise above basic daily survival. When they drank, these burdens appeared to be insignificant, and they felt as if they were floating above them, as if in love, or in a daydream. Aurore felt that her intellect and perception were diminished when she drank, so she almost never indulged in anything stronger than milk, and she perceived Hyppolite and Casimir's drunkenness as a deadly disease that had struck them down and made them into helpless newborns. She did not attempt to rescue them from it, because all of her moves towards criticism only depressed them more, and this led them to drink more, and to sink further into an unperceptive stupor.

Living with two alcoholics that stood up until six in the morning drinking did permanently rotate Aurore's schedule, so that she made it a habit to work at night across her life. She preferred working in Marie-Aurore's boudoir because it only had one door, and could not be used by anybody that wanted to go somewhere else. In this small room, Aurore had her herbarium, collections of butterflies and pebbles, a hammock and a desk in an armoire. It was here in those desperate years that Aurore wrote her first experimental stories. She wrote one called, "The Life and Death of a Familiar" about a cricket that resided in this boudoir with her for a long time, until he was crushed in a window by a house servant. She also started writing a novel by mimicking the popular romantic style of her day, and the speed with which she managed this project made her realize that she could attempt making a living from professional writing, even if that particular project was too rough, and she never attempted selling it. She felt more and more an urgency to find a profession to fall back on because life at Nohant had been suffocating her for years, and she felt that she would reach a desperate conclusion if she did not find an escape route.

Aurore's confidence in her professional abilities grew as Nohant peasants began coming to her seeking help with illnesses, and as there was no other doctor in the region willing to take on gratis clientele, Aurore was the Deschartres substitute for these people. A few had seen her years earlier working by Deschartres side, and when a couple came and were helped by Aurore, more followed until there was a steady stream of patients. Aurore took out the medical and pharmacy books from Nohant's library, and with their help and from-memory, reset bones, stitched wounds, and prepared syrups and ointments. As she was helping all these people for free, she started wondering if she could do the same for money for wealthy clients in La Chatre, but when she queried her acquaintances in that town, they all laughed at the suggestion of paying a woman-physician, or asking one to attend them when they were ill. This frustrated Aurore, so she started thinking of ways that women typically made a living in French society. In the next few years she worked through several ideas, but she did not settle on novel writing until much later, as a last resort.

***

The general elections of 1827 that decided the makeup of the third legislature of the Second Restoration awoke a political split between Aurore and Casimir, which allowed Aurore to rebel politically against the injustice of her situation.

On November 17th and 24th, only those who were tax-paying citizens were allowed to vote in this election, and this group was composed of only 94,000 people, out of the millions of others who lived in France, but could not vote. The tally when the election was done was that the left won 170 seats, ultra-royalists won 125 seats, and the right won 75 seats. The ultra-royalists wanted to return to absolute monarchy, repeal the Charter that created a constitutional monarchy, and otherwise to assure a return to the pre-revolutionary system. The left portion of the vote varied greatly in degrees of left-thinking. On the extreme left were republicans, who supported the rights of workers, and included both socialists and outright revolutionaries. The middle-left included constitutionnels, who were for the Charter, but against giving the populace the right to vote. Those who were on the right were the liberal royalists, who supported the monarchy, and also wanted to raise taxes to support the bourgeoisie middle class. In other words, while only the upper and upper-middle class bourgeoisie and aristocrats voted in this election, the left that was either outright anti-monarchy or for a constitutional monarchy won the majority of the Assembly. This meant that the next three years were full of political friction between Charles X and the Assembly, until he dissolved his leftist assembly in 1830, an act that sparked the 1831 revolution. Of course, there were other problems, besides this friction, for Charles X, as he was a converted libertine, who previously regularly frequented brothels and hit the bottle, but who spent his time as king on enacting ultra-rightist policies, including bringing back the sacrilege law, offering the death penalty for blasphemy, and working to return to kings claiming divine rights.

Casimir was the Mayor of Nohant and the sub-prefect for the district at the time, and he now decided that he wanted to enter the wider political arena, by supporting a campaign of the regional candidate that wanted to join the Assembly. Casimir joined the liberal royalists party, which united what was previously the liberal and bonapartist parties. Despite these roots and the name, the liberal royalists were on the right, and supported monarchists, rather than asking for a return to Napoleonic rule.

In contrast, this was a period when Aurore first joined the winning leftists, aligning herself with the revolutionary republicans. Aurelian was also a rightist royalist, so Aurore initially had few contacts on the left as most of her extended family and friends were firmly in the royalist camp. Aurore began her gradual movement towards the left because her social views were in opposition to those of the upper class in her region. As part of his attempt to gain a central position in the liberal royalist party in his district, Casimir rented a townhouse in La Chatre, where he began organizing balls and political gatherings. For the first few meetings, he succeeded in inviting the top liberal royalists in the region, who all gushed about his expensive dinners, festive entertainments, and beautiful guests. He then made the mistake of asking Aurore to help organize the next gathering. He gave her a list of guests that he wanted her to write specialized invitations for. He also explained that she could not invite anybody from the political left or from ultra-royalists, and she certainly could not invite anybody from the middle or lower classes, as the top liberal royalists never attended events where anybody but the "best" members of society would be present. Aurore listened to these directions, and realized that she really wanted to spill sand into Casimir's crystal glass on this occasion. She once again did not state that she agreed with his directions, and instead of following them entirely contradicted them. She invited members of all three political factions, and she invited a few people that were the scandal of the town, or were in the middle class, and had never been invited to a society party in the history of La Chatre. Thus, upon arriving at the ball, the warring political parties found themselves face-to-face with each other, and there was a long deadly silence over the hall for many minutes, before the guests started gossiping with outrage about this highly inappropriate mixing. Aurore included the following song she wrote about how she saw this gathering, which she called the "democratic ball," in her autobiography:

> Seven days go by.
> They fill the punchbowl high.
> They wax the ballroom floor.
> The host is at the door.
> Three new guests arrive, whose colors are suspect—
> In the town they all were asking
> Whether everyone was masking
> At the sub-prefect's.

When the tallies from the election came in and showed that the leftist republican party vote a majority, Aurore felt an irresistible urge to go to Paris to meet these radicals and to become involved in some way in their movement. All she was doing at Nohant was practicing pencil and water-color portrait making, and her commissions for these dried up when she staged the democratic ball.

Aurore arrived in Paris in December for a two-week trip. She wrote letters to three medical academics, all in their fifties and at the top of their careers, who she wanted to consult regarding questions that had come up during her medical practice over the prior few years since she started practicing. She also wrote to some of the well-known republicans in Paris, but they did not take them seriously, as they were coming from aristocratic woman. The doctors, on the other hand, were eager to meet with a young lady that was attempting medicine and who wanted their advice.

Her first visit was with Augustin Jacob Landre-Beauvais, who was serving on a professorship at the Paris polytechnic school, and was known for diagnosing and defining rheumatoid arthritis. He was removed from his academic post a few years later, in 1830, by King Louis-Phillip. Dr. Landre offered detailed explanations of the symptoms, causes and possible cures for arthritis, on which Aurore took notes, asking several clarifying questions, and asking about several related diseases that she had observed in her patients.

The second stop was at Dr. Husson's office at the Paris Hotel-Dieu. Aurore came across Dr. Husson's research into using animal magnetism to put patients into a trance, where they couldn't feel even very severe pain or burning. Aurore asked him questions about practical applications of this technique to her peasant patients, who had to have major surger-ies performed, but Dr. Husson could not demonstrate this strategy on the spot, and Aurore decided that it was a hoax.

Her final stop was with Francois Joseph Victor Broussais at his military hospital of Val-de Grace, and she was squeezed in between his morning duties as a physician, and his afternoon teaching duties. Dr. Broussais' research interests were in the interdependence of different organs, and in the same year when Beauvais was fired, 1830, Broussais was appointed as the professor of pathology for the Faculty of Medicine and Health Services. Francois' lecture interested Aurore more than all the others because he had a wide grasp of the function and interaction between the different organs, and he offered her a good deal of practical answers to the list of questions she brought with her. The conversation was so engrossing that when his lunch hour was over, and Dr. Broussais made his excuses and was about to curtsey and exit, Aurore blurted out, "Dr. Broussais, this has been an amazing learning experience, I simply can't leave Paris without thanking you in some way, why don't you let me take you out for supper tonight?"

"Mme. Dudevant, that is very kind of you. I would be delighted."

"I will have my coachman pick you up after your last class. He will wait for you at the main entrance."

Aurore was twenty-three at the time, and her affair with Aurelien was continuing. She had hoped to meet with Aurelien on this trip to Paris, but his duties kept him too busy on this occasion, and Aurore found that she was in need of romantic entertainment, but without a gallant knight. After marrying an older man and becoming the mistress of another older man, Aurore was in this period of her life clearly attracted to wisdom and maturity, and was not concerned with the outwards appearance of the men she became attached to. Casimir was chubby, and while Aurelien had a gentlemanly charm to him, he was not the ideal of classical beauty. But, her sudden attraction to Dr. Broussais was not something she could not possibly have explained. This might have been the only time in her life that she had sexual relations with a man in his mid-fifties, including her later affairs, when she was of an advanced age herself. The attraction stemmed in an odd combination of elements. First, Aurore recalled meeting Dr. Broussais at the Palace in Madrid when she was a little girl, pretending to be a male aide-de-camp to Murat. He was thirty-six at that time, and working as an army doctor. He was brought into the Palace after Murat started to suspect that he was being poisoned, and ordered all of the Spanish doctors to be removed from his staff. After Murat recovered, Aurore recalled hearing him give a brief lecture to Murat and his advisors regarding the medical books he had released earlier that year, *History of Inflammations, or Chronic Inflammations* and *Review of the Medical Doctrine.* He told Aurore that at that particular time he was working on his third and last major academic book, *Irritation and Madness,* which was released the following year. They spent the supper discussing these books, and Aurore explained that she was the aide-de-camp to Murat, and that she recalled hearing his lecture there, which amazed her and sparked her earlier interest in medicine. She suddenly realized, as they discussed that early meeting, that she had asked Deschartres to show him how he performed medicine because she recalled how easy it was for her to understand Dr. Broussais' lecture even when she was only four. In addition, Francois had a magnetism about him that is necessary in all great professors. He was used to attracting the admiration of his students with his finely designed suites, with his gently combed hair, by making seductive eye contact, and with his general relaxed, yet pointed demeanor. Every moment of a conversation with him was engulfing, offered new information, and brought various reflections and questions into Aurore's mind.

On their ride back, Aurore leaned in and kissed Francois gently on the mouth. As he was a hot-blooded Frenchman, he returned the kiss with energy, and then used all his years of experience with love-struck ladies and medical expertise to kiss Aurore in all the right places, and to massage her shoulders, back, and legs in a way that relaxed all her reservations. Aurore redirected the carriage to her empty apartment, and they had a long, sensual night together.

Exactly nine months later, in September of 1828, Aurore gave birth to Solange. Casimir must have suspected something, as the married couple had not had intercourse for five years. Aurore did not abort the baby because Dr. Broussais had a brilliant mind and she wanted to see a child of hers that would inherit some of that intellectual intensity. She also hoped to encourage Casimir to divorce her by flaunting her affairs, but Aurelien was too conservative to have ejaculate inside of her, as he was constantly working to avoid the risk of an illegitimate pregnancy. This second birth was an easy one, and Aurore even spent a couple of hours as she was having birth pains making shirts and bonnets for the coming baby.

Casimir was showing signs of outrage long before the birth, and after Solange was born and the shape of her head did not resemble either Aurore's or his own, his frustration became complete, but he did not find it in him to shout at Aurore about it in the household because Hyppolite, his wife, or a member of the staff was always in earshot range. A few months into this pregnancy, Casimir began an affair with Pepita, a Spanish maid, who took care of Maurice, and would take over caring for Solange after her birth. Pepita had enormous breasts, strong thighs, back hair, and thick lips. She flirted with all the men around her, and had first come to France as a mistress to an aristocrat. When he tired of her, she found employment in the Dudevant household. Casimir resisted having affairs with members of the household staff up until that point, as he was attempting to keep them separate from his domestic life, even renting the house in La Chatre for this purpose. But, after looking at Aurore's growing stomach over dinner one evening, he reached a breaking point. That night he went into Pepita's room with a bottle of wine, and as he anticipated, after a single glass, Pepita was receptive and he relieved his frustration in a few satisfying minutes.

After Solange's birth, Casimir felt more frustration than a short rumble could satisfy. Whereas before he would quietly and quickly get the act over with, he began a ferocious new technique. It developed when he was in the small chamber next to Aurore's bedroom, which belonged to Pepita, and they were carrying on as usual, when he suddenly heard Aurore turn a page in a book she was reading. He carried on, then he heard another page turn, and another, and another. It seemed that every time he went in for the plunge, Aurore turned a page. Finally, Casimir groaned loudly, just to be louder than the page turning. Aurore took a bit longer than previously to turn the page, but then moved on. Casimir then began plunging into Pepita with all his might, uttering extraordinary grunts at every penetrations. Pepita joined in by breathing loudly, and yelling out "Ah, ah, aaaah, oy, uy-yuy-yuy!" and the like. Aurore sat there quietly for around five minutes, as she was reflecting about love, sex, and relationships, and then when her reverie reached an end she once again turned the page of her book. At this, Casimir ejaculated and nearly passed out on top of Pepita.

The next morning, Aurore and Casimir sat down to eat golden croissants and black coffee. Casimir was visibly distressed, as it appeared as if his scheme of unnerving Aurore had not worked, and she once again remained impenetrable to all attempts at disrupting her perfect composure. Finally, Casimir broke down, "So, it seems Solange is our little miracle baby."

"How so?" Aurore asked, looking up from the coffee she was sipping.

"It's a bit of an immaculate conception, don't you think?"

"How do you mean?"

"I mean isn't it perfect that you could deliver nine months after your trip to Paris, where you probably met with your good friend Aurelien?"

"I did not meet with him in Paris nine months ago."

"Then, who did you meet in Paris nine months ago?!" Casimir said, boiling over with rage at this new suggestion that the father was some other man, and not the man Aurore had been seeing with his semi-consent.

"I didn't *meet* with anybody nine months ago in Paris. You know I went to consult with doctors about the ailments I was having."

"And where were these ailments, in your lower regions?!"

"I really don't appreciate your raised tone, and these suggestions!"

"And I don't appreciate holy births under my roof!"

"After the night you had yesterday, don't you think we might see a few new holy birth under *our* roof?"

Casimir could not think of a retort for that comment, so he dropped the remainder of his croissant, and retreated to his room. This conversation silently outraged Aurore, but she thought that considering the nature of the Solange's birth, the interaction she just had with her husband wasn't as bad as things could've gotten. The conversation didn't progress much further over the following years, and Casimir never publically contested Solange's legitimacy. A few months later, in the spring, Aurore and Casimir even went on a holiday together to Bordeaux with their two children. But in the fall of 1829, Aurore went to Perigueux alone, saying that she wanted to spend time with her friends Felicie Molliet and Zoe, but really spending the entire time in embraces with Aurelien.

This prolonged tete-a-tete with Aurelien returned Aurore's thoughts to finding a way to make a living to escape the confines of her marriage. Aurore's new scheme was design and painting of ornamental birds and flowers on snuff boxes, cigar cases, fans, tea chests, and work boxes of chestnut, which she covered with varnish. But the materials were very expensive, and sales too slow. She might have had more luck with selling these if she shipped them abroad as France was famous for its luxury and skilled finished good, including silks, gloves, and porcelain. Be that as it may, Aurore's design venture failed, and if it hadn't Aurore might have remained a fine local designer, and might never have attempted publishing a novel.

While Aurore was exploring her decorative venture, in December of 1829, Hyppolite replaced Casimir as Pepita's lover. Casimir found out about this turn of events in the following months of January, when he returned from Paris, to report that a cargo vessel, *Jeune Caroline*, was given to him as an investment by a swindler and that he had lost ten thousand francs on it. They all had a family meeting that evening about the matter, and Casimir agreed to give Aurore the one thousand francs in spending money that was guaranteed her in their marital contract. Before the meeting was over, Aurore ordered the firing of Pepita, saying that she fed Maurice wine and bread in the village while he had indigestion, but really because she overheard the argument earlier that day between Casimir and Hyppolite regarding Pepita, and it sickened her beyond her tolerance limit. Pepita's job as nurse to the children was taken up by Andre's new wife, Francoise. Andre was the young man who had accompanied Aurore on rides when she was a child, as he remained at Nohant across his long life, and remained as Aurore's trusted servant. The news that Pepita was fired was satisfying enough for Casimir because he wanted to spite Hyppolite and because he already started a flirtation, which later turned into a full affair, with his servant, Claire, who was similarly loose with her affection.

Early in May of 1830, Aurore visited Solange's father, Dr. Broussais, in Paris, and the two had a nice dinner, but Aurore did not tell him about the timing of Solange's birth, and they focused their conversation on medicine, and this time did not go to Aurore's apartment afterwards. On the following few days, Aurore went to Parisian museums on her own, studying masterful paintings, trying to understand the techniques they were using. Afterwards, she would do a bit of painting in her apartment, and upon failing to capture a unique style that would be worthy of the great masters, she suddenly switched from art to studying the elements of modern romantic novels, and this activity would engulf her imagination for decades to come. But on this particular trip to Paris, Aurore was too preoccupied to actually begin a full novel because of the sad turn her relationship with Aurelien de Seze was taking. On May 15th, Aurore traveled from Paris to Bordeaux to see Aurelien, and suddenly saw deep wrinkles in his forehead, as he told her about his father's recent death, and his depression made their physical encounter a tragic affair that barely reached a conclusion. By the time Aurore departed from Bordeaux for Nohant, she knew that her affair with Aurelien had come to an end.

Chapter 12

The July Revolution and Jules Sandeau

The events that led to the July Revolution started at least as early as in 1829, when Michel de Bourges, also known as Louis Michel-Chrysostome, during the burial ceremonies of a French deputy who was killed by a member of the Royal Guard, delivered a thundering funeral oration that nearly caused a pro-republican, or rather simply revolutionary, riot. Bourges' and Aurore's paths would later cross, but they were not yet in the same circles. The crowd was shouting, and was about to storm those who represented the monarchy at the meeting, when they were stopped by a regiment that entered the hall. Bourges went underground after this because he anticipated that he would be arrested as a rebel-riser. Bourges was born from humble roots, or that of a woodcutter, who happened to have been murdered by royalist fanatics three decades earlier, before Michel's birth in 1797. Michel worked his way up from these humble beginnings to working as a tutor and only completed a law degree in 1826. Then, he represented clients that included deserters, and others down on their luck. By 1829, he had married a wealthy wife, and this arrangement allowed him to focus on social and political causes, instead of lawyering to pay the rent.

Before Bourges could be captured, the July Revolution descended on France between July 26 and 29, in 1830. Charles X was overthrown and Louis-Phillip won his thrown in a royalist anti-Bourbon dynasty and pro popular sovereignty coup d'etat. The Revolution began when bourgeoisie business owners learned that according to the new Saint-Cloud Ordinances, they would no longer be able to run for the Chamber of Deputies, and in return stopped lending money and closed their factories, causing a spike in unemployment. At the same time, newspapers, which had been ordered to stop printing by the Ordinances, refused to do so, and in response there was an attempt by the police to seize these contraband papers, but the police force was prevented for carrying this out by the mob which once heated up continued to cause havoc over the next three days until there was a change of regime. During this brief Revolution, Michel de Bourges took the unexpected role of helping to prevent bloodshed, and persuaded a royalist general to surrender without a shot.

In the days after the insurrection, there were reports that a royalist regiment from Bourges was marching on the rebel town of La Chatre, considered to be rebellious because their top politicians were liberals. So, the liberals of La Chatre, led by Casimir, Hippolyte and the republican Jules Neraud, improvised a National Guard company of 120 men, and prepared to do battle in military gear, and armed with flintlocks, bayonets, and sabers. When it became clear that nobody was marching on La Chatre, Hyppolite created a fictional account that a house on Rue de Seine was being leveled by a cannonade, and this put the "National Guard" on high alert for many hours, before Hyppolite finally confessed, amidst his own laughter, that he had made the story up.

While her husband was leading the Guard, on July 30th, Sand went to Le Coudray to meet with her friend, Charles Duvernet and a group of other far leftists, which included Gustave Papet, Alphonse Fleury, and a young man they mentioned, whom she was meeting for the first time, Jules Sandeau. The latter was sitting alone under a pear tree reading a book, in contrast with the agitation among the other members of the party, who were all engulfed in a debate how they should use the July Revolution to their advantage, here was a man who found a classical book to be of more interest than the drama of the moment. Aurore sat down next to him, and to be polite he bowed his head and they chatted for a bit. Aurore was as flirtatious as she could be, and initiated hints that she was interested in an affair with him. Jules told her that his father was a collector of royal taxes, and that he was studying at the Royal College of Bourges, where he recently won literary and drawing prizes. He was beginning to gain some repute at his young age of nineteen. Jules realized his legs were cramping from sitting under the tree and talking for such a long time, so he invited Aurore for a walk, and as they strolled under gentle willow trees, their hands touched as Jules helped Aurore over a branch on their path. Both of them immediately felt a sensual response to the other's thin and soft fingers, and they simultaneously blurted out.

"I believe I love you Aurore."

"I feel so much love for you."

They laughed at this coincidence and then kissed gently on the lips, holding both hands. It would be another three months before they began a full-blown sexual relationship because Jules was not as experienced with such love affairs as Aurore was. Half a year later, Aurore realized that she had to separate from her husband because she could not imagine being away from Jules for more than half of a year. This decision was made more immediate when she found Casimir's will, which stated that she would get nothing upon his death by "curses," and this outrageous maneuver made not only a residential separation, but also a divorce an urgent necessity, as she became aware that her husband was openly hostile to her financial interests.

Three days later, in December of 1831, Aurore went to live in Paris with the hope that she could make a living from popular writing. Casimir was still engaged in an affair with Claire, and was seeing some other ladies in La Chatre, so he agreed to let Aurore spend half the year in Paris, partially because he assumed that she could not survive there on only 1,500 francs in allowance for six months, but Aurore assumed that it would be enough because her mother had lived in Paris on 3,000 francs for the past decade. In addition, she planned on splitting some of her expenses with Jules, and he also managed to afford living in Paris on a small allowance. To save money while she searched for an apartment, she lived in Hyppolite's apartment for the first week she spent in Paris.

To keep up appearances, Aurore rented a garret on Quai Saint-Michel, in a house that stood before a bridge opposite from the Morgue. This garret consisted of three small rooms, and a balcony, where she began growing a pot of Reseda to match her neighbor, Mme. Badoureau's orange tree. The trouble was that this place stood at the top of five flights of stairs, which seemed romantic when Aurore first looked at its fantastic view of the Seine and the monuments of Notre-Dame, but turned out to be a painful daily climb. The place cost only 300 francs a year to rent. Aurore only hired a caretaker to help her with the house-work for fifteen francs a month, which was a big change from the army of servants that Aurore had at Nohant. To avoid cooking or hiring a servant to do it for her, Aurore had her evening meals brought in from a cheap neighboring restaurant. She also decided on washing and ironing her clothing herself, as she had done it before at the convent, and this was a major way to save money. While Aurore went through a lot of trouble to arrange for the furnishing and cleaning of this Saint-Michel garret, her real apartment was in Jules Sandeau's rented furnished room in a boarding house-hotel on the Quai des Grands Augustins and Rue Git-le-Coeur.

Aurore spent the majority of her first three month in Paris in Jules' room, but her family obligations meant that she had to move Solange in with her. When she was not engaged in amorous activities with Jules or taking care of Solange, Sand was constantly trying to find work, but all she managed to arrange was having a small portrait of her caretaker on display at the café at Quai Saint-Michel, on the ground floor, under her garret, but it did not sell, nor generate other portrait commissions.

Aurore was not able to write her first published novels in the garret because it was too uncomfortable, so she only began her professional writing venture when she went back to Nohant later that year. Meanwhile, it was winter in Paris, and she was struggling merely to survive the months she was allowed to spend in the city without giving up on the idea that she could have an independent residence for half of the year. On this first trip she was still hopeful that she could write in the city, and even tried doing it at the Mazarine library, but it was freezing there, and too noisy because of all the old hoboes that slept sitting up at the tables. Walking around Paris to Jules', to the library, and elsewhere in the middle of the winter naturally brought Aurore down with a cold. The same extensive walking also destroyed her expensive shoes, so that she had to buy boots with iron heels, and change her clothing from feminine to masculine for the sake of convenience. She began wearing a long, gray, square redingotes, with trousers, a vest, a gray hat, and a wide wool tie. Aurore mimicked Jules' fashion in these choices, and he accompanied her when she hired a tailor to craft them, helping to pick out the items that would make her look convincingly like a little boy starting his courses at the university. The outfit allowed Aurore entry into all the places where women were barred, like the pit in the Parisian theaters, where she could engage in raucous fights with the rebel. The only thing she had to learn to do to pass as a boy was what she had already been doing naturally since she was a child, or avoid coquettishness, and all other lady-like mannerisms.

The affair with Jules was the first one that Aurore had that was both intellectually and sexually fulfilling. Aurore realized that the reason she could not become excited with Casimir and allowed her relationship with Aurelien to cool was because they were older than her, and she felt like they had to be the ones that worked to please her in bed. She spent several years in Nohant living a nun's life, and this type of seclusion and mental inactivity was not to her taste. In the first weeks in Paris with Jules, she knew she had made the right decision to move to Paris and to become engaged not only with Jules, but also with his revolutionary friends, who had just won the July Revolution and suddenly felt a burst of creative and intellectual freedom, which had been suppressed with censorship and other laws across their earlier lives. Most of these young students and artists were born right after the Revolution, or they were only children when it took place, so they were raveling in the spirit of liberty, and in the possibility of a brighter, romantic and idealistic future. Aurore looked at their intercourse as a handshake between equal friends. Because Aurore and Jules saw each other as friends, their intercourse frequently resembled a wrestling match among a couple of boys, as they would straddle each other violently, beating and scratching, as they rolled with laughter and ecstasy.

The circle that Aurore entered frequently met to plot and converse at a restaurant called Pinson's on Rue l'Ancienne-Comedie. This "group" was really a section of the Society for the Rights of Man, an organization that was split into groups of twenty people per group. While they met regularly in these small groups, they could also be coordinated into joint political rebellions, and this was how they carried out most of the republican or leftist revolutions from across this period in French history. The section of the society that Aurore joined included many politicians and writers who were later elected to the National Constitutional Assembly of the Second Republic, after the Revolution of 1848. Among those elected in 1848 was Alphonse de Lamartine, who she called Planet in her correspondences to avoid implicating him, and who was elected as an MP a couple of years later in 1833 and stayed in politics across his life, while also contributing literature to the romantic movement. Another later member of the Assembly in this group was Francois Rollinat, who was closer to Aurore's age, and also happened to write romantic poetry. Jules Sandeau was far from matching the other members in radicalism, and joined the group primarily for their literary merits. This group was partially funded in their social gatherings by a wealthy land owner from Berry, Gustave Papet, who met Aurore when she was inquiring regarding work as a physician, and asked him about his practice because he also ran a free clinic for his peasants. Gustave pulled the other members of the group together by inviting them to stay at this Ars Chateau and otherwise supporting their creative and political ventures. Another key member of this group, from Aurore's neighboring La Chatre, was Alphonse Fleury, a lawyer and banker, who became a Government Commissioner after the 1848 Revolution. When Aurore met with this group after the July Revolution, they were regrouping from organizing the coup d'etat, and preparing for the aftermath of this event. They now met regularly in Paris, as political developments meant that there was a need for coordinated action.

The group was led and organized by Alphonse de Lamartine, who was a founding member of the Society for the Rights of Man, and who collected monthly fees from the other members to sponsor their rebellious activities. It should be noted that in this period, writing political novels could be as radical an action as starting a revolution because of the tight censorship laws in France. One of the radical novelists and play writers among them was Henri de Latouche, who Aurore always called Delatouche, and who was also from La Chatre. When they first met, he offered free tickets to the entire club to watch his new comedy, *La Reine d'Espagne*, or *The Queen of Spain*, which was poorly received because of its radical criticism of the Spanish monarchy. Delatouche began mentoring Aurore, and helped her with her early literary commissions. Aurore attended this performance dressed as a woman, and happened to run into Baroness Dudevant during the intermission in the lobby. The Baroness was shocked to see Aurore at that Parisian theater, when she knew that Casimir was still at Nohant.

"Good evening Madame," Aurore uttered, curtseying to the Baroness.

"Good evening Madame, but why are you here without Casimir? Did he come to Paris without informing me?"

"I am staying in Paris alone at the moment."

"I see, so is it true that you intend to publish novels?"

"Yes, Madame."

"Oh my goodness! What a funny idea you've had."

"Yes, Madame."

"It's great that you have found a way to amuse yourself, but do you seriously intend to put my good name on the covers of your silly novels?"

Aurore had assumed that she would use her real name, but suddenly she did see a need to use a pseudonym if her mother-in-law was this hostile to the idea of associating with a writer. "You are right, of course, I would never use the Dudevant name on one of my covers."

"Very good, Madame, very good," Baroness Dudevant moved away from Aurore with a nod of the head.

When Aurore got back to her box seat, where Delatouche, Jules and others were waiting for her, she summarized the meeting she just had quietly to Jules.

"What pseudonym do you plan on using?" Jules asked.

"You know the publisher that asked you for a new book under your Jules Sand pseudonym?"

"Yes."

"You don't have one ready yet, and I've finished *Indiana* before I left Nohant, and need the money. So, why don't we edit it together and sell it as dually authored by Jules and George Sand?" Aurore wrote *Indiana* in the three months she was temporarily back at Nohant earlier that year. Three months was enough for her to finish *Indiana*, and to start a couple of other projects that she fully developed later on. She had prepared for concentrated and rapid novel-writing when she wrote earlier novels and plays, most of which she discarded because they were merely training exercises for these rapid bursts of productivity that she would have across her life, as she habitually wrote novels like others do the dishes or exercise, from start-to-finish, without editing, and without stopping to consider if she was going astray.

"As if we are brothers…"

"Yes, or cousins."

"It's a good idea. Let's see what the publisher will say about it."

The intermission was over and the play started again. And just like that, Aurore had gained the name she carried across the remainder of her life, and by which she is still popularly known, George Sand. The publisher liked these pseudonyms, and thus George had sold her first novel before the end of her first experimental year in Paris, making 1,000 francs on the deal, and this victory gave her the courage to continue publishing romances for many years to come. What Aurore did not know, and Jules forgot to mention to her, was that he chose the name Jules Sand, not only because it was a shorter version of his name, but also because he admired the bravery of Karl Sand, a Germany political assassin, a fact that came back to hurt George's reputation when she had a literary reputation that could be damaged.

Meanwhile, Aurore was dealing with a cholera epidemic that killed six people on the first floor of her building, including her landlady, but did not go any higher. She was also facing critics of both sexes that were telling her that women should make babies, and not novels, including M. de Keratry and his wife, Mme. de Keratry, but George thought that Keratry's own novels were done in bad taste, as one of them depicted the rape of a dead women by a priest, so she ignored these bitter critiques. To escape from the glum reflections about her gender and chosen profession, Aurore kept busy by taking all assignments that came her way, including accepting Delatouche's offer to edit his newspaper, *Le Figaro*, for fifteen francs per month, a task that she was particularly excited about because it let her spend more time near Jules, who was also employed at this paper. While Aurore barely made any money from editing, she was able to put her work into print, as in the single month of March, 1831 this paper published at least three of Sand's articles on a violin virtuoso, Paganini.

As with most of the projects that the group of rebels that George belonged to did, right beside the pieces about Paganini, George published a column purported to be a decree by the Paris prefect of police, which on one occasion commanded all citizens capable of bearing arms to guard the Palace Royal later that night. While this message was disguised as a joke, it could have brought a mob to "guard" with weapons the King's Palace, and this mob could have progressed from guarding to attacking the Palace in a new coup d'etat. As a result, this announcement angered the new King, who seized all copies of *Le Figaro* and filed a lawsuit against the paper. George was tempted to confess that she was the author of this contentious piece to gain fame, but like most of the other rebels in this click, real names were not revealed to the public and frequently not even in private communications because these rebels hoped and succeeded in gaining public office and public repute, which would have been impossible if they were jailed for sedition. The case ended up dying when the prefect of police dropped it, and George's name was not forcefully uncovered.

It was around the time of this Palace guarding fiasco, when a new member joined George's political club. Delatouche brought Honore de Balzac in, as he was one of his many disciples, but the two had a falling out, partially over their influence over George, and Balzac satirically used Delatouche's knowledge of wallpapering in his 1835 novel, *Old Father Goriot*. Honore de Balzac was still relatively unknown when he entered this group in 1831, but his fame was partially assisted by his campaign to become the leader of the French Republic, which ended with a near fatal fall he had a year later in 1832, but meanwhile won him a good deal of radical leftist friends, including George. On their first meeting at the restaurant, Balzac had read a quote from a novel he had just published, *The Wild Ass's Skin*, which was spoken by a Carlist, or somebody that wanted to reestablish the Bourbon line of succession in Spain, "'Despotism pleases me; it implies a certain contempt for the human race. I have no animosity against kings, they are so amusing. Is it nothing to sit enthroned in a room, at a distance of thirty million leagues from the sun?'" Some members in the group liked this passage and laughed, while others found fault with it; the latter did not sit well with Honore, who typically found criticism to be personal affronts. George did like these passages and saw the sparks of greatness, which only turned into fame for Balzac two years later with the publication of his best-selling novel, *Eugenie Grandet*, with which he started his *Human Comedy* series.

While some members of the group were skeptical about him, George expressed her admiration, so Honore invited her to visit him in his apartment on Rue de Cassini, where he rented a mezzanine between the ground and the second floor. Right before George's visit, Balzac had been paid for *The Wild Ass's Skin*, and he used this money to transformed his poet's-rooms into magnificently designed boudoirs, with silk-lined walls bordered with lace. The two had great dinners, made up of boiled beef, melon, whipped champagne, and ices, in these boudoirs, and looking around George sensed that Honore was sacrificing food (when guests weren't there), and other necessities to afford making his home look luxurious for his honorable guests, a flaw that had ruined several earlier business ventures of Balzac's and that eventually led to his early death. When George came over, Balzac would start talking about the book he was working on, and then he would talk about his character, or his views on business or political developments, so that George barely had time to put a word in, and simply listened with interest, soaking up lessons about self-reflection and continuous in-looking discussion from this great writer. George adapted some elements from Balzac's realistic style and inserted self-examinations into her novels because of this influence. George also adapted Balzac's workaholic writing technique, as both worked without the use of drugs or alcohol, under the pressure of tight deadlines and financial need. On a few occasions, Balzac made it up to George's fifth floor apartment, but these efforts nearly killed him because of his large bulk.

The death of General Jean Maximilien Lamarque on June 1 of 1832 was cause for a meeting of the "club" on the evening of June 2nd. George had met the General on several occasions, at aristocratic family gatherings, and more recently among republicans, as he became a leftist in his final years, supporting the independence of Poland and criticizing the monarchy. Alphonse de Lamartine gave a detailed explanation on the significance of the General's death, and that there was a chance he was poisoned, as he was only sixty-one and in otherwise good health when he died.

"There are several Polish refugees, I think one of them was named Frederic Chopin, who were working with the General towards Polish independence, who want to hold a demonstration of some kind, and some have expressed a desire to even riot…"

While George and Frederic Chopin did not meet on this occasion, this was a period when Chopin first entered her orbit. The prior year, in September of 1831, the Battle of Warsaw, a part of the Polish-Russian War, led to the collapse of the city of Warsaw in which Chopin resided at the time, and which he had to flee to avoid the aftermath. Chopin moved to Paris as a refugee at this point, one among many middle and upper class refugees that could afford the trip to Paris. Because Chopin was a recognized composer, he became friends with radical politicians and artists soon after his arrival, and those among Parisian artists who were for Polish independence were also for revolutionary actions within France.

"When do they plan on this rioting?" George asked, curious to find out how those types of rebellions were organized.

"They have suggested a few possibilities, but the best one I heard is doing it during General Lamarque's funeral."

"Isn't that disrespectful towards the dead?"

"No, I'm sure the General would approve. There are also other refugees, unemployed prior factory workers, and some other radicals who want to join us."

"Would we lead the charge?"

"We usually stay in the background and deploy the troops. If any members of this club were caught, it would be a major blow to the republicans."

"Where will the funeral be again?"

"Outside of the Palace."

"Hm… why don't we re-direct the procession by blocking the road towards Place de la Bastille?" George asked, as if she just came up with a unique twist to one of her novels.

The group agreed that this was the best course of action, and they discussed the details of the plan, forwarding secret messages to the members of the other sections of the Society. Before they departed, Lamartine handed each of them a protective vast for the forthcoming conflict.

On June 5th, George left Solange with her neighbor and met the other members of her club at the procession. Because they began by what appeared like a peaceful demonstration, George was at the front, in her boy-student outfit, helping to re-direct the casket. There were several strong men that pushed and shoved those that carried the casket and those around them, while George merely argued with a few people in the procession, encouraging them to lead the casket to the Place de la Bastille in the name of "liberty" because the General would have wanted the honor to pass through that square, where the Bastille once stood, before the Revolution. With slogans, cheers, shouts and nudges, the team managed to lead the procession where they wanted them. When they got to the Place, a few scheduled speakers gave orations about the need for Polish and Italian independence. None of the members of the Society spoke, as they would have been recognized. Then, George waved a red flag she was carrying with the words, "Liberty or Death," and ran away from the center, as the refugees and workers began a riot, firing several shots at the troops, who fired back. George managed to get out without a scrape, and rejoined the other members of her club, as they gathered at the edge of the street to study the outcome of the confrontation. They decided to spread out to rally more rioters to their aid, and went in different directions, ahead of the mob. George ran through city streets, shouting for people to join them, "We will dine at the Tuileries tonight!"

But, hours went by, and while rioting continued, George soon realized that it was dying out instead of spreading. Some strangers she met appeared to realize that she was a woman, so she started to feel uncomfortable that exposed on the streets. She rejoined the members of the Society at their appointed rendezvous point, and since it would look suspicious if she failed to pick up her daughter from her neighbor she was told to go back home. George only had one incident on her way back, as she just made it across the bridge at Hotel-Dieu, before she saw that right behind her, the seventeen insurgents who had seized the bridge, were suddenly surrounded by the national guard regiment, which began cutting them to pieces and throwing them into the Seine. She saw the last two being captured, glancing backwards, as she ran into her building. She looked down from her balcony to check what happened, and she saw the two remaining insurgents getting shot. Trembling, but working to appear composed, George changed clothing from her boy's outfit, for a dress, and knocked on her neighbor's door. Mme. Badoureau, who worked as a teacher, did not appear to notice anything unusual about George's appearance, and surrendered Solange without an inquiry.

"I'm so glad you haven't retired yet. I'm so sorry to intrude on you this late," George fired out as she was curtseying and beginning to re-treat back into her own apartment.

Meanwhile, the organizers made a few more efforts across the night and into the following morning to raise a successful rebellion, but it siz-zled out and the leaders just managed to get away before the chief refu-gee rioters were seized. Chopin happened to leave with the organizers, before this final clash. In total, a couple thousand people died, with equal losses on both sides.

On the next morning, George once again left Solange with the neigh-bors, saying that she had to go out to buy the day's food. She wore her best dress to look less suspicious as she went directly by the armed sol-diers along the bridge at Hotel-Dieu, and trembled every time she heard the firing squad striking another found of shots at a new band of rebels being executed on a nearby street. George went to the Quais hoping to see some of her Society friends in action, but only saw the King march-ing with his troops to show that he had won the day. This outcome was devastating, and the club's meeting that evening was one that began with a silence, and barely got off the ground, as the only good news was that nobody out of their twenty members had been killed or injured. They had expected an overthrow similar to the July Revolution of the previous year, so this total defeat set them back, and a new revolution took over a decade to materialize.

In the meantime, George helped by going to the morgue to inspect the cadavers to determine if some of the rebels that had not been ac-counted for were dead, or possibly imprisoned or on the run. The sight of a pile of human bodies at the morgue distressed George, despite the many ailing bodies she had previously seen during her medical practice, and she became a vegetarian for two weeks because she couldn't stomach the smell of blood.

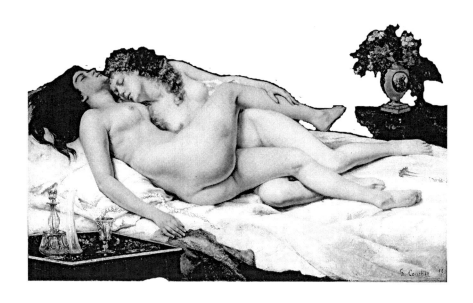

Chapter 13

Fame and
Mme. Marie Dorval

Before George had a chance to adjust to life in Paris without the possibility of an immediate republican take-over of the government, she was forced to stay in Paris by the sudden popular and critical success of her novel, *Indiana*. The plot of *Indiana* reflected many of the personal struggles George was facing, as she wrote it in the middle of a revolution, when she had to write what she knew about, and did not have time to plot ahead or to make things up. Indiana Delmare, a noblewoman, is in a marriage that is so devoid of passion that it is making her physically ill, and to escape she falls in love with Raymon de Ramiere, who has already impregnated the maid, Noun, who commits suicide when she suspects that Raymon will leave her for Indiana. Indiana at first leaves Raymon, but then returns and when she discovers that he only feigned loving her she is about to commit joint suicide with her cousin, Sir Ralph, when they discover that they love each other, and settle together on an isolated island farm. The radical Parisian critics applauded the statement *Indiana* was making against the Napoleonic Code's strict rules against divorce and for the status of minors for all women, which could force women into suicide. They had believed that "Monsieur G. Sand" was a man, who justly sympathized with women. They would later turn on her, once they discovered her read gender, but this was a period when they were in ecstatic oblivion.

While George's literary career was taking off, her relationship with Jules Sandeau was coming to a screeching halt. He kept grumbling that he didn't deserve the credit for a novel that was primarily George's, and the solution he proposed was for them to stop their collaboration. Because George knew that two cousins or brothers suddenly severing writing relations would look suspicious and might reveal her gender, she was upset by this suggestion, and when Jules insisted, she suddenly no longer saw him as a chum that she could trust, and her romantic feelings for him faded as well.

When she suddenly became famous, she was introduced to Francois Buloz, who had just become the editor of *Le Revue des Deux Mondes*, which had an enormous financial backing, which allowed him to win a competition against other major publishers for George's future short stories, which included *Metel-la*, a couple of years later. Buloz published only the best French writers in his magazine, including Victor Hugo, Alfred de Musset, Balzac, and Alexander Dumas, pere, and standing in this group brought George Sand into the top echelons of French literature, a rank she did not lose even after her gender was made public.

George spent the earnings from *Indiana* and *Valentine*, a whopping 3,000 francs, on a better apartment, and a new servant. She moved into the new apartment on Quai Malaquais in 1833. The place was a paradise composed of a garden with blackbirds and sparrows. The place was so luxurious that the local beggars interpreted it as a sign that George had money to give away and launched a campaign to liberate her from it.

If you plan on traveling to Rome, you might be warned about gangs of children that swarm foreigners, and while pretending to be playing or begging for money, clear all pockets of their possessions. But, those gangs of children are indeed childish when they are compared with the organized gangs that surround and feed on celebrities, or anybody else that clearly displays wealth. If you are not aware of the complex schemes these gangs typically play, it is likely that you have not entered their radars. If, on the other hand, you start to notice that people bump into you by accident, and suddenly declare their love for you, or declare that they admire your shoes, or your last novel and the like, then there is probably a scheme brewing. Most criminals get by on stealing cars or carriages, they might get caught and sent to prison, or executed. But, organized criminals have worked in around the same way since long before George's time through the present. Different members of the gang specialize in different parts of the scheme. Some might pretend to be sick or dying children, others might pretend to be their grief-stricken mothers, while others are engaged in finding new prey for the whole gang to swoop on. If one of them asked for alms and received a few pennies, they would hardly be better off, but if they can pressure with their numbers, their persistence, or with their mind games, a person to giving the bulk of them alms on a regular basis, then they have found a continuous stream of funds that can feed the whole gang, if they find several targets that pay up on demand. Most of their targets are likely to have had negative experiences with these types of schemes before, and flatly refuse all alms from the onset, which might or might not cause the gang to lose interest, but it certainly prevents the target from being victimized. But, targets like George Sand present a unique situation, where the target is interested in helping the poor, and feels that even if the gang is playing a game on her, she still has a responsibility to help. If she refused all who asked her for charity, word might spread across the country that she is stingy, and does not support the plight of the poor.

Immediately after George moved into her new luxurious apartment, a ring of beggars swooped in, and began a steady assault on her residence. One day a servant would announce to George that a former artist was at the door that had hit hard times, and was asking for some funds to get back on his feet. On the first couple of times that George heard a version of this story, she let the artist in, and gave some small amount to help a fellow artist out. But, on the fourth time that the porter announced a variation on these theme, George exclaimed in outrage that he was not to announce similar visitors in the future, and that he is to immediately turn them away, telling them that George Sand was busy at work. Another common trick was for these beggars to offer subscriptions, showing a list with false signatures, attempting to get her to subscribe to something that didn't exist, hoping to get the money, and never return. George became especially upset once when she was introduced to sisters of charity, who was wearing a clear imitation of a nun's gown that Sand knew perfectly well the correct appearance for from her days at the convent. One story that made George come to the door just to take a look at the absurdity of the scene was when she was told a rebel, who had escaped from prison after being convicted in the June Revolution was hoping to get her assistance. George had met or seen most of the rebels involved in that uprising, so she had to inspect this claim, but it turned out that it was not a refugee, or one of the workers, but some drunken hooligan, and after listening to a bit of his ridiculously inaccurate story, George gave a forced laugh and shut the door in his face herself. George was least offended, and continued to give some alms to infrequent visitors who were just poor drunken idiots, and did not pretend to be anything else.

George was constantly amazed at how much time and effort this organized gang spent on figuring out when she came and went, when she received money from her publisher, and all other aspects that affected her money. It seemed to George that the only way they could know all that they knew was if most of her household staff was assisting them with information. But, their machinations were so complicating that George did not think too much about them, as she had too much work to be done on her novels.

What troubled George more than all these visits from strangers, was that sometimes men and women who were friends of hers in the better circles of artists and politicians in Paris also practiced complex schemes that were aimed at her money. More than a couple of her lovers threatened suicide to remain with her or in parallel with a request for money. Some would gradually explain that they had lost money gambling and that they would be beaten up or shot if they did not find some funds to cover these debts. Finding these types of liars, manipulators, and brutes in her bed, or in her boudoir over supper hurt George so deeply that she became emotionally detached and began to see the people around her in a very realistic light. She had to accept that money motivated the actions of most people who did not have enough of it, and knowing this motivation meant that from the artists in residence to lovers on vacation, George had to guard her heart from romantic notions about love that surpassed material interests.

***

A few years after the Terror, in 1798, Marie Delauney, who was later popularly known as Marie Dorval, was born in an impoverished and ailing broken family in the port city of Lorient, which had seen hard times across the Revolution and would continue to remain in financial ruin across the starting Napoleonic Wars. Her father abandoned the family when Marie was five, and her mother died of consumption a few years later. A girl had few options, and finding no employment, aside for singing in the choir of a work called, *Joseph*, and seeing that her equally aged lover could not provide for her or protect her, Marie married Alain Dorval, an elderly actor, when she was fifteen, but the marriage only lasted for five years before Alain's death, and left Marie with two children. Thus at twenty, to support her family, Marie began acting in provincial stage or traveling companies, and barely scraped by for a decade, a period that featured her in the role of Fanchette in *Le Mariage de Figaro*, in the comic opera at Nancy, and other high-drama roles. She used a single white dress all of her parts for years to save money. Her first success only came in 1827 in the play of a radical liberal writer, previously imprisoned for sedition in his plays and novels, Victor Henri-Joseph Brahain du Cange, or simply ducange, *Trente ans, ou la vie d'un joueur* (*Thirty years, or the life of a player*). The average salary for Parisian artists in various disciplines was 5,000 francs per year, with those at the top, like Balzac and Hugo, earning around 10,000 francs, a sum that at her peak Marie surpassed working all gigs that came her way and making up to 15,000 francs per year, as if to make up for all the years she spent struggling without returns. A string of successes brought her to the attention of one of the most prolific vaudeville play writers of her time, and also a theater and political columnist, Jean-Toussaint Merle, who was only a bit over a decade older than her. Their paths crossed because Jean had served as the Director of the Theatre de la Porte-Saint-Martin in Paris in the years leading up to Marie's first major theatrical success. After two years of marriage to Merle, in 1831, Marie was as physically ill by the arrangement as the heroine of *Indiana*, and this was when Marie met George.

At that moment, Marie was once again acting in radical plays. One of these was Victor Hugo's *Marion Delorme*, about an actual historical courtesan, and which was censored out of the theater after the first performance in 1831 by King Charles X. The second play Marie was simultaneously involved in might have been a real-life reenactment of the first. Dorval got the leading part of Adele in Alexander Dumas' *Antony*, which premiered in May of 1831, by agreeing to a love affair with the author, who was also courting her acting rival, Mademoiselle Mars, for the role, but the latter later dropped out, leaving the job to Dorval. The play was as controversial as Hugo's, because it had adultery as its central plot, but it wasn't banned.

It was in May of 1831, during the phenomenal performance of Dumas' *Antony*, that George was first deeply impressed with Marie's performance. It was her first year struggling to make it as an artist in Paris, and she was working to sell her first novels, editing for pennies at *Le Figaro*. Since Marie had been involved in extramarital affairs across her two marriages, as she frequently had to give herself to win the best parts, and found lovers to entertain her or to give her gifts her husbands could not afford, she was particularly honest and emotional in this performance. The audience reacted by becoming ecstatic and shouting, and fainting, and screaming with joy and terror. Marie's style of acting was to portray extreme excitement, both on the sad and happy notes of the performance. When she portrayed her anxiety over losing Antony, she twisted her face in agony, and fell to the stage in horror, throwing her hands up, and writhing her whole body with the most frightful agitation. When she pronounced her lines, she screeched them out to hide her husky voice. She also rolled her r's with pounding stress because she wanted every syllable to be heard in the back of the theater. In the final death scene, her face broke out in such a torrent of tears, and her hands flew in such over-exaggerated tragic gestures, that George was amazed that this same actress had just laughed symphonically at the beginning of the same play.

It is very uncommon to go to the theater and see an actor that invests their emotions and bodies entirely in the performance. Most actors are visibly laughing at themselves through their onion-induced tears, or are saddened by the role they are playing when they are supposed to be overjoyed. To be believable, actors frequently have to choose roles that perfectly reflect their own turmoil and feelings. If the part fails to match the actor's state of mind, both fail to convince the audience of their dramatic reality. Modern films frequently allow actors to remain stoic across the story, as they merely react to physical challenges, like car chases and monsters that threaten them. If an actor is allowed to show tears, fear or other intense emotions, these are typically in response to experiencing real physical pain, as they are thrown in a bucket of ice water, or hang by their fingers off a rooftop. When they show happiness, they are either engaging in ecstatic sexual intercourse, or eating chocolate. The camera looks too closely at the actor's face and can detect all signs of emotion, so anything but a blank stare can betray an emotion that contradicts the required feeling in that dramatic plot point. At the time when Marie played Adele, the audience was not a foot from her face, but was further than a few rooms away. This meant that actresses could perform repetitive gestures and general facial expressions that conveyed the intended emotion without becoming lost in the emotion themselves. But, Marie was too personally invested in the parts of courtesans and cheating wives that she was playing in this period for it to be possible for her to simply throw her hands around mechanically, without actually feeling the meaning of the tragic words she was uttering.

As a writer, George was amazed to see this much emotion infusing another writer's play. If this was one of her plays, she would have wanted just that level of intensity on the stage. She was also amazed at the emotional response she felt to Marie's tears and movements. She did not scream or faint, but she felt her face flush and cool to the movements Marie was playing, as if she was executing a finely tuned and precise sonata. The acting nearly overpowered the brilliant lines Dumas had written, so that it wasn't clear if it was the actress or the play writer that were pulling the strings, or caused the audience to erupt in profuse applause at the end. George took Jules' hand and squeezed it with passion when Marie fell after being stabbed with a knife in the final act. After the applause had died, she wanted to go back stage to check if Marie was all right. She knew that she wasn't actually deadly injured, but she wondered if Marie was traumatically hurt emotionally by running through all those ups and downs. It would not have been difficult for George to have gained access back stage as she was already in the same literary circles with Dumas, but she resisted and instead took a carriage with Jules to his room. She began kissing him aggressively in the carriage, as if she was starving and needed sustenance from his embrace. Their intercourse went on for hours, as George could not reach a release to the ecstasy she was feeling. George had not had a single partner that was concerned with her satisfaction or release, and even if Jules was a more dexterous lover, and his fingers were a bit more nimble than most, the scratching and biting was not concentrated in the place that would have brought George out of her maddening frustration. They spent four hours wrapped up together, and rolling between the bed, the carpet, and the window, until Jules deadly exhausted having reached climax half-a-dozen times. He was pale to the point of being bluish-white. His thin arms could barely get off the bed. He lay there at an odd angle across the bed, nearly suffocating as he couldn't move his mouth up from the pillow enough so that it would get adequate air. Meanwhile, George was nudging him with her big toe, fully awake, and more frustrated and energetic than ever. George turned and crawled over to see Jules' face. He had closed his eyes, and had passed out.

George folded her head onto her arms, and sat there for a few moments, contemplating if she could go to sleep. She decided that no amount of rum would be enough to knock her out, so she put on a silky nightshirt, and sat down at a small table. She dipped her pen in the inkwell, and looked down at a blank, beige piece of paper. She thought about writing a scene for the novel she was working at the moment, perhaps a clandestine meeting between lovers, but glancing over at Jules' body on the bed made her lost interest in further reflecting on such encounters that night. Suddenly, as she glanced out of the window at the black night outside, she recalled the performance she had seen that evening, and all the other actors, the words, and the aristocratic audience faded, and she just saw Marie flying across the stage, as if she was running on coals in Dante's

Hell. There was only one string of words that belonged on the piece of paper in front of George:

Dear Mme. Dorval:

I was at your performance of Antony *earlier today. It was the most magnificent and stunning interpretation of Dumas' words that I could have imagined. Dumas is lucky to have found an actress that could capture the soul of his piece with such intense emotion. I have frequented many shows in Paris, but I have never seen an actress as dedicated, and passionate about her craft than you are. Thank you for putting all of yourself into the act, and making me feel more vibrantly alive than I have felt in a decade. This is why I am in Paris, trying to make it as a writer, to inspire violent feelings in my readers. I hope that if I ever write a play that will find a producer, you will do me the honor of acting in it. If you have a few extra moments, and you would like to amuse yourself a bit, I hope that you will visit me in my garret, so that we can discuss the theater, art, love, and all the things that you would make a delight by your mere presence.*

Once again, thank you for your brilliant performance.

Yours truly and fully,

George Sand/ Aurore Dudevant

Once she finished this letter, and put it with the stack of letters that was due to be sent out on the following morning, George finally felt relief of the tension that was tightening her chest, and she went over to the bed, turned onto her side, in the corner that Jules wasn't occupying and promptly went to sleep.

In a couple of days, when George was chatting in her garret with Jules, Marie ran into the living room, fluttered right up to George and threw her arms around George's neck, exclaiming: "Here I am!"

George was amazed by the abruptness of this encounter, which made her giddy with glee, as if a character of a fantasy had flown out of the page and was kissing her cheek. George flushed red, as she studied Marie's adorable slip, and the strange broken feather at the top of her hat, which bobbed as if it had broken off amidst Marie's run across Paris to her apartment without Marie realizing that an accident had happened.

"Mme. Dorval! What an amazing surprise! Please have a seat," George pointed to a chair, and Marie flopped down into it, inhaling a gulp of air that she had been missing along her climb up five flights of stairs.

"It's such a delight to meet another woman artist! Aren't there few of us in Paris? And your friend, who is he?" she said pointing with her thin, tiny finger at Jules, who was surprised by the meeting, as George did not tell him she had written to Dorval.

"This is my friend, Jules Sandeau, or the Jules Sand that I'm writing with."

"Splendid, it's wonderful to have somebody to work with. Are you too married?"

"No, dear me, I'm married to Casimir Dudevant. Jules still has his liberty."

"Isn't it wonderful to be young and at liberty?! Well, you two simply must join me and my family for dinner Sunday night. They would really enjoy meeting a couple of Parisian artists."

"It would be a much greater delight for us to be in your company," George said, fluttering her eyelashes.

They chatted a bit longer, and then Marie flew off, saying that she had a rehearsal that afternoon. George and Jules attended the dinner on Sunday, and it flew by in interesting conversations between Jean-Toussaint Merle, Marie, George, Jules, and the couple's three children, two of whom were also young actresses. At the end of the evening, Marie invited George to visit her on her own at a time she knew her husband, Jean, would be away at a newspaper office, the children would be at school or with tutors, and the staff would be taking their afternoon break. She did not invite Jules to accompany George on this second visit, and George did not think to invite him.

Marie was sitting in a thin dress, which accentuated all of her abundant curves, with her enormous eyelashes and giant blue eyes, on the edge of her bed when George entered. Marie pointed for George to sit on the bed next to her. They talked for a long time about their lives, youths, travel, different types of theatrical troops, and the best way to captivate an audience in a comedy or at a tragedy. George was intoxicated by this conversation, and the smell of lilacs and roses that cluttered dozens of vases across this spacious room. She leaned back against a stack of pillows and looked up at Marie, who turned around and propped herself by the elbows on the bed, her luscious breasts pressed firmly by the fabric of the bed. She threw off her little shoes and dangled her thin feet in the air, as if she was once again a fifteen years old girl. George looked over at Marie, listened to her ringing laugh, watched her back curving slightly with each giggle. And suddenly, as if she was tasting an irresistible ice, George bent down and kissed Marie on her forehead. Marie trembled with pleasure, and pulled herself up till her lips were on a level with George's. They kissed tenderly, and both felt as if for the first time the kiss felt perfect against their lips, as both of their lips were thick, but soft, and the skin was of the same material, and had the same sweet taste. Marie reclined against the bed, and George moved towards her face on her elbows and continued the kiss, massaging one lip at a time, and then gently pecking both lips together, then slowly moving in tiny kisses all across Marie's face, and chin, and forehead, and hair, and neck, and focusing on an erogenous zone, the one that she herself preferred to be kissed, but was kissed too infrequently without directions. They took turns kissing each other and caressing the other's skin, and their dresses fell off, like flowers past their bloom. They dived under the sheets, and wrapped up in an embrace, and then started kissing breasts, and finally kissed clitorises, and focused in those areas for an hour each, until they erupted in trembles, and sighed as all their frustrations and worries were swept away in the ecstasy.

After they lay back, resting for a few minutes, they chatted a bit more, and then with a peck on the lips, George stood up, got dressed, helped Marie to get dressed and headed home, as Marie's family was about to return. Their affair lasted in this calm and ecstatic way for over a decade, as both of them found just the satisfaction that was missing from their relationships with men. Neither of them got involved with other women because there was nothing missing from their erotic affair. Both of them continued their stormy relationships with men, but they moved between men as if moving between decorative arrangements, while despite Marie's occasional screaming tantrums, and George's moody silences, they had found ideal mates in each other, and could not imagine severing their personal and sexual relations.

Because this affair lasted for nearly two decades, it is surprising that critics have doubts to this day if an affair took place. Marie and George were discrete, and without servants, friends or family seeing them in a passionate embrace, the enormous quantities of time they spent together could be explained as friendly visits. The rumors about them started because their male partners, and others, who were involved in a complex web of sexual relationships that made up the Romantic Movement, were jealous of the knot between them, as it was the strongest of their entanglements, and hurt the prides of those others who could not figure out how they were deficient. One of these jealous lovers was Alfred de Vigny, who started seeing Marie at around the same time as George because Marie was in a romantic mood that year and flew on rendezvous not only with George, but also with a few other men, of whom Alfred was the most persistent. The second jealous lover stemmed from Marie's participation in Victor Hugo's *Marion Delorme*, wherein, similarly to indulging Dumas to participate in his play, Marie also indulged Hugo's lust.

Hugo went on to other mistresses, which included Juliette Drouet, who was fond of intrigue and gossip, and who would have moved a theater to keep Hugo in her embraces. Hugo himself helped Juliette to spread rumors about George and Marie because he was outraged that a critic called Janin had called George's over-dramatic *Indiana* the *best* book ever written, and he thought that this was preposterous when it was compared with his great novel, *Notre Dame*, or equivalent to calling it a "whore," in comparison to George's legitimate wife of a novel. The circle of friends to which George belonged plotted revolutions and love affairs with the same focused strategic intensity, and gossiping about who was involved with whom on any given week was both essential in conversations among friends, and also cause for violent outburst and even duels, as George was soon to learn.

Troubles started descending on George Sand on all sides after 1832. Her son, Maurice, began studying in college and she was appalled when she inspected his dormitory by the fact that his used uniform caused a skin infection, and the lack of chamber pots and prohibitions on relieving oneself outside sickened him. George took him to her apartment, and was amazed to find that he had taken after her, enjoying sedentary studying and art, without the need to go out to enjoy himself in Paris.

At the same time, George once again felt a glum mood descending on her, and she wrote in *Lelia* about an ornamental tomb and fountain under cypress trees at Ormesson, a place she visited shortly after her marriage. This simple scene brought tears to George's eyes as she wrote it because she was reflecting about the mad jumps between different men she had made in recent years while trying to escape her marriage, without being able to actually cut her marital ties.

The attacks against George's character began about a year after the positive wave of critical reception. The first item to hit the news was that George was actually Aurore, a woman, and this outraged all of French society worse than if they had found out that she was an anarchist. Then, lesbianism rumors spread, and suddenly she was some kind of a sexual radical. Then, everybody was outraged that she was expressing her alliance with German assassins with her name, and it really seemed that George was a republican revolutionary that was running amok and writing scandalous fiction. Even George's mother wrote to her to criticize her outrageous morals, sending some of the most outrageous critical notes that George hadn't found on her own to her attention.

The worst blow for George was when on March 2nd, she found Jules in an uncomfortable position, deep within his washerwoman at his tiny Rue de l'Universite flat, which hardly allowed the space for such embraces on top of the rusted sink. George was not exactly committed to Jules at the time, so she withdrew, shrugging her shoulders, but Jules shouted after her, "No! It was just one time! It doesn't mean anything!"

"I just don't want to play second fiddle with a man who is involved with the help again. I mean Casimir might have been with every maid at Nohant. It just sickens me to think about you in the same... positions."

"I can't lose you over this! I'll kill myself first!" Jules shouted, as George continued her descent down the stairs to the exit.

At that moment those words were empty and ridiculous. Why would a healthy man with so many young and attractive washerwomen at his disposal kill himself because he has lost an older partner, who was not only married, but otherwise involved as well? But, as George tossed in her bed that night she started to worry that there might be some truth to the threat. Perhaps, she had underestimated the influence she had on Jules. They had been drifting apart since he declined to publish with her, so George felt miles away from him emotionally, but perhaps Jules did not have a heart that bounced back as readily as hers. George had suffered too many heartbreaks in her first years to feel the blow of loss as deeply as most sane and well-brought-up people of both genders. Her heart was similar to the chest of a prize-fighter who has been hit in the chest thousands of times, and who had built up muscles that were actually nearly as strong, and more resilient than stone, which allowed him to be hit there repeatedly after the first few injuries, without further serious damage. Marie was made out of a similar material, which allowed them to chat about the crazed men they were seeing, without becoming jealous. So, that morning, George wrote to Marie and told her to watch over Jules, who she assumed would go to Marie for help to try and reconcile the flame of their relationship. George hoped that Marie would mother little Jules, who was still at school after all, and she told Marie about his suicide threat. But, before going to Marie Dorval for mothering, Jules did indeed attempt suicide via a dose of acetate of morphine. The attempt failed because he vomited it, and shortly thereafter Jules went to Italy to recover. The trip actually helped Jules to clear his head, and he did not make attempts to rekindle their romance, and this made George curious to see Italy with its miraculous curative powers.

Chapter 14

Duels, Infidelity, and Alfred de Musset

Of all of George Sand's love affairs, the one with Alfred de Musset was the most traumatic, passionate, and affectionate, and it
left a deep impact not only on the remainder of both of their
lives, but also on their families, and on the literature that they left behind.

A year before George began her literary and political work in Paris,
in June of 1830, Alfred was a twenty years old dandy *fashionable*, with
bright blue eyes and fine blond hair, dressed in a silky waistcoat, elegant
black top hat, and velvet revers. He met a married aristocratic lady at one

of the gambling tables he frequented. He had a few affairs prior to this one, but he found that the mature age of the woman, her experience, and the nobility that spoke through her manners, words and actions drove him mad with desire. She was slightly consumptive, but it only added a tragic paleness to her skin, and enlarged her eyes in contrast with her thin face. On the night they met, Alfred walked her to her carriage, and then they took a trip around Paris. She succumbed to his advances, as he was young, beautifully dressed, finely cologned, and certainly more excited about the encounter than her elderly husband. They had a few nights together in Musset's apartment, before he escorted her once back to her house, when her husband wasn't there. At the doorstep he found another gentleman his own age, who was waiting for the object of Musset's affection. Musset was outraged as she told him not to make a scene, but opened the carriage's door, clearly showing that he was within and upset by another man's presence.

"Who may I ask are you?" Alfred asked, stepping out of the carriage.

"Count de Rhine, and who do I have the pleasure of speaking with?"

"Alfred de Musset."

"Am I interrupting something? I thought I was here to give you a music lesson. If you are otherwise engaged, I can come another time…"

"No, no, Alfred was just dropping me off."

"I beg your pardon!"

She nearly pushed Musset back into the carriage, and told the driver to take him elsewhere, and went back to the Count, taking him by the arm, and leading him into her house.

It suddenly became clear to Alfred that the lady in question was toying with him simply because she hoped to explain her amorous interests, and to arouse some jealousy in this rival suitor, who might not have otherwise been aware that when she invited him for a music lesson, she was really interested in a tete-a-tete. Thinking about the depth of his betrayal in the carriage that night, Alfred was taken with a seizure that left him rigid as if he was dead for at least a minute, and when he recovered he saw red, and wanted to run back to her house, have his way with her for the last time and then cut them both to pieces.

Alfred was one of those men who never learned to suppress primitive violent urges. Sexual desire came to him with violent physical reactions that suppressed his ability to logically evaluate the best course of action to gain what he wanted. This tendency towards animalistic grabbing and seizing is common among men who have indulged in alcohol or mind-altering drugs for a lengthy period of time, as they are used to always being in a daze of confusion, where they only have the strength of mind and body to response with their muscles and teeth. Somebody insults them, and they might actually run up and bite them on the nose simply because it was the first thing that came to mind.

On that particular occasion, he was already too far from the rival and from the object of his desire to plunge at them with a knife, and after he slept off his alcoholic rage, he simply put the affair behind him, but was left with a scar on his heart which was preventing him for marrying, put him to womanizing, and was inspiring great works of art, as only one of his poetry collections was published before this early tragic love affair, and the rest of his poetry, plays and novels followed it.

Three years after this unsuccessful love affair, Alfred was as dandily dressed as ever, sampling ices with a group of his romantic writer friends at the Café Tortoni, which was also a favorite meeting place for George, who on this occasion happened to be there as well, and as their two tables had several members who knew each other, Charles Saint-Beuve suggested a merging, and before long they were all chatting about the political and artistic news of the day. Victor Hugo, who was sitting at George's table, was at first horrified at this invitation, as Charles had recently had an affair with his wife, but soon he recalled the positive review Charles had given him years before this incident that led to a catapulting of his fame, and he decided to endure the trial.

Meanwhile, Charles chatted away, as if unaware of this awkward coincidence, and introduced Alfred to George, saying: "Here is the great writer of *Indiana*, and here is the applauded author of *A Spectacle in a Chair*. I'm sure you are familiar with the other's works, and will have an interesting time discussing them." Charles then turned to a couple of other members of the party that he thought should be introduced, and explained who they all were. Alfred knew what George's name must be, but George had to get Alfred to give his with some guile. He happened to have a copy of the poetry collection in question with him, and he gave it to her. She reviewed it, reading the first poem, "The Reader," which ended with:

> If you dislike it or not, it will close without a rancor;
> A boring show is quite common,
> And you will see mine without leaving your chair.

With an introduction like this, George simply had to read the rest, so she asked Musset if she could borrow it, and since it was uncommon to find a lady who was this interested in his poetry, and who might have offered serious literary criticism of his work, he gave it to her with delight, saying that she could keep the copy. It was not obvious to either of them at that moment that they were destined to start an affair. George was always around intelligent men, and tried to behave casually with most, as one of the chums. Slipping from friendship into a sexual relationship typically involved a good deal of effort on the man's part, and Alfred was too much of a womanizer to consider making a great effort with any one woman.

**

Sometime after the initial meeting between George and Alfred, in April of 1833, George was writing the final pages of *Lelia*, and was reflecting if she was truly a lesbian and that she could not be satisfied with men. In addition, she thought she might have lost her ability to love, or if the muscles she had to develop over her heart to survive the loss of Aurelien and Jules were now so thick that while she could perform the motions in an affair, she could no longer let herself slip into the tide of love.

After the failed June Revolution, George's republican club transitioned into meeting at salons, instead of at the small restaurant they used to plot their political maneuvers. Those who were members of the club before remained, but they were also joined by members of the current administration, and by other members of the liberal Parisian society who might not have been revolutionaries, but enjoyed meeting rebellious writers and social thinkers. They met in the homes of some of the wealthier members, and sat in a semi-circle in velvet and gilded chairs, sipping on tea, eating pastries, and chatting on much lighter topics, while solidifying alliances. One of the new members brought in was Prosper Merimee, who at this time served as the private secretary to the minister of finance, Comte d'Argout, and later wrote a novel that was turned into an opera that was inspired inpart by George Sand, *Carmen*. Merimee was a generalist, who dabbled in everything from novel and play writing, to archeological excavation, to historical, linguist, and folkloric research, and finally semi-professional womanizing.

George was among only three other women at one particular salon, and Merimee had already seduced two of the other women, and made an unsuccessful attempt on the third. Thus, he gradually made his way towards her chair and sat down beside her. Seeing a handsome thirty years old bureaucrat sit next to her, George was curious to learn more, so she struck up a conversation immediately, and they quickly found many common interests. When he mentioned his name, George recalled hearing it before among her friends, and she knew that a couple of them would be interested in bringing him into their close circle, so she invited Merimee to with a group of them at the Opera that weekend for the showing of Giacomo Meyerbeer's *Robert the Devil* (*Robert le Diable*), one of the first and best native Parisian operas, and one that deals with a Faustian deal with the Devil over a marriage. George and Merimee sat in a box full of George's chums, and George gave Merimee a detailed commentary on the piece during the intermission, as she had seen that opera a couple of times before. In contrast to George's usual habits, she brought Solange, five at the time, with her to this performance because she thought she should begin exposing her to the arts. Solange had fallen asleep in the Second Act, and despite being awakened and fed a pastry during the intermission, she went back into a solid slumber, and Merimee had to carry her on his shoulders down the grand staircase of the grand Opera house. Merimee was a perfect gentleman, escorting George and Solange home, and scheduling a new social meeting with George at her door. They met a few times in the next two weeks, a time when they built a friendship and a working relationship that lasted for a couple of decades after this point.

As if recalling that George was a woman, Merimee suddenly decided to return to his initial idea and to attempt seducing her. He asked George to accompany him on a walk along the Seine, and she was delighted by this proposition, as she typically avoided walking alone in that part of Paris, and Merimee's escort would allow her to see the river under the stars. They strolled along a walkway by the Seine for some time in silence, studying the river and the distant buildings. Soon they came within sight of the Ile de la Cite, an island that made George think about Venetian islands, where Jules went to forget her. They strolled along the Pont Neuf bridge onto the Ile, studying the Notre Dame, the Louis IX's Sainte-Chapelle, and the Conciergerie prison, all of which looked sinister in the light of the dim lamps, and recalled the night of the June Revolution in George's memory. They went back along the bridge, and back along the Seine, headed towards George's residence. George was wearing her masculine student uniform. The walk had energized her, and she felt alive and vibrant, and she started chatting with Merimee about architecture and excavations, but Merimee gently guided the conversation away from these sober topics and onto a few compliments about the great shape she was in, which got George onto her good old horse Colette, and they made a plan to go riding when they would both be in the countryside. Merimee then once again started guiding the conversation back to the point he was getting at: "What I was trying to say was that you look beautiful in the moonlight."

"No, in what I'm wearing, I doubt it."

"Indeed you do look better in that outfit than most socialites look in the best dresses of the court."

"How democratic of you."

"So, I was wondering if you are disposed to perhaps engage in a tete-a-tete?"

"All right, I am disposed, if that's your wish, and it will give you pleasure. But, you should know that with where my mind is at the moment, I will not respond pleasurably to it."

"Why don't we attempt it, and perhaps it won't be as bad as you suppose."

"Very good, here we go," George said, and they made their way at a steady pace to her apartment. George was hungry, so she asked for her servant to bring in some supper from the regular neighboring restaurant that she used, and within half an hour it was delivered. During that intermission, George went back to chatting about archeological digs with Merimee, and he easily slipped into that discussion, also forgetting about the anticipated intercourse. They ate supper, still in the midst of this debate, and then George took Merimee into her room, and had her maid undress her in an armchair, just as she would have if she was a soldier undressing in a changing room full of other boys. Merimee tried to see George as a seductive woman, but there was something jarring about all this, as in his two decades of womanizing he had never seen a woman behave without any coquetry whatsoever. The maid had finished, and left, and George was now sitting, completely naked and with her hair down, in an armchair, looking at him quizzically, uncertain what he was waiting for. To explain the next move symbolically, George got up and got under the sheets. Merimee started to feel as if he was the last horse out of the stalls at a race, so he took of his boots, and all the other layers of his clothing, and walked over to the bed in the nude and also got under the sheets. The time that had elapsed and Merimee's strange hesitation made George completely limp, and she had never been less attracted to a human before, or since. Then, instead of kissing her, Merimee attempted to stir her by caressing her breasts. George could see his enormous black eyebrows in the candlelight, and she realized that he was only a year older than her, but that his body had aged more than hers and that the wrinkles under his eyes, and the thinning hair over his gigantic eyebrows were interesting features in a study of character, but were not the sort of thing somebody wanted to see amidst sexual intercourse. She thought about Marie's soft lips, and her sculpted breasts, and then she looked down at Merimee and recalled seeing his genitals, as he was walking over to the bed, and she could not have reached down to help Merimee prepare for the act even if she was a courtesan. It would have been rude and would have ruined a building friendship to have told Merimee about her predicament, so she just lay there waiting to see what would develop. Merimee attempted caressing George's thighs, but did not feel his organ rising to the occasion. He had a similar thought process to George's, and he also didn't want to say something rude that might have ruined a political alliance, so without saying much of anything he acted as if the caressing had fully satisfied him, nodded, said that he had an early morning meeting, and left George alone in her room, where she fell asleep in a few minutes.

That morning George woke up laughing, recalling the events of the previous night. It was the most ridiculous sexual encounter she had ever had, but because it was extremely ridiculous, it was a show she wanted to see again to understand what had happened. She also felt bad for Miremee, and did not want him to think that she did not appreciate his attempts, or that she found to be unattractive. She wrote a letter inviting him to make a second attempt that evening. To which Miremee replied with a short note, *You have an incurable desire to please everybody you meet. You should collect yourself, and focus on your own desires.*

This note struck a chord with George, as it made her realize a problem that might have been the cause of her numerous affairs, without finding one that pleased her fully. This line of thought led her to Marie Dorval, so she went over to her place and described what had transpired. Marie only saw humor in the events that George detailed, and the two were rolling with laughter for an hour, before George departed with a sense of relief. Their shared laughter implied to Marie that George considered the affair to be a farce that could be shared, if not with the public at-large, then with their small circle of friends. So, when on the following morning her lover, Alfred de Vigny, entered her boudoir and began caressing her breasts with his hands, she couldn't hold it back and blurted out the story George had described. Alfred laughed so hard that he could not restart his advances for at least an hour and managed to proceed only after shooting a glass of whiskey. Later that day Alfred had lunch was Alexander Dumas, and the two discussed the two plays they had out in the Parisian theater, *Stello* for Vigni and *The Tower of Nesle* (*La Tour de Nesle*) for Dumas. When they were talking about the Tower of Nesle, Dumas mentioned that he had first seen it walking along the Seine, and this made Alfred burst out in rollicking laughter, but puzzled Dumas, as they were discussing melodramatic historical semi-tragedies, and it seemed there was no logical cause for the laughter. Seeing Dumas' quizzical look forced Alfred to confess what he was thinking about when he heard Seine mentioned, and Dumas immediately pictured the scene and laughed until tears came to his eyes. That evening Dumas went to the same salon where Merimee and George initially met. George was sitting on one side of the room, and Merimee on the other, and both were attempting to maintain serious philosophical conversations without glancing at the other. Dumas was sitting in the middle of the room, and as usual he was surrounded by a circle of his collaborators and admirers. Finally, he couldn't stand talking about anything else, and he delivered an abridged version of the story to the dozen writers and politicians around him, who all bubbled in suppressed giggles, as anything louder would have been highly unusual at that particular respectable salon. As a punch line, Dumas added, "Merimee is five feet, five inches…" The story quickly spread across both sides of the salon, and suddenly George heard the punchline repeated in the seat behind her. Immediately realizing what the joke was about, she initially felt an urge to jump into the Seine from embarrassment, but she managed to compose herself, and simply excused herself and went home.

George did not immediately retaliate against Dumas for spreading rumors about her publically, but it was in the back of her mind across the following months before it boiled over in a major incident. Meanwhile, on June 15th, George once again met with Musset at the apartment of Florestan Bonnaire, a financial backer of *Revue des Deux Mondes*, and thus an affiliate of her benefactor, Francois Buloz. George sat next to Musset and relayed her thoughts about the poetry book he gave her. On this occasion, George was wearing a bolero with a gem-studded dagger dangling from her waist belt. Once the two were settled in a comfortable conversation, Musset asked what Sand did with the dagger that she came armed with. She explained that she usually dressed in a man's attire, but since she couldn't do that for this occasion, when she was meeting with Florestan, she needed the dagger to protect her in place of a boring and expensive servant. This exchange made George blush, as she suddenly felt bad about displaying a weapon at a friendly dinner, so by the time they finished drinking coffee, she had hidden the dagger out of the guests' sight. Musset justly took this to mean that she was lowering her defenses and might reciprocate if he made an advance, so he kissed the hand that she extended him upon parting for a handshake.

The memory of George's tanned hand and her admiration for his poetry stayed with Musset, so when he got to his family house on Rue de Grenelle Saint-Germain, he copied the following verses from a poem he was writing, *Rolla*:

Do *you* regret the age when, in majestic grace,
Fair heaven amid the gods made earth her dwelling-place;

When Venus Astarte, child of the mighty sea,
Rose from the bitter wave in virgin purity?
The time, when drifting nymphs lay on the river's breast,
And with their wanton laughter vexed the lazy rest
Of fauns stretched out to sleep upon the reedy shore?

He sent the poem to her, and when the two met in a couple of days, he showed her the rest of the book, which was a dark philosophical work about a debauching man that commits suicide for a moment of purity, to escape his sinful existence, a complete contrast with the poem about the chair that he had shown her earlier. Because George was reflecting on glum subjects herself at the time, she suddenly felt a strong emotional response to Musset that she thought she might never feel again, and invited him to visit her at her apartment at night on June 18th.

George had been reflecting about what went wrong with Merimee and she decided to attempt a bit of coquetry. She sent her servants away after they let Musset in. He walked into her room to find her in a pastel negligee, sitting cross-legged on a cushion, puffing on a pipe of Bosnian cherry-wood, and listening to a few exotic birds twittering. Musset, in his turn, had heard the rumors about her encounter with Merimee in that same room, and he decided to attempt gallantry to match her attempt at coquetry. He dropped dramatically onto one knee before her and made a stage gesture of amazement looking down at the Arab babouches on her tiny feet. He made an extremely slow gesture with the tips of his fingers and touched the edge of one of the babouches, as if to inspect the fabric. George felt the extremely light pressure on her toe, and smiled, anticipating further progress. Musset pressed more of his hand onto the soft shoe, but at this moment Gustave Papet, the wealthy physician from George's district, and Gustave Planche, the Swiss poet, walked into the room, unannounced, as there were no servants in the main living room to greet them.

To explain what happened next it should be noted that George and Gustave Planche had a brief sexual affair a couple of months earlier. George was embarrassed by this surprise, but she thought that the affair with Planche was like a handshake between friends, and that he must have moved on to other engagements, as she did. When Planche fell on her couch and stretched out, as if he was at a harem, George started suspecting that he was not happy to find a rival at George's place at that hour of the night. Musset simply thought that Planche was awfully rude to be lying back in that fashion in front of aristocratic company. Suddenly, Musset recalled where he had seen Planche before. Musset was seducing a young girl at a ball and kissed her shoulder briefly during a waltz, and Planche had been in a neighboring pair of waltzers and spread the rumor that Musset had no shame and was kissing shoulders in public.

"What are you doing sprawling on a lady's couch? I thought you were concerned about public manners," Musset asked, outraged.

"What are you doing sitting in a yoga position on a lady's floor?" Planche retorted.

Musset suddenly realized that instead of getting up, he had sat down cross-legged on the carpet next to George's feet. He now stood up, and sat in a nearby chair.

"I was just admiring the carpet. I plan on buying from the same merchant for my room."

"Which merchant is that?"

Musset looked at George for some help, but she twisted her eyebrows, not wanting to get involved.

Planche took some chocolates out of his pocket, and stretched them towards Musset. "Here I think you'll like these. We just had a whole bunch of these and it was inspiring."

Musset thought that this was a peace offering, and decided that since they were George's friends, it was best to accept it. He broke off a couple pieces of chocolate and sat back down in his seat, eating them slowly. It was an odd type of chocolate that he had never had before. As he was chewing them, he wondered why Planche had not offered George any. George did not appear keen on trying them, and she had just temporarily left the room to put on a coat over her revealing outfit.

They chatted a bit about different opera musical styles, and about the coming age of romantic poetry, when suddenly Musset started to feel violent stomach cramps. In a few moments he was stretched out on the second couch, just like Planche.

"Now who's casual in social circles," Planche joked looking over at him, writhing in pain.

Meanwhile, the cramps were only getting worst, but Musset could not imagine asking George to use her restroom, so despite nearly passing out upon standing up, he excused himself and went home, where he experienced violent diarrhea.

"The doctor was right a couple of those chocolates and there goes three-days' dinners," Planche whispered to Papet, as Musset was leaving the room.

Musset didn't realize that the chocolates were laxatives, but he was embarrassed by the incident, so he stayed away from George for about a week, which turned out to be eventful. During a literary luncheon a couple of days later, Dumas made renewed jokes about George's Merimee affair, with her within earshot, which enraged her. She stormed out, followed by Gustave Planche. They discussed the matter at George's apartment. Planche had heard the Merimee joke that was being passed around, and George filled in the details, explaining how she was offended to have her name mired by Dumas, who was treating the relating of the story as a theatrical performance. Upon Planche's proposal, they went two days later to the offices of the *Revue des Deux Mondes* because Dumas was working there at the time. George stormed in, stood upon Dumas' desk and said,

"I demand an apology this instant!"

"What for?"

"For the rumors you have been spreading about me."

"They are not rumors they are the truth, and I have it on very good sources, all of whom confirm it."

"So you will not retract?!"

"No. I'm not apologizing for relating the truth."

At this point Dumas looked around the office, and saw that a couple dozen of the most respected writers and editors of the day were glaring at him, all having assumed that he was spreading false rumors about George, who appeared to be a victim being gravely offended.

Dumas clearly saw that there was need for decisive action and stormed downstairs, where he found paper and an ink pen and wrote the following letter, which he gave to Planche, as soon as it was done:

Dear M. Planche:

It appears that I am being accused of acting indelicately by speaking the truth. I believe that I acted justly, and that there is no fault in my actions. I feel offended to have been asked to apologize, and since Aurore Dudevant is a lady, and she has brought a gentleman, the above-addressed, Gustave Planche, with her, this seems to indicate that she is demanding to be satisfied and that M. Planche has volunteered to stand for her in the proposed duel. I accept this proposal, and will be available to stand under arms, once M. Planche confirms that he accepts the consequences and makes arrangements for seconds, the time the duel is to take place, and other details.

Truly Yours,

Alexander Dumas

Upon glancing over this note, Planche was about to pummel Dumas with his fists, but the operator of the publication where they were having this exchange, Francois Buloz, separated them, and led Planche out of the building.

George and Planche departed. Planche was a bit white from this encounter, as he was suddenly realizing that Dumas must have been serious about the duel, while in his home Switzerland such threats would have been made in jest. George was also disconcerted about the encounter. She expected an apology, and instead her friend was being threatened with a potential death in a duel. But, there was nothing to do now but go home and return to work. So, they separated and both went home to continue writing their individual projects.

Planche did not come to visit George in this interim as he hoped to convince Dumas that he was not George's lover. Meanwhile, Musset took this opportunity to write to George on June 23rd, alluding to the forthcoming duel lightly, and since a light joke was better than Planche's silence, George agreed to meet with Musset on the next day. The two met in private for a couple of nights, and then Musset took George to the Tuileries Gardens, acting like a perfect gallant gentleman, and making all the gestures and saying all the right words that suggested his cherishing love. This was a unique development for George, who was used to initiating the romance in her relationships, as Musset was taking over as the prancing peacock.

A week passed with Musset and George engaging in an intensifying romance, when George heard the report from Planche that he and Dumas had chosen seconds and weapons for the forthcoming duel. George was surprised that the duel might actually come about, and she wrote to Planche explaining that she was involved with Musset and that it wouldn't be appropriate for Planche to duel for her honor, as they were not involved in an ongoing liaison. Planche was relieved that George saw it that way and he conveyed this message to Dumas, saying that he could duel on George's behalf, but that he was only her *friend*, and not her *lover*. Dumas replied that carrying on with the duel under those circumstances was ridiculous, and that he had clearly misunderstood the relationship between George and Planche, and that if Planche felt it was fitting, he could call Dumas a "fool" in his next *Revue des Deux Mondes* article, as that was clearly the case. Thus, the duel was cancelled, and Planche retreated for some time out of George's life, exhausted from this dramatic incident.

George only needed a couple of weeks to recover from the threat of a duel before it was a minor incident far in the past. After the publication of *Lelia*, George worked non-stop to release five other major novels that year, including *Andrea*, *Jacques* and *Leone Leoni*, some of which were previously finished, but all of which required proofreading, and various other fine touches before they could be released by the printer. This meant strings of business meetings, constant correspondences, and long nights at the writing table finishing these works. It was the most intensive writing year of her life, but she did not take time off across most of it because she was determined to make enough money to become more independent of her husband, who was becoming increasingly hostile as news about her various infidelities were reaching him. When George was sitting down at the table to write a new romance, she started noticing that she felt cold and pragmatic about depicting the affair, and this was highly problematic when she had to depict the intensity of the high-drama romance between a given pairing of lovers. Marie was too involved with de Vigny to offer her the inspiration that she needed to regain her trust in love, and the near-duel with Dumas had frightened away some of the other suitors that were attempting to be near her previously. George wanted to feel less like Lelia and more like her old self, and the only subject that could help her in her research on sexual arousal and loving relationships with men was Alfred de Musset. George wrote to Musset on July 30th, inviting him over in the middle of the night, and the two chatted until dawn, when Musset finally had the bravery to once again attempt getting on his knees before her. He told her that he wanted to experience a pure love, as if he was reciting from *Rolla*, but looking at George with sad eyes, and then he told her about his dreams for writing grand novels about what was at the essence of real love, and how difficult it was to be a romantic in a materialistic and sex-crazed world, and his eyes broke with a couple of tears, as he kissed her hands. The hours they had spent talking intimately had been just what George needed for foreplay, and she felt her body responding to Musset's kisses, and her back arched like a leaf, as he began kissing her cheeks, and she surrendered with joy to this young gentleman, who seemed genially happy to receive her assistance, kindness, and love.

George had a pile of work on her desk, but after a couple of nights with Musset, she pushed it to the side, writing a few brief notes to her editors, asking for extensions, and departed on August 5th, with Musset for the forest of Fontainebleau, traveling down the Seine in a riverboat. At first the country setting brought them together, but then when they were alone on moss of the rock formation of Franchard, Musset suddenly started telling George about another woman who he had brought to that same spot. The mention of another woman brought George into the present, and she suddenly saw that she was a loose woman alone with a womanizer, and that they were involved in yet another affair for both of them. So, when Musset asked her if she wanted to walk together to a place where he found a great echo, George asked to be left alone instead.

As Musset was scaling down the mountain, he realized how his revelation about the other woman must have sounded to George, and he decided to take a drastic dramatic measure to regain her affection. He screamed out in terror, which as he hoped brought George down the mountain to his side. As she was approaching, he began shaking, as if he was having seizures, and George bent down to comfort him. He gradually relaxed his muscles, resting his head on George's thighs.

"What happened?" George asked, frightened by this weakness in a grown gentleman.

"I thought I saw a ghost walking towards me, and it put me a fright."

"Oh, my darling. He's gone now?"

"Yes, you scared him away."

Musset developed this story into his need to be mothered by George over the following week, and she took care of feeding, clothing, and washing him in a way that satisfied her maternal instincts, generated joyful intercourse, and kept them from engaging in any more fights.

On August 15th, Musset and Sand returned to Paris to celebrate the release of Musset's poem, *Rolla*, with the publisher that they shared and a large group of their associates. Planche was there and clearly observed that Musset and George were together, a fact that was confirmed by Marie Dorval, in whom George had confided. Ten days later *L'Europe littéraire* published a piece by Capo de Feuillide that compared *Lelia* with Marquis de Sade because both heroines were full of "mud and prostitution," Planche was personally offended because he previously published a review that said that *Lelia* would, "start a blazing revolution in contemporary literature." Thinking back to the fact that his withdrawal from the duel with Dumas might have led George to fly into Musset's arms instead of his own, Planche challenged Cap de Feuillide to a duel. Unlike the previous occasion, this time Francois Buloz and Emile Regnault were actually invited to act as Planche's seconds, and the group went to a secluded corner of Bois de Boulogne, and even exchanged a few miss-fired shots.

George was kept in the dark about the progression of these events, so both she and Musset were annoyed when they learned about a rival for George's intimacy fighting a duel without consulting either of them. To retaliate, Musset wrote a long "epic" poem poking fun at the duel, where supposedly men fired at each other from six hundred paces and missed melodramatically.

George continued mothering Musset, as he moved out of his parents' house and into hers. They entertained each other by sketching, sharing their writing, and George sang Spanish and Italian operas. One issue that developed early on was that Musset woke up early and began working very gradually and slowly, and George woke up at two in the afternoon, and once she started writing in the evening she worked furiously through the night until she met her extraordinary goals. George was at the peak of her fame, and George's writing schedule was frequently pushed into the night as distinguished guests came over for dinner. On one evening, they were joined by Professor Eugene Lerminier and a member of the British House of Commons, along with Alfred's brother, Paul. Planche wasn't alone among George's friends to play practical jokes on new guests. On this occasion, Alfred dressed up as a maid and was extremely clumsy while serving dinner, even spilling a pitcher of water on Professor Lerminier, all without the guests noticing that he was a man dressed in women's clothing. Cross-dressing was not popular in this period, so people were not likely to look closely when detecting unusual curves, or their lack.

After enough time in Paris for George to have finished and sent to the printer a new book, they once again took a trip for a couple of weeks to the Fontainebleau forest. Yet another month in Paris brought some additional funds, and George decided to splash some of her money on her budding romance, as Musset acted bored in Paris, and she thought a trip to Italy might be just the thing to rekindle their passion. They set out in the middle of the winter, on December 15th of 1833, which was a horrid season to make a sea voyage, or to live in a seaside country, but it was when George had saved enough money, and their relationship reached a breaking point. They took a steamship from Lyon to Avignon, and during this trip George caught fever, which meant that she was barely conscious when Musset pulled her along with him to see Pisa and Camposanto because he was doing research for his new play, *Lorenzaccio*, which was based on Sand's historical notes about the 1537 Conspiracy. George contributed her own knowledge of insurrections and conspiracies to these notes, without explaining to Musset these details, as he was an apathetic moderate, and did not involve himself in the republican plots that George was continually working on. George was still sick when they arrived in Venice's San Marco square in a gondola on the night of January 3rd, but as was her custom since she survived major illnesses as a child, she did not seek medical attention and worked to cure the illness herself, continuing to engage in strenuous travel as if nothing was wrong. Despite the crushing migraines and fever, George was revived by the canals, bridges, and magnificent architecture of Venice. While there were islands with architecture on them on the Seine, here the entire city was within a jump of the water, as there was hardly a building that was not standing near a canal, as the canals were really the streets of the city, used for transportation via boats and gondolas. Looking out of her Hotel Danieli balcony, she saw a gothic church, a small square and a canal below. She could take in this scenery whenever she reached a moment of hesitation in her novel, looking at it for inspiration.

On the morning after their arrival, George felt sick and was both inspired and felt pressured financially to begin writing, so she put paper to pencil. Seeing her starting to write a few lines, Musset threw a fit, as he couldn't imagine how she could plan on staying indoors and writing when they were in Venice, and could spend the day exploring that ancient city. It seemed to him that with only two weeks of planned stay, she could've written her novels on her return to Paris. George, as usual, did not engage in a shouting match, and instead just continued her writing, after briefly expressing her intention and inviting Musset to take in the sights on his own. Bubbling with frustration, Musset rented a gondola and journeyed on his own to the museums, palace and free-standing architecture at the Piazza San Marco, then going over to the island of Lido. Musset's list of places to visit included some of the places he read Byron had visited in Venice before him because he admired that great poet and wanted to follow in his travel footsteps. Thus, he went to the convent of San Lazzaro, the Mocenigo Palace, and the Fenice opera. Then, Musset decided that since Byron had described the beauty and vigor of Venitian women, he had to try them as well, and for this he visited aristocratic salons, where he started flirting with wives, daughters and courtesans alike.

Musset looked like a model from Sandro Botecceli's "The Birth of Venus" at the time, with his clear, soft complexion, blond hair and blue eyes. George looked like a pretty strong young brother of Carmen, the gypsy, with black hair and black eyes, with her hair tied back with a scarlet sash, and smoking too many fine Venitian cigars.

Back at the hotel, George was frustrated that to keep up appearances of the two of them being friends, she had to rent a three-bedroom apartment, so Musset could stay in a separate room. George was writing as quickly as she could, hoping to finish and send in a project to generate additional funds to pay for the unexpected expenses that Musset was running up. Musset's wild run through the "sights" of Venice lasted for around four days, until during an unusual visit that George accompanied Musset on to their hotel's casino, Musset told her that he did not love her any more. With all of her previous lovers, a declaration like this or clear womanizing would have spelled an immediate end to the relationship, but on this occasion George's resolution and her ability to physically get away from Musset were impinged by her fever, and by the fact that he had succeeded in making George feel like the responsible mother of a spoiled child, who had to be supported or he would not manage to survive on the mean streets of Paris. George could not take the next ship out, and leave Musset to dig himself out. She had to stay until their planned return date, and at that point take Musset back to Paris, and deliver him to his parents for their care. The emotional turmoil of having to stay in the same apartment with Musset that she was paying for while he stated his intention to find a new love affair was so traumatic that George's health declined, and on the next day after Musset's confession, George called a doctor in to bleed her, but he clearly was not used to this practice and kept missing the vein, which made George even sicker.

Chapter 15

Mardi Gras and Pietro Pagello

While there were no tests adequate to make a clear diagnosis at the time, the timeline suggests that George caught typhoid in the first days of the steamship trip to Italy on around December 15, which meant that she cycled through all four weeks of the disease's stages by January 15th, when her symptoms cleared. George's fever in early January and attack of dysentery at the end of January suggests that it is also possible that she might have caught typhoid at the beginning of January. The delirium that comes with typhoid can be mild or sever, and clearly George experienced a minor delirium, which seemed relatively normal to her because if you recall the events in her life up until that point, delirious tragedy and euphoria were the normal feelings she experienced across the time she spent working as an aide-de-camp at four for Murat, to assisting the June Revolution, to her suicide attempt in childhood, and through all the other plunges and spikes that make up the fabric of George's life. She had also been sick with rheumatism, skin-insect infections, fevers, cramps, two pregnancies, and an enormous list of other complications, through all of which she kept working on her studies, on her writing, on her singing, and otherwise never slowed down in the face of expected bounds of illness. If she was delirious, she put this delirium into the mad shouts and exclamations of the characters in her novels, and did not yell aloud for Musset or anybody else for help. What is a bit strange is that having drunk the same water and eaten the same food during their steamship trip, Musset only displayed symptoms of the disease on February 4th, and his symptoms began to clear on February 15th, when they are only supposed to worsen based on the standard four-week progression of the disease, as naturally the fever is only supposed to subside after the third week (without antibiotics).

When on January 11th, George called for a doctor from the hospital to come and visit her, she was seen by Pietro Pagello, who was twenty-seven at the time, and whose father was a silk merchant that ran one of the top literary salons in Venice. Pagello was among the top doctors in the region, and he was promoted from being an assistant surgeon at the Hospital of San Giovanni e Paolo in 1834 to being the primary surgeon at the Hospital of Belluno starting in 1862. Still, he did not detect typhoid and only saw a regular fever in George, for which he assisted her with a more precise bleeding than the previous doctor that saw her in Venice could muster. This bleeding might have taken some of the bad blood out of George's system because she returned to writing her novel on the following day.

As George went back to work, after spending a couple of days with her at the Hotel, Musset once again felt the urge to explore Italy, so he left her and went to a show at the French consul, where he met some indulging dancing girls on January 13th. His return to debauchery despite her illness hardened George's heart, and she decided that for the sake of her novel she had to permanently close the door between their apartments.

She had sacrificed other relationships for her art, and when any personal relationship stood in the way of her artistic ambitions, the person always lost, and the demands of her work and art won. Some might think that workaholic and putting art and work first is a tragic character element, but it was the happy solution to George's circumstances. Her personal relationships were always plagued with tragic scarring, as those closest to her betrayed her trust by womanizing, abusing the bottle, assaulting her, and hurting her in varied and surprising ways that always left her emotionally battered. Even in her best friendships and love affairs, the people she was intimate with were unfaithful, manipulative, or had other personal flaws that made them toxic elements in George's life. In contrast, the job of writing romantic novels was consistently satisfying, and always delivered the fruits that it promised, including fame, financial rewards, and emotional satisfaction in creating finely crafted novels. People who never attempt complex book writing or ceiling fresco painting or the various other tasks that consume an artist's whole life, cannot understand how interpersonal love is deflected into love for one's art. In other words, two monkeys are perfectly happy in a jungle today in a family with children, and they love each other, physically and emotionally, as they have intercourse, groom each other's backs, and help find food to keep their members of their family unit fed. But, if one of those monkeys grew up in a situation similar to George's, she would have lived in a broken home where her mother beat her, and then left her with a distant relative monkey, which also beat and abused her, and which then sold her off into marriage for a banana, and this marriage was then interrupted by a gang of other female monkeys with which her intended mate carried on, while she ran away from this "family unit" to find other male monkeys in a distant tree, continuing her search for the right mate across dozens of horrid and abusive mates until her dying days. You might see how for this second hypothetical monkey, lasting "love" can only be found in a romantic novel, and that a love of art and work can be the stabilizing and satisfying constant in a chaotic, mad, and violent world.

Musset was oblivious of the emotional turmoil and final crash that his womanizing and rejection caused George, so on January 15 he went to a masked ball at Baron Gina's Venetian palace, and for the after-show made love in a hooded gondola to an expensive courtesan. After engaging in similar affairs for the next five days, Musset caught a venereal disease, which he let George examine, as she was the doctor between the two. She did not have any other cure to give him, but suggesting that it was time for them to leave and go back to Paris, as their two planned weeks were up. Musset objected that he wanted to finish a poetic book he was working on first, since George had barely seen him touch a pen since they arrived in Venice, she thought obligated to support this sudden isolated burst of creativity, and could not force an artist away from his inspiration.

A week later, Musset was still insisting that he had to write, while he was spending most of his time amidst the revelries in preparation of Mardi Gras, as masked ladies and gentlemen began appearing in the piazza, and some early parties commenced. Musset overindulged and as George was recovering from an attack of dysentery on February 4, Musset's typhoid fever suddenly became apparent.

The experience of taking care of an invalid or somebody deadly ill or insane for a period of two weeks is one that is brutal for an artistic personality. The first challenge is that while having typhoid yourself might not keep you away from your novel, a lover having typhoid can force even the most focused woman to maternal distraction. Alfred would scream in delirium, and George would have to stay by his bedside for hours, even long after he stopped screaming just to make sure that the attack had subsided, and that it would all not take a sudden turn towards disaster. Doctors don't experience a similar problem, as most doctors approach a given illness as something that has to be diagnosed, treated, and then left alone to heal. This is how George approached the many patients she saw as a doctor at Nohant. But, despite being around sick people since she was a child, assisting Deschartres, the bond that Musset forged with her when he asked for her assistance by expressing, uncharacteristic for most men, weakness glued her emotionally to the nest by his side, and threw her into violent depression as she worried he might die. Thus, George could barely write a word and this was the usual cure she took for her ennui, so she was depressed for the entire two weeks without a hope for a cure. George had never allowed herself to feel that much sympathy for any human being in her life, amazingly this included her two children, from whom she could separate for many months without feeling that without her they could reach a tragic end. But, in parallel for this overwhelming maternal death-grip that Musset had on George, this same emotion prevented George from seeing Musset as a lover, or imagining any future sexual intercourse with him. It was as if he became her newborn child and imagining intercourse with him was incestuous and grotesque. In addition, knowing that he was a hopeless womanizer with a venereal disease, meant that engaging in intercourse with him would damage her health, and that engaging in such a close personal link with a man who would be sure to move on to other women upon the first opportunity but who was now the most dear person in the world for her would have been a pain that she could not endure contemplating.

Musset did not see anything grotesque about George's body just at that moment, and he was traveling in a different direction, as her continued care for him spiked his attraction, and he was feverish with desire to grab her and to be as far inside of her as he could get. George did her best to repel his advances, but, on February 10, he was mad enough to jump out of bed completely naked, in front of Dr. Pagello, and to run all over the bedroom, chasing George, grabbing her in his arms, then trying to hold on as she would wring herself out of this embrace, and then running after her again.

"Oh! Give me a kiss or I shall die from wanting you! The fever is a love fever! Come to me my George, my dear, my darling, be with me!"

George and Pagello watched in amazement as Musset managed to keep this up for six hours, varying the running and grabbing with shouting regarding his demands for sex, singing love songs, and convulsing on the floor, the bed, and out on the balcony. At one point, Musset managed to hold onto George long enough to squeeze his lips into hers, and then as he was attempting something that started as a caress of the neck, he began strangling her, with their lips were still locked. Pagello used his student assistant and between George hitting Musset with her free arms, and the two doctors pulling him by the collar of his shirt, they finally wrestled him off her, and subdued him by holding him down by arms, legs and torso to the bed.

Musset's attempt at strangling George was not an isolated incident, but it was the only one that was witnessed by Pagello and his assistant. Musset was the product of extensive abuse of alcohol over at least a decade, together with a malicious and sadistic nature. The illness stripped away his reason, leaving behind the animalistic instinct that came out when he was intoxicated. But, in his delirium he was mistaking George for a rival male animal, and not treating her in a manner which might have convinced a female to permit mating. He was shouting that she was a prude, inexperienced in bed, and he was hitting and wrestling with her as if she stood in his way towards tribe-dominance. The insults, while they appeared to be requests for sexual favors, and reverse-psychological maneuvers to get George to feel bad about falling behind in love making, were really aggressive grunts, barks, and chest-beatings meant to intimidate George into submissiveness. This is where people complicate animalistic instincts. George was a powerful woman as a doctor, a successful professional writer, a matriarch, and various other positions that put her on top of the social hierarchy in contrast with Musset who was comparatively on the bottom. Musset felt that he had to reassert himself and to fight with George for dominance, and this urge was mixed with his need for intercourse with the same party that was his rival. George wrestled with Jules, and rather enjoyed a bit of a struggle between chums, but Musset was too ill for her to attempt beating him up without a guilty conscience. If she was the woman in the interaction, then an aggressive approach called for the survival instinct of kicking the male off her, and yelling for him to go elsewhere. A monkey that does not fight off an overly aggressive mate can become the victim of a serious attack from behind. For all of these reasons, Musset was charging at a rival, and George was retreating from a fight and repelling her mate's violent sexual impulses.

On Mardi Gras' Pancake Tuesday, February 12, as the streets were noisy with party-goers, Musset developed a bronchial inflammation and pneumonia, and started coughing up blood, all frequent accompanying symptoms of typhoid fever. Dr. Pagello took all of the curative measures he could think of, including applying suction cups, and putting cold compresses on his forehead. Musset imagined that the compresses were an attempt to bury him alive under them, so he screamed that he was being murdered. When he was given sedatives, he spat them out because he thought that they were trying to put him to sleep so that they could murder him in his sleep. But, despite Musset's objections, Pagello managed to apply the necessary cures, and on the following day Musset felt better. Pagello must have indeed applied some miraculous cures if he managed to cure in a couple of weeks an illness that usually took a month to clear up, but then he was one of the leading surgeons in Italy.

As Musset was starting to feel better, George felt a weight of responsibility lifting off her, and she suddenly started noticing the handsome Doctor Pagello, who had been assisting her through a couple of the toughest weeks in her life. George had a habit of requiring a new love affair to recover from an old one that she hoped to abandon. She needed to switch addictions, or to find a new pleasure before she could surrender the old one. If Dr. Pagello wasn't there, she might have returned gradually to once again feeling a sexual attraction for Musset, and this might have been a time when she could've enjoyed becoming intimate with him again, diving into a sea of raw passion that was unleashed during the illness. But, George felt that Pagello was a calm, logical venue for her to project the pent up frustration and love, so that she was not investing in a destructive relationship that would rip both Musset and her to pieces, but instead was escaping for Pagello's calmer waters. On the night when Musset first felt better, George suddenly found herself at her writing desk again, after weeks of being forced to stay away from it. She intended to return to writing her novel, but instead found herself looking outside the balcony and thinking about Pagello. The pen naturally found its inspiration, and George wrote a letter where she expressed the warmth in her heart for the dear doctor, and a hope that he might feel the same way, without any certainty that this was the case. She mailed the letter that night, and Pagello arrived at ten the next morning, as if only to look in on Musset, and checking him for a few moments he declared that he was still improving and then took his leave, whispering for George to follow him. George had put on her best gown before his arrival, in anticipation of what she couldn't possibly expect, so she quietly followed Pagello out before Musset realized that she was going.

Later that day, George saw the Piazza San Marco for the first time, and was amazed at the fine pastries served at the little cafes that Pagello recommended, and at the variety of foreign merchants, including Turks and Armenians, that called Venice their regular port-of-trade. George spent the next couple of weeks with Pagello and her long absences would have become too apparent to the recovered Musset, if his friend Alfred Tattet had not arrived in Venice with his mistress, the actress, Virginie Dejazet, and started keeping Musset entertained. Musset was partly fooled because he had never seen George at the start of a love affair from a distant perspective. From an outside perspective, Pagello and George might have been continuing their discussions of medicine at Pagello's hospital, instead of doing it by Musset's bed, and boring him all the while. But, few days passed into the outings that Pagello and George were taking together before they were in each other's arms, and engaged in very gentle and calming intercourse. Things might have continued this way, with George spending most of her days at Pagello's apartment, if Alfred Tattet did not reach the end of his stay on March 14, which meant that Musset would no longer have a friend to party with, and he suddenly looked more closely at the "friendship" between George and Pagello.

Musset was fully dressed and recovered and sitting at the living room table, talking with Tattet, who had just informed him of the forthcoming departure. Pagello was standing by the balcony, with George within arm's length of him.

"Who is going to accompany me to the salon tonight then," Musset asked, looking around the room.

"There will be plenty of people there," George replied, trying to suggest a solution.

"And what will you be doing tonight?" Musset asked, suddenly suspicious.

"Research for my 'Notes from a Voyager' project. I want to see some of the other islands…"

"You never wanted to go see the islands with me!"

"I felt too ill, and now I would like to study them."

"So, you've been going to see the islands without an escort?!"

"…No," George said after a moment of hesitation, "Pagello has been escorting me."

Pagello turned pale, as he was recalling the last time Musset had raised his voice during his feverish rages.

"Why are you looking so glum Pagello? And you George, what's bringing a shadow to your brow?!"

"You are imagining things, please calm down, or your fever might return!"

"My fever stopped weeks ago, you're trying to hide your guilt!"

Musset grabbed a sharp knife that was lying on his lunch plate and rushed at George and Pagello, "I'll kill you both here and now, if you don't tell me immediately why you are both looking glum!"

The last part of Musset's demand was muffled as Tattet rushed at Musset and wrestled him to disarm him. Tattet then stood between Pagello and Musset, touching both of their chests, as he was forcing Musset off Pagello.

"I challenge you to a duel! Pick your weapons, or she'll know you for the coward that you are!"

Pagello shook his head, and had to muffle a laugh as the situation was so overly dramatic it had become ridiculous.

"Ah! Now you're laughing at me! And you, George, you haven't denied it! I can see now what has been going on right under my nose, you shameless whore!"

"Please Alfred, you must still be feverish, you aren't acting rationally. Please calm down," Tattet was saying, holding Musset back. Finally, he got tired of pushing Musset back, as he was taking a few swings at Pagello with the knife, so he restrained his arms, by pulling them behind Musset's back, and led him despite his struggles into his own adjoining room.

Tattet spoke with Musset for some time, explaining that there were other women in Venice, and that he might be seeing something that wasn't really there between Pagello and George until Musset calmed down, and said that he would be all right, and that Tattet could depart without worrying that he would shoot or stab Pagello or George.

While Musset promised to calm down, as soon as Tattet left, he returned to shouting like a madman when she would return at night from her tete-a-tetes with Pagello, and frequently entered her room at night when her light was on and she had told him that she would be working, but he suspected Pagello had snuck in via the window to have a rumble with her. Once, George opened her eyes because she heard a rustle in her sleep and saw Musset circling her bed, barely dressed and brooding. She pretended that she was still asleep on this occasion to avoid starting a row in the middle of the night. Even after Musset returned to his own amorous exploits on March 17, he continued to hassle George with his suspicions about Pagello. On the next day, Musset saw a light at night under George's door and rushed in to find George writing a letter, which she hid before Musset could grab it.

"You can't be rushing into my room every night! If you don't stop this madness, I'll put you in asylum!" George shouted, flustered from the near-discovery.

"You'd go that far to be with him?" Musset asked, and was too over-come to continue, so he retreated back into his own room.

He was sitting up in his bed, when an hour later he heard what sound-ed like George's footsteps outside. He rushed to the window in his dress-ing gown and saw George, wrapped in a shawl, quickly walking away from their hotel. Without putting on shoes, Musset ran down the hall and into the street, and ran barefooted over the cobblestones after George. She jumped into a gondola, and because the driver was asleep when she sat down next to him, Musset had just enough time to jump into the gon-dola with George, before it took off.

"What are you doing you madman!" George screamed out, horrified that Musset might stab her right there in the gondola.

"I've had enough speculations. I'm finding out tonight what you have been up to! You're going to have to either drag me to an asylum, and I'm sure you won't have trouble keeping me there with how I'm dressed, or you are going to show me exactly where you are going!"

George did not reply, and the gondola slowly made it to the island of Lido. As soon as the gondola stopped, George jumped out and run across the port and into a small cemetery, where she collapsed on a bench, ex-ploding in torrents of tears.

Musset ran after her, and was surprised that the cemetery was empty. He sat down on the bench next to George and crossed his arms, listening to her weeping for a couple of minutes.

"Just give up, you are not going to be able to meet with Pagello to-night unless you confess what you've done! Admit that you are a damned fool, and that you've betrayed me!"

"I am a fool, Alfred, and I've done something awfully foolish."

Musset was startled by this news, which he had gone to all that trou-ble to obtain. Both of them dropped their heads, and after George dried her tears, walked back to the gondola and then glided back to their ho-tel. Pagello had come to the front entrance to the hotel for his schedule meeting with George, and between his presence there at that hour, and George's near-confession, it was now painfully clear to Musset that he was right in his suspicions. Then, Pagello and George walked Musset back inside, helped him to wipe of the bleeding soles of his feet, and put him back into his bed. Pagello and George exchanged looks, and Pagello nodded in response to George's inquiring glance.

"Alfred, it's all true, what you have been suspecting, and what I have refrained from telling you up until now. I did not think you were well enough for this news. I'm sorry, Alfred, it was intolerable of me to have done what I did when you were barely recovered. I hope you will forgive me for my misdeed," George said rapidly, hoping to say everything before Musset interrupted with the curses she expected were coming.

Alfred did not have any curses left in him. He knew that he was unfaithful to George across their time in Venice, and he could not justly lay blame on the infidelity entirely on George. Looking up at Pagello, he saw a calm, gentle, brilliant doctor, a man who if not a match for George, was certainly more fitting than him. He recalled nearly stabbing both of them several times, and all of his other assaults and harassments, and he could not think of a reason or a way for George to stay with him.

"You are the right man for her Pagello," he finally said. "I should've gone back to Paris months ago. I'll go as soon as I can, so you can have some happiness in this beautiful city."

"Oh, Alfred, I wish this all turned out differently, what a nightmarish few months this has been," George said. Alfred took George's hand and put it in Pagello's. A couple of tears broke out in George's eyes, and she kissed Alfred goodnight.

After a silence, when all three of them were lost in their own reflections, Pagello left the hotel, and George went to her own room for the night.

***

Musset left a couple of days later, as soon as he could arrange the trip. George had just run out of money, and while she felt guilty about breaking Musset's heart with her affair with Pagello, she also felt as if Musset was leaving when she no longer had the funds to sponsor his Italian adventure. She was now the one in need of financial assistance and was relieved out of her predicament by Pagello, who used his own and the resources of his friends and family to show George the best side of Italy, and to help her create a setting where she could write productively, while taking some trips to see the most romantic sights in the region.

George was not only interested in Pagello because she wanted to escape her painful love for Musset, but also because he was one of those gracious, seductive, irresistible Venetian men. It's a type that can't be bred anywhere else. Something about the constant proximity with the sea, classical architecture, and travelers from around the globe that makes the natives of that city magnetic to female visitors. The same cannot be said about the men of Israel or Rome, or many of the other internationally famous cities. Venetian boys somehow just have the genes that sculpt them like Roman statues, perhaps the sea air conditions their hair, and exfoliates their skin. And Venetian men, even fishermen past-fifty, have a calm wisdom, confidence, and dexterity that seeps romance and gallantry. Pagello was one of these men, and he was as calm as the waters deep beneath the surface of the sea, in contrast with Musset's constant stormy moods.

It was the beginning of spring and as usual in this time of the year, George felt simultaneously sexual, creative and exploratory drives seizing her. Pagello took her out of the hotel she was paying for immediately after Musset's departure and at first put her up with his friend Lazzaro Rebizzo, an aristocrat with a recreational passion for poetry. On the next day, when Pagello suggested a trip, George gladly agreed, and they hyped through the Tyrolian Alps, sailed across the Venetian archipelago, and then stopped for a few days at the place that belonged to Pagello's parents in Castelfranco Veneto, a small town full of medieval architecture a few hours inland of Venice. The town reminded George of Nohant, and Venice was an improved version of what she dreamed Paris would be like before she started spending half of her year there. When George moved into Pagello's place on their return from this excursion, she was refreshed and ready to jump back into her work, and within a few short months she wrote works that were published across the following two years, *Andre, Jacques, Mattea*, and the first of the *Lettres d'un Voyageur*. Pagello worked days at the hospital, so she had a motivation to wake up earlier than usual and shifted her schedule to writing when he was out, instead of at night when he was asleep. Surgeons did not make much in those days, so George had to adjust to frugality, as Pagello frequently bought sardines and shellfish from the Venitian fishermen, and cooked it himself, instead of dining out. If she needed to buy candle wax, or if she had to go out to explore Venetial sights, she rented a gondola with an old, crippled gondolier, Catullus, who at 15 francs per month made more money than she did as an editor in Paris. George was delightfully stranded in Venice for five months before she finally received the "misplaced" letters and bank notes from Buloz, that were sitting on a shelf there for months before a postal employee finally surrendered them to her, as if Venice did not want to lose her, and was holding on to her ticket home. George immediately used this money to pay her creditors, and to plan a trip back to Paris where republican events had recently moved in a direction that demanded her participation.

***

George did not read newspapers or visit salons as regularly in Venice as she did at Nohant or Paris, so she only heard vague news about a renewed labor riot in Lyon by the *canut*, or the silk workers. The previous Canut labor riot in 1831 was one of the causes that pulled republicans together after decades I relative non-aggression on behalf of this rebel faction after the French Revolution. The first riot had attracted an enormous army of workers, but the king had sent a military force that outnumbered them in such proportions that they gave in without a fight, but their brief overtake of the town inspired many of the later international Industrial labor revolts. In the second riot, the quantity of canut that participated was so enormous that they did not surrender without a fight and the government seized ten thousand of them as part of its suppression of the uprising, many of whom were deported, but a two thousand were imprisoned in Paris, with a few of these released early on, but one hundred and twenty-one kept in prison across the following year until the Mammoth Trial in 1835, in which George was to play an active role. The Society for the Rights of Man, to which George continued membership, was responsible for organizing all of the waves of the canut uprisings. Lyon was in the center of France, and one had to pass through Berry to travel from Lyon to Paris, so republicans in Berry were instrumental in these actions.

The wave of anti-republican suppression that followed the rebellion in 1834 cooled off by August, and it was time for George to return to offer her assistance to the cause, and to pick up on her work. On August 2, Pagello accompanied Sand in a hired carriage. George dressed like a shabby boy, with linen pants, a cap and a cotton shirt, to be more comfortable on this journey, which took them slowly across Lake Garda, the Simplon and Geneva. George's first task upon reaching Paris was attending Maurice's college awards ceremony on August 16. George's second scheduled meeting on the following day was with Musset, who had been exchanging letters with her over the previous months and knew about her arrival. Pagello supervised this meeting for George's safety, in case Musset's madness would return when he saw her again in person. Seeing that he was not trusted, Musset was particularly cautious and polite, and humbly kissed George's hand upon entry. The meeting left Musset with a bitter taste of disappointment, and upon returning home he realized that he could not remain "friends" with George, and had to make an attempt to seduce her again. George agreed to see him without Pagello on August 21, and at this two-hour meeting Musset did his outmost to charm her by complimenting one of her recently released novels, and begging her to renew their intimate relations.

During the first meeting, George had the impression that Musset had recovered his senses and that he now saw her as a close maternal friend, to whom he was grateful for assisting in a time of hardship. Her relationship with Pagello had now survived several intense months of travel, which surprisingly created little friction between them because

Pagello was one of those men who take things easy, and let them roll over him. He had the constitution of a city physician, who has seen thousands of mad and screaming patients, and for whom it would have taken an extraordinary hardship to get him to respond with anything but composure and practical reasoning. George was at the top of her fame, and his family saw his relationship with her as an achievement equivalent to becoming a doctor. He also felt that since he started having a relationship with George, it was a matter of honor for him to see it through to an end that George might name, and he could not have imagined staying behind in Venice, and letting George travel back to Paris alone. When George expressed an interest in seeing Musset again this was not entirely surprising as he knew they were exchanging letters, and as he was a student of both medical and mental conditions, he anticipated that George and Musset might slip back into their interrupted affair if neither of them could manage to stop writing friendly love letters. However, Pagello had not acted logically when he went to Paris with George because he had to take a long sabbatical from his medical practice, stopping his chief source of funds and risking losing his position. He had to determine if George and Musset were indeed about to reunite because if that was the case, he could not spend more than a couple of weeks in Paris. So, when George gave him a letter, on the next day after their private meeting, destined for Musset's eyes, Pagello opened its seal and read the single line written on it, "I must be yours, it is my destiny." The line was particularly offensive to Pagello because he had discussed a potential divorce and remarriage with George, and her somewhat positive reply encouraged him to think that she took their relationship as a mature affair between a committed couple. The letter suggested that she was deeply in love with Musset, and thought so little about their affair that she gave it to him, as if he was a live-in lover delivery boy. But, it was a long carriage ride to Musset's place, and by the time he arrived his brief burst of anger had subsided and he decided that it was for the best for him to have learned the truth at that moment and that regardless of what became of George's proposal, it was time for him to head back to Venice.

To return to George, she could feel that Pagello was tense about being in Paris without clear employment, and that he was anxious to settle there or to head back home. She assumed that his hospital and familial duties would win over. She also leaned on Pagello when she was destitute in Venice, and now she once again had her finances in order and wanted to use her liberty to find pleasure, rather than a second marriage, before she managed to leave the first. When Musset confessed that he still desired her, she felt the old passion returning, and the feeling of maternal fondling receding beyond her memory. George had a very weak memory when it came to what she had written in her romance novels, and what transpired in her actual previous romantic relationships. All the reasons and emotions that meant a break with Musset was necessary for her survival had disappeared after months with Pagello, and only his soft kiss on her hand and all the memories that it brought of their intimate moments remained haunting her.

On his part, Musset had retreated from Venice because in the few days he was sober and well he realized that he had been behaving like a raving lunatic. He did not have a reaction like this in his first failed love affair, and this sudden violent rage and yearning had caught him by surprise. If this was a normal affair for either of them, it would have ended when Musset stated in Venice that he wanted to seek other women and that he no longer loved George. Because the two of them were locked up together with few people to talk French with for a few months, and because they had shared near-death experiences, they could not stop romantic correspondences. So, if there was still love between them, Musset could only conclude that there was still a sexual attraction, and so he proposed a rejoining, which George could not refuse because she felt a similar need to materialize a loving feeling into a loving physical contact. Musset flew directly over to George's place and the two had very ordinary and uninspired sex together because they had dropped the coquetry and gallantry that initially charmed them both, and were both suddenly nerves and saddened by their bodies linking fully again, as it reminded them of moments when they had been ecstatic together, and that now there were too many injuries between them for them to be able to link emotionally when their bodies were intertwined.

After they separated, they both lay on the backs looking up at the high ceiling of the hotel room. George had already arranged to leave for Nohant on the next day, and she could not cancel those plans.

"I have to head out for Nohant tomorrow," she said glumly.

"Tomorrow?" Musset echoed.

"I told Casimir that I would, now that I've taken Maurice out of college. There is no reason to stay in Paris that I could explain to him."

Musset was hit with the horror of the situation. He was in bed with a woman who had a husband, a steady lover, and several other lovers she saw casually. He had not been with anybody else since returning from Venice as exchanging letters with George kept him satisfied, and he suddenly felt a new burst of energy that resulted in a higher literary output of his life. He was being made a buffoon out of by the woman in bed with him, who was now mocking him and saying that she would be the one to leave him after a night of passion.

"I'm actually leaving too… for the Baden-Baden spa," Musset finally replied, naming the first place that came to mind that would sound romantic, but also suggestive of possible clandestine meetings.

"Ah, I haven't been to that spa before. Will you get that whole body wrap they do at those?"

"No… I plan on bathing naked in the hot tubs."

George noticed some of the sarcasm in Musset's tone, but then considered that bathing in the nude would be amusing, so she smiled and didn't reply.

"Should I come by in the morning before you depart to… help you relax before the trip?"

"No, my dear Alfred," George said, turning over to her side to face him. "But one day, I'll be yours again for twenty-four hours. Destiny will bring us back together."

Musset did not have the strength to turn towards her or to retort for a few moments as he reflected on what she was saying. While they had an opportunity for intercourse on the following day, she was rejecting him, and was not promising to renew their relations when she returned for her usual months-long stay in Paris, but only that they would be together for only one more day. *Is she trying to seduce me by threatening to only be with me once more?* Musset found all this to be extremely repelling as the grunting ape inside of him returned. He would win the final battle with this powerful rival. She would be the one missing him, and he would be the one moving on to other lovers.

"Perhaps I will do you that honor, but I have an early morning tomorrow, so I should get going."

Musset jumped out of bed, displaying his naked form from its best angles in the candlelight, as he strutted and turned seductively and yet as-if coolly to put on the layers of his clothing.

"All right, have a good trip," George said casually, and Musset could hear her turning to go to sleep as he was leaving the room.

Both of them took their intended trips on the following day. George had said that she could not meet with Musset on the following morning because she had scheduled an important meeting with Pagello for it. Musset had mentioned that the letter she sent to him was opened in his reply and there was only one person that could have opened it. George met with Pagello and the two had a consultation about the medical symptoms of disintegration they were detecting in their relationship. George said she couldn't trust him if he felt a need to read her letters. Pagello said the obvious point that she was inviting an old lover into her bed before she had ended her affair with him. Then, both made several other points that clearly showed that there was no way for them to move forward, and at the end of this weighed and calm discussion Pagello packed his things and departed for Venice, saying that it had been a pleasure to meet and be with a great writer like George Sand, and that he would always treasure the memory of the splendid trips they had together. George complemented Pagello on his cheerful and composed nature, and thanked him for all the help he offered her in her time of need. They kissed on the cheeks and on the lips, and George saw him off as he got into his carriage and drove off to continue his brilliant medical career.

When George arrived at Nohant, she found a steaming Casimir, who had not seen his wife in nearly a year between her stay in Paris and her extended trip to Venice. He was writing letters encouraging her to stay in Venice when she was away, but he thought that she would take these as mockeries they were intended to be, as he was sure she was supposed to run out of funds half a year earlier. How could she have found the money to stay in Venice for so long? As her husband he had full access to all of her financial records, and while she was clearly running up debts she could not have paid off for the first months, she somehow managed to pay all of these bills off prior to leaving Venice and on top of this afforded accommodations that were not reflected in these bills. Clearly she had to have had a lover who took care of her in Venice. Who was this lover? Some Venitian dandy?

George arrived at night, and slept in her own room, so that Casimir did not have a chance to query her about all this in private. After sleeping for around twelve hours, George woke up mid-day and joined Casimir and the children for an early supper. Looking over at her daughter Solange, George realized that she was unusually quiet, in total contrast with the infant terrible that she was before George left. While Solange was no longer a baby, and was receiving lessons in polite manners, she was not simply polite, but docile. George considered what could be causing this docility. Casimir was clearly angry, and looking over at George with rage that was about to break out, but he was not paying attention to the children, and George could not suppose that he had suddenly taken an interest in raising them and that a change in behavior could be attributed to his parental efforts. Maurice was now a young man, who was receiving outstanding marks in college, and showing literary interest. Maurice had also been away from Nohant for most of the year, so he couldn't have traumatized Solange. George continued her brief detective project by looking at who else was around. She noticed the servants who were bringing in supper, and those who were carrying out the plates, and a couple who were cleaning her room in the distance, to get it done before she returned from supper, and would have needed to be left in peace to work. All of them were docile, helpful, and wanted to serve the masters of the household. George finally stopped her gaze at Julie, a servant who was assigned to Solange, and who was sitting on a chair at the side of the room, with furrowed eyebrows and a long frown, knitting a sock, and glancing over at Solange to check on how she was eating. She was constantly smirking or grunting upon looking up at Solange, which made Solange twitch, fidget and look down at her plate with embarrassment. George was immediately reminded of her fear of Rose, and realized that Julie was clearly hitting Solange and berating her in a similar manner, which while it rolled off George's skin was causing Solange to become fearful and docile, instead of turning rebellious and self-confident, a reaction the same treatment brought out in George. She was studying Julie for several moments now, and had put down the fork with a piece of quail chest on it to give her character analysis her full attention. This suddenly brought both Julie's and Casimir's attention to her, and when they both frowned at her, she couldn't help it and blurted out, "What have you two been doing to Solange?! Why is she so tame?!"

"We've been raising her while her mother was on a pleasure trip!" Casimir shouted.

George looked closely at Solange's wrist and noticed a small red mark. "And what's that? Are you going to tell me she got that mark by accident?!"

"It's just a little bruise. Children play. She could've fallen…"

"Solange, did you fall dear, how did you get that mark?"

"I don't know… I might have fallen."

"She doesn't know. She knows very well how she got it. She's just too afraid to say it with Julie glaring at her!"

"You are just shifting blame onto Julie when you are the one who's been running around engaging in all sort of outrageous behaviors!" Casimir's face was red, and he had stabbed his quail in the chest with his knife, leaving the knife upright in the bird as he threw down his napkin to invest all of his energy into a screaming match with George.

"Your accusations will get you nowhere. You don't have any proof. I was in Venice. I was writing. I have four completed books to prove it!"

"You are a spoiled whore! You were in Venice whoring yourself out for your dinners!"

"How dare you call me that in front of Solange, when I could hear you in Julie's room last night! You keep forgetting that Solange's caretaker always stays in the room next to mine!"

"Your dare to make an accusation like that in front of our whole family, and the entire household staff!?"

"It looks like I did dare, and I'll go further to insist that Julie leave this household immediately. She's fired. I don't want her anywhere near Solange!"

"You can't fire her!"

"Solange, dear, would you prefer if I found you another nanny, or would you like to keep letting her hit you?" George said attempted to quiet her tone to let Solange reply without fear of retribution.

Solange nodded.

"Yes, you think Julie should be let go?"

"Yes…" Solange mumbled, looking down at her plate timidly.

"There you have it. Go pack your things Julie. It's time for you to find another position."

Casimir was still fuming, but he had run out of retorts, as Solange's agreement meant that if he insisted on keeping Julie, he would be complicit in the abuse of his daughter. Julie looked at Casimir for a while until the silence became awkward, and then she stood up, put her knitting down on the chair, and retreated into her room to pack her things, as she was ordered to do. Julie's exit resolved the immediate argument, but Casimir's insults rang in George's ears, and it became clear to her that a divorce was now an immediate necessity. But, practicality won over and George remained at Nohant for the following three months, or the usually agreed on term, without making any sudden changes. She worked to avoid being around Casimir as much as possible, and focused on her writing and on raising her growing children.

On November 1, without waiting a day after the first of the month, George departed for Paris again with Solange, whom she placed in boarding school, freeing her apartment for potential romances.

George was going to the salons she frequented, the literary dinner parties, and was meeting all of the other piled up obligations she had for meetings with publishers, reviewers, fans, and business associates that were scheduled for this period. But, she still had too much free time, and when she was sitting down to write in the evening she was brought back to the memory of her affair with Musset, as if her memory was wiping out all those other love affairs and leaving only one as the sole sincere and overpowering romance of her life. This was a glum thought, so George went to see Marie Dorval to find ecstasy and comfort with her.

They kissed and caressed each other with their usual friendly repose and sensitivity, and were both relieved of the frustrations of the prior months of absence from each other's embrace. But, then Marie suddenly threw a fit about George's long absence, and asked questions about the affairs George had in Venice, knowing that it would give her pain to hear George recounting the new lovers, and new adventures she had without her. And George was sad to hear about Marie's relations with her husband and de Vigny, and both felt a separation between them soon after their bodies parted contact. George said a few words in an attempt to apologize and to bring the conversation back to a positive note, but Marie was in one of her tragic fits now, and she burst out in tears instead of being calmed. George retreated, and felt more emotionally frustrated upon returning to her apartment than she had been before she left to see Dorval.

She was back that night, alone, with an ink pen ready, but unable to write about any other type of love than the one between her and Alfred. So, she gave in, and wrote a letter to Musset, inviting him to visit her.

Musset had indeed taken a trip to the spa to avoid George finding out that he had made the trip up to correspond with hers simply because he was outraged that she was leaving him. Watching nude and semi-nude bodies, and letting his friends lead him to a couple of courtesans for amusement eventually brought him back to the bottle, and got him back into his revelry and womanizing. An access of both had stupefied him enough for him to have forgotten about George temporarily not because he had a short memory, but because he was barely conscious for the three months that passed since he last saw George. Now he suddenly received a letter from George at his parent's house inviting him for a new tete-a-tete. Was Pagello still in Paris? Would he supervise this meeting? Musset considered these and other questions and returned to the last thought he had as he was leaving George's hotel room three months earlier. He wrote the following letter:

G.

You are a notorious, low, deceiving, cheating, outrageous woman! You have laid waste to my young life, and you have ruined me for all other women, until I can't imagine marrying because I imagine I might marry somebody like you! I hope that you will finally suffer as I have suffered since I've met you. Leave me alone, and torment yourself with your miserable company!

Alfred Musset

George re-read this letter a few times, and suddenly felt more guilt for a man who was once her lover than she ever did before. Jules, Pagello and others simply withdrew and moved on to other love affairs, and never wrote to her of any heartbreak, or pain their affair might have caused them. George assumed that men enjoyed rolling around in ecstasy and then moving on to another conquest. Because in her early adventures with men she frequently found them to be unfaithful even as they were proclaiming their love, she had concluded that men were all naturally unfaithful, and that trusting a man to be more than a strutting peacock was an irrational womanly thing to do, and she had decided that she was not meant to be a woman. Her heart was hardened and masculine just like the clothing she chose to wear, and she had become comfortable with her dominant role and with taking her pleasure without risking becoming emotionally overwhelmed by any one man. Her strategy of switching romantic partners had worked for curing her of past infatuations, but it was suddenly backfiring as an emotional attachment to one man was casting a sinister light on the rest. She wrote a sad letter in reply to Musset's, expressing her sympathy, and apologizing for hurting him, and saying that she was a woman destined to be miserable in love, and that she was already suffering, and had been suffering for a very long time, without really feeling the depth of her misery, which was now bubbling to the surface. This letter was more frank and expressed a sorrow that Musset did not realize George was feeling, so his affection fluttered back into his heart and he flew to George's apartment on the next day. Musset's call startled George because she had expected that confession to be the last letter she would send to him, and that it was an apology and a final goodbye. She was not emotionally prepared to receive him, so she told the porter to deny him entry. Over the next couple of days, George alternatively felt embarrassed by denying him entry, and earnest to run over and see Alfred, until the latter urge won and she ran over to his townhouse. She was happy to see that Alfred opened the door and in moments they were in Alfred's room, wrapped in a long embrace. George might have had an orgasm for the first time that night with a male partner because she felt her skin response to his kisses with an intensity that she did not think was possible. She had let herself relax and fall into ecstasy, as her guard uncharacteristically fell aside.

Unlike in romance novels, they did not find perfect ecstasy for eternity. They broke up. Then, Musset moved for a week back into George's apartment. Then, he overheard Gustave Planche, his old rival for George's affection, making fun of him by saying that he was cuckolded in Venice at a literary salon he attended with George. Musset smacked Planche with his glove, and was set on fighting a duel over a period of two days. A few days before the scheduled duel, George confessed to Musset that she did start an affair with Pagello before she told him about it in Venice. This outraged Musset, as all his delirious speculations were proven to be true, and he told her it was over. He also explained that he does not plan on defending George's honor since the truth was that she had none, and so George succeeded in preventing a duel once again. After thinking about his situation for a bit, Musset insisted that George return all of his letters because he had decided to write a novel about their affair. When a writer asks another writer for research materials, it is unthinkable to deny the request, so George gave him all but one of his letters, which she thought was too graphic and too personal. Musset sent a servant to pick up the letters, and did not send any notes, or otherwise acknowledge her existence in the next few days. This silence after she had surrendered her private letters to his authorial hand meant that he was planning on writing the worst kind of slander or the exact truth about their affair, either of which would have meant that George would be ousted as being a loose woman who has had countless affairs. Because she was planning to file for divorce from her husband and because she was trying to get more money from him if they were going to stay together, having documented proof that she was unfaithful would have devastated her case. In addition, there were already rumors that she was scandalous, and now the critics would have a new armory to fire at her, which could have meant that her publishers might stop publishing her work, saying that her personal life was censorable.

At first, George attempted to keep her composure, but as a couple of days passed, she could not write, and she did not want to meet with any of her friends. She slept in much later than usual, trying to escape from these reflections in sleep, but her dreaming thoughts were about Musset, and she always woke up exhausted from struggling to fall into unconsciousness as images of Musset kept surfacing to pull her out of it. On November 19, George woke up at 2pm, drank a glass of milk, and could not eat any of the snacks that her servant brought in from a neighboring restaurant. There was a tall pile of mail on her desk that had to be answered, and she kept thinking there was a bill in there that hadn't been paid, but she didn't have the energy to plow through the pile to figure out what might be outstanding. She stared at the pile of papers, picking up one at a time and staring at the letters without being able to focus on the content. Finally, she put them down and lay back down on her bed. She picked a few tresses of her hair up with her fingers and twirled them nervously. She had not cut her hair since she left for Venice, or for almost a year now, and they had grown out to a length that she was not accustomed to as she usually had a bob, or hair down to her shoulders, which allowed her to pass for a boy when she couldn't hide her hair under a hat. She spent too much time around those that preferred she dressed as a woman, or in her room writing in Venice to have considered cutting them. Now she realized that they were the sort of hair Marie Dorval, or some of the finer society ladies had, seductive, flirtatious, and sensuous. She sat at the mirror of her boudoir, and looked at them, as they fell wildly over her naked shoulders and neck. If she had seen herself on the stage of a play house, she would have written a letter of admiration after the performance. She found a pair of scissors, and at first she brushed her hair carefully, lined the scissors up at a straight angle, as she saw her maid doing, and cut across the line of hair. As she studied the job she just did, she realized that while it looked like a straight line when she was holding the hair down with her brush, when the hair was loose, they were falling all over the place. She knew that if she attempted to cut the back of her head, they would be completely crooked in the back. Was she hysterical as she proceeded to cutting her hair into a crooked bob all around her head? Women cutting off their own hair, and failing to do it in a straight line is frequently used as a symbol for madness. But, George knew she had to finish the job or she would have looked ridiculous with only a front section cut, and she also knew that her maid could fix the hairstyle on the following day. She just really needed to feel a surge of masculine power at that moment, but when she saw the crooked haircut she saw what she just did as a mad act herself. The madness was not in the sin against good taste, but in the fact that she was now looking with longing at the cut strands of hair lying on her thighs. Instead of seeing these black locks, she was imagining Musset's blond hair, and she suddenly yearned to run her fingers through them, and to smell them after he had a scented bath, or after they had been together all night and they were damp, and they smelled like the essence of his soul. George walked over to her closet and opened it. She kept a collection of bones there that she used for research into human anatomy, a study she pursued with the help of those three doctors, including Solange's father, who she had met all those years ago, and met with periodically at their schools for consultation. Among these bones were three skulls, and as she looked at these yellow skulls of a man, a woman, and a boy, she saw the cadavers at the morgue that she saw piled up after the failed June Revolution, and she thought about all the men that she was partially responsible for sending to their deaths, as she managed to escape suspicion because of her sex, class status, and cunning. Were her lovers suffering a fate similar to those cadavers as she worked through several men each year, unable to find satisfaction, unable to chain herself to any one of them, unable to give up her true love for her writing and her ambitions for power and revolutionary change for the sake of a committed relationship with any one of them. She recalled the one time she had the courage to jump into the river with Colette as a child. She had just retired Colette from active service that year, and she felt as if with Colette a part of her, which had learned the lesson to not jump when she wanted to because somebody might be under her who will die with her, was also retiring, and that she once again had a longing to find total peace and to escape the miseries she was causing herself and others.

Knowing that Musset enjoyed symbolic communications, and wanting to express how she was feeling with a couple of immediate symbols, if Musset would not, as she expected, let her relay everything she was thinking and feeling. George had found that in her communications with brilliant men of her time, she usually listened, and they talked, and the only chance she had of being heard was in her writing, where she could not relay the exact truth at the risk of execution for sedition, or social execution for her promiscuousness. There was a moment when she looked at the hair that fell to the floor when she stood, and searched around the room for somewhere to dispose of them into, so that the maid would not be horrified by the mass when she entered in the morning. At that moment, George's first thought were the skulls in her skeleton closet, but this thought vanished when she actually opened the closet and started thinking about the cadavers. Yet, now when she was reflecting further, she returned to her original idea and decided that she could solve both problems with one gesture. She gathered the hair from across the floor, and placed the bundle into the woman's upturned skull.

It was now around 6pm, and George wrapped the skull in a shawl and took a carriage to Musset's house. Musset's porter opened the door, and she gave him the skull, taking the shawl off, and then leaving without giving a verbal message. The porter recognized her and carried the skull and hair into the dining room, where the Musset family was having dinner. Musset was sitting next to his new mistress, a young actress, who screamed as the skull was displayed by the porter over Musset's shoulder. He recognized George's hair immediately.

"Did she bring this herself?" he asked.

"Yes, Sire, but she has gone," the porter replied.

Musset noisily stood up, pushing the chair backwards, and took the skull. He went into the living room to be alone, and there he buried his face in the tresses inside of the skull and inhaled their natural perfume. Her scent brought him back to his maddening love for her, and he ran over to her apartment, and for two days they did not surface far from her bed. Then, Musset once again felt that he needed to escape that mad romance, and he left Paris, without telling George, who found out when she flew over to his house, and was told he wasn't in the city. George briefly left for Nohant, but within a week of arrival received a new apology from Musset, which she finally could not accept because her heart was overwhelmed with pain, and she explained this in a letter to him, including in the package the blond locks of hair that he gave her after they reunited upon his receipt of her black tresses. She had been smelling and touching those bits of hair as if they were a drug, or the face of a beloved, and she had to be rid of them and all other reminders of Alfred, or she was going to sink into permanent lethargy and depression. But, only a month later, she was back in Paris, and renewed her affair with Musset, fighting through her last defensive maneuvers, but unable to end permanently a relationship that was bringing her to emotional peaks she previously thought were only possible in Shakespearean tragedies.

It was only on February 12, Mardi Gras, a year after the time when George and Alfred's affair was meant to end, when he declared he no longer loved her, and then fell ill with typhoid, thus prolonging an affair destined to be brief and explosive into one that kept burning and exploding for a year past what any carcass could have endured before being left in cinders. Musset had sent her an invitation to meet his new actress mistress at the Masked Ball at the Paris Opera on Mardi Gras, and included with the invitation a domino and a black satin mask. He wanted to match George's symbolism, but he did not want to scare her away with something threatening like a dog's paw. George was flattered to receive these gifts, and was curious to see a masked ball at the Opera, so she went on her own. Alfred saw her coming in because he was waiting for her, and then he began a loud conversation with his mistress and her friend in the lobby, where he was poking fun of his "cuckolding" in Venice, using George's real name, Aurore Dudevant. George could see that several of the rich and aristocratic patrons of the opera were nearby in the lobby and that a couple of them were surprised to overhear such scandalous news. George did not have Planche or any other friend to defend her, so she left the Opera house, and went home. Musset had finally committed the biggest sin a lover could have performed in an affair with a socialite, married woman, and a break with him was now a matter of survival for George, not because the affair was hurting her heart, which always managed to recover, but because it was now a threat to her finances, her work, and her social position. The anger that George was feeling flooded over the old feelings of sympathy, as she now realized that she was the real victim in that violent relationship. She finally managed to return to her work, and to her political schemes. After working steadily for a couple of weeks, her mind returned to Alfred, and she had one final symbolic message for him. She sent a caged bird to his mother with a goodbye note. She knew that Musset would never commit to her because his parents would not have allowed him to marry an older re-marrying woman. She also wanted to say that Musset was caged, but that she was free and that she would not allow herself to be caged for any man. George felt strong and confident when she sent this message, but after the message left her apartment, and she knew the affair was finally over, a deep depression came over her again. On the morning of April 5, her most radical, most famous and most dear friend visited her at her apartment. Alphonse de Lamartine listened to her troubles, and told her that the only solution was for her to change locations to a place where she could work in peace, away from the troubles that had piled up in France. George agreed with his wise council and even traveled to Nohant to make an informal will that asked for her friend, Mme. Decerfz, to take care of her children if she was going to have an "accidental" death during her travels in the East. Since the trip to Venice brought typhoid fever with it, she fully expected that an extended trip to the East would quickly end all her suffering in the most dramatic and adventurous way she could imagine. But, as she was heading out, her republican friends called her away from her fantasy of a hermit's death and to the real political tragedies that she could actively help to prevent by staying in Paris.

Chapter 16

The Mammoth Trial, Divorce, and Michel de Bourges, or Everard

George was ready to depart for the East, and thought that this was her destination when she got in a carriage on April 7 of 1835, and found Alphonse Fleury, one of the central members of her "club," waiting for her there. He had come in from La Chatre and was led into this carriage out of his own by the porter when he said that he could wait for George in her carriage. It was unusual for one of George's political friends to come to Nohant, and this clandestine meeting suggested that a major plot was brewing. George did not ask any questions, but Fleury understood that she must be curious and explained that they were heading for Bourges, a couple of hours away for a chat with Alphonse de Lamartine, who had come up with some new ideas for how to resolve George's predicament. They arrived in a country inn at Bourges, and had dinner in a private room with Alphonse de Lamartine and Everard, officially known as, Michel de Bourges. They began the conversation with the personal topic that was driving George mad of late, her divorce. But, before they had finished eating their grilled chicken, they switched to discussing the Mammoth Trial, and the approach Everard was planning to take in his defense of that radical group, which was affiliated with the Society for the Rights of Man, to which all present republicans belonged. It became apparent to George why Lamartine had brought her to that inn for that conversation with Everard, she could solve both of these legal problems by developing her legal skills and exchanging services and lessons with the top lawyers that were working on the Mammoth Trial. She could teach them about official writing, and help to compose their court documents, while they could research all possible ways for her to escape the horrors of her marriage.

When she suggested an exchange of services, Michel was goggled-eyed and flattered that the author of *Lelia* wanted to trade literary and legal secrets. They commenced a debate where both were pulling the other party towards their extreme, legal logic and literary art. They also discussed the possibility for a socialist revolution in the near-future, but Lamatrine was saddened to report that they did not have the resources to get those who were imprisoned for the Mammoth Trial out of prison by violent means, and that they had to resort to legal means, something that was new for the group, but a strategy they all embraced as a unique way to avoid bloodshed in a revolution that might fail.

They all traveled together to Paris, where the trial was set to commence, and George and Everard took up residence at the Hotel Jacques Coeur, in separate rooms. Everard had brought his legal library with him from Bourges, and he let George study his books on French law, the Napoleonic Code, case law, and various other books on the rules, procedures, and laws of the French legal system. He also regularly clipped newspaper articles regarding the Canut uprising, and passed them to George for her review. From these, George learned the details of the widespread protest over minimum salaries in Lyon, and the massacres with bayonets and cannon of the rioters by the government's troops. Arrest warrents were written for 420 of the rebels on February 6. Everard also gave George books on the "social question," including radical socialist pamphlets that argued for the literal division of property by taking it from the rich and giving it to the poor. Everard was an agrarian, and believed that the rustic life was ideal, and supported a return to agrarian law, where farmers in earlier pre-industrial and pre-feudal times worked to feed themselves and their families, without the need for giving a portion of their earnings to the government, and without relying on the industrial complex for salaries. George did not support the idea of giving away her Nohant estate to the poor, but she also thought that the rustic agrarian life was a beautiful ideal. In a way, George was taking a set of law courses with Everard, as the two debated and discussed the various books that George was reading in the evenings. George also lectured to Everard during those times about the rules of literary and rhetorical composition, as Everard typically had to argue his cases in small courts, without presenting written arguments, and now suddenly had to offer major pamphlets with his legal reflections.

After a couple of weeks of legal research, George had come up with a few basic points to present to Casimir as part of their divorce negotiations. Everard advised her that the best option would be if Casimir went along with the split, as forcing him into a divorce went against most laws and precedents of the period. She returned to Nohant, where upon being asked under what circumstances would be be willing to split, Casimir offered to double the current allowance she had for spending half the year alone in Paris to 3,000 francs in allowance for her and Solange. This meant that she would have had to stretch her allowance twice further because Solange's education alone cost 1,500 francs annually. Hyppolite intervened in this discussion and counter-offered 6,000 francs, which would have left Casimir with 10,000 francs. Casimir saw the logic in this amount, as being a sum that was realistic for George living permanently in Paris. But, before he signed the papers that George drew up, he realized that the costs of running the Nohant estate were too high to afford them on only 10,000 francs. He spent his own small inheritance on bad business dealings, so the sum he would receive as part of this deal would have to permanently sustain all of his annual expenses. He proposed that George should get Nohant and pay for its maintenance, while he would receive 7,000 francs annually to live in Paris. George realized that this deal would give her just enough to afford living on her ancestral estate in comfort, so she edited the agreement and presented it to Casimir. He signed it, but before the ink was dry, he was thinking about how George needed to dress as a boy and lived in relatively small apartments in Paris, and he started doubting that living in Paris with only basic essentials would satisfy him. When he expressed these doubts, George tore up the contract and retreated to Paris to consult with Everard and to come up with a better strategy, as it became clear that Casimir was only negotiating to see her hand, and that he would never give up a portion of his income in exchange for their permanent separation.

George was back in Paris a week before the Mammoth Trial started. George rented a studio apartment, *la mansarde de bleue*, which sounds more romantic than what it was, or merely "the blue attic." This studio was visited regularly by their extended circle of republicans, which now included a new member, the twenty-four years old Hungarian composer, Franz Liszt, who had been engaged in an affair with the married Countess Marie d'Agoult for over a year at that point, and had both republican and personal interests in common with George. Everard had spent that time organizing his legal briefs and papers. Seeing him buried in his legal paperwork, George immediately put her own legal troubles aside, and helped him to work through the various minor laws and rules that he had not yet fully analyzed, summarizing her research findings in briefs she gave him in the evening. At the end of a week of this work, the first day of the trial finally arrived on May 5. This first date was only a preliminary hearing, which was followed in three weeks by the week-long trial sessions between May 29 and June 4. On all of these dates, George put on her student outfit, and slipped into all of the court sessions, before the House of Peers, which was serving as an extraordinary court of law in this constitutional law dispute, in this disguise, without being asked to leave, a feat as women were not allowed in the chambers. This trial lasted for a week because 164 of the accused insurgents had to appear, many of whom had to be questioned, cross-examined, defended, and investigated. Anybody that has not attempted to be an examining lawyer for a day cannot imagine what a week in this court of Peers would have been like. Everard was the lead lawyer, so while his associates could stand back, he had to be alert at all times, and had to immediately reply if there were any irregularities, and had to lead all of the cross-examinations, and all of the interactions between his labor side and the House of Peers. It should be noted that the House of Peers in this period was comprised of over 150 hereditary lay peers, and ecclesiastical peers, and included most of the members of the royal family, who did not attend all sessions, but a few of them did make appearances for this special trial. Thus, any number of these aristocratic and church-affiliated figures could suddenly ask Everard questions, and otherwise interrupt the flow of the proceedings. While there were many rules of order in place from the Napoleonic Code, hardly all of those present knew them.

George had to sneak into this finely designed and domed assembly chamber, which was crowded on an average day with two hundred officials, and several dozen accused men standing trial. Since her family had close relations who were members of the House of Peers, she was recognized by a few of them during the trial. One of these distant friends was Duc Decazes, the Chief Referendary of the House of Peers, and he contributed to informing the guards that George had his own special permission to be present at the hearings. The reason for Decazes' willingless to allow George in is also explained by the fact that one of the active peers even carried the name M. Dupin. Thus, during the trial, George shamelessly waved to the prisoners who were her close friends. Nobody made a move to remove her because she was the only woman there, and neither her relations nor her revolutionary associates considered her to be "legally" a woman. She typically sat in the row directly behind Everard, and made a few whispered suggestions when he lost his composure, or was uncertain about the best legal move.

Everard frequently lost his composure. Unlike all of the other republican lawyers, despite a decade of radical legal battles, this was his first Parisian trial, and the first time he was in the same room with members of the reigning aristocracy. He had met some regional aristocrats, and had won regional trials across his decade-long legal career prior to that point, but he did not know that he was facing an enemy that did not play by the rules that they written. The other republican lawyers did not want the responsibility of being the lead because they knew that assassinations, poisonings, and executions without a fair trial were still common, and that they had to step lightly when they threatened the king, barons, or the church publically in open-court, because while they could only make legal retorts there, the other side was willing to kill thousands of rebels to avoid raising workers' wages, and they were just as willing to press false charges against lawyers that stood in their path. Thus, the other republican lawyers argued that they had to make a perfectly reasoned legal argument that would not have left any gap for the opposition to explore in a counter-offensive. All they had to prove was that the workers' protest was a right guaranteed them by the ideals of post-revolutionary France, or that there was no proof that those men who stood trial had committed murder or were indeed the leaders of the rebellion. They wanted to win the case quickly on technicalities and specific legal maneuvers. However, Everard insisted that they had to use the case to wage a political battle against corruption in French government that was apparent from the Peers' disregard for written rules and procedures. This disregard of procedures was an intentional maneuver intended to disorient the republican lawyers, and when Everard wrote and published a pamphlet of complaint which stated, "It is our moral duty…, and we fill it with proud satisfaction, to declare in the face of the world that, so far, we have shown ourselves worthy of the sacred cause to which we have devoted our freedom and our life... Persevere, citizens... The infamy of the judge makes for the glory of the accused," a statement that was followed by 110 forged signatures from the top republicans of the day, the Peers used this document to find Michel de Bourges guilty of contempt of court, if not sedition, and charged him a 10,000 francs fine, and put him in prison for a month, taking the best republican orator off the case. Only one other republican came forward to take responsibility from the manifesto from May 11th that accused the judge of infamy, and this was another defender, a doctor, Ulysse Trelat, who for some reason the court determined to be the primary author and convicted to pay a larger 11,000 francs fine, and to serve three years in prison. Everard had accused the House of incompetence, when in truth they only feigned ignorance to hide their malicious disregard for laws that weren't in their favor. Right before Everard was convicted, the Trial began descending into chaos, where defenders were refusing to testify on their own behalf because they did not believe that their testimony would be treated fairly by the extremely this biased court.

While the trial was not going well legally, it stirred a sexual passion in George, and she offered herself to Everard on the night of the first hearing, and the two were lovers across the trial and long after it. George was stimulated by Everard's impassioned shouting, gesticulating, and the great power of his mind, and wanted to calm his storming and release his frustration.

After Everard was convicted, on June 15, he abandoned the rest of the arguments to the other republican lawyers and retreated temporarily to his home in Bourges. There was only one forthcoming trial in August against those who were accused of producing exposives for the rebels. The final judgement would come in August 13, when there were 72 other convictions, aside for the early convictions against Everard and the second defending speaker. George's contributions were not as welcomed by the other lawyers, so she returned to Nohant, and invited Michel to visit her there while Casimir was away on "business." George later loaned a house in Bourges temporarily to be with Everard as he dreaded the forthcoming incarceration, and became unusually jealous, pressing her to take more radical steps to finalize her divorce. At the end of July, Everard even snuck into George's Nohant bedroom at night and they spent four days without servants in Nohant in close embraces. They were interrupted when Casimir came back a day earlier than expected and found them alone in George's room together. He became enraged and nearly shot Everard, before he ran outside and managed to hop in a carriage and escape. While George reported that she stayed out of this case between Everard's conviction and the remainder of the case in her autobiography, she also hinted that she had snuck into prison to see Everard. But, while her romantic passion for Everard might have been admired by her romantic readers, it is certainly more believable that she snuck into prison on July 12 to assist with the escape of 25 prisoners from Sainte-Pelagie, to keep them from harsh prison sentences that were handed out a month later. George and a group of her republican friends bribed a night guardsman and slowly snuck into the prison, waiting in dark cells themselves before the coast was clear and they could lead the prisoners out without detection. George also assisted with the plotting for an event that her son, who was now mature and friends with the children of the Parisian aristocracy, happened to see from a very different perspective.

In July, Maurice wrote to his mother to inform her that he has witnessed the Fieschi's attempt to blow up the Citizen King Louis-Philippe's carriage with an "infernal machine." Maurice was with his friend, Charles d'Aragon, and with a young lady that he was courting, who later became the Empress of France, and they were chatting, while occasionally glancing over at the procession of the King passing during their visit to the Comtesse de Montijo. They suddenly heard a loud boom, and saw the commotion of the guard rushing to check on the King's safety. The proximity of her son to this plot that she had a hand in startled George, and she was compelled to use a similar assassination attempt in the novel she was finishing for Buloz, *Engelwald*, which could not be released under that name, and which depicted an Austrian assassin who wanted to eliminate Napoleon. George had got the idea that such subversive rebellion was legal from reading Walter Scott's rebellion novels about the Jacobite rebellions in eighteenth century Scotland. But, on this occasion she learned that the same symbolic statements of anti-tyrannical protest were counted as sedition in French, as she was under police surveillance for months after she sent her proofs to Buloz, and came closer to becoming a political prisoner than she did when she actively engaged in revolutions. Instead of taking the surveillance as a warning on September 15, George called Louis-Philippe a "crowned log" in her sixth *Lettre d'un voyageur*, so that she was officially blacklisted as members of an "anarchist committee." Since she was indeed a member of the central revolutionary movement in France, George found the surveillance and blacklisting to be ridiculous because she could continue to publish radical pieces and insults against the King without any other repercussions than these statements of political dislike.

While George was hardly concerned about the surveillance, she could not engage in direct rebellion against the crown, or meet with the "club" at the salon they were all members of at the time. Thus, she returned to Nohant and focused her energy on striking an agreement for the separation from her husband. A string of back-and-force negotiations and trials followed. On October 4, George once again had a meeting with Casimir, and asked him how he wanted to edit their previous agreement for it to be something he could sign on permanently. Casimir said that he wanted to stay in his house in Berry, so George gave him more space and spent a couple of weeks in her garret in Paris, where she came up with a new contract that gave Casimir still less than what he was offered before, only half of George's income, which sent him into a rage, and he demanded to be the sole master of Nohant. Knowing that Bourges was scheduled to serve his sentence in a few days, starting on November 3, George scheduled a meeting with Bourges, Gustave Papet, Duteil and Rollinat to get their legal advice on the matter, and they all believed that a legal separation without an open contestation and divorce was still preferential. They also advised her that she had to stay away from her conjugal domicile to demonstrate that she was physically separated from her husband. Duteil offered to serve as the mediator in their separation negotiations because George was clearly bringing out an emotional response in Casimir when she was presenting the contract versions to him herself. These maneuvers at first appeared to work, as on November 12, Casimir signed the proposed separation agreement and resigned from his position as Mayor of Nohant.

Because George's allowance was frozen or rather uncertain during these negotiations, and because she could not remain at Nohant, she stayed with Duteil and his wife Agasta for a few months in their La Chatre home. Duteil's extended family lived in this house, including his seven children, so that there were fourteen at their nightly dinners. George felt obligated to baby sit the children, playing charades and parlor games with them, and then she chatted with the adults of the family after the children went to sleep, so she had to push her writing schedule back to later hours than she ever kept previously, working between 12am and 4am. However, even in those late hours, the Inn of La Boutaille across the street was noisy, as circus performers, and other drunk and disorderly customers carried on in loud song, thieving, and yelling inside and outside of the Inn through all hours of the night.

After spending three months in this hellish domicile, where she was hardly able to produce novels at the rate that would have helped her make a living in that difficult financial time, George finally heard a decision from the court on February 16, 1836, in her favor, granting her separation, possession of Nohant and the custody of both of her children. The children were still in school in Paris, so for a full month, between February 17 and March 20, George was delirious as she was completely alone in Nohant. She was so tired of having an enormous family living in a cramped house, that she dismissed all of the servants, and only had Andre's wife bringing her food and other essentials during this period. George might have had a restful and productive second half of her life. She might have contributed to drafting key legal manifestos and documents. She might have become the first recognized female doctor and medical researcher in France. If she had managed to hold onto Nohant at that point, when she was free from all overpowering love affairs, she might have regained her composure, and might have turned to the philosophical and rhetorical writing projects that she started to see as more fitting for her mental constitution than romance novels. But, she was only destined to be completely free for a few days out of her long life.

On March 20, George was called over to Paris because M. Dudevant had found two servants that George fired to be alone at Nohant, and because they were disgruntled by being dismissed after years of service, they dictated statements that they had seen Aurore Dudevant with several lovers over their time at Nohant. This new evidence re-opened the separation hearings, and a new trial was scheduled for May. George was terrified that this evidence would leave her with nothing, so on the day before the trial, May 10, she borrowed 10,000 francs and was planning on escaping to America if the court ruled against her. Because of Everard's skillful maneuvers, and brilliant legal research, it turned out that the evidence that M. Dudevant presented of George's infidelity actually meant that she was indeed both scandalous and injurious to Casimir's character and person, and this in turn meant that Casimir could not have any reason to stay married to her unless he was solely interested in keeping hold of her money. The judge agreed that the marriage in these circumstances was immoral and illegal by all religious and judicial rules he knew, and he upheld the prior separation terms. The trial was a public spectacle, and the proceedings were published, including the accusations against George, and Casimir's own infidelities, and as a result George became infamous. For his part, Casimir again lost his composure, and continued the legal fight even after this point when it seemed clear that he had no recourse for winning. Casimir's new case was filed in Bourges, so George had to spend the summer with the Bourgoing family in their country cottage in Bourges. She dressed as a society woman to attend the Bourges trial on July 6, 1836 to dispel the gossip about her questionable sexuality and manners. The presiding judge, M. Mater, heard additional evidence from Everard, including M. Dudevant's 1831 letter to George, "I am going to Paris; I will not stay with you, because I do not wish to inconvenience you any more than I wish to be further inconvenienced by you." Everard explained that the letter once again proved that Casimir's only reason for staying in the marriage for the five years following 1831 was to have access to George's money. Casimir barely sat through a full day of brutal legal examinations and maneuvers by Everard, who was fighting this case with the same rebellious energy as he used in the Mammoth Trial, and indeed this time he was even more emotionally invested in seeing a just outcome. Before the day was done, he was tempted to raise his hand and withdraw the case to be able to leave that courtroom and retreat to his drinking and womanizing in peace. So, when the judge dismissed them all at the end of that hearing, Casimir immediately told is lawyer to drop the appeal, and this withdrawal got the judge to finalize the divorce on the following day.

George finally took full possession of Nohant on July 26, Saint Anne's Day, and celebrated the occasion with all of her local friends by dancing in the garden under the elms. While George might have remained in Nohant across the year, if she only had her preferences in mind, Maurice wrote to her in August with news from Paris that demanded that she remain involved in Parisian political affairs. Maurice had become close friends with the twelve years old, a year younger than Maurice, and the youngest son of King Louis-Phillipe, the Prince, who Maurice called Antoine, and who was officially known in that period as the Duke of Montpensier. Antoine was forced to flee France for Spain during the 1848 Revolution. Maurice reported that he and Antoine had spat on the heads of the national guardsmen from a gallery above. Maurice had told George that he was also a liberal republican, and now he was fraternizing with a leading democrat prince in line for the throne, and humiliating honest guardsmen in the process without apparent shame. Some re-education was necessary, so George took Maurice and Solange with her to Geneva for two months starting that September, and when Maurice returned to college, she stayed at the Hotel de France in Paris to watch over his political progress. Her republican friends might have staged a coup d'etat at a time and place when Maurice was even closer to royalty than he was during the last assassination attempt, and George needed to keep track of developments to be sure to warn him or take him away from the center of the action when a new rising was to develop.

Chapter 17

A Decade with
Frederic Chopin

Since George was in Paris, she returned to her regular salon visits, and she met Frederic Chopin for the first time when she was sitting in a room across from him at Mme. D'Agoult's salon on November 15, 1836. Goerge attended the same salon a month later, and met Chopin there again.

Meanwhile, in December it started to look like her concerns regarding Maurice were founded as he started showing symptoms of poisoning, which the doctor diagnosed as enlargement of the heart, but George suspected was a near-death homicide attempt, as he had violent headaches and pains in other parts of his body. The doctor recommended stopping his classical education, and since it meant taking him away from the Prince, George agreed, which meant that Maurice was spending more time at home and was preventing George from having tete-a-tetes in her apartment without him discovering them.

George was forced to sneak away to Bourges when she was supposed to be traveling to Nohant for a clandestine meeting with Michel at the end of December. This encounter did not go well because the details Michel read when he was assisting George at her divorce trial showed George in a dark light, and he accused her of having affairs, while they were together, with two men that hardly played any part in George's life, Gustave de Gevaudan and Scipion de Roure. He demanded she return his letters because he was afraid that they might end up in the press, like so many of George's other affairs, and this sent George back into a deep depression as she knew that the affair with Michel was coming to a tragic end, which arrived in March, when in a scene repetitive of her last encounter with Jules, George found Michel in an embrace with a fat, and horrid looking "singer." This memory kept George away for a few months, but she asked Bourges for a new meeting on June 7, and they spent a few days together in a country house, without George finding any joy or release in the encounter.

The romance was over, and George was in need for a new flame, and the first person who came to visit her back in Paris was Bocage, and she knew that he had been in love with her for the four prior years that they had been friends, so George suggested an affair, and one was promptly on the way. Bocage was an actor, a few years older than George, and George had first been impressed with him when she saw him in the same play where she discovered Marie Dorval, *Antony.* He was in George's republican "club," and visited the same salons, but because of her relationship with Marie, George did not think of him as a potential partner until that moment. This affair became awkward when Liszt was shocked enough by seeing the two friends flirting with each other that he made a joke about it to Bocage, who repeated it to George, who was outraged and told Liszt to refrain from joking about her personal life. But, while she was outraged by such jokes, she also saw an affair with such a long-time close friend as ridiculous, and thus it did not last long.

A week after this fling, George found out that her mother, Sophie, was dying. Sophie had not seen her daughter for over a year, and the two met very infrequently across the years when George was married to Casimir. The portion of the inheritance that Marie-Aurore left for Sophie meant that she could afford to live in her Parisian apartment with a couple of dedicated servants, and with all the necessities, and some luxuries that she needed. Her daughters were all married and she was free to change her hair color and dresses without them judging her spending habits. She did not want to go near Nohant, as screaming at her grown daughter with her husband at the table was not something that she wanted to attempt. She had never had independence before, and while she did not want to use this independence to write books or because of any other ambitions, it was her life-time wish to enjoy complete leisure and rest. She would wake up pretty late, have the maid help her bathe and arrange her hair and clothing, then eat a full brunch of croissants and tea, then take a trip in a carriage to the shops to buy some trinkets or clothing that was new that season, and then return home to try on these new acquisitions. In the evening, she would get a foot-rub, eat duck or seafood for dinner, with napoleons or other pastries for a snack. On some evenings, she would invite some ladies over and play cards, or go to a restaurant with them, or otherwise amuse herself. Sophie was happier in those last years than she had ever dreamed of becoming, and she did not have any need for further maneuvers because she had just enough money to live out her days in the most blissful inactive retirement.

Amidst all this joy, Sophie suddenly started feeling pains in her stomach, and when she called a doctor in to examine her, he concluded that her liver was tumefied and told her that she had to be in a hospital if there was any hope of prolonging her life. She had not saved very much money, as she lived for the present and bought all the luxuries her allowance afforded. So, she picked the smallest room at the private hospital where she was taken, telling her daughter Caroline that this was to avoid people finding out how rich she was and stealing her money. The room's air was dense with bodily fluids, and the steam caused by a July heat wave, and the sheets hadn't been washed in over three prior patients, all of whom died on the bed. This was the moment when George rushed in, as she was informed of this development when she was at Nohant and had to take care of the business of leaving her children with caretakers and Nohant in good hands before she could make it over to see Sophie.

From George's perspective, in the year since she last saw Sophie, her mother had aged so much that she looked as if she was a hundred. Sophie was indeed exhausted from staying in that hospital room, and she was thrilled and hugged and kissed George upon her entry because she knew that her daughter would get her better accommodations, which she immediately did, renting a spacious apartment overlooking a garden. George brought in the best doctors in the hospital and they reported that the disease was too far progressed for them to be able to do anything else for Sophie, so George took her back to Sophie's home to make her comfortable. On the trip back, they went to Chaps-Elysees because George thought that it would cheer Sophie, but while she smiled and tried to look energetic, the historical locations did not interest her in the least, and when she thought it was appropriate to do so, she said she was tired and asked to go home. One of the other reasons Sophie looked old was because she had stopped eating because of this disease, and now she ordered an enormous dinner, but didn't eat it, just looking at the fancy dishes that she had been eating all these beautiful years in Paris. After dinner, George took her into the garden, and she sat there thinking about beautiful dishes and beautiful dresses she saw earlier that day in Paris. Amidst these reflections she looked up at George, who looked pale, and she imagined what George must be thinking about, probably something about how tragic death was, or about life after death, she recalled these reflections from the novels of George's she had read. She suddenly felt as if she needed to respond to these unspoken serious reflections, so she said that she had stopped being devout, and that she did not want a priest at her deathbed. As she thought, this pleased George, who was indeed thinking about how horrific death was, and about all the deaths she had seen, and about the misery of a life spent without any major achievements, and ended amidst obscurity. It was at this moment when the meeting between mother and daughter was interrupted by news that Maurice was attempting to kidnap Maurice while George was away and put him back into school before he was well. George immediately decided she had to go back to prevent this outrage. Her mother supported this decision and told her not to worry, and that she would be well enough soon to go to Nohant to stay because it now belonged to George.

"Upon your return, you will find me cured," she said and they kissed goodbye.

In the morning, when Sophie woke up, she asked Caroline to do her hair because Caroline was there and her maid seemed uncertain if she should return to her daily grooming schedule. Caroline did a fine job, and Sophie was delighted when she looked at her thinning face in the mirror. She was thinking about the hairstyle she arranged on the day she met Maurice, when exhaustion seized her, and the mirror fell out of her hand, and her body had finally reached a state of complete rest. George arrived a day later, and was devastated that she had missed her mother's final moments. She stayed for the funeral, which was attended by a small circle of family and friends.

The death of her mother brought a new lack of care for society's opinions into George's perception and choices. On November 20, 1837, she began a relationship with Felicien Mallefille, who was a decade younger than her, had a black mustache and beard, was a play writer, and was tutoring Maurice and Solange in history, philosophy and theology. The affair started lightly as a bit of fun, but that winter she was down with liver troubles and rheumatism, which left her right arm temporarily paralyzed. This illness, and some returned negotiations over money with Casimir, kept George from fully engaging in her affair with Mallefille, who she saw daily, when he was taking care of the children. After half a year in this little amusing distraction, George was in her regular spring heat and when she met Chopin again at a salon on May 8, 1838, she suddenly saw that he was a much better match for her than Mallefille. She adored Chopin's piano compositions, and she felt an urge to help him by inviting him to stay at Nohant, or to be around Chopin regularly to hear him playing the piano.

Chopin had a similar aversion towards the opposite sex as George did, thought she attempted to suppress it by repeatedly jumping into affairs with a wide variety of different men. George enjoyed being the one doing the seducing and after weeks of her attempts, they finally consummated the affair on May 15. On the following morning, George sent Mallefille on a two week river-boat excursion with Maurice to Le Havre, and upon his return, George was certain that her affair with Chopin would last, and she informed Mallefille that their sexual relationship was over. In the same conversation, George also asked Mallefille to write a review of Chopin's recent composition. This change of topic was preposterous, so Mallefille justly suspected that an affair must have started between Chopin and George. He investigated this on the following night by waiting in a carriage outside of Chopin's door and surprising George as she was exiting after their intimate meeting. He grabbed and tossed George out of the way, and she ran away afraid that he might do more damage. Meanwhile, Mallefille started pounding on Chopin's door, until he was restrained by Albert Grzymala from assaulting Chopin who had opened his front door. Days later, on June 2, when a fellow tutor, Alexandre Rey, criticized the scandalous affair, Mallefille angrily challenged him to a duel to defend George's honor even if he was no longer with her. This duel was fought without a loss of blood, but left a mark on George's conscience. It made her realize that there had now been half-a-dozen duels fought over her honor, and the carnage she left among her past romantic partners was looking like a massacre. She decided that she would attempt to commit to Chopin for the sake of both of their health and safety. Since Chopin was a brilliant composer, and the two had an easy chemistry, this turned out to be an easy goal to meet.

Chopin had now been a refugee in Paris for a few years, and while he was starting to become recognized in musical circles, his financial situation was lacking, and he happily accepted George's offer for the two of them to take a trip to Spain with George's children, as he hadn't had the funds to temporarily leave France to see the world on his own. The party departed on November 7, once again too close to the coming winter. While George hoped for the best, she knew before they left that Chopin might have been consumptive. The worst fears proved to be well-founded when after spending the first week in a Spanish villa, the cold and windy house caused Frederic to catch a cold, which turned into bronchitis when a new Prussian stove started smoking charcoal, and soon Chopin was coughing up blood. In two days, this dire symptom was combined with a storm that had made their Wind House uninhabitable, and their landlord, Senor Gomez, insisted that they evacuate out of the house because having somebody who was clearly consumptive staying there meant that they would have to burn all of the sheets and furniture to avoid infecting the entire neighborhood. George complied and moved the group to a Carthusian convent that had been abandoned since an 1835 decree because it had fewer than 12 monks on the premises. There were two guardians at the convent besides them, and it was extremely cold, and Chopin's symptoms worsened into a pulmonary infection. While they barely had any furniture, Chopin did cart his enormous expensive piano with him, and he spent desperate nights at this piano, composing harrowing music, including *Preludes.*

One of these evenings, Chopin was sitting at the piano. His fingers were artfully moving among the keys, painting tears, raindrops, and a funeral in one composition. George was sitting on a wooden chair. The wind was wailing through the open windows. George leaned back a bit, and in moments she was seeing a string of amazing forest pass by on the white wall behind Chopin, one majestic forest with leaves and flowers that didn't correspond to any natural foliage, another a tropic, and then one from her native Berry. The horrific reality was disappearing and George entered Chopin's musical mind and got lost there for the hours that Chopin spent at the piano before his cough disrupted his concentration.

They were forced to stay there for three weeks, while crosswinds of the storm made travel impossible. They had time to talk in moments when Chopin was well enough for the discussion about their affair, and Chopin explained that he had a couple of women he was courting with intent to marry them. George did not understand that Chopin had been courting and flirting with many women over the years, but had never had the courage to commit to any of them, and that his willingness to be with her was the biggest commitment of his life. Instead, from George's perspective, he was a young man who was hoping to find a suitable match, and who would never have considered marrying a woman with her romantic past. So while George did not engage other men during her affair with Chopin, she also always assumed that it would end one day when Chopin finally proposed to somebody else.

The Spanish excursion continued amidst tragic lice infections, thievery of goat milk and continuous diluvial rains. Only after a two months stay in this freezing hell did George finally manage to finish a novel on February 5, and to get a loan for their return trip. The group had to travel in the cargo compartment to Barcelona because a hundred squealing pigs were housed at the top of the ship, which the captain hoped to keep healthy by keeping them away from the consumptive Chopin. The whole sea trip lasted for over two days, but finally they arrived at Marseille and Chopin was examined by the first doctor he had seen since the slump of his symptoms, Dr. Cauviere, who confirmed that Chopin was indeed consumptive, and prescribed bleedings, and eating white meat and water tinged with red wine. They spent three months in Marseille, and then a few days in Genoa, where Chopin was up for vising museums to break the monotony and because he remembered why he had wanted to go to Spain initially. Then, they finally returned to Nohant, and Chopin spent that and the following dozen summers there, recovering from consumption and composing brilliant masterpieces. George also rented an apartment on Rue Pigalle with two pavilions and a garden to be near Chopin's new apartment on Rue Tronchet. Despite apparent separate living arrangements, Chopin frequently lived with George in her apartment because she acted as his nurse.

George left politics behind as she was caring for Chopin. When the two were in Genoa, on May 12, 1839, George's friends, Armand Barbes and Louis Blanc, attempted a failed coup d'etat, and her absence during the plotting that went into this scheme meant that her "club" was hesitant to rely on her with new projects that came up after she returned to Paris. Meanwhile, in 1842 a new law began the expansion of the French rail system, and improved transportation between Paris and Nohant, making the trip an easier one for all those who escaped the city in the summer. Years flew by, as if they were suddenly also traveling via the rail instead of by horses. Suddenly it was 1843, and the major event that summer was that Chopin's family came to visit Nohant because they were mourning the death of Chopin's father. The other development from that period was that Maurice, who was now twenty-one, was in love with a girl that George had adopted years earlier, Pauline Viardot, a twenty-three years old, who was ordinary in appearance, but was such a close family friend that Maurice had gotten to know her better than others. One more year of these little family dramas sent George into a depressed spin, as she escaped to the place where she had made a shrine for Corambe, and reflected about the great ambitions she had given up for her family and friends. Instead of writing great masterpieces, she believed she was writing flighty romances rapidly only to make money. Instead of fighting with the other republicans in the brewing revolutions, she was nursing a single composer on a country retreat. Love had destroyed what she could have become.

Another year flew by, and in 1845, George found herself writing *Lucrezia*, without being conscious of what this novel wanted to tell her about herself. It was written in a period during the last summer that Chopin spent at Nohant, when he stayed in his room for days, weeping, breaking his pens, changing each measure a hundred times, so that he had spent six weeks on one page, only to return to the original version. Watching Chopin unable to progress with his work reminded George of watching Musset spend days on a few lines of poetry. George never had a period like this, as she wrote books steadily since her first novel through her last composition, and only stopped when depression or illness disabled her. This new novel was about a thirty-years old actress, Lucrezia Floriani, who resembled a mixture of Marie Dorval and Sand herself, with children and many prior lovers, who falls in love with Prince Karol, who has been mothered and spoiled and who fails to appreciate her love, which leads to her tragic death at the end. If Chopin had been looking for himself in all of the romantic heroes in George's novels over the years, he would not have remained in that relationship for that long, so when he reviewed her proofs initially he did not see the similarity between Prince Karol and himself.

Then one night, George was holding Jean-Jacques Rousseau's *On the Social Contract*. Socialism was re-awakening in Paris before the up-coming 1848 revolutions. But in that spacious living room, with a few decorations from before the French Revolution, on that cooling summer evening Chopin was composing Polonaise in A-flat major, Op, 53. Un-like many of his earlier pieces, this one was moving along at a violent rhythm. He was hitting the keys, as if striking blows in a revolt against something. He had been re-reading Sand's *Lucrezia Floriani*, and sud-denly some comments his friends had made about a similarity returned to him. He wanted to show her that he was still vital, alive. He wanted to demonstrate the speed of his virtuoso playing. His hands moved on a particularly aggressive string of violent notes. There was sweat on his chin and forehead. He could feel bloody mucous building in his chest, and that he would soon have to stop, excuse himself and go to the bathroom to clear his throat. But he had just visualized a resolution to the climax he built into, his fingers rolled down the keyboard. They hopped off nearly a foot off the surface of the board, and down, and then a final note. He wiped his nose with a soft napkin and stood up, feeling a bit of pain in his back. George was not alone in the living room, and the entire audi-ence applauded with amazement and clear fascination. Chopin knew that he would never be able to bring himself to stay at Nohant again. Sand was applauding with the others, but her gaze was distant as if she was still daydreaming. He was too familiar with her daydreams, but a sparkle of romantic love appeared to be missing, or was it his hurt pride that misinterpreted the same signs because Sand's fictional portrayal of their decade-long committed friendship was an appalling nightmare when he compared it with his own romantic notions of the same period.

After *Lucrezia's* release in 1846, Chopin never returned to Nohant. Rumors and facts about George's affairs were flying across Paris, and her break with Chopin finally got her publisher to over in 1847 the enor-mous sum of 100,000 francs for a five volume autobiography of George Sand's life. George was disposed to confessing because she also felt that the break with Chopin was a monumental event in her life, and that she now had to reflect and evaluate her actions to understand herself and to defend herself before the jury of her peers. She wrote the first volume up to her own birth in the first year, escaping into researching her ancestors to avoid what she suddenly realized was a life that could not be described honestly without the risk of immediate imprisonment and execution.

Chapter 18

The 1848 Revolution and the Minister of Propaganda's Residential Lovers

Only half of George Sand's life was over by 1847, but less is known about her affairs and revolutionary actions across those long three decades that followed. The love affairs were calmer, without duels or skulls. Her revolutionary activities were successful, and those who succeed in revolutions have more to hide than those that fail. George was the matriarch of her estate, and she reigned with certainty, surrendering control when she needed a manager to assist her with the daily business. It was the best part of George's life, when flighty lovers chasing young skirts retreated, there was nobody contesting her inheritance, and she had finished her studies, and now practiced medicine, legal matters, business, and political maneuvers, and the literary craft with equal ease and skill.

While George escaped from the worries of falling into illogical loves, her children were only now ready to begin courting their marital partners. Solange and Maurice married later than George had expected because George's violent divorce from Casimir a decade earlier had shown marriage in its worst light to the products of this marriage, and they were both hesitant about entering unions before they were psychologically ready for marital warfare. In June of 1847, when she was nineteen, Solange began to be pursued by her first suitor, Fernand de Preaulx, who was also flirting with George's goddaughter, Augustine Brault. Fernand was tall, strong, with long wavy hair, blue eyes, but neither intelligent nor rich, and he switched to Solange because he assumed that she had a

larger dowry. There were a lot of speculations about complex interlock-
ing triangles between the different members of the household, but those
intrigues are meant for a separate novel that would focus on this next
generation of Sands. The flirtation with Fernand ended in half of a year,
which he spent at Nohant, eventually begging for Solange's hand in marriage, which she finally flatly refused.

That spring George and Solange went to Paris together and met
with a sculptor, Auguste Clesinger, over a decade older than Solange,
but an expert in artistically executed seduction. Since he was familiar
with Sand's work, he flattered her and asked to do their busts, later also
sending a free sculpture that George admired in his gallery, with a note
of interest in Solange. This direct interest from a sculpture that George
admired led her to invite him to reside and do some of his sculpting at
Nohant that hot summer, and he immediately joined them at Nohant, and
proposed to Solange on his first day there. The fact that Clesinger had a
studio in Paris and made a living from his art suggested to George that
he was independently wealthy, but it turned out that he was one of those
suitors purely after money that she had rejected in her youth. Solange did
not have a similar instinct and accepted the proposal. On May 18, Casimir
arrived to spend a couple of nights, and George pulled a tendon in her
leg rushing to avoid seeing him in the living room. On May 19, Solange
and Clesinger were married at the Nohant chapel in a private ceremony
attended only by immediate family members, in part because George was
still recovering from the strain and had to be carried in. After spending
a couple of nights at Nohant, the couple departed for their new Parisian
apartment, but within two weeks it was obvious that trouble was brewing for the new marriage. On June 3, Solange reported that Clesinger
was taking advantage of her loving disorientation in the first weeks of
the marriage to run up over 12,000 francs in debt on jewelry, the tailor,
servants, hired carriage, and other luxuries, and this amount was only
what went over the extraordinary sum Solange was given as a dowry that
he had squandered in only two weeks. George refused to give any more
money because she had nothing else she could offer without sacrificing
her own well-being, and this sent Clesinger into a malicious social ram-
page, as he tried to create a rift in the Sand family. Events reached a violent end when on July 11, Solange and Clesinger followed George back
to Nohant in an attempt to get a loan from her to cover their mounting
debt. George had flatly refused to offer any more assistance and retreated
to get some work done in her room. Meanwhile, Clesinger was saying
that Augustine was a flirt and that she did not deserve the large dowry
George was planning to offer her, and threatened to forcefully back and
ship Augustine away from Nohant. Eugene Lambert, the family's paint-

ing tutor, was in the living room when this argument was going on, and he interrupted on George's behalf saying that if George had a right to offer Solange a dowry, she also could offer one to Augustine. Clesinger felt that this comment was disrespectful towards his wife, so he raised his fists, then grabbed a hammer from a table, and swung it at Eugene, but he missed when Eugene nimbly jumped aside and kicked Clesinger violently in his stomach with his foot. Maurice started asking both of them to calm down, but at that moment George returned from her study and, without saying a word, came right over to Clesinger and sharply slapped him across the face, and then attempted to wrestle his hammer out of his hand. Maurice tried to help his mother, but Clesinger was swinging the hammer to keep it in his hold.

"I'm going to kill the both of you!" he was shouting, wild-eyed. This exclamation made George temporarily loosen her hold and Clesinger got the hammer free. George started tugging on his hair, and Clesinger, now maddened by all these attacks, nearly hit Maurice over the head with the hammer, when George slapped him even more violently, so that he was disoriented for a few moments.

"You bloody dyke!"

Clesinger leaped at George and punched her with his closed fist with all his strength in the chest. George jumped back, putting a bit of pressure on her chest because it was ringing with pain. Seeing that his mother was now being beaten, Maurice had enough and he grabbed his pistols from a neighboring room.

"I'm going to shoot that bastard like the bitch that he is!" he was screaming, as he was walking back with the pistols.

At this moment, Jean, a young manservant who was hired a couple of weeks earlier and had not seen that kind of a violent altercation in any of his prior aristocratic places of employment decided that it was his duty to intervene at that point and he tacked Clesinger and pinned his arms around his back, pushing him against a wall. The curer was in the garden across this debate and only had the courage to enter when he heard somebody tackling Clesinger, and when he entered he helped restrain Clesinger against the wall. At the same moment, Victor Borie saw the enraged Maurice, and fearing that he might be mad enough to shoot Clesinger even after he was restraing, he pulled the two pistols out of Maurice's hands. As a side-note, Victor Borie was George's new lover, and kept the post of artist in residence and intimate partner between 1847 and 1850. Solange was speechless across this entire encounter, but now she saw that if she didn't say something the family might file charges against Clesinger or something else might transpire, so she put her hand on his shoulder and said, "My dear, when you hit my mother, you became the one at fault here, so go to our room and compose yourself." Clesinger saw that he had no supporters in the household, and retreated to their room, as asked. On the next day, Clesinger and Solange departed for La Chatre, from where they wrote in asking for Maurice's horse and Chopin's caliche, but receiving new rejections, attempted to spread rumors about George's cheapness towards her children in the city of La Chatre, where hundreds of residents turned up on the street to hear their accusations. Chopin then sent a note to George expressing his sympathy with Solange's argument, which cooled the last of George's feelings for him.

The violent altercation with Clesinger was the last time that George was assaulted in her own house and to make sure that it never reoccurred, she severed all relations with Clesinger and Solange, at least for the time being. Refusing to see, help or interact with somebody that hurt her sent a message to the other members of her household, the beggars that circled her looking for charity, and to the French artistic and political circles that she was no longer going to submit to abuses. If George had lifted her defenses years earlier, she might have had a smaller household, but she would have avoided all those years of pain, which came from her failure to see abusive and manipulative people as cold and calculating. Of course, while George attempted to shield herself, she remained vulnerable to influences and attachments until the end, always hopeful, despite clear proof to the contrary. But from this point forward, her skin had thickened to a near-bronze density. She had forgiven Musset and others too many times with the assumption that their madness was involuntary, but she knew now that if she did not have logical responses to violations, people would keep exploiting her liberal views on proper human behavior to win money, love, or other things from George.

The turbulent events in her own household made George restless and when she returned to Paris for the winter, she joined in the pre-revolutionary preparations that her "club" was wrapped up in. She was a bit out of shape now, having given up riding regularly with Colette's retirement, so instead of marching in the front lines with a flag, she worked behind the scenes across this revolutionary period on creating propaganda pamphlets, manifestos, and articles under various names and anonymously to inspire a larger following of rebels who would finally be numerous enough to overthrow the monarchy, and not simply to replace one monarch with another. The entire "club" was now more mature, held higher political offices with wider influence, and their organization of the 1848 Revolution in February went as flawlessly as a coup d'etat can go. Louis-Philippe abdicated, and the Society was finally able to take a leading role in national politics, becoming the members of the Provisional Government of the Second Republic, which held power for four years after the 1848 Revolution. Of course the Provincial Government was soon overrun by the moderates, as the radicals lost an election, still there was a major shift following the 1848 Revolutions unlike in the string of revolutions that came in the previous couple of decades. This phenomenal success in Paris also sparked other 1848 Revolutions across Europe, as it indicated that the liberals finally had enough support to succeed. A few weeks after the overthrow, George suddenly saw Chopin in a crowd and clasped his trembling, icy hand, before he ran down the stairs and out of sight, and the crowd pushed George further up the stairs to the political meeting she was attending that afternoon. The temperature of the hand brought out the doctor in George, so she stopped by the salon of Charlotte Marliani at the Square d'Orleans, which George knew Chopin frequented, and he was indeed there, and informed her that she was now a grandmother, Solange having had a daughter, without informing George of this development. Solange was partially unwilling to talk with George during that period because Princess Anna Czartoryska had just spread the "rumor" that during an altercation between George and Solange's husband, George was heard to blurt out, "She's not legitimate. She's not M. Dudevant's. So, she has no innate right to an inheritance." Solange's parental background did not come into full light, but Solange was shocked by this news that she was hearing for the first time, and outraged with her mother for contributing to the spread of such accusations. The coldness in Chopin's voice prevented George from sympathizing with his illness, and she did not see him again before he departed Paris for London to escape post-revolutionary violence on March 18. The two did not exchange letters in the following months, as George was busy with her revolutionary work, and it was a tragic shock to her when she found out on October 18 of 1848 that Chopin had died in London the day before from tuberculosis. George had feared this news for over a decade, had tried to keep Chopin healthy for the same of art and that great man, and now she did not even know he was on his deathbed because the feud with her daughter meant that she failed to convey that information to her, preferring to see Chopin die in poverty and misery to giving way in her dispute with her mother.

The pain over helplessly losing Chopin was only one tragedy that displayed the horrible nature of humanity amidst the final triumph of democratic ideals. Before learning of Chopin's death, George learned that March of the death of her half-brother, Hyppolite, who had slumped further and further into a drunken stupor over the previous decades until he was completely mad and imbecilic, and in his total lunacy believed that George's republican friends wanted to assassinate him, without being able to come up with any financial or political motivations for these actions. George had only exchanged letters with him for years, and felt as distanced from him as from Sophie when he reached this gradual death, the meaning of which only suggested that a life of complete drunkenness was as meaningful as the life of a moss that spends its short existence hitting glass until it finally finds the flame.

In the decade that George spent in relative seclusion with Chopin, she continued to publish books, and always had the ambition of starting a radical journal or a press of her own, similar to Dickens' journals, and to many other literary figures who transitioned from publishing their work with others to publishing it independently across the middle of the nineteenth century, when there was a ready market for new publishing ventures. In part radical and socialist writers like Dickens had to found their own ventures because conservative publishers frequently censored out works with radical messages. In George's case, her long-time publisher, Buloz, rejected a new novel she sent to him, *Horace*, because it was too radical in demonstrating Leroux's doctrines in fiction, so in 1841, George founded the radical, symbolist *Independent Review* with Pierre Leroux and Louis Viardot, which survived for a few years by serializing not only *Horace*, but also George's *Consuelo*, and the works of other symbolist novelists, but failed to turn a profit equivalent to what other publishers could offer. In 1844, she founded the socialist Berry newspaper, *The Pathfinder*, or *Eclaireur de l'Indre*, hoping to communicate with the proletariat and to raise them to revolution with its pages, but it did not see too many issues or sales, especially not to the poor, who couldn't afford the luxury of buying a radical paper. In the midst of the 1848 Revolution, similarly to Marx's writing of communist political pamphlets, George was writing several anti-corruption and pro-workers' rights, socialist manifestos, including *To the Rich*. She spent March in meetings in her role as the unofficial Minister of Propaganda of the republican party, with Victor Borie accompanying her around Paris for safety and then waiting in the hallways, while she was in meetings until 1am. Several of the top republicans were campaigning to put George Sand on the official election ballet to elect her to the National Assembly, but she refused to run because she thought that her victory before women had a right to vote in France would have been a political farce.

In the same period, George founded a journal, *The Cause of the People* (*La Cause du Peuple*), which only saw three issues before it was censored out of print. The second issue of *La Cause du Peuple*, from April 16, 1848, began with a signed article from the editor, George Sand, which was titled, "Socialism," and exclaimed, "...Sovereignty resides in the people and cannot reside elsewhere than in people. Sovereignty is the government of all... Our duty is to exercise this right, and as we cannot conceive a right without practice, the right and responsibility are inseparable and indivisible." The worst offense George committed in this period was her contribution to issue 16 of the *Bulletins of the Republic*, where she called for open insurrection if republicans failed to win in the forthcoming elections. Despite George's best efforts, the republicans did fail and the moderates won the April 23 election. The bloody repressions after the election were injurious towards republicans, as the proletariat did rise up on George Sand's and other socialist calls to insurrection on May 15, but they were overwhelmed by the moderate opposition that then proceeded to suppress the rebels to prevent further insurrections. Because she had called for an open insurrection, the Society put her into a leading role for organizing the insurrection on May 15 in Paris. She helped to spread the message via a few key messengers to those who were eager to participate and then she led the crowd of demonstrators into the Chamber, and once again she only barely managed to get out of the way as the National Guard bayonetted the crowd to clear the Assembly Chamber. George was there with a few male revolutionaries, who did not have the female gender to disguise them and so were jailed, these included Blanqui, Raspail, Armand Barbes, and Pierre Leroux, the latter was the editor of George's *Independent Review*, so finding him among those arrested casted a shadow over George, and her Parisian apartment was violently searched in the repressions. As a result, George was forced to retreat back to Nohant, but still wrote another thirteen socialist articles for the *True Republic*, until the press was put under strict censorship and George had to remain relatively silent in the following years, writing subversively rebellious novels, instead of openly rebellion with calls for revolt in signed articles.

George retreated at the right moment, as immediately after she left for Nohant and became engulfed in writing her autobiography by the end of May, on June 1, the Parisian radicals barricaded the streets in a new insurrection attempt, but did not have enough supporters in their ranks and 1,500 of them were massacred, 12,000 arrested and 5,000 deported by General Cavaignac. Reading about these repressions, despite some republican winnings in the election convinced George to focus on her writing and on her estate because the French political stage was finally too depressing for her to contemplate a chance for positive change.

George missed the wedding of her goddaughter, Augustine to Charles de Bertholdi in Nohant amidst all these violent events, and she contributed an enormous sum to her dowry without attending the ceremony on April 12. Despite the dowry, Augustine's father published a libelous pamphlet against George a few months later, on June 5, called *A contemporary: the Biography and Intrigues of George Sand*, which the Minister of Justice, whom George had met when her grandmother fed among the retreating troops during the Cossacks' attack on Paris, had to help George seize for its untruthful and malicious comments. Just as George managed to suppress one attack, on June 23, the details about George's participation in calling for insurrection was made public by Ledru-Roll-in's assistant at the Ministry of the Interior, but yet again George managed to escape with her head.

The only other lover that George had during her decade with Chopin was Marie Dorval, whom she continued to see occasionally on her stays in Paris. Their romantic friendship was informal, and never escalated into duels, so George maintained it, without becoming engulfed in it. When Marie Dorval started to decline in 1847, in the midst of performing the lead role in *Marie-Jeanne*, because of a perforated lung, she exchanged a few letters with George, but the news did not seem dire, and George was beginning to be involved in pre-revolutionary activities, so she was not able to give the matter her full attention. While her health turned at this point, Marie's emotional troubles went back to 1831, when Marie and George had just met, and Marie's daughter, Gabrielle, who was only sixteen at the time, fell in love with a consumptive called Fontaney and ran away with him to England and got married there, against Marie's better advice. Gabrielle fell ill and died within weeks of their arrival in London, and Fontaney only had enough strength to return and die in Paris. These events devastated Marie for many years, but she was slightly cheered when her other daughter, Caroline married a young actor called Rene Luguet, and her third daughter Louise also found a decent husband. Just as the Revolution had upset the lives of Hyppolite and Chopin and brought their deaths perhaps a bit earlier than would have happened naturally, the Revolution also upset Mme. Dorval, who was struck with terror during the post-insurrection repressions, and these fears were intensified by the sudden death of her grandson, Georges on May 16 at 2 Rue de Varennes. Marie was able to raise her spirits high enough to attempt a new acting job a year later, but on April 5, of 1849 she fell ill in a stage coach heading to Caen for a show. That night when Marie examined herself in a mirror, she was struck by how old she looked, with two missing teeth, and in her simple black dress. Then, at that late hour, Rene Luguet suddenly burst into her room to announce that she would not get the lead in an upcoming production, but that the company was willing to offer her 300 francs in allowance. The news that she was now so repelling that she could not play a lead and was being offered charity instead devastated her and after going to sleep that night, she refused to get up again. The next morning, Marie was diagnosed with fever and an ulcerated liver, the latter was apparent by the blood in her feces. A few weeks passed amidst this illness, and on April 20, Rene was so frightened by Marie's pains that he fainted a few times from watching them. It was after Rene recovered from his second faint that Marie started telling those gathered about her love for her dear George Sand.

"What a beautiful, pure heart George has always had. There are so few people that can love people as she does. She is the one great love in my life. Don't you all love her, isn't she worthy of the best love?" Marie's daughters nodded, and Rene, who knew a bit more about the nature of the "love" between Marie and George, nodded with more contemplation.

"Was it Marie that suggested the name George for that poor grandchild that died?" Rene reflected silently.

A few weeks later, a year after little George's death, Marie wrote to her daughter, Caroline, asking her to shield his room for the day, and to put flowers in it to commemorate the occasion. Then, despite her ailing condition, on the following day, May 17 of 1849, she took a stage coach to Paris, which overturned in the night. This trip was the final blow, and Marie died on May 20, saying that she knew that she was dying and that she was resigned to this sublime event. George found out about Marie's death on May 23, when she received a letter from Caroline Luguet, and wrote the only chapter of her autobiography titled with the name of only one person, "Mme. Dorval," devastated with grief over the loss of this closest friend and lover, who she could no longer help or console.

George wasn't alone in this period, as Victor Borie, was still living at Nohant, and their affair was still vital. But, Marie's death left a gap in George's heart and later that summer, when she met Hermann Muller-Strubing, a thirty-seven years old, plump and muscular, German refugee scholar-musician, who was imprisoned for radical activities for seven years, George invited him to come and stay at Nohant, despite Borie's continued presence there. A few months after the addition of this new resident, Borie started to suspect something was amiss and to rekindle his relationship with George did what he knew would best catch her attention, founding a new weekly, *Le Travailleur de l'Indre.* However, a couple of months after the start of the venture, on December 22, when the first issue was released with statements favorable to the working class, authorities seized it and condemned Borie to a year imprisonment and a 2,000 francs fine, which he escaped by fleeing to Brussels, and staying with a painter friend, Luigi Calamatta, as finally his affair with George became more dangerous than the rewards it offered.

Meanwhile, Hermann was already in-place and ready to assist George both musically and intimately, and they had a few splendid months together before on April 15, of 1850, George began a new affair with Maurice's friend, Alexandre Manceau, a gray-eyed, thin and frail, thirty-three year old, amateur play writer. In the absence of Marie Dorval, George was looking for exactly what Manceau was willing to offer, but both Borie and Hermann would not provide... Can you guess what this was? Without being indelicate, Manceau was one of the only men George was ever with who understood that penetration does not bring a woman to a climax, and he kissed the correct organ to achieve this glorious resolution to their intimate encounters. George also appreciated that he prepared her pillows, brought her slippers, and otherwise pampered her by massaging her body, and helping her bathe. After decades of looking for a romantic partner who was attractive, gentle and caring, she finally found a young man who made her completely happy.

Perhaps one sign of the degree of George's happiness is that she managed to tour Paris on December 1, during Prince Louis Napoleon's coup d'etat, without having an urge to assist the republican generals that were imprisoned in these actions. Her only maneuver upon hearing of the start of repressions on December 4 was to retreat to Nohant with Manceau to keep both of them safe. Then, from the comfort of her study, she wrote a letter to the President of the new Republic, which was passed down to Napoleon III by her old cousin Rene de Villeneuve, whose wife had held the infant Napoleon III in her arms during his baptism. In addition, George had written a kind letter to Napoleon while he was imprisoned, which cheered him, and made him read a few of her novels after he was released, which impressed him greatly. The letter asked for mercy for the arrested republicans, and in response Napoleon invited her to meet with him in Paris in January. Since she was invited by the President into Paris, she was not afraid of the raging repressions, and promptly returned to the city. While she did not want to be entangled with the events, it seemed that she could not sit by while her old colleagues were massacred.

While George was in Paris, she took the opportunity to repair her relationship with Alexander Dumas, after their violent break decades earlier over Dumas spreading the rumor about Merimee's failure to perform in bed with George. George now dedicated her new play, *Moliere*, to "The author of *The Three Musketeers.*" Dumas had moved on to writing brilliant romantic novels over the previous decade, and reading them in her free time George developed an admiration for his artistic talent that was stronger than her embarrassment over Merimee. Upon being shown this dedication by Buloz, Dumas invited George to dinner, and the two talked about their rebellious children. Dumas son, Dumas fils was in Russia at the time, courting Lydia Nesselrode, a married woman. Dumas then sidetracked into another reason he had invited George over at that particular moment, as apparently his son had found the letters that Chopin and George exchanged in Poland, and was asking what he should do with them. George asked that the letters be brought into France, and she was relieved after she received and burned them, as she was writing in her autobiography that Chopin and she had a chaste relationship, while the letters offered graphic proof to the contrary.

Amidst these meetings with old friends and enemies, George had waited long enough for Napoleon to be ready to receive her on January 30, 1852. Napoleon was delighted to see her, and took her hands, as she begged him to be fair to the republicans, and he could not help but schedule a second interview so that he could spend a bit more time with this still beautiful black-haired author of *Lelia*. Napoleon also gave George some positive comments about his intended treatment of republicans, which George took around to Parisian ministers to make sure that the Prince-President's wish for clemency was translated into actual loosening of repressive policies. George had a few days to wait before the second interview, and the ministers' offices closed at night, so she had time to go to the Theatre du Vaudeville, to meet Dumas fils for the first time during the entr'acte, who was there for the premier of his grand play, *The Lady with the Camellias* (*La Dame aux Camellias*). A couple of days later, on February 5, George met with Napoleon for the second time, and as a result of these efforts that April, Emile Aucante and Ernest Perigois were released from prison, and the order for Fleury's arrest was cancelled. Emile Aucante even moved into Nohant that May to make sure that his safety was guaranteed. These were amazing achievements when one considers that during these repressions, 27,000 people were arrested and 10,000 were deported by Napoleon.

This effort exhausted George's political energies, and she returned to Nohant to be pampered by Manceau, in the comfort of her books and her writing. Life was not without its dramas, as in April of 1854, Solange's husband, Clesinger found out that Solange was having an affair with her cousin, Gaston de Villeneuve, and immediately began divorce proceedings, demanding full custody of their five-year old daughter, Nini, who he nearly kidnapped and took to Paris, while Solange retreated into a convent. Half a year later, in December of 1854, the court issued a legal injunction sanctioning the separation and putting Nini into George's custody at Nohant. Clesinger was outraged and frightened by this decision as it meant he might lose his daughter and George's allowance, so he took Nini away, saying that he wanted to take her to a boarding school, but got her sick with scarlet fever during a winter carriage ride, and two weeks later, after Solange finally won Nini back, the child died in her arms on January 13. This violent and deadly conclusion to her marriage devastated Solange, and a few years later she started traveling around Europe with wealthy and aristocratic lovers, as she had lost faith in marriage and wanted to find light entertainment to escape in from her troubles.

Then in the year when Gustave Flaubert's *Madame Bovary* was brought to court for outraging public decency, 1857, Alfred de Musset died, in part from his continued womanizing and alcoholism. Learning of this death, George found it difficult to concentrate on other topics, and did not see a reason not to confess when the man who might be offended was gone. So, in May of 1858 she finished *Elle et Lui*, about their hyper-dramatic affair. She had been thinking of writing a reply to Musset's vengeful, 1835, *La Confessions d'un enfant du siècle*, but had refrained to avoid a back-and-force literary battle. She had now forgot to take into account the possible offense her book might give to Musset's brother, Paul, who in 1859 published his reply, *Lui et Elle*, a parody on Sand's *Elle et Lui* that once again defended Musset's position in the affair. George let the debate stand there, having said everything she needed to in her previous autobiographical works and in her 1858 novel on the affair.

A few more years flew by, and the major event from 1861 was that Alexandre Dumas fils came to stay for the summer to Nohant because he was depressed about his love life, and about the failure of his artistic ambitions. Dumas had brought his friend, Marchal le Gigantesque, or le Mastodonte, with him, and he was delighted to find that over the following few months George and Marchal begal an affair. Marchal was 182 pounds, told good jokes, and was a year younger than Maurice; in other words, George's lovers kept getting younger as she was getting older. George was entertained by Marchal and jumped into this new romantic adventure because Manceau, who had been consumptive since George met him, was now growing sicker, and would be somewhat incapacitated for the last four years of their affair before his death.

The big news in the spring of 1862 was that Maurice finally decided to marry, at thirty-eight, to Marcelina Calamatta, a nineteen years old daughter of George's old friend, Luigi Calamatta. Their civil wedding ceremony was on May 17. This wedding made Maurice suddenly conscious about the fact that his mother and her residential lover, Manceau, were still in control of Nohant, even when he was the Mayor of Nohant, and was certainly old enough to accept responsibility for business matters, in addition to political affairs. On November 23, 1863, Maurice exploded at Manceau, demanding that he leave and that he was not the master of Nohant. George decided to avoid the confrontation and offered for Manceau to stay in her Parisian apartment until she could join him in a couple of months. When Manceau and George returned to Nohant on March 16 of 1864, after having seen a premier of Sand's play in Paris that was attended by the Emperor and the Empress, they found Maurice as cold as ever, so a month later George left this glum household to be alone at Gargilesse, without servants, to once again work on her novel in complete peace. This was a week just like that month she had spent alone at Nohant after her divorce, when George refreshed her depleted energies by being somewhere without any outside distractions, and only the wind and the rustling grass and trees to take her away from her reflections. Those brief moments of peace brought George back to herself and she returned to Nohant to continue her battles with her friends and family. A few months later Monceau began coughing up blood and it became clear that his condition was quickly regressing, so the couple stopped intercourse to preserve Monceau's strength. Meanwhile, George flew back to Marchal, her "big fat baby," for a quick fling. It was on August 21 of 1865 when Monceau finally died of consumption, spending his last days writing a novel with George to avoid the darkness of the approaching end by escaping from it in art. A few months after this, George's spirits were recovered and she jumped into a full liaison with Marchal, and began writing a novel about this affair called, *The Last Love*.

George was entertained in the last decade of her life by great writers, composers and artists, including Gustave Flaubert, with whom she vacationed in 1866, and who later came to visit her at Nohant in 1869, and again in 1873. On the latter meeting, Ivan Turgenev also came along to converse with the great George Sand.

Having reached the ripe old age of seventy-two without a break in her literary production, George was suddenly interrupted on May 15 of 1876 by a constipation that continued for weeks without any movements, which led to vomiting and sharp gastric pains. Operations were attempted, but without results, and it was difficult for George to speak through her tightening throat on June 7. Some of the words she said on her deathbed puzzled those present, "Love live greenery." Everybody understood her comments about her coming death, and her goodbyes, but many pondered about how "greenery" fit with "love" or "live." The three words in the slogan of the French Revolution were, "liberty, equality, fraternity." Was she trying to recall these three words and only managed to come up with their substitutes? Instead of "fraternity" "love," instead of "liberty" "live," and instead of "equality" "greenery?" Perhaps, George's deathbed version is more profound than the original. George had spent seventy years fighting for equality and liberty among revolutionaries, but she was supplanted from power on her estate by her male son, and she could not gain a political position in the government she risked death and imprisonment to bring about because of her gender. She had also seen several revolutions that revolved the system from one corrupt government to another, without moving France towards actual equality or liberty for the people. She did have plenty of greenery though at Nohant and on her travels abroad, lots of nature, which she worked to describe with passion and conviction in her romantic novels. Life was now ending, so it seems that she uttered this word satirically as well. But, had she found "love?" She must have been thinking along these lines in her last moments at 9am, on June 8, right before she lost consciousness. She looked around at her extended family and resident artists, and there wasn't a lover among them. Marchal was alive and well, but he was absent, and he would not make an appearance at her funeral. At the funeral, Victor Hugo would say that George was an "idea" that would continue to "live" after her death. This idea cannot be a romantic one about tragic true love that lived in George's novels. The idea has to be about the strength a woman needs to survive revolutions in her heart as she keeps hoping for love after the next revolution, but keeps finding only more of the same tragic loss and disappointment that came with all of the previous turns of the wheel. The idea must also be about hoping for more than "greenery" from life, and struggling for "equality" and "liberty" against millenniums of oppression and constraint.

Glossary of Characters

Marie-Aurore de Saxe: (1748-1821) George's grandmother, the Countess de Horn

Jean-Jacques Rousseau: (1712-1778) the lover, before George's grandfather, M. Francueil, of Mme. Louise Florence D'Epinay

Archbishop of Arles, M. Leblanc de Beaulieu: (1753-1825) George's "bastard uncle"

Emperor Napoleon Bonaparte: (1769-1821) Emperor of the French between 1804 and 1814

Maurice Dupin de Francueil: (1778-1808) George's father, military officer

Sophie Dupin: George's mother

George Sand, or Aurore Dupin: (1804-1876) novelist, and revolutionary

Casimir Dudevant: (1795-1871) illegitimate, George's husband

Aurelien de Seze: (1799-1870) Deputy Prosecutor General, George's lover

Louis XVIII of France: (1755-1824) King

Hyppolite Chatiron: George's illegitimate half-brother

Dr. Francois Joseph Victor Broussais: (1772-1838) physician, George's lover and the father of her daughter, Solange

Jules Sandeau: (1811-1883) novelist, George's lover

Honore de Balzac: (1799-1850) novelist and playwright, George's friend

Marie Dorval: (1798-1849) actress, George's lover

Alfred de Musset: (1810-1857) poet, dramatist, novelist, George's lover

Prosper Merimee: (1803-1870) dramatist, archeologist, historian, the one who didn't rise

Alexander Dumas, pere: (1802-1870) novelist, dramatist, George's "friend"

Alexander Dumas, fils: (1824-1895) dramatist, Dumas' son, George's friend

Gustave Planche: (1808-1857) critic, George's lover

Dr. Pietro Pagello: (1807-1898) Italian doctor, George's lover

Michel de Bourges: (1797-1853) lawyer, politician, George's lover

Baron Maurice Dudevant/ Sand: (1823-1889) writer, mayor, George's son

Prince Antoine: (1824-1890) youngest son of King Louis-Phillipe, Duke of Montpensier

Felicien Mallefille: (1813-1868) novelist, playwright, tutor, George's lover

Frederic Chopin: (1810-1849) Polish composer, George's lover

Solange Dudevant/ Sand: George's daughter

Louis-Napoleon Bonaparte III: (1808-1873) President and Emperor of the French Second Republic

Images

Front Piece: "Aurore Dupin," pastel by Aurore de Saxe.

Introduction: "George Sand," by Francois Theodore Rochard.

Chapter 1: "Marie-Aurore de Saxe," anonymous pastel.

Chapter 2: "Bonaparte Crossing the Grand Saint-Bernard Pass, 20 May 1800," by Jacques-Louis David, 1802.

Chapter 3: "Napoleon Bonaparte," by Henri Félix Emmanuel Philippoteaux.

Chapter 4: "Joachim Murat," by François Gérard, 1800-1810.

Chapter 5: "Maurice Dupin," anonymous portrait.

Chapter 6: "Napoleon's Retreat from Moscow," by Adolph Northen.

Chapter 7: "Augustinian Monastery of Quebec," drawing.

Chapter 8: "Jean-Baptiste de Belloy," anonymous portrait.

Chapter 9: "Casimir Dudevant," anonymous photograph, 1860s.

Chapter 10: "Reception of Louis XVIII to the Town Hall, 29 August 1814," by Theodor Hoffbauer.

Chapter 11: "François-Joseph-Victor Broussais," by Antoine Maurin.

Chapter 12: "Jules Sandeau," by Henri Lehmann, 1858.

Chapter 13: "The Sleepers," by Gustave Courbet, 1866.

Chapter 14: "Alfred de Musset," by Charles Landelle.

Chapter 15: "Doctor Pietro Pagello," anonymous portrait.

Chapter 16: "Michel de Bourges," anonymous portrait, 1835.

Chapter 17: "Frédéric Chopin," anonymous photograph, 1849.

Chapter 18: "George Sand," photographed by Nadar.

OTHER ANAPHORA LITERARY PRESS TITLES

PLJ: Interviews with Best-Selling YA Writers
Editor: Anna Faktorovich

Inversed
By: Jason Holt

Notes on the Road to Now
By: Paul Bellerive

Devouring the Artist
By: Anthony Labriola

100 Years of the Federal Reserve
By: Marie Bussing-Burks

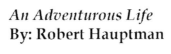

River Bends in Time
By: Glen A. Mazis

Interview with Larry Niven
Editor: Anna Faktorovich

An Adventurous Life
By: Robert Hauptman

Lightning Source UK Ltd.
Milton Keynes UK
UKOW04n1606190514

231927UK00001B/12/P